D0397926

Caller of Lightning

THE ARCANE AMERICA SERIES
Uncharted by Kevin J. Anderson & Sarah A. Hoyt
Council of Fire by Eric Flint & Walter H. Hunt
Caller of Lightning by Peter J. Wacks and Eytan Kollin

Caller of Lightning

❖

PETER J. WACKS
AND EYTAN KOLLIN

CALLER OF LIGHTNING

Copyright © 2020 by Peter J. Wacks and Eytan Kollin

A Baen Book

Baen Publishing Enterprises
P.O. Box 1403
Riverdale, NY 10471
www.baen.com

ISBN: 978-1-9821-2463-2

Cover art by Dave Seeley
Maps by Randy Asplund

First Baen printing, June 2020

Distributed by Simon & Schuster
1230 Avenue of the Americas
New York, NY 10020

Library of Congress Cataloging-in-Publication Data

Names: Wacks, Peter J., 1976- author. | Kollin, Eytan, author.
Title: Caller of lightning / Peter J. Wacks and Eytan Kollin.
Description: Riverdale, NY : Baen Books, 2020. | Series: The Arcane America
    series
Identifiers: LCCN 2020008739 | ISBN 9781982124632 (hardcover)
Subjects: LCSH: Franklin, Benjamin, 1706-1790--Fiction. | GSAFD:
    Biographical fiction. | Fantasy fiction.
Classification: LCC PS3623.A28 C35 2020 | DDC 813/.6--dc23
LC record available at https://lccn.loc.gov/2020008739

Printed in the United States of America

10 9 8 7 6 5 4 3 2 1

Dad, this one is for you. You are missed.
—Peter

My dedication goes to my present and my past.

The present is my beloved. Denise, my wife, thank you
for your boundless patience, your cutting wit, and your love. Of
all things, you are what fills my life with joy, appreciation,
and just enough apprehension to make life worth living.

My past is my father. Dad, my love of history is founded
on you and the library you had in your study. It was a place
of learning where I learned about history and all its fascinations.
My discussion with you made this book and many other books
and stories possible. Thank you.
—Eytan

✛⟺ ACKNOWLEDGMENTS ⟺✛

First and foremost, I wish to acknowledge my friend and partner in this endeavor, Peter Wacks. Peter has been the driving force behind this novel. His dedication, willingness to learn the details of history, and driving energy have made this book what it is. I cannot say that I always appreciated losing some arguments about historical trends, but I loved the discussions that led to this book being what it now is. Thank you, Peter.

Second, I wish to acknowledge the brilliance of J.A. Leo Lemay. He was a professor of English. To his glory, he wrote what I consider one of the, if not *the*, finest multi-volume biographies written in the English language. Its attention to detail and breadth of subject is staggering. This man did not simply list the books Benjamin Franklin read as a child. He read them, analyzed them in the context of Franklin's childhood and future writings. This is just the merest example of the effort Professor Lemay put into his work. The tragedy is that this man died after completing volume three. The last four volumes remain uncompleted. I can remain grateful for what we have whilst mourning the man and the works he did not have the time to complete.

—Eytan

I never know what to say in these things, because I feel like no matter what I do, I'll miss something or someone. I also wasn't expecting to write one of these . . .

So, I'm going to go super obscure. One of the hardest parts of writing something in the past is understanding how language was *actually* used and how it impacts what you read in timely accounts of said history. The second thing—where do you draw the line between historical accuracy and what the modern reader can palate before it detracts from the story? On that note, I want to acknowledge two old books that helped in the construction of this book. The first is Francis Grose's *Dictionary of the Vulgar Tongue*, originally published in 1785. Between that and the second book, *The Scoundrel's Dictionary, or an Explanation of the Cant Words Used by the Thieves, House Breakers, Street Robbers, and Pick-Pockets about Town,* published in 1754, I really got a grip on the conversational flow of English on the streets during the 1750s. Look them up, if you are so inclined. They are a lot of fun.

—Peter

Caller of Lightning

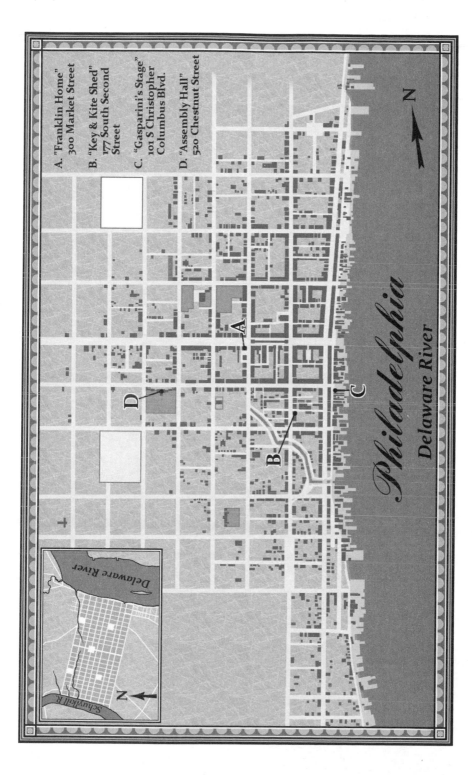

A. "Franklin Home"
   300 Market Street

B. "Key & Kite Shed"
   177 South Second
   Street

C. "Gasparini's Stage"
   101 S Christopher
   Columbus Blvd.

D. "Assembly Hall"
   520 Chestnut Street

Philadelphia

Delaware River

N

Delaware River

Schuylkill R.

N

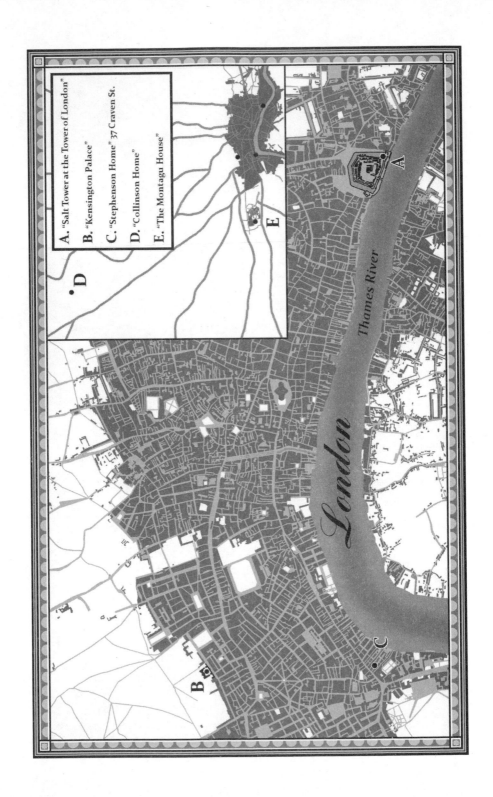

A. "Salt Tower at the Tower of London"
B. "Kensington Palace"
C. "Stephenson Home" 37 Craven St.
D. "Collinson Home"
E. "The Montagu House"

London

Thames River

"In going on with these experiments,
how many pretty systems do we build,
which we soon find ourselves oblig'd to destroy..."
~ Benjamin Franklin, August 14th, 1747

My Dearest Son,

   I have ever had Pleasure in obtaining any little anecdotes from my Ancestors. Should you e're find your way across the Veil between our Sundered Worlds, or the Veil between Life and Death, as I fear may be the truer, I imagine it might be equally agreeable to you to know some of the Circumstances of my Life which I never shared with you, as Fathers so often do not find voice to share with those whose responsible guidance and care they have been charged by Providence. As last we saw each other was when you were with me in England, in a Moment most disagreeable, and afore the time in which our Worlds could no longer touch, there is much with which you are unacquainted.

   When I reflect on my Life, it induces me sometimes to say that were it offered to my Choice, I should have no objection to a Repetition of the same Life from its beginning—only asking the Advantages authors have in a second edition to correct some Faults of the first. So I might, besides correcting these Faults, change some sinister Accidents and Events of it for others more favorable. Chief amongst these would be our Separation in England before the Sundering. But since any such Repetition is not to be expected, the thing most like living one's life over again seems to be a Recollection of that life, made durable as possible in writing.

   Hereby, too, I shall indulge the Inclination so natural in old men, to be talking of themselves and their own past actions as grand Stories; and, perhaps to gratify my own Vanity, the beginning of this Memoir is the same as the Day I discovered the existence of the Arcane. Forgive my Desires, but, with all Humility and Dignity intact, I shall impart this as I remember it, this story of a Key, a Book, and a Bell, rather than the more traditional Bell, Book, and Candle and perhaps in that remembrance gain back one of the Days I have lost with you. Though a poor Substitute for your Presence, we must all make do with what is Real, and leave the intangible to Dreams.

~ Benjamin Franklin, July 17th, 1777
Letters to a Lost Son: An Accounting of the Sundering of Worlds

Part 1:
A Candle

About a candle in the form of a simple Key,
which is a font of electric fire.

1752

The
Franklin Home
Philadelphia,
Pennsylvania Colony
June 10th
✠ ✠ ✠

As frequent Mention is made in the News Papers from Europe, of the Success of the Philadelphia Experiment for drawing the Electric Fire from Clouds by Means of pointed Rods of Iron erected on high Buildings, &c. it may be agreeable to the Curious to be inform'd, that the same Experiment has succeeded in Philadelphia, tho' made in a different and more easy Manner . . .

~ *Benjamin Franklin*
The Pennsylvania Gazette

❖ 1 ❖
How Fortunate

Thunder rumbled in the distance.

Ben Franklin slid the window curtain aside, discarding the letter he had just opened and read. It fell from his fingers to the floor, settling on an untidy, ankle-high pile of handwritten journals recently sent from the estate sale of the Widow Eversleigh in London. They were purchased for Franklin by his dear friend Peter Collinson. Despite the diaries having been sealed inside oiled paper during their journey across the Atlantic, ostensibly to protect them from moisture and salt air, a rankly nidorous scent wafted up from their tattered leather covers.

Franklin excitedly called to his son as he stared at the approaching—and uncommonly heavy—evening storm clouds. "Today is the day, Billy. Come, help me gather the supplies!"

His gaze drifted across the rooftops, tracing the gray and black skyline. The long spell of light rain was breaking at last in favor of harsher weather. In the distance, lightning stabbed through the clouds. He could see the colony's bright red flag snapping boldly in the wind, and the sign hanging over his laboratory door bounced on its chains as errant gusts tugged at it.

"Look at how the electric fire dances so brightly in the heavens tonight! Grab the rope, kite, and the rest of the kit, Billy. Hurry now! I have a modification I must make."

The stout forty-six-year-old turned from the window and was surprised to learn that he had been talking to himself. Minutes before, as Franklin had eagerly opened the letter from Collinson, his son William had been organizing books of royal law on the far side of the room. It was a shared family passion to find ways to fight the Penn family's stranglehold on the colony and improve the conditions generally of the people living in Pennsylvania. Now his laboratory was empty save for Ben himself, though the lamp his son had been using still burned, merrily lighting the desk.

For being a grown man, Ben reflected, the boy could certainly sneak about.

Another rumble of thunder sounded, spurring Franklin to action. "Peter!" he yelled as he began sifting through the container crates that housed his extra supplies. "Attend!"

The head of the household slaves poked his head in from the connecting anteroom. "Mr. Franklin?"

Ben grunted as he carefully shifted a box of glass jars, ready for conversion into Leyden jars, to one side. "Why haven't we taken these over to Mr. Loxley? No, never mind, forget that I asked. We can deal with them later. Find that wandering boy of mine and tell him it's time to attempt the experiment." Peter started to leave, but stopped short when his master continued talking. "And tell him to hurry! If I'm any judge of these things, we have perhaps thirty minutes before the storm is upon us."

"Yessir, Mr. Franklin. I'll find him straight away." Peter ducked back out of the laboratory.

After going through several crates and boxes, Ben finally gathered what he needed for his newly conceived alteration, but the prepacked box with the actual experiment continued to elude him. Stepping back to gather both wits and memory, he pulled a kerchief from his breast pocket and dabbed his forehead in frustration. "Damnation, William, will you hurry up? I don't want to have to wait 'til Fall to test this methodology, and we might not get another storm this season."

A shout echoed from the hall. "Coming, Father!"

Face flushed, William Franklin hurried through the doorway. He was a handsome, fine-featured man just into his twenties, with curly dark hair that hung to his shoulders.

"Where were you off to?" fussed Ben irritably.

"I'm sorry, Father. I do know how important this is. You were lost in that letter, and I needed more penning ink for the ledger, so I went to get it. Then I heard you shout and, realizing your plan, knew that I had to change into something more appropriate." William adjusted his immaculate undress jacket.

"Very pretty. I cannot find the kite, Billy, or anything else we prepared."

"You had me put it away. For safekeeping, you said." The young man shimmied behind several large stacks of different weights of papers, then vanished from sight as he leaned down for a moment. When he stood again he was hefting two boxes from which copper wire and two pieces of shaped cedar extended. "Here. This is everything you directed me to store."

"Indeed, my boy, that is what's needed. And here is the modification I just devised." Ben held up a spool containing a short length of silk rope.

William paused, brow furrowed. "I trust that you'll explain later." He awkwardly shifted round as he wiggled out from behind the stacks of printing press paper. Emerging with the two boxes, his shoe cuff caught on the boards of an overflowing paper box and tore a small run in his cotton leggings. William paused, mouth pursed, and closed his eyes. Taking a deep breath, he forced a smile. "We haven't much time, correct?"

Ben slid his glasses down the crook of his nose and stared over them at his son's leg. He raised one eyebrow slightly and pursed his lips. "A gentleman is never seen in public as less than composed."

William took another measured breath. "Yes, sir. I've fallen victim to your overstuffed boxes. Not for the first time, and nor, would I wager, the last. Rather than change again, perhaps one of your own sayings is more applicable?"

"Indeed. Haste makes waste! A little more care and your hose would still be whole."

William worked his mouth soundlessly, words lost for a moment in the face of his father's admonishment. "Actually, sirrah, I had intended to say that a plowman on his feet stands above a noble on his knees, and we have work to do. But you are aright. Of course."

Ben frowned as he squinted through his reading spectacles. They would never serve, outdoors, so he took them off and put on the pair he kept in his coat pocket. "Much better," he said. He finally took note of the overly composed look on his son's face and the complex emotions it sought to disguise. "I am sorry, Billy. My nerves are on edge to try this experiment, and I have been more than a little unkind to you over a triviality. Can you forgive me?"

"Of course, Father." William continued, though a little stiffly, "If you would, in turn, refrain from calling me 'Billy,' as you know how much I dislike it. Shall we depart?"

Franklin clapped his son on the back, "Sorry, sorry. I'm not myself."

"Then who are you?" William relaxed, shifting his burden.

"There is the wit! Well done," Ben replied with a smile as he took up one of the boxes for himself.

The two men, each carrying their own load, hurried out of the laboratory. "Peter, douse the lamps!" Ben yelled over his shoulder as he and William ran into the windy evening. They moved quickly through the market district, toward Society Hill and the banks of the Delaware River. People cleared the way for them—the good folk of Philadelphia were well used to the Franklins chasing around town for one reason or another, and in any case were eager to escape the increasingly foul weather themselves.

The Franklins hurried toward a small field a third of a mile away, on the edge of the dockyards and only two blocks off the river. Just outside it they passed the Loxley house, a unique tan dwelling, currently under construction, with the walls of the second floor pushed back from the façade of the home. The street-facing side of the second floor had been turned into a balcony capped by a lightly peaked roof, which was supported by two cornices that looked like they belonged on a frigate. Those who knew the house's history understood that this architectural curiosity was actually the case— the roof supports had once adorned the HMS *Adventure*.

A small wooden stand-up, eight feet on each side, awaited them in the middle of the field, far from the homes surrounding it. One wall was missing, giving the structure an open face. It was here that Ben put down his box and began preparations.

William stopped beside his father and hurriedly rummaged through his own box. Practicing this in his father's laboratory had been one thing; assembling the components of the experiment here in the open wind, even partly shielded by the walls of the stand-up, was quite another. He extracted a steel spike with a loop on the end and placed it on the ground just as his father tossed the silk rope to the back of the shed. Then he picked through his box and carefully pulled out a bundle of cut cloth, also silk.

Thunder rumbled, closer now.

Both generations of Franklin worked quickly and silently, unpacking the pieces of the kite and the Leyden jar with which they hoped to capture the electricity that Ben had theorized hid in the clouds above. Sporadic drops of rain blew into the stand-up, tickling them both. William crossed the two pieces of cedar, clamping them together, then tied off the cross-section. Next he stretched the silk diamond taut on the cedar cross, forming the body of the kite, and fastened it firmly in place. Then he began to attach a length of thick, straight, copper wire to the kite's upper tip.

Ben examined his son's work and grunted. "I believe something isn't right here," he said, nudging the steel spike with his shoe tip. He then studied all the supplies at hand, frowning. "William, can you go ask Mr. Loxley for a smaller connector for the Leyden jar?"

"I can, yes." William jerked tight the knot tying the hemp string to the kite. "Is there a reason I may know that the spike we brought is no longer suitable? To better guide Mr. Loxley?"

Ben scratched at his chin. "Ahhh. I'm not sure. But..." He paused, carefully framing his thoughts before continuing. Thunder rumbled in the near distance and Ben glanced back, then continued hurriedly, "...if I am correct about the nature of the electric fire above, I suspect—no, I fear—that use of a full rod will draw too much of the fire upon us. That would not have been a problem with my Christ Church plan, but as that structure remains sadly unfinished, we must look to the storm and a kite instead. I am sure, though, that proper application of thought will yield a safe manner for us. So..."

William pursed his lips momentarily as he propped the kite up inside the shed. "Are you sure a smaller connector will draw less electricity?"

"I believe this to be the case. One wouldn't wrestle a cask of brandy simply to quench a morning's thirst. Rods of steel or iron like this one are used to draw the fire from the sky and safely divert lethal strikes. We only wish to test the properties of this fire, not kill ourselves in the process."

"That would be for the best, yes. I will be quick." William set off jogging back to the Loxley house, while the elder Franklin continued to work.

With the kite unpacked and assembled, and the hemp string attached, there was little left to do but apply the new modification he had conceived. Franklin unwound the silk cord and set about tying it to the hemp, a little above the terminus where a kite string would typically be held in the flyer's grasp. Once that was complete, he carefully positioned the Leyden jar inside the shelter where it would be easy to access yet remain dry; an increasing worry as the rain pelting the stand-up grew heavier.

Hearing steps approaching though the grass, Ben looked around the corner of the stand-up and saw his son and another man trotting towards him.

"I say, Ben, today is the day?" shouted Benjamin Loxley, holding an oilcloth jacket over his head to stay dry.

The elder Franklin grinned. "Indeed, Benjamin, it is! I could use one of your keen insights into a more suitable connection device, provided Mrs. Loxley isn't too upset with you for abandoning her in a half-finished house with the storm overhead?" He waved to the woman watching them from the covered second-story balcony, and she waved back.

Loxley stepped into the stand-up and put his jacket to one side, taking care not to dampen any of Franklin's equipment. He was a solidly muscled man, his size attesting to his deftness with a hammer, but belying his equal skill with compass, pen, and rule. In Franklin's estimation, Loxley had no equal in Pennsylvania as draftsman and artificer. It didn't hurt that the two were close friends.

"Not you, too! I'll finish the house soon enough, but it is more than adequate cover for now. Jane will have none of the damp, I assure you." Loxley laughed and reached into his pocket, withdrawing a stout metal key. "William explained your need, and I thought of this. Will it do?"

Franklin examined the key closely, turning it over in his hands. It was a simple thing, unmarked and undecorated. "Perhaps," he mused. "Interesting. Not iron or steel, at this weight, though by appearance it would seem otherwise. Is it a known alloy crafted for a purpose or simply a happenstance mixture?"

Loxley smiled. "Clever as always, Ben. You hold the key to a shop I recently closed in London. In a moment of humor last year, I had it cast from the same batch of metal as the colony's new Assembly Bell on order from Whitechapel Foundry. Just a little keepsake. Mr. Charles was kind enough to let me include it in one of his shipments from London. The copper content is near one-half—after the iron I had them add into the mix—and should be high enough to serve your purposes without overdoing it. It seems poetic, too, though some might disagree. I do hope it will serve, as I'm afraid I have nothing else on hand to offer. There certainly isn't time enough for me to fashion anything new for you, and it should suit your purposes well."

"Poetic indeed, that we capture fire with the essence of our colony's future bell, made to celebrate the past. This is perfect. Thank you, Benjamin." Franklin handed the key to William, who passed a loop of hemp string through the circle of the key's handle and knotted it in place firmly, just ahead of the attachment to the corded silk.

"That's my work done, then," said Loxley. "I'll be up on the balcony with Jane. Dry. As in not wet. Best of luck, my friend!" With that, he lifted his oilcloth coat back over his head and ran home, grinning madly with the intensifying rain nipping at his heels.

William picked up the silk rope. "Now?"

"Yes," Ben said. "Stay in here and maintain a firm grasp. Do not step outside—we must keep the silk cord dry as an additional protective barrier from the electricity. I will get the kite aloft." He took the kite and its tail in one hand and the coil of hemp in the other, then marched firmly away from the stand-up.

Back turned to the wind, head lowered to avoid the pattering rain, Franklin played the hemp string out behind him as he walked. Once far enough, he stood still and looked up, lifting the kite to an advantageous position, while still holding its string taut. He stood for some time, growing increasingly wet, vision blurred by the drops of water running into his upturned eyes and gathering on his glasses.

As a particularly brisk gust ruffled and whipped at Ben's coat, he risked releasing the kite. The wind did its job, lofting the silk diamond and its copper-wire conductor upward. Ben controlled the climb carefully, easing the string through his fingers foot by foot, then yard by yard, until the kite was fully ascended and riding steadily in the heavens. When he finally let go, the arc of string lifted well above his head. Something primal happens, a universal thrill of childish delight, when a kite catches the wind. This emotion took hold of both Franklins and they whooped in delight. Back in the stand-up, the silk cord pulled tight in William's excited grasp. Loxley's high-dangling key, now exposed to the elements, danced on the line.

"Nicely done, gentlemen!" Benjamin Loxley shouted to them through the rain, from the safe cover of his house's balcony.

"And pray do make sure that this endeavor stays under your control, Mr. Franklin!" Jane Loxley added, with a teasing smile.

The two Franklins quickly regained their composure and focused on the experiment. William controlled the kite and Ben returned to the stand-up, soaked near to the skin but taking absolutely no heed of it; his attention was fully on the sky as the clouds turned black and the raindrops fell thicker and faster. "The time is almost upon us, William!"

The rest of the world faded from Ben's attention as he watched stray hemp fibers along the kite string slowly lift, then stand on end. A spark jumped off the end of the key, and his eyes widened. Carefully, tentatively, he stepped forward and reached out his hand, balled into a fist, with the second knuckle of his index finger jutting forward. Another spark jumped from the key, this time to his finger. The sting that came with it was familiar to him from years of laboratory experiments. God's lightning and Man's spark were one and the same, different in degree but not identity. *Electricity!* Ben gazed at the key in wonder.

"Can we transfer it to the jar? Is this the moment we capture fire from the heavens?"

"Indeed, William. We are, together, a modern Prometheus, stealing electric fire from the gods." He spoke with a raised voice to be heard through the rain pelting against the stand-up.

"That sounds rather grandiose." William grinned at his father. "If you won't mention my torn legging at the alehouse, I won't tell anyone of your muddy shoes."

"My word on that, as parent and gentleman."

Ben picked up the Leyden jar, one of his own modified designs, then stepped back into the storm and held the jar's projecting metal rod to the sparking key. Though invisible to sight, the jar quickly charged until the tip sparked over. Grinning like a child, Ben stepped back into the shelter and placed the jar, with great care, in the box it had come from. "We've done it, my boy. We've captured electricity without spires made of iron. With just hemp and silk."

"And Mr. Loxley's key."

"And Benjamin's key, yes, but that was needed only to transfer the electric fire to the phial. You saw the hemp strands rise, lifting as the fire in the kite string grew. Wet hemp, dry silk, and a bit of copper in the sky were sufficient to our proof."

"I *am* amazed. Pray do not think otherwise. Though I have a question . . . " William caught Franklin's eye, then tugged on the silk cord he was still tightly holding. "If we are keeping this portion dry in order to remain safe, how do we bring in the kite without danger, and without waiting for the storm to pass?"

The question caught Ben by surprise. He held up a finger and opened his mouth, then closed it and scratched at his chin, thinking. William had seen this process often enough while assisting his father in the laboratory and knew better than to interrupt.

"You're right," the elder Franklin finally said. "While spooling it in, of course the soaked string will carry fire with it. We would be exposed at every touch. Allow me a moment, please."

"Of course," William replied wryly. "I have nowhere else to be."

"You could simply let go, I suppose. No, that is a bad idea. Hmmph." Ben studied the hemp string and saw that it was rapidly building up a charge again, as the kite bobbed and danced in the electrical fire's airy home. Light flashed behind the clouds, a sign that powerful strikes of lightning might at any moment cut through this portion of the storm. Even one such bolt striking the kite could be disastrous.

"Hurry, please, sirrah," said William. "The water dripping down the hemp has begun to dampen the silk in turn, and I most definitely feel the wet."

"The solution is simple," Ben assured his son. "We will not have to wait out the storm. But I shall need your coat."

"*My* coat?"

"Mine is soaked. Yours is comparatively dry—dry enough, certainly, to provide a barrier against the fire for as long as it takes to reel the kite in."

"I understand."

Holding the silk cord tight in his right hand, William let go with his left and sought to shrug that arm and shoulder free from his coat's embrace. The effort was both comical and almost entirely ineffective, giving William momentary reason to regret his fondness for good tailoring.

Ben reached out to assist his son, and the world flashed bright.

Franklin's heart seemed to stop in his chest as the evening suddenly stilled. Every detail of the storm was clear, in vivid relief, as if he had lifetimes to idly examine them. A thousand hovering drops of rain fell, each one a clear crystal pearl with its own small reflection of the vast spark in the sky. Most importantly, he could see the electrical fire itself, the one moving thing in an otherwise unmoving world—a spectral force clawing inexorably downward along the kite string toward the pale white hand at its end, below.

In that instant, Franklin understood William was about to die.

It had been sixteen years since Ben's first son, Francis, had been taken by smallpox at the age of four. Time had done nothing to heal that wound. Nothing. *Not William, too . . .*

"STOP!"

Ben threw his left hand up, fingers splayed against the force of the descending electrical fire. He felt the weight of it pushing him, and instinctively pushed back with every ounce of stubbornness in his soul. To his surprise, the dangling key began to glow with a color he could not name. Points of the same impossible shade danced like will-o'-the-wisps around his fingers.

Above him, the electrical fire slowed in its course down the burning string, then stopped. Ben squeezed his fist tight . . . and watched the fire leap from the string and flee back into the clouds. Lightning, striking in reverse, opened the sky and leapt from the silk and copper.

Thunder rolled away in echoes. The blazing kite fell towards the earth as the rain once more poured from the heavens. Motion resumed as a frozen world stuttered back to life, and a cold wind danced across Franklin's face.

William stopped struggling with his coat and dropped the dampened silken cord, laughing. "There's that, then. Not a problem after all, though we'll have to get a new kite."

"How fortunate," Ben said. The most intense hunger and exhaustion he had ever felt overcame him, and he collapsed.

The
Stevenson Home
Craven Street
London, England
June 10th
✥ ✥ ✥

❖ 2 ❖
Laws of Motion

House by house and yard by yard London yawned, turning away from daytime commerce towards nighttime and warmly lit hearths. Smells of cooking stews and sweet breads mixed in the evening air with leftover traces of soot and horse manure along the walkways of Craven Street. The buildings here were dark red brick, with white-painted first-floor siding. Tall windows at the front of each home allowed occupants a view of pedestrians and other goings-on, while interior curtains of varying quality, neither too rich nor too poor but comfortably between, softened the ebbing light and shielded the owners from passing view.

The façade of the Craven Street house numbered 7—but receiving mail at 27, because it was the Stevenson home, the 27th inhabitants of the street—was one of the brightest and cheeriest on the block, despite the oddly confusing numbering system used by the Spur Alley post. Rumors of dark undertakings inside its walls were popularly whispered among the neighborhood's other inhabitants, who, like most London gossips, showed more imagination than sense when confronted with a family that did not readily mingle—and offered rooms to boarders to boot. None of these bandied tales were true, of course; though other mysteries, unguessed and unsuspected, did hold residence there.

On the second floor of the Stevenson home was a room filled with books, few of which could be found among the sellers' stalls in St. Paul's Churchyard. In that room, a girl of thirteen received her lessons—lessons few knew existed, and even fewer received, unless they were young noblemen of very particular families.

The girl wore a white dress with a yellow ribbon and sat primly on a stool next to a table. Her feet kicked idly and ceaselessly back and forth as she read carefully from an old handwritten journal. Her tutor waited for her without concern, filling the time by writing in a booklet of his own. On the table between them were several stacks of leather-bound books, a folio of unlined paper, some yarn-wrapped square pencils, and a small, elaborately engineered orrery.

When the girl finally put the journal aside, the man paused his notetaking and looked up.

"And so, Polly, on review. According to the works of Myrddin Emræs, separate from the study of religion or the mystical, precisely what is natural philosophy?"

"Umm. The study of all things known in the physical world?"

Her tutor, a clean shaven, very angular man who somehow still managed to seem warm and soft, raised an eyebrow at his pupil.

"In nature, rather," she corrected herself, "and how that study is both organized for human understanding, and determined in effect, by certain functional laws and taxonomies. That's not quite how it's written, but I believe that I conveyed the essence. Right?"

The girl's voice wavered only a little. Young Mary Stevenson encouraged people calling her by the nickname "Polly," as she felt it gave a more innocent impression, and adults were clearly more forgiving of children than young women. A sharp and calculating mind hid cheerfully behind her careful mask of precocious charm. With Mr. Overton, however, she felt no great reason to hide, so apart from occasional accidents of habit, by and large, she did not.

"Very good. And which taxonomies are part of Myrddin's natural philosophy, then?"

She furrowed her brow. "Well, all of them. And none of them. Context matters here. He describes philosophy as a process of questioning, not just a collection of facts—as a means to fuse mind and spirit with observation of the worlds around us."

"Exactly! It is only through the exacting discipline of questioning nature that we form a better understanding of it. Now attend," Mr.

Overton lifted the orrery with one hand and turned a key in its base with the other, then put the machine back down. Six sphere-tipped wire arms began to move at their own geared pace around a larger central sphere of polished brass, modeling the solar system. "Through the tension of an inner spring, I set this device, alike to Lord Boyle's, in motion. By what law is it moving?"

Polly squirmed in place as she thought. Her eyes looked to all the nooks and crannies of the library. She fidgeted with the white fabric of her dress, then picked through the books in the stack before her until she reached the one on the bottom, which happened to be William Gilbert's 1600 treatise *On the Magnet and Magnetic Bodies, and on the Great Magnet the Earth.* The text was actually in Latin, but Polly translated the title quite without thinking, Latin having been one of the first things that Mr. Overton had taught her.

"Well..." She finally looked back to her tutor. "There is a problem with that."

"Go on." Robert Overton was a gaunt and angular man, with eyes that seemed to see beyond his apparent thirty-odd years of age. Despite fashion favoring a clean face, he wore a short beard, which, along with a knowing smile, was currently concealed behind steepled fingers.

Polly took a deep breath as she idly flipped through the pages of the Gilbert book without looking at them. "What do I do if the question has more than one answer, please?"

Overton unsteepled his fingers and beamed. "If you believe there is more than one answer, you must share all those you have identified." He ran a finger around the orrery's copper base, then turned the key again a single time, renewing the vigor with which the tiny planets orbited the miniature sun. "Tell me, Polly, have you found that which you think can answer the question?"

The girl nodded. "The orrery moves, as do the planets, according to Newton's First Law. By the first law, you acted upon it by winding the key. The gears inside push each other as the spring unwinds. When it is unwinding, it keeps pushing, which we see as the planet's moving. That's why it is no longer at rest?"

Overton nodded encouragingly. "Correct. Please continue."

"By the third law, it moved in an opposite reaction to the winding of the key, I think? Or maybe the gear? Or..." Polly chewed her lip, thinking carefully. "Newton's first plainly covers the mechanics of the situation. If you had asked me about the planets themselves, and not the orrery, I could stop there and be whole. But I think this is a trick question. Myrddin Emræs addresses things more fundamentally."

Polly held up her hands and made a rough circle with her fingers, squinting as she tried to visualize the gears. Her tongue poked out between her lips, and she moved her hands around, fiddling with imaginary clockworks. "So . . . by the law of your choice. The law of your *will*. The planets move as they shall, and it is not in human hands to change their course. But this is different. *You* decided to wind the key. A thought—intangible, formless, weightless, without measurable being—is what set the orrery in motion."

"And how, exactly, is that observation meaningful? The key is there. Anyone could wind it. It wasn't my thought that did the winding. That was the work of three fingers and a wrist."

"Your fingers would have been just as still as the orrery, without the original generative thought. In Myrddin's terms there *is* more to consider here. I don't know what . . . but *something*. I'm sure of it."

"While being somewhat inaccurate, that was quite well done, Polly! Your interpretation of the laws is faulty, however. While you see past the simple into the complex, your vision is still clouded. We will address that in other lessons. When you can verbalize this insight more clearly, and in greater depth, the—"

He stopped abruptly, blinking, and went pale.

"No. It cannot be . . ."

Polly tilted her head, staring at Mr. Overton. This was odd. Her tutor had never done anything like this before. It seemed to her, suddenly, though his body was in the room with her, his eyes stared at something leagues away.

Then he shook himself and was back as though nothing at all had happened. "Please excuse me, Polly. I'm sorry. I abandoned your instruction mid-sentence."

Polly waited expectantly, intensely curious about what had made her tutor lose focus.

As he opened his mouth to resume, there was a rapping at the door.

"Mr. Overton?" The voice of Polly's mother, Margaret Stevenson, came faintly through the thick oak. "Can you take a moment? An important missive has just been delivered for you."

"Of course," he called back. As he opened the door he looked toward Polly with an expression too stern to be taken seriously. "Reflect upon your answers and the text, please," he instructed her.

Margaret peered around the doorframe and caught her daughter's eye, smiling encouragingly.

Once both adults had stepped out of the room, Polly scrunched her eyebrows. "What are your secrets, Myrddin Emræs?" she said to herself as she stared at the orrery. The spring inside had almost completely unwound—the device barely moved, now.

After a moment a bead of sweat dripped from her brow down along her cheek. "Laws of motion dictate that motion can be calculated, but the calculating act itself...the *thought*..." she murmured, tracing imaginary letters in the air. With no visible touch, the orrery began to speed up. Polly smiled and leaned forward, narrowing the focus of her attention. Inside the metal base the crunch of a breaking gear could be heard.

The orrery halted abruptly.

Polly rocked back and almost fell off her stool. "Bugger," she said, regaining her balance and smoothing her skirt. She guiltily glanced around the room to make sure no one was hiding in the shadows, ready to yell at her for cursing. Realizing how silly that was, she sheepishly looked back to the broken orrery. Her little secret sometimes had unexpected results.

Nodding once to herself, she squared her shoulders and sat primly, awaiting her tutor's return, pretending nothing had happened.

The Loxley Home

Philadelphia,
Pennsylvania Colony
June 10th

✣ ✣ ✣

❖ 3 ❖
He Must Be Told

The storm outside was finally abating. Clouds passed, leaving a starry night in their wake.

"Mr. Franklin?" Jane Loxley leaned over the snoring man. "Ben? Are you aright and just asleep?" She retreated from a particularly loud and forceful inhalation, though with a slight smile. The elder Franklin's somnambulant soundings were answer enough. "I shall take that as a 'yes' then, that you are kipping down here until morning."

Benjamin Loxley's study was much the opposite of Franklin's. Where Franklin's was dense with clutter and experiments and the tools of several trades, this room was controlled and highly organized. Books were fewer in number and contained to just one shelf, while most of the wall space was used to hang carefully levered sketches and diagrams. There were no piles of any sort. Drafting supplies sat in small crates at the back of the desk, and two chairs, as well as the divan, surrounded a small table intended to support socialization with clients.

Jane yawned and stood. Being careful not to wake her accidental lodger, she tucked a thin cotton blanket over him. "Very well then, your further care is in the hands of my dear Benjamin. It's too late for me." She walked out of the study, leaving the supine Franklin, and the divan he lay upon, behind.

In the house's spacious kitchen, she found her husband and William Franklin engaged in intense conversation over the cook's cutting table. Pulling out a tray from the cabinetry, she started to collect slices of bread and cheeses for the two men.

"I don't understand," William said, in aggravated consternation.

"Neither do I," Loxley admitted.

"I wish he'd wake up. Perhaps he could conceive an explanation."

Both men stared at the key on the table. It looked harmless enough, but sparked lightly whenever either of them brought their fingers near. The furrowed lines in Loxley's brow deepened.

"I have crafted more of the Leyden devices than I might count, as well as sundry other tools, for your father. While I haven't his grasp of the underlying principles of the electric force—I know that nothing in those principles explains *this*. Ten jars and still the key sparks." Loxley pointed to the counter across the way, where two ranks of Leyden jars sat in formal rows.

William took a sliver of cheese while Loxley continued.

"Ten! The electrostatic globe that Caspar Wistar and I built to your father's specifications will create such a charge quickly enough, but you must turn the crank firmly and steadily to do so. This key is something else. Plain metal may convey charge, William; it doesn't *hold* it. Yet we have now used this key to fill every Leyden jar in my possession, with no apparent diminution of its capacity." He shook his head. "I admit I'm uncomfortable with its presence here. What if it discharges its load back to the heavens?"

In the silence following this question, Jane stepped up next to her husband and leaned her head against his shoulder. "Benjamin. I love you, and honor both our friends as if they were part of my own family. But it is nearing midnight, and we have precious few hours before it will be time to wake again. I must abed."

"Ben shows no sign of waking?"

"Lazarus slept less deeply before resurrection, I suspect, though he was surely quieter. Here are snacks for you and young William. If you don't eat them, store them safely till morning in the waiter and you can have them for breakfast. As I can only guess at how late you will stay up, I'm afraid I will certainly be away by the time you rise. Until you do retire, please see to Ben and William as needed."

Benjamin nodded at his wife. "Once again, you are the only of us to show sense. I apologize in advance for the uselessness I will surely weigh upon you tomorrow, my dear."

"My apologies, Mrs. Loxley," said William. "We did not mean to impose."

"Hush. It will make a fine story to share," she said, smiling. "Half the pleasure in knowing your father is getting to talk about him." She pointed to the Leyden jars, a dimple visible in one cheek. "But please put those away, yes? I would like my kitchen back."

"Sleep, my dear. And don't worry. I'm sure Ben will want to take all of them to his workshop."

Jane nodded, leaving the two to their muted conversation. She picked up a small tin candle lamp with ornately-holed sides and mounted the stairs to the second floor, then walked to her bedroom. By her expression, something was clearly on her mind. She took off her small blue cap and black ribbon, placing them on a wooden ball in her closet, then tied the ribbon out of habit as she spoke quietly to herself. "Just what have they done?"

She went through her nightly ritual in a state of mild distraction, considering the problem. First she removed her gown, taking care with its rows of fabric gathered at both sides and the close-fitting elbow-length sleeves decorated with lace *engageantes*. This she smoothed out on the bed, straightening the crisscrossed blue ribbon over the stomacher and folded for wear on another day. Then she took off her matching petticoats, lifted the wooden busk from the front of her stays, and reached behind herself to loosen them enough to shrug out of. Lost in thought, Jane sat down at her dressing table and finally took off her stockings. Dressed now only in a plain white cotton shift, she let down her hair and was at last ready for bed. But her mind still fretted, and one finger traced the circular scar on her hip through the weave of her shift, over and over.

He must be told, she thought.

Jane picked up her candle lamp and left the bedroom.

Her mending room was at the end of the second floor hallway. Once inside she closed the door, lit the waiting sconces, and pulled a small wooden chest from its hiding place under her darning station. The deep lacquer finish of the chest glowed with dark cherry accents in the flickering candle light; there was a stylized etching of a many-branched tree in the center of its lid. Opening the box she removed quill, ink, and paper, which she set to one side as she sat down before her table. She paused, gently biting her own lip, and tucked an errant strand of hair behind her ear.

What I do now cannot be undone.

Nevertheless, she opened the bottle of ink and took quill in hand. Her conclusions were certain. *I'm sorry, my dear husband, but there are powers here beyond us. We must distance ourselves from the Franklins.*

She dipped the quill's point and began to write. By the time she was done, her first careful words were already fading from view.

The Franklin Home

Philadelphia,
Pennsylvania Colony
June 27th

✤ ✤ ✤

✤ 4 ✤
No Good Being Trouble

The scents of just-cut spring onion, mashed corn, and fresh baked bread filled the room. Jemima was beginning the preparations for a meat pie, minding the corn porridge on the fire as she did. She wiped a bit of sweat from her brow with her sleeve and looked over at her husband, Peter. He and King—a seventeen-year-old slave who was the most recent addition to the Franklin household—were quietly going about their duties on benches near the fire, one applying dubbin to the household's leather shoes, the other polishing the silverware.

Despite the similarities of their work, their demeanors could not have been more different. Peter was engaged in his task, the silver, in a contented mood. As he polished, he sang hymns. Jemima smiled softly to herself. It had taken years to get him to stop singing songs of the old gods, particularly Shango, and embrace the music of their master. She knew in his heart of hearts the Christian god sat behind the old gods, but he at least left room for both. For her.

At this moment, he sang the hymn "The Pharisee and the Publican," which he had learned from a hymnal his master had printed some eleven years earlier. Jemima loved her husband's voice, but wondered if the choice was intended to provoke, rather than lift, spirits. It was easy to take it as criticism of the younger slave.

The Lord their different language knows,
And different answers he bestows.
The humble soul with grace he crowns,
Whilst on the proud his anger frowns.
Dear Father, let me never be
Join'd with the boasting Pharisee . . .

King ignored Peter, or pretended to. He worked the household shoes over, as if having to clean and polish them was both insult and injury. He sighed. He fidgeted impatiently. He banged the waxy lampblack dubbin down between applications. Even the way he handled the brush was an assault, as though the bristles would cut leather instead of shine it. To Jemima, his anger was as clear a scent as anything in her cooking pot.

"Peter!" she called when her husband finished the hymn, and before he could start another. "You have much more to do there? I could use some meat from the cellar."

"It's pretty good where it is." He examined the gleaming silver service and nodded with satisfaction. Then he went to his wife, gave her a squeeze around the waist, and headed out back to the cellar. "I'll return real quick."

Jemima started slicing turnips as she turned to frown at King. She was so practiced with her cutting knife that she didn't have to watch her hands as she prepared the vegetables. "What is it that you are up to there?" she asked.

King bent over his work, switching from brush to rag, suddenly diligent in his efforts with the shoes.

"You heard me." Jemima put down the knife and stepped over to the young man. She put her hand on top of his head. "You seem a bit out of sorts, child. The Lord has blessed us with a beautiful day. Why don't you enjoy it?"

King used his hand holding the wax rag to sweep her hand away. "It doesn't matter, and I'm no child."

"All right, then." Jemima went back to her own work with a single sad shake of her head. *Mind it*, she told herself. *King is not Othello. You can't take him into your heart like he is your child, even if he is of an age. It won't bring Othello back, and it don't seem this one is looking for a mother.* She absently rubbed her rejected hand on her apron, wiping the lampblack off. But she couldn't let it go. "King, it may or may not seem like it matters—as need be. What does matter is your outward manner. Right now, what I see is something I'm not going to suffer all day. I have enough to worry on without you upsetting the masters."

King's jaw clenched and his grip on the shoe tightened. Jemima was about to say something more when Sally Franklin walked in carrying a half-grown ginger kitten in her hands. At just nine years old, Sally was buoyantly sure of herself. She wore a huge grin and almost skipped as she walked.

"Miss Sally! What are you doing in my kitchen with that animal? Shoo!" Jemima fetched a broom from the corner and pretended to sweep Sally out.

Sally giggled. "I just needed milk for Kitty. Isn't he beautiful?" She held him up for display, his rear legs dangling in the air. The kitten yawned indifferently.

"You know your mama said you weren't to make this one into a favorite. We need a good mouser, not a plaything."

Sally nodded in solemn agreement. "Oh, but he is! Mouser is even his name. You're going to be a mighty hunter, aren't you, Mouser?" She looked the kitten in the eyes. It contemplated her, completely unperturbed by her awkward management.

Jemima favored Sally with a skeptical look but put away her broom and busied herself pouring milk from the daily half-pint into a saucer. With a mock frown she handed it to the little girl. "You know there's not a lot of milk in the house, Sally. This is supposed to be only for coffee and tea."

"Yes, but I want him to grow up to be big and strong, you see. Bigger than any dog! I'll feed him and tend him every day." Sally draped Mouser over the crook of one arm—the kitten didn't so much as twitch at the transfer—and took hold of the full saucer carefully with her now free hand. With a happy parting shout of "Thank you, 'Mima!" she vanished back into the interior of the house.

Jemima returned her attention to King. "Don't think I've forgotten *you,*" she said, as she put the sliced turnips to one side and started pounding more flour into pie dough. "It is one thing to be down in the doldrums. Anybody can get in a mood. But this behavior of yours is not a benefit to anyone, least of all yourself. You need to find a secret place. Somewhere to hold your thoughts away from showing them."

King stood up in anger, his work forgotten. He turned on the older woman, eyes wide and all the hotter from the effort he made to keep his voice under control. "I need a *secret* place, do I? A secret place where I can remember the old gods of home, maybe?"

Jemima just looked at him, saying nothing.

"Or where I can be more than I am? How about that? Can I choose who I talk to, and when, in this secret place? Can I go there and stop pretending I'm just a *thing*, some object the masters own, same as they own these boots? What I need is a bugger-all *place* where I can do more than dub shoes or haul sacks of flour!"

"That's fool talk, and you know it."

"Maybe so. But I'll not live and die under such a guise as you and Peter are content to."

"Content?" said Peter from the doorway. He stood there holding the meat he'd brought back from the cellar. "Master Ben is better than some. At least he pretends at guilt. But he isn't going to manumit you if you destroy the tranquility of his home. Mind that."

King spun in surprise; fists clenched. His jaw moved as though he had something else to say, but the plain sadness in Peter's eyes stalled him.

Peter walked past, shaking his head. "Put those fists away, boy. They'll only get you killed if you use 'em. Fists is a weapon for the weak."

King scowled in anger. "They use them on us."

"That's what I just said. A weapon for the weak. At least they provide for us, King." Peter handed his haul over.

Jemima took the salted meat from her husband. "Provided for is something, not nothing," she said to King, trying to get through to the boy. "You don't know how it can be. Mr. Franklin hired Peter out a couple of years ago. I didn't see him for *six months*. There's no good being trouble to anyone, as all it does is cause trouble for all."

King glared at her and left the room, abandoning his task.

Without a word, Peter picked up the dropped rag and set to finishing the shoes. There were other tasks still to get to, and at the end of the day, the first rule was always to make sure the work was done.

The Franklin Home
Philadelphia,
Pennsylvania Colony
June 27th
✤ ✤ ✤

✤ 5 ✤
So Very Clever

Ben Franklin closed his eyes and pinched the bridge of his nose, hard, pushing back against the latest wave of a most pernicious headache. "I swear this'll be the death of me," he spoke to no one in particular. For a second he recalled a saying he had considered, but rejected, for the pages of *Poor Richard's Almanack*: "Talking to one's self is the surest way to be certain of having the listener's attention. If one does not, then one shouldn't be talking at all."

It was late at night and the heat was just starting to cool. Franklin leaned back in his chair and unbuttoned the top button of his three-button shirt, then stretched the muscles in his neck by moving his head in loose circles. After a time his headache began at least to recede, if not fully clear. Ben brought himself level again in his seat, opened his eyes, and stared once more at the Key.

He wasn't entirely certain when he had started to capitalize the word to himself. Definitely, he had made the mental shift sometime before the Key filled its thirty-seventh Leyden jar, though. There seemed no end—so far it had exhausted all his available supply of the storage devices. At that point, he had cleared the ledgers and law books from the desk William customarily used, and now its surface held only the Key. It emitted a soft ringing hum he could hear every time he focused on it, which no one else could apparently detect, and continued to glow with an unnamable light that only his eyes could see. But no one could miss the odd, intermittent sparks that danced round it on a schedule of their own conception, leaping merrily to any idle finger that came near.

The story of the kite and the storm was all over Philadelphia now, but Franklin had sworn his son and wife and the Loxleys to utmost secrecy. Until he understood it, Ben wanted no one else to know—and so far, it had defied any and every test he could conceive.

The frustration was maddening. The Key brought him back, again and again, to his memory of the frozen world, the lightning strike, and the threatened death of his son. It was a painful thing to relive. Children never truly grow up in the eyes of their parents, and William was no exception. He had earned the rank of captain in the provincial troops at just sixteen years of age and was a handsome, sought-after young man. Yet to Ben he was still rosy-cheeked little Billy, who refused to be put down and wanted his hugs. Franklin could acknowledge and accept the young man who bore his famous name with such stiff formality and decorum; but standing between the two of them, always, was the child who laughed from the tops of trees and played scotch-hopper and battledores in the street.

In Franklin's memory of the moment, it was the boy as well as the man holding the wet kite string. The fear that Ben had felt as he watched the lightning reach down the twine, strand by strand, inexorably carrying with it his son's bright and burning death . . . the ferocious denial that had risen in turn from somewhere deep within . . . these things had changed him. The *Key* had changed him. And now he could do . . . *things*. He didn't dare speak the word "magic," as that seemed completely and utterly asinine.

Yet still . . .

He splayed the fingers of both hands flat on the table to either side of the Key, some six inches away. Immediately the light that only he could see shone brighter, the humming sound increased, and a ripple of small sizzling sparks danced from the Key's plain metal curves. Franklin brought his fingers together: the light and humming increased. Slowly, carefully, he eased his hands closer to the Key, keeping his palms to the table. With every inch, the phenomena grew more vivid, the sparks longer and more energetic. When they finally touched the skin of his hands, tingling in small bites, he stopped and tried to grow comfortable with the sensation.

"This will never do," he admonished the Key lightly, as if it could hear him. "I do not dispute your nature, whate'er it may be, but if we are entwined, then you and I must find our way to a more accommodating partnership."

Straining with the effort, he sought the same emotion and resolve in him that had repelled the lightning, intent this time on consciously moderating their strength. "Come alive, come alive," he whispered, reaching within. Face red, the veins on his temples throbbing with each heartbeat, the Key's power hot against his fingers, he imagined himself holding the reins of a frightened horse he sought to calm. The image achieved little: if anything, the Key's sparks grew more intense instead of lessening.

Finally he gasped and slumped back, his hands coming away from the table. The Key quieted and went mute: sparks gone, hum gone, only the slightest of glows retained.

Franklin closed his eyes. Headache or no, exhaustion took him and he dozed off sitting in his chair. He was woken by a hand massaging his shoulder. He smiled groggily, "Debby."

She reached past him with her other hand, setting down a Betty lamp on the edge of the desk, next to his, which had gone out. "You didn't come to bed. Still obsessing over the Divine Spark you have received?" Deborah Read Franklin was a stout woman in her mid-forties, just two years younger than her husband. She dressed and acted simply and was comfortable with who she was.

Ben favored his wife with a warm, if tired, smile. "You've known me since I was seventeen. When have I ever been prone to ascribe to the miraculous that which could be calculated and measured with reason?"

"Ha! Just because you're stubborn enough to pretend deafness, don't assume God isn't speaking to you. And if this is not the Divine, then what? Witchcraft? The Devil?" Her massage dug into his shoulders as if to accentuate her point.

"This is a taxonomy of energies we are unfamiliar with, that is all. Logic and reason shall guide me. As always."

"Yet you're scared, husband, because I think you know it is something more."

"Pfaw. What have I done to deserve a tongue lashing from my own helpmeet?" It was a defense he often rallied to when she had him dead to rights, and he knew it.

"If you didn't want a woman with opinions, you should have found some Whitechapel maid to tend you during your time in London. Someone, perhaps, who would have been impressed by the muscles of a young man who could throw paper reams but had no fortune. But you didn't, did you?"

He chuckled. "It's the mind that makes the woman. Can you imagine me with someone lacking in opinions? It'd be worse than trying to stay awake at a reading of the Assembly minutes, save that the torment would extend *ad infinitum!*"

"You think you don't deserve that?" Her hands tightened and loosened, digging into his weary muscles.

"I wish you had come with me."

"I will never board a ship, Mr. Franklin. Dismiss the notion. I have nightmares, and, frankly, I feel faint just talking about it now. But to my point—which you sidetracked me from—your certainty that the world is just a puzzle to be solved shone from the first moment I met you. Dare I say it is fundamental to your nature? There you were, always half a step from running into something, completely distracted and preoccupied by your head. Your hands went about your labors on their own. It made you so handsome. But I always knew when you were close to your hard-sought solution, whatever it might be."

"You were? How?"

"Because you would start muttering under your breath in Latin, all unaware."

"Did I?"

"Yes. Exactly as you were doing in your sleep just now, when I came to find you."

She stopped massaging his shoulders and stepped to the side so she could look him in the eye. "Ben, you must open your heart to belief. Believe you are worthy of this gift. *Believe* you can summon God's will. If all else fails, then throw in a little Latin for good measure."

He smiled warmly. "I may grab a quick bite and work for another hour. I promise to think on what you've said."

She bent over and kissed his cheek. "Jemima and I have banked the fire in the kitchen, but there is fresh bread for you in the breadbox. There's no milk or butter, thanks to Sally. I told her she couldn't make a favorite out of that kitten, but this evening I found her dressing it in a bed gown, feeding it butter, and treating it as a baby. I fear next she will fashion a pudding cap and leading strings."

"Well, I can think of worse things for her to do. Perhaps I shall bring her down to keep me company."

"Benjamin Franklin, don't you dare. And don't stay up all night, please. You may think you have the energy of youth, but you don't. Remember that Newton saying you like so much; 'Genius is patience.' Well, patience gives you time for rest."

"Time aplenty for sleeping in my grave," he answered, pursing his lips wryly as his gaze drifted away, latching onto the tools on his workbench.

"We shall see. Good night." Quite aware that her husband was once more fully distracted by the puzzle in front of him, she did not expect or insist on a response. Taking her Betty lamp with her, she departed quietly.

Once more sitting in solitude, Ben's thoughts turned inward. In the seventeen days since the experiment, he had not been idle. Upon awakening at Loxley's the morning after, he had seen the ten filled Leyden jars and heard the testimony of his son and friend. That the other two men heard no sound from the Key added to the mystery, but even these were nothing to the moment they had all observed when he casually reached down to pick up the Key, meaning to drop it in his pocket, only to find a Vesuvius of electrical fire leaping up to greet his hand. Nothing like that had happened with either William or Loxley; when each subsequent attempt by Franklin engendered the same response, it had fallen to William to carry the Key home with them, wrapped for safekeeping in a sheath of thick leather.

Each morning, Franklin rose from slumber with fresh ideas for experiments. Each night, he surrendered to sleep later than the evening before, more frustrated by how little he learned. William helped as he could; for the rest Franklin managed, through trial and error, to work out ways to conduct his tests without ever touching the Key directly. Ever the improviser, he had found it comparatively easy to modify the wooden galleys and type tools of his printing trade in order to move and hold the Key as required.

Working thus, he had weighed the Key in comparison to several uncharged fellows, finding no difference when compensating for mass and volume. This did not surprise him; as he already knew, there was no difference in weight between a charged Leyden jar and an uncharged one.

Next, he clamped an odd contraption of brass and glass lenses, affixed with moving arms on a pole, to the edge of the workbench. Then he had taken to examining the Key under those magnifying lenses, focusing different lights upon its surface and recording detailed notes of any observable discolorations or imperfections, no matter how small. This, too, yielded nothing.

The non-generative keys he examined by way of comparison all showed the same natural flaws. From there he sought to exhaust the Key's apparently endless charge, first by filling all the Leyden jars that could be obtained, then by immersing it in water, and finally by running it direct to ground through conductive wires. These trials achieved nothing, which only complicated his confusion, since the usual problem with electrical experimentation was managing to generate and keep, on hand, a sufficient supply. Nothing in Franklin's experience or reading even mentioned the problem of overabundance, let alone offered an understanding of it.

And then there was the matter of the filings.

That test had taken William's help. Wearing blacksmith's gloves, at Franklin's direction, the young man had taken a steel file to the Key, carefully rubbing along the center of the stem to extract a collection of shavings. In short order, there was a small but visible pile. Franklin intended these for various chemical and temperature tests, having wondered if grains of the Key would still carry some force from the whole, proportionally or not; and whether heating might reduce the force's strength, as hot metal had long been observed to lower in conductivity. But when the two had examined the Key's stem, curious to see what underlying material had been exposed, they were startled to see it still utterly unmarred. As for the shavings themselves, they were bright silver, not the brownish-black of the Key.

Franklin, turning over the file, had found it ruined. All its teeth were shaved off smooth over the course of his son's strokes.

Nothing he'd tried since had been any more effective or shed any further light.

But as Debby had reminded him, genius is patience. Sitting alone in the dark, listening to his house settle and breathe in the night, as even well-made houses do, Franklin considered this instruction and the man who had written it. Newton—scientist and alchemist both, inventor of calculus and believer in the astrological sway of planets . . . what would that great and contradictory man have done, faced with Ben's current mystery?

There would have been some Latin muttering then, right enough.

Of course, Latin had its advantages. As a language it was more precise than English, and therefore a powerful tool for analysis and expression. There was good reason Newton had written his *Philosophiæ Naturalis Principia Mathematica* in Latin instead of English. Ben considered the Third Law, most commonly translated by his countrymen as *For every action there is an equal and opposite reaction*. But that wasn't precisely so. Newton had actually written *Actioni contrariam semper & æqualem esse reactionem*, which more accurately meant *For every action there is always a reaction of equality in the opposite direction*. The issues of magnitude and direction were interrelated, and critical to a proper understanding of the forces involved—

A notion blossomed in Franklin's thoughts. It was much too simple to credit. Yet turning it over in his mind, he could *feel* the rightness of it. Breath hushed, he spoke his first words in more than an hour. "Oh, my Debby . . . so very clever, girl." He rubbed his hands together. "And you too, Master Newton."

Without bothering to light a lamp, Ben returned his hands to the workbench on either side of the Key, this time keeping them palms up. The humming began and the Key's residual glow brightened, augmented by an occasional visible spark.

Taking several deep breaths to relax himself, Franklin cast out the memory of the lightning bolt and his fear. He focused his will and his belief into a single wish. *Whatever you may be, I don't reject you; I welcome you. "Et ego recipiam vos."* Warmth rushed through his palms and the humming quieted.

He waited a moment, then brought his open hands toward the Key as gently as if it were a flower. This time sparks neither erupted nor snapped at his flesh. Warmth spreading throughout him, emanating from the Key, spread far and fast. He could feel it radiating, and there was no world for him other than this moment, which stretched on for he knew not how long before his hands, traveling leagues instead of inches, finally came to rest clasped round the Key.

Snatching up a ledger, he began taking notes, never noticing young Sally sneaking away from the door, bored of watching him journal. She glanced down to Mouser, "What was that strangeness? What did Papa say . . . *Et ego recipiam vos.*" She whispered to Mouser, who purred in her arms, watching her intently. She felt a wave of warmth wash over her, like the kitten was a tiny oven. "How odd. Well, Mouser, I accept you!" She giggled quietly.

The next morning, Debby walked into the workshop, blanket in hand. She draped it over her husband, asleep at William's desk, then picked up the stack of papers he had written through the night and, carefully tracking the words with a finger, began reading.

The Great Bridge
Boston,
Massachusetts
October 4th
❖ ❖ ❖

✦ 6 ✦
Taught by George

Overton wrapped his overcloak tight against the night's chill. He had grown out a ridiculously curly moustache and pointy devil's beard for this disguise, but the frost still nipped at his cheeks and nose. An overcast sky blanketed the stars and moon, leaving only a few pockets of light dimly illuminating the sleeping city. Below, the sound of the Charles River gently echoed as it welled against its banks. It would be two hours still before the populace began to wake, and more fires would scar the serene stillness and hush of night.

He rubbed his eyes and sped up, stifling a yawn. It had been months since he had felt the call of a new artifact being forged but he had been unable to depart for the Colonies until he was sure the King's men were no longer watching him. It felt like days since he had slept. Now that he was here, he had simply to make his way to Philadelphia, and find the artifact Jane Loxley had warned him about. Shadows kept him company on his walk, illusory pedestrians stepping in and out of focus as his vision played tricks on him.

He paused for a moment, making sure he was alone, then muttered to himself, "*Bæran.*" The darkness melted away. It was not that he had summoned a will-o'-the-wisp, or open flame, but rather, he had summoned light that only he could see. And as his vision pierced the shadows, he realized that one of the phantom walkers hiding at the edge of his vision was no mere distortion of the eye. He spun to confront the wraith, but the shade was ready for him.

"*Macht kleb!*" echoed across the bridge.

Invisible hands grabbed Overton's wrists and yanked him back till he dangled precipitously over the water. A stream of pure force smashed into his abdomen, knocking the wind out of his chest. Overton let his head loll, inviting the attacker to come closer.

The shadows simply faded away from a man, dressed in simple clothing—though of high quality—who stepped forward with his hands clenched about empty air. Overton immediately understood the man's magic. "You were taught by George."

The man nodded, and spoke with a north London accent. "Yes. And I've been sent to collect you and the objects of power. You have committed treason and will be brought before his Majesty to receive judgment."

"I see. Is that all?" Overton studied the man, taking in every detail.

The man paused, confused. "I'm sorry. What?"

"Is that all? Is there a particular object you seek? Did the King tell you who I am? Are there more of the King's Guard here?"

"How did you—" he glanced over his shoulder to the other side of the bridge. It was all the confirmation Overton needed.

"*Æris!*" Overton spoke the word calmly and a gust of wind bowled the man over.

The guardsman struggled to his feet, hurling clamps of unseen force at Overton as he kept repeating the phrase, "*Macht kleb!*"

Overton countered with wind strikes each time, casually swatting away the other's rudimentary magic. "That's the problem, you see. George never teaches his students more than one or two things. He is too scared of what you might do if you touched real power."

"*Macht blic!*" a second voice joined in the fight and an arc of lightning smashed silently through the night and caught Overton full in the chest. He flipped through the air backwards, his head banging against the rail of the bridge. Barely catching himself before tumbling to the river below, he managed to collapse on the walkway. Everything was stained white and his ears rang.

And the two guardsmen stood side by side, walking calmly toward him. Pushed to his limit and beyond, by both exhaustion and having his head solidly rung like a bell, he gave up on being gentle. "*Abrecan, ád dwæscan.*" He slammed his hands down on the bridge, focusing on his assailants.

Both men froze. Their eyes went wide and their mouths gasped for air. Below their skin, the veins that carried their lifeblood began to glow as fire sparked and consumed them from the inside out. Within seconds, their skin flaked off, so much dry parchment, and all that was left of them was a pile of dust.

Overton sucked in a huge breath, took a moment to collect himself. Lest he get caught by more of the King's men, he quickly gathered the ashy remains into a pouch and vanished into the night.

The Plumstead Warehouse
Philadelphia, Pennsylvania Colony
October 17th

✣ ✣ ✣

✤ 7 ✤
Dextrous of Hande

The crude wooden stage occupied most of one end of the warehouse, in an area normally taken up by bales of Carolina cotton and the latest crates of goods coming into the city from Europe. Late afternoon sunlight from vents in the ceiling mixed with smoky torchlight and the glow of candles in reflective metal sconces. Together, these illuminated the performers, who had just that day arrived in Philadelphia, in a shroud of tantalizing mystery for the watchers.

After this portion of the show, tonics and such would be for sale until evening time, when the main body of the troupe would put on a translation of *Il Vero Amico*, the newest play to make its way across the ocean. Meanwhile—the celebrated Callista Family Acrobats having completed their display of tumbling, balance, and strength—the audience's attention was now wholly occupied by the antics of a middle-aged man with a curiously long and curly moustache and beard combination, capped by oiled-back hair, who was dressed in garish blue-and-purple robes. Capering about the stage with him was his comically bumbling assistant, a bewigged boy wearing a bedraggled Italian gown at least twenty years out fashion. Propped against the wheel of a cart at stage right was a large sign that read:

✤ GASPARINI THE GREAT ✤

— IL MISTERO DEI SECOLI —
The Most Dextrous Of Hande, The Greatest
Entertainer Since Isaac Fawkes
✤ MYSTERY OF THE AGES ✤

Gasparini spoke to the audience in Venetian-accented English, gesturing at the new props his assistant was clumsily unloading from the cart. "As you can see, good friends, I have three pails—One! Two! Three!—and a single watermelon..." The boy stumbled at the watermelon's weight; Gasparini righted him mid-pratfall and continued. "At least I *hope* to have these necessities, assuming my not-so-lovely assistant can find her feet!" With that, he placed one of the wooden buckets over the watermelon, hiding it from view; then gestured to the boy to sit down on the bucket, which was accomplished with considerable flouncing of the rumpled gown's skirts.

"I know you have all seen the magic of the cups and balls, perhaps even as performed by Isaac Fawkes himself! But you have never seen anything like this, gentlemen and...um..." Gasparini squinted at the audience as though he was having trouble finding someone. "*Si, si*, ladies, such beautiful Philadelphia ladies! And free spenders, *no*?"

The seated assistant idly withdrew a recorder from the floppy sleeve of his gown and began to play a vaguely mysterious tune. Gasparini stopped him with a mock slap to the back of his head, which jolted his wig forward; the audience laughed loudly while the two performers exchanged an elaborately escalating series of glares. Gasparini sighed loudly, wagging his finger. "Not yet, Giuseppe...I mean Giuseppina, *si*, that's what I meant! Wait for me to gain a connection to the *mistica*, you silly thing, and *then* you begin the *musica*!"

Franklin gently elbowed his son. "I say, this is marvelous. Much better than last year's performance."

William nodded. "Is he really as good as Fawkes?"

"Not a patch. But we must take what we can get, here, and he *is* lively."

The traveling company was a welcome respite in the midst of intense times. The Pennsylvania Assembly had petitioned the colony's owners, the Penn family, to contribute from their holdings to locally collected taxes and fees, towards local matters and needs.

To no citizen's satisfaction the Penns had refused, and the dispute was in clear danger of escalating. The Proprietors were bluntly refusing to pay taxes themselves, as well as using the taxes collected from others in a method the Assembly balked at. With pressure building, a chance to ignore the colony's problems and simply laugh was a welcome relief to many: the entertainers would find generous and needy audiences here.

Gasparini now hefted a bottle filled with a bright pink fluid over his head, striding the stage like a tiger. "Once I drink this *tonico mistico*, derived from the meat of the watermelon and the essence of waters obtained from the lost temple of Solomon, I shall be able to make the fruit disappear!" There was an obligatory gasp from the crowd, mixed with challenges of disbelief.

Gasparini brought the bottle to his lips and drank, leaning back further and further, until the pink fluid was entirely consumed. Then he straightened, and, as his assistant played, he lifted the other two buckets up—to show the audience they were empty—before slamming them back down again with great thumps upon the stage. In this lifting-and-dropping manner, he reversed the buckets' relative positions, placing one at the other side of his assistant, then both, and then worked them back to their original places. At no time did the boy move from his perch or pay any attention to his master at all, remaining fully focused on playing.

Finally Gasparini stopped with a flourish and addressed the crowd, "My esteemed friends, which bucket do you think the watermelon is under?"

A din of shouting voices made plain that the audience knew nothing had changed, and the watermelon was still under the seated boy. Gasparini crooked a dramatic eyebrow and snapped his fingers. The boy in the dress immediately stood up, stopped playing, and backed away from the bucket. Gasparini, smiling mischievously, lifted it to reveal . . . nothing.

The crowd gasped.

In quick succession Gasparini lifted the other two buckets, and the audience gasped again when the watermelon was found under the last one.

At that, without another word, the magician launched into the rest of his act. The boy in the dress stood to one side, playing faster and faster, as Gasparini lifted and moved buckets at will, his robes swishing dramatically. The watermelon appeared first here and then there, under a different bucket every time. As the music grew more intense, a second watermelon was found, which Gasparini rolled to one side. Moments later a third watermelon joined it, and then a fourth. The audience's applause grew louder with each addition.

The music stopped. In a series of flamboyant motions, Gasparini turned all the buckets right-side up and placed a watermelon in each, then stacked them in a clumsy, ill-balanced tower. That done, he snapped his fingers twice and kicked the buckets over. As they tumbled and rolled noisily on the stage the onlookers could see that they were all now completely empty.

Thunderous applause followed, along with foot stomps, whistles, and shouts. The grinning magician basked in this acclaim for a moment, then clapped both hands together above his head with a shout of "Presto!"

At this the three missing watermelons fell from the rafters, narrowly missing the boy, who jumped back in unfeigned surprise. They smashed as they hit the stage, spraying seeds and red-pink pulp in all directions.

Ben blinked rapidly and brought his hand to his chest. The Key, which he now wore under his shirt on a chain, had begun to warm when Gasparini had completed his act's first move.

The magician and assistant bowed to the crowd while the acrobats from earlier set up a table to sell watermelon tonic infused with "Solomon's Gift." William Franklin moved forward to join the queue, but Ben caught his arm.

"No."

William was surprised by his father's reaction. "Why not? As you say, the tonics are harmless enough. Just sweet tasting waters, yes?"

"This is different. Quietly, please, step aside with me."

William gave him a look. "Father . . ." he began.

Franklin interrupted. "I know, I know. But step aside with me nevertheless."

William followed his father out of the warehouse. Outside, William breathed deeply of the cool autumn air with its hints of tobacco smoke and hearth fires and said, "You are obviously troubled, Father. Why?"

Franklin rubbed the Key through his shirt. Its metal had started to cool as soon as they had exited the building. "Somehow, whatever that man was doing made the Key come alive. Painfully so, in fact. I do not know how or why, but I prefer to avoid whatever agency was in use."

"But this . . . this is marvelous! A clue! We have so many questions and no answers. Your investigations have offered no—"

"I have gained greater control."

"Yes, yes, but no *understanding*. If there is a connection between what this mountebank was doing and the Key, then he might know something useful!"

Franklin shook his head "My boy, we are men of thought. Men of philosophy. Through observation and questioning, that is how we will find our answers. Not from some strolling button-buster."

"I do not understand," William frowned. "It seems foolish not to just go *ask* him."

"And how would you proceed? Mr. Gasparini, welcome! Do you like our colony? I do hope so. And tell me, please—was that business with the watermelons just a trick, or was it dark magic? Can you throw fiery sparks with your hands like my father has learned to do?"

"Surely discretion offers more options than those," William rejoined. When distracted and flustered, his father could become a most unkind person.

The elder Franklin thought for a moment. Why *was* he so hesitant to approach the wandering magician? In place of his usual clarity of thought he found nothing but muddle, and an unexplainable urgency to be as far from the Plumstead Warehouse as possible.

Meeting his son's eye, he said "Perhaps. The thought that intrudes upon my process is that we would risk being spoken of poorly by our peers, though I know this is not true."

"Then you have no reason."

"No reason I can yet name . . . which does not reduce my certainty. Until I know more, we will avoid this man."

William was taken aback. He has never known his father to be anything other than fearless and inquisitive. This sudden reticence shook him . . . but taking in his father's expression, he nodded and acquiesced.

The two Franklins walked in complex silence through the

Philadelphia streets until they parted company at Society Hill. Ben continued towards home, lost in thought, while William left for an evening of drinking and merry distraction with his friends.

They did not speak again upon the topic for weeks.

The
Blue Anchor Tavern
Philadelphia,
Pennsylvania Colony
November 28th
✣ ✣ ✣

✦ 8 ✦
The Hands of Our Enemies

Jane Loxley wore a full-covering cloak, overdress, and low-heeled buckleless shoes identical to those she had purchased for her maid earlier in the season. With the hood of her cloak pulled up against the snow and wind, and a covered basket in hand, she was able to pass through the afternoon streets as unnoticed as any servant. Not that recognition was so great a risk, but when engaged in the Society's business, it was always better to exhibit care.

At the Blue Anchor Tavern, she found her Lord waiting at the back door. He opened it for her without a word, and they entered together. Inside, the goodwife and her two helpers scurried about the kitchen, tending to multiple stews, warm cider pots, and a bank of meat pies that were being prepared for the evening rush.

The tavern staff took no notice of the two cloaked intruders, or of the sudden gust of chill November wind that accompanied their entry. Jane, seeing this, understood that they were *glamoured* and chose to stay silent. The very first time she met her Lord she had tried to make conversation with him in a similar situation, and her voice had broken the spell, revealing their presence to those passing by. That was how she had learned all acts of magic have their limits. Even his.

A few moments later they stepped into his room at the top of the stairs.

He closed the door with care and finally spoke. "You were quite right sending the letter; I applaud your instincts. This Franklin fellow is potentially troublesome."

"Thank you, Lord—"

He stopped her with a look. "No formal titles—or especially numbers—please. I am 'Signore Gasparini' here, merely a traveling entertainer; as you are simply 'Mrs. Loxley.' I have raised wards against interruption, but they rely upon convention and appearances."

"Yes, Signore." Jane acknowledged his instruction with a swift nod. "What do you command? I would not wish Mr. Franklin harm—in fact, he is a dear friend of my husband's—but he is not one to limit the bounds of his curiosity. There is no telling where the exploration of his accidental discovery will take him."

"Indeed. The man attended my show five times during our performances here, and he was clearly studying me in a way his fellows were not. He sees and feels more than they do."

"He always has."

"Not like this, I wager. Somehow, something has opened his senses—something more than mere proximity to the star metal. I sought to tempt him to come to *me* by using more real magic and less illusion each time he watched, but it did not work. Indeed, I may have driven him away. On the last attempt he left the audience mid-show and never subsequently returned."

"If Mr. Franklin is so gifted, perhaps he should be brought into the fold? Our numbers are small, and few of us have actual skill, despite our knowledge."

Gasparini shook his head. "He does not sound like one to be 'folded in' to me. I am planning to discourage him, as I am able, after I learn exactly what he has and what he does or does not know."

"There is also the son," Jane added. "They are fairly inseparable."

"I see no reason to suspect that William Franklin is attuned to the available magic. Much like your husband, he has no sense for it and would be better served kept in the dark. But the father is a different matter. If we do not take action, he might someday serve our enemies."

"Surely not. There is a natural opposition."

"You are young, Mrs. Loxley. In my time I have seen hunger for power overwhelm much greater walls."

The bitter note in Gasparini's voice was new to Jane. It both hinted of mysteries and warned against their exploration. She gently pushed a finger against her hip while thinking, tracing out small circles. "We have six years before the comet comes. Can you keep Mr. Franklin in check that long? Or must you . . . "

Gasparini smiled. "Kill him? No. First we will see if discouragement suffices. As long as he stays in the Americas, he is not a serious threat—a concern, yes, but not a threat. In a certain light, I might even be able to use his placement here to our benefit."

"So you will wish me to continue to observe and to report."

"As you can, yes. But Mr. Franklin was not, in fact, the primary reason for our meeting."

Jane looked at her Lord quizzically. "Then what was?"

Gasparini took a sheet of rough paper and a pencil from the room's small desk and sketched while talking. "The Society faces a more immediate difficulty. In response to your letter, I traversed from England to the residence I maintain in Boston with an artifact I call the Manydoor, then traveled from there to here as Gasparini."

"The Manydoor?"

"Yes. It is a series of door handles that all connect to each other, no matter where in the world they may be. Now, as I prepare to return, I have received word that my Boston lodgings, and several other homes on the street, have burned down during my absence."

Jane's eyes widened in surprise. "But there are preventions—"

"Yes. There are. Rather, there were." Gasparini looked up from his drawing and focused on Jane intently. "Our opposition is skilled, and these fires are their doing, I'm sure. I was set upon by two of them on my travels here. Somehow they followed me. Despite my shields, they must have detected the use of the door and determined that the risk of exposing this ability might be worth the reward. According to my agent within the civil authorities, a search through the debris revealed no hardware from the house at all. Everything—including the door handle—was gone."

Jane sought to control the fear that rose within her. "The Manydoor is in the hands of our *enemies*?"

"Calm yourself, please. It may be so, or it may not. I am informed that urchins and other scavengers are routinely chased away from burned-out homes and businesses. It is possible that one such has taken it, unaware of what they carried."

"How can I help?" Jane asked.

Gasparini handed her his finished drawing, a careful rendering of an intricately shaped metal door handle. "Once I am done with Mr. Franklin, I must return to England, and, without the door handle, I will have to take passage on a ship like anyone else—there won't be power enough to traverse without aid until the time is upon us." Gasparini shrugged. "It is not ideal to lose so much time to idleness, but there is no choice. While I am shipboard, I must rely on someone else to manage the search for the Manydoor. For that task I have chosen you."

Jane knew that her surprise and uncertainty were self-evident. She studied the drawing intently, making no attempt to hide what she was feeling.

"You honor me."

"I do not. You are best suited for this among our colonial fellows and have earned my trust—and this commission—through your own intelligence and capabilities. Use the Society's resources here as you must, under my Seal. The task is clear, if not actually simple—do your best to locate and recover the lost handle for the Manydoor. Failing that, seek any indication of a trail."

"I will, Signore. I will also keep my ear to the ground for gossip of people disappearing unexpectedly and without a trace, as could easily have happened to someone taking it by mistake. Any such report might help us narrow down the location." She paused before continuing. "Is there anything else I can do?"

"This alone," Gasparini answered seriously. "There are few enough objects of power scattered across this world, and the Manydoor is singular amongst those artifacts. Nothing else has its power, reach, or focus of ability. Better it be lost or destroyed than in the possession of our foes."

"I'll find it."

"If you don't, my task in London will be—" He clenched his jaw. "Just see that you do, Mrs. Loxley."

The
Franklin Home
Philadelphia,
Pennsylvania Colony
December 1st
✤ ✤ ✤

✥ 9 ✥
Mind Your Anger

Ben Franklin shivered as he sat in the yard outside his kitchen, huddled naked under a blanket as was his morning ritual. He often rose at five to allow for the solitary thought he felt ensured a productive day; on this morning he particularly wanted to have time to himself. True dawn was still more than an hour away. The stars above him were undimmed, and to the east only a first elusive hint of light was cresting the horizon. Behind him, inside the house, the rest of his family slept. Even the servants were still abed.

He sipped a bowl filled with watery, warm porridge, a breakfast habit he had adopted in London in his early twenties. Other workers at the press would drink beer on waking up to avoid getting sick from drinking fouled city water. They also believed the beer gave them much needed energy in the form of golden liquid bread. Ben had different ideas. Not liking the way morning beer stripped him of his faculties and made the world seem less sharp, he devised his porridge recipe that used boiled water instead. Satisfied with the results, he swore by his recipe to this day.

He chuckled as he reminisced. Back then, he had lent weekly wages to other press workers at a modest profit—a practice that simultaneously controlled, and enabled, their beer intake. He had built the foundation for his first fortune, a few pennies at a time, on other people's drunkenness.

Ben took another sip of porridge. Though it was quickly cooling, there was still enough warmth to spread across his stomach as December's cold pinched at his cheeks and nose. He rubbed his belly, absentmindedly feeling the curve of hanging flesh. He poked his finger into his belly button and wiggled it for a second, then sighed. How he missed the flat abdomen and unending energies of his youth!

But that was another world, and long ago. He could only reflect on it for so long before returning to the more pressing concerns of the moment.

The taxation problem, for one. The Penn family withheld monies earned by the colony, flatly refusing to follow the laws set by the Assembly, much to the colony's detriment. It was vexing. The Assembly had a duty to protect the people, even if that duty meant standing up to the proprietorship, and Ben could not help but feel ineffective in all the ways he publicly and privately sought to change this situation for the better.

William, for another. Though he couldn't ask for a more dutiful son, behind the appearance of filial devotion Ben sensed increasing doubt, and the shadow of serious disagreement. In all honesty, he felt compelled to admit that William was becoming a stranger to him, as if a void had opened between them that might never be bridged... a void first noticeable in the aftermath of the experiment, and one which only grew with each new piece of mastery he attained over his magic.

Magic was the center of it, of course. The Key was the center of everything, the sign that he was no longer the man he had been; even as he had no idea of who, exactly, he now was, or what sort of man he might become tomorrow.

Porridge or not, I'm cold, he thought, reaching for the Key where it hung around his neck, beneath the blanket. He stroked the plain metal with chill fingers and said, quietly, "*Et calor*," whereupon a gentle heat radiated outward from the Key, warming his bones and dispelling all discomfort. *Could the press worker do this? The printer for hire? Or even the much-lauded statesman and inventor? Who am I now?*

He prided himself on being a rational man. Yet magic was clearly, inarguably, real, and greater than natural law: he could not argue with the evidence of his own senses and experience. It excited and frightened him to face something beyond the ken of his mind; indeed, beyond the ken of natural philosophy as it was commonly understood.

He took a final sip of the porridge and placed the bowl next to himself on the bench. Above him the first golden ray of dawn speared the sky, reflecting through the clouds in a pale web over Philadelphia's architecture. Though it was only light, it seemed to Ben that a second city existed in the sky, with golden, pink, and red walkways of sunbeams—paths of the angels, never meant for mortal eyes. He wasn't deeply religious, preferring reason to faith, but this sight still spoke to his soul. Mornings like this made it difficult to not see God's hand in every aspect and beauty of nature.

Grunting, he pulled the blanket tighter. He felt like everything was coming to a head. It was only a matter of time before the Assembly and the Penn family would require intervention from the Crown. The Key, the lightning, his own abilities . . . only the good Lord might know what was in store for the future of natural philosophy and the study of electricity.

A sound from his workshop disturbed him.

Roused from thought, he spoke in a forced whisper—loud enough to carry to the workshop, but no further. "Peter? King? Jemima? Is that one of you?"

Silence was his answer.

Ben's eyes narrowed. He stood, clutching the blanket one-handed, and tried to stay quiet as he inched around the corner of the house toward the workshop door. As it came into view, he heard another slight noise and all thoughts of politics and philosophy fled. There was definitely someone sneaking around within his workshop!

Who would dare?

He eased up to the door and wrapped his fingers around its handle, peering through the glass panes. There! A shadow, darker than the others, was doing something near his desk. With a quick twist of his wrist, he yanked the door open and jumped across the threshold. Shards of glass flew as the window broke upon the door's hard impact against the wall.

"Who goes there?" He shouted. "This is not your place to be!" Without thinking, he dropped the blanket and picked up his cane, leaning by the inside of the door, which he brandished with both hands. "And you better be ready to pay for that window I just broke!"

A tall man—all angles and shadows—stood by Ben's desk, holding one of the decaying journals Peter Collinson had sent the previous summer. By his manner he wasn't at all surprised to be discovered. Calmly, without even bothering to look up, he continued to scan the pages in his hand. "One of the lost journals of Myrddin Emræs. One chronicling the founding members, and numbers, of his society, no less. How odd to find it *here.*"

The man spoke with a decidedly Venetian accent.

Franklin slowly lowered the cane in shock. "Gasparini? The itinerant magician? . . . what are you doing here? This is my home!"

Gasparini held up a finger in the direction of Ben, still not looking away from the journal. "One moment please, Mr. Franklin. I am here to correct one of those small mistakes that fate, in its blind fashion, will make upon occasion. You are in possession of a most unusual Key. I require it."

"You are trespassing, sir. You will leave my house *now*, with *nothing*, or I will hold you here while my slaves bring a constable."

"I don't think you fully understand what is happening here, this is not a requ—" The magician, as he spoke, finally turned to face the outraged Franklin. "*Mio Dio!* Did you realize you are completely naked? What a strange man you are!"

Ben lifted the cane again, ready to swing, and took breath to shout.

With idle unconcern, Gasparini waved the fingers of one hand in Franklin's direction and said "*Slæp.* I had assumed the Key would be stored here among your things . . . but I see you are *wearing* it, instead."

In an instant, Ben tottered backward and slumped against the wall beside the door, dropping the cane as his body slid to the ground. He could still see and hear, but he no longer had control of his muscles.

"You see," said Gasparini as he approached, "you are an infant in this world, Mr. Franklin. And as such, this Key and this journal, they are not for you. You'll hurt yourself and others should you continue."

Red tinted the edges of Ben's vision, and he could feel the blood pounding through his body. *Stand, damn you!* he screamed inside his own mind. He tried to force his lips and tongue to form the Latin word for "stand," but only a breathy whisper issued from his mouth.

"And now I will take what I have come for."

The magician knelt down, reaching for the Key.

NO. The thought was not a cry of desperation, but rather a command, echoing in Ben's mind. He felt magic surge through his torpor-stricken muscles, coiling like a serpent around his heart.

Before Gasparini's fingers could touch it, a single actinic tongue of electrical fire leapt up to meet them. The bolt sizzled as it wrapped around Gasparini's hand and arm and then, for all Ben could see, appeared to *squeeze.* The man fell back in surprise, crying out as he jerked his arm away. Thin tendrils of smoke rose from ragged burned strips in his coat sleeve.

Still unable to speak, Ben felt his palsied features form a savage smile.

Gasparini's eyes flared with anger to match. He stretched his hand out toward Franklin, clearly intending to try again, and Ben could hear the Key come back to life, humming loudly—even threateningly—like some guard dog crouched and ready to protect its master. Electric fire crackled and sparked in a dozen colors along its surface.

Gasparini narrowed his eyes, studying the prone Ben intently. He moved the fingers of his hand as if trying to turn the tumblers in a lock, listening intently to the subtle changes in the hum that resulted. At last he stopped, frustrated, and let his arm fall to his side.

"Interesting. You've made the artifact part of you."

"*G-g-etttt youuuuu . . .*" Ben finally found a shred of voice, exulting as he felt the fingers of his right hand come together in a fist.

Gasparini stood and retreated two steps, then took a moment to dust himself off. "You have done something you should not have been able to do, Mr. Franklin. If there was the slightest chance that you knew how, I would stay and try to learn what you are. But you clearly don't and would, I suspect, discover more in the exchange than I adjudge safe. We may yet speak, under different circumstances, when I am ready—and you are not." He retreated further, to the desk, and picked up the journal he had dropped there. "'Tis almost a pity that I cannot leave this with you, just to see what you could grow into. But it would risk too much."

He held the journal from one corner, between the tips of his thumb and forefinger, and said "*Beswæle.*" With that word, it flashed brightly into a small fireball. The timeworn pages flared up in a heartbeat, and Gasparini dropped the burning covers and spine, now bereft of their content, to the ground.

Brushing his hands off, the traveling magician walked to the door. He paused and squatted down at a safe distance, meeting Franklin's eye.

"*Excæ . . . ,*" Ben raged quietly.

"*Si, si.* You do not like me. In your position I would not like me either. As to the sleep power, well—a normal man would have been rendered *inconscio* for a full day, but you are no normal man, clearly. I suspect you will be fine in an hour or two, so long as you don't burst your own blood vessels trying to yell like that. You really should mind your anger. It is not healthy at all." The magician patted Ben's cheek, then stood and walked to the open door. "*Cessa la tua*, Mr. Franklin. I will see myself out."

Ben heard the door creak closed, then nothing. He tried again to move; sparks crackled around the Key and his weakly clenching hands for almost a minute before he was too exhausted to continue. As consciousness faded, two thoughts fought through the growing fog of sleep: a determination to examine the remaining journals Gasparini had not found as soon as awareness returned; and the curious observation that when the Key had caught the magician by surprise, he had cursed in an unmistakably English accent.

1753

The Stevenson Home
Craven Street
London, England
February 12th
✣ ✣ ✣

❖ 10 ❖
The King's Law

Polly watched in frustration from the receiving room on the first floor as the Thomas Lobsters of the King's Company First Guards stomped by her. Piece by piece, they collected and packed the second- and third-floor possessions of Mrs. Stevenson's lodger, then removed them from the premises.

"I don't understand, Mother."

Margaret hushed her daughter. "He has violated the King's law, Polly. We are lucky they are only taking Mr. Overton's things and not us as well."

The red-coated guard who stood between them and the hallway, keeping them in the receiving room, chose this moment to finally speak. Surprisingly, his voice revealed a posh north London upbringing. "He's a criminal, my dear. Nothing but a scoundrel and common cur headed for the gallows."

Polly bit her lip and grabbed her skirts to conceal the involuntary fists she was making. She was fuming and could barely contain herself. During the six months of Mr. Overton's absence she had continued her studies by devouring the fascinating contents of his books at will, leaping from volume to volume as curiosity pushed her ever deeper. She had come to think of them as her own. And now these loud, pompous men in the colors of the King were taking all her treasures away.

She narrowed her eyes, ignoring the guard. "What if he comes back and finds his property gone, Mother? Shouldn't we be protecting it? He is *our* lodger and these men—"

"Polly, don't," Margaret interrupted, all too aware of her daughter's tendency to say the most inappropriate things at the worst times. The guard interrupted, sparing her an inevitable verbal joust with Polly.

"Little girl, if he dares come back here we will kill him. That's the order." The man swaggered over and stood before them, glaring down at Polly. "The order from the King. And if you hide him, or anything *of* his, you'll be in trouble too. Deep trouble, with, I repeat, the King."

Margaret tried to step between the guard and her daughter, but he shoved her aside. The Stevenson matron banged her shoulder against the wall and bit down a cry of pain. She knew better than to give this man a further excuse to be a bully. She just had to pray Polly would not enflame the situation.

The guard shoved his face up against Polly's till their noses were almost touching. "D'you understand? I need to hear you *say* it."

"I . . . I . . . " Polly's eyes were tearing up, though she knew it was from anger as well as fear. She ground her teeth. "I understand, sir. If he comes here, I will tell the watch."

"The *watch*?" He took both her arms in his big hands and shook Polly once, roughly. "No, not those Bow Street plodders of Fielding's. You come to the Guard and tell *us*, understand?"

"Please, good sir—" Margaret tried to interject again, but the guard ignored her. He shoved Polly back then poked her hard between her collarbones.

"Only us!"

Polly nodded sullenly. It was taking every ounce of self-control not to use her will to break his finger in half.

"Good," said the guard, misreading her tears as fear, rather than the barely contained rage they were. He turned his back on Margaret and Polly and returned to his post at the room's entrance.

Polly stood bravely, not wanting to give the guard any form of satisfaction, but Margaret blew that plan by kneeling down and wrapping her arms around Polly.

Polly pulled away sullenly, then under her breath mumbled a small chant to foul his stomach. It was a petty vengeance, she knew, but brought enough peace to her soul to avoid any larger violence. In an hour the man would have far more to think about than his polished buttons and high-toned, superior manner, and serve him right!

Grounds of the New State House

Pennsylvania Colony
March 10th

✛ ✛ ✛

✥ 11 ✥
By Order of the Ass

The ceremony in which the Assembly's new commemorative bell was to be sounded was held on one of those strange spring mornings where the air is crisp and cold, yet the sky so clear and cloudless that the beating sun roasts anyone daring to stand still beneath it. Humidity clung to the grass and every other surface—most importantly, to Ben's skin and clothing. Like many around him he was overdressed for the weather, having assumed that the week's general overcast skies would persist.

Now he wished he could strip off some layers, but refrained. On the Philadelphia docks, perhaps; but not in this place, among this well-to-do company. Perhaps not even on the docks, actually. He was far from the muscular youth who could throw paper bundles, as much as he wished the sight of his rather large and pale belly wouldn't be so improper in this crowd. He imagined the assembled masses running and screaming, climbing the scaffolding of the Assembly Hall's half-constructed bell tower to escape the sight of his unclad belly. His lips twitched, but he held the smirk in. Though gazing around at the fifty-odd people present, Ben noted wryly that he wasn't the only person dabbing sweat away.

He turned to address his son, who, despite being immaculately dressed, showed no sign whatsoever of discomfort. Franklin marveled quietly at the sight. "Well, William, though the weather is not agreeable to me, I cannot say the same for the occasion."

"Indeed, Father. But mind your step," the young man warned, carefully avoiding a pile of animal scat. "The lawn is somewhat aerated."

Ahead of them, cradled in a stand that raised it above ground for testing, was the two-thousand-pound bell. Standing next to it was Isaac Norris, leader of the Pennsylvania Assembly, looking as proud as if he had cast the bell himself, using metal he had personally mined with his own bare hands—and not having simply ordered its creation in London, using funds appropriated for the task by the Assembly. Franklin could not begrudge the man his pride of accomplishment: Speaker Norris was a man so successful in business that he had been able to retire in his forties, after which he devoted himself to Pennsylvania politics with a fervor that equaled Franklin's own dedication to natural philosophy and experimentation. In doing so, Norris had followed the trail blazed by his own father, who had been elected Speaker of the Assembly in his day. Like his father, and like Franklin, Norris's devotion to the colony ran deep.

Ben nodded briefly to Norris as he and William approached the bell. They were close enough now to make out the two bold rings of raised type which circled the upper portion of the bell's waist. From this angle, the top line read:

LEV.XXV. V X. PROCLAIM LIBERTY

And below it,

IN PHILAD^A BY ORDER OF THE ASS

Even knowing that the word in full was "assembly," Franklin could not help but chuckle at the sight.

William raised an eyebrow. "You are in high spirits today," he observed.

"Indeed I am. This is a masterful display. I would have thought to frame the words, rather than run them in a circle. As it is, every crass-minded jack will be making jokes. I must do something with this in *Poor Richard's Almanack.*"

William stared at the bell, puzzling. "I consider myself well-lettered, Father, but I don't see your point. Isn't it simply a biblical quote to honor the liberty that, by the grace of God, we all enjoy as Christians?"

"It's right there. Right in front of you. You really don't see it?"

"See *what*?"

Franklin pointed, smiling. "It's a bit *ass*-inine, don't you think?"

William's back stiffened. "Are you implying that I lack sense? This is certainly not the thanks I'd expect for coming out to assist you with your secret experiment today."

Ben immediately regretted his words, though it was William who was missing the joke. "Nothing like that, William. It's just . . . well, look again. Read what is visible from where we are standing, and fill nothing in. Not 'Assembly,' then, you see, but . . ." He waggled his eyebrows and laughed again, this time louder and slightly nervously.

William did as instructed, finally noticing what he had missed. "Ah. How droll," he said, his back even stiffer. The acknowledgement contained not even the slightest trace of humor.

Franklin was saved from making matters worse by the approach of Speaker Norris. "What about our bell brings such mirth to Philadelphia's most famous son?"

"I won't be the most famous for long if you keep up your good work, Isaac," Franklin said smoothly, deflecting the question.

Norris beamed at the compliment but was not to be deterred. "Come now, Ben, I would share in thy mirth if it is not too delicate a thought to share. Perhaps something more on thy outlandish stance that we should become a royal colony instead of remaining a proprietorship?"

William turned slightly, offering a hand to the Speaker of the Assembly. "Mr. Norris. It is a delight to see you. I'm afraid my father was having a bit of a jest at my expense. Hardly worthy of repeating in public; it was simply a minor education on the nature of the inscription you have chosen for this marvelous new bell. He would have it framed differently to better show the quote you have chosen in a single reading, rather than requiring one to walk a full circle."

"Well," smiled Norris, "I didn't consider that. We allowed them to perform the setting of the letters in the manner they thought best at the foundry, under the predetermination that they be around it." He glanced sidelong at the bell and his chest puffed in pride. "But upon reflection, I believe that this arrangement creates a deeper meaning."

"What meaning would that be?" Franklin asked, genuinely curious.

"Well, the circular nature of the inscription carries with it a certain unendingness that is symbolic of the liberties we have gained through William Penn's Charter of Privileges. It gives physical form to our very foundation as a colony, and the invitations to live here presented by William Penn to the Friends. Families like the Janneys and Yardleys, and even my own, who were led to Penn by the like of Fox and Barclay, then escaped oppression . . . it is an unending circle of faith and life—what better reason could there be? After much discussion in the meetings, that was the reasoning we landed upon." Isaac's cheeks flushed, as he appeared to realize he was speaking as if at a podium or lectern, rather than casually among friends.

Franklin was used to Norris slipping comments about William Penn into nearly every conversation, a habit that all too often generated argument. Both men wanted to hold the Penn family accountable, but Norris did not share Franklin's wish to dissolve the proprietorship—he simply wanted the Assembly to hold a stronger position in the balance of relative power.

Rather than rise to the bait, intended or not, Ben glanced sidelong at his son. William, well aware of the longstanding disagreement, responded smoothly to his father's cue.

"No one could possibly see it otherwise, Mr. Norris. Beyond that, however," he continued, "I am sure all who hear the bell shall carry those words of wisdom, and that liberty, in their hearts each and every time it sounds."

Norris broke into a huge grin and slapped William on the shoulder. "Astute as ever, young Franklin. But now, my apologies. I must retreat in the face of social obligation and speak to other guests as well."

As Norris excused himself to hobnob with the next group approaching the bell, the Franklins walked around it to the opposite side. Ben felt the Key's warmth and tingling under his shirt, a sensation he now took completely for granted, paying attention to it only when it changed in response to some aspect of his ongoing investigation. Despite Gasparini's intimations, study of the remaining journals had yielded little, as they were written almost entirely in a hodgepodge of languages that Ben could not read, or in some cases even recognize.

He found himself increasingly stymied in the face of passages like:

Þā heofansteorran gedrif heofonbéacen hrægnlo-cabrægnioca bellique saccager et rend abismera des artefacts ᛗᚠᛋᚾᛗᛋᚾᛏᛗᛏ séo gemærung dont sera mort á tous. Hit insegel unálífedness. ᚠᛁᛦ · ᚻᛗᚱᚾᛏᛗ ᚠᛁᚠ · ᛏᚠ · ᚻᛁᚻ · ᚱᛗᚻᛏ.

Ēadiġ bið se wer þe ne gǣð on ġeþeaht unrihtwīsra, ne on þām weġe ne stent synfulra, ne on heora wōlbærendum setle ne sitt; ac his willa bið on Godes ǣ, and ymb his ǣ hē bið smēaġende dæġes and nihtes. Him bið swā þām trēowe þe bið āplantod nēah wætera rynum, þæt selð his wæstmas tō rihtre tīde, and his lēaf and his bladu ne fealwiað ne ne sēariað; eall him cymð tō gōde þæt þæt hē dēð.

As yet unwilling to present them to outsiders for translation, he had returned to his own more methodical approach of trial, error, and experimentation. The Key, according to Benjamin Loxley, had been cast in part from the same metal used to make the Assembly's new bell. It was therefore imperative that Franklin obtain a sample for comparison. Was there something special about the specific iron that Loxley had ordered added to the mix? Ben couldn't see how, and hoped not, as there was no chance of ever obtaining any of it. But as for the other substances in the Key, the bell offered a ready abundance.

The bell was under the awning of the State House, strapped to a massive yoke of American elm, and propped up by four beams. As Franklin moved closer, William shifted back, taking up position according to the plan they had laid out. Now anyone looking their way from this side of the awning would see only William's back, and nothing of his father's doing. As William waited, he kept careful lookout to the sides, and occasionally behind them, in as poised and diffident a manner as possible.

Standing now directly before the bell, Franklin paused in surprise. Though there had been no noticeable change in the Key's energy, the unique humming sound he associated with it was now marginally louder in his ears . . . and the sound was not coming solely from the Key, but from the bell itself as well.

Might there be some inherent power here, too? This unexpected possibility set his mind racing.

Acting quickly, he removed a small steel file from his pocket. With his right hand, he scraped the file back and forth against the inside edge of the bell's lip; while with his left, he caught as many of the ill-gotten shavings as he could. Once he judged he had enough for his purposes, and a bit more, he transferred the filings safely into his pocket. A brief glance showed this test had not duplicated his original attempt with the Key: the file was unmarred, so the filings were indeed bell metal. A notable difference already! Ben's excitement mounted.

He pocketed the file, his original purpose accomplished. But there was yet the curious matter of the bell's humming to consider . . . *what if . . .*

Placing hand to chest over the hidden Key, he focused his attention on the sound. The rest of the world fell away from his senses, until there was only the hum and the Key and the bell, and nothing else, not even the grass beneath his feet.

Gently, he whispered "*Calor . . .*"

He felt the Key spark against his skin. For just an instant the bell glowed in his vision, while the air around and above it shimmered. The hairs on his arms responded, standing on end.

Franklin blinked. He called back to his son: "Did you . . . "

"Did I see heat rising from the bell as it sat in chill March air? Under an awning? Fully shaded? Yes, Father, I did. Thank God the effect was brief." Then, less calmly, "Can we *go* now?"

Franklin didn't reply. It was like that moment in the storm when everything had stopped for him, yet somehow utterly different. Time felt as if were spooled like a string around his will; he felt caught in it just as much as it was captured by him. All the while, the hum from the bell increased precipitously in volume. Under his hand and against his skin, the Key suddenly blazed with force, and he could feel the hairs not just on his arms, but also on his legs and all the rest of his body lift in place, tingling. Without consciously realizing it, he put his hand to the bell's rim, gently touching its surface, and traced a path upward from that point to just below the circular inscription. He felt a strong jolt, and jerked back in surprise.

"Father! Come along now!"

William's voice was directly in his ear, and his grip firm on Ben's shoulder, pulling him away.

"How . . . what—what just happened?"

William kept his voice low. "I don't believe anyone else saw or heard, but there were *sparks*, and you just stood there for a full minute, mumbling to yourself. In *Latin*. Here—" he handed his father a kerchief. "Put this against your mouth. Your nose is bleeding."

"I remember none of that . . . a full minute, you say?" His voice was muffled but clear through the cloth.

"At least. If not longer."

As they moved away from the bell, Ben's head began to clear, though his nose wasn't letting up. The two Franklins finally stopped under the shade of a tall sycamore tree, far enough away from the milling groups peppered across the lawn to avoid any surprise encounters.

"Much better," said Franklin, seating himself on the grass with some relief. "You say no one saw?"

"Not that I observed. You merely appeared overwhelmed, as if you were about to faint. That is why I went to you. Whatever happened?"

"I can only guess. Some reaction to proximity between the metals, perhaps? We know the bell was forged from part of the same stock as the Key. We know the Key has properties beyond those we understand; observably the bell does, too. I have more questions than ever, no answers, and frankly I grow weary. I need rest." He examined the kerchief, which was now almost fully stained. "Perhaps we should depart."

A hush came over the crowd as Speaker Norris stood before the awning and held up both hands. The sounding ceremony was about to begin.

"After this," said Franklin, amending his suggestion.

In a commanding voice, Isaac Norris addressed the gathered crowd. "We come together to hear the sounding of our new bell, this bell which commemorates fifty years as a colony since we drafted our constitution!" He was interrupted by a round of cheering. "With many thanks to God, and with thanks to our Assembly, and above all to you—the people of Pennsylvania, who have toiled for fifty years—"

For the Penn family's benefit, thought Franklin.

"—to build a land where any dream can be achieved, I give you . . . the Pennsylvania bell!" He reached under the two-thousand-pound casting, grabbed the leather strap affixed to its clapper, and gave a righteous pull. But the tone that issued upon the clapper's impact was no resounding clang, but rather a harsh metallic thump with barely any resonance at all, followed by a loud and terrible cracking.

All present reacted with dismay, seeing that a small but unmistakable crack was now visible along the rim of the bell.

William looked at his father and raised an eyebrow. The crack was exactly where Ben had first touched the bell, moments before. Neither Franklin missed the implication.

Ben returned the bloody cloth to his nose as he watched the questioning crowd move in to surround an unhappy Isaac Norris.

"Let's go, William. This is making me dizzy." Franklin accepted his son's help in standing, then set a determined pace away from the Assembly building, towards home. He saw two local foundry owners, John Pass and John Stow, heading to join the conversation as he and William walked in the opposite direction.

Craven Street

London, England
June 1st

✜ ✜ ✜

✦ 12 ✦
The World Will Change

Polly awoke to a gentle night breeze cooling her. She sat up in bed, confused. Hadn't she shut the window? In her groggy state of mind, she wasn't sure.

"Young Miss Polly, please don't take fright." Mr. Overton's voice floated to her out of the darkness.

Polly rubbed her eyes, acclimating to this sudden consciousness. She knew she should have been surprised, but somehow wasn't. For several days now she had felt as if her tutor were somewhere nearby, unseen and unannounced. "Is that really you?"

"Indeed."

"I didn't think you would return to London." She was finally able to make out the shape of him, standing by the window, limned in moonlight—and now she remembered shutting the casement after all. "You're hunted by the King's Guard! They stole all your books and belongings, and were very mean to me." She sat bolt upright.

Overton came forward and sat down on the edge of her bed. He was smiling, though to Polly's way of thinking his eyes spoke more of sadness. "I know. You mustn't worry about it. The King seeks for the same things that I do and wants something he believes is in my possession. It wasn't here, so they won't be coming round again. Neither you nor your mother are in danger."

Polly looked at him doubtfully. "I don't understand. He is the

King. Shouldn't you want to help him, or shouldn't he just ask for *your* help?"

Overton's half-smile faded. "Were only the world that simple. You are a bright girl; you know better than that."

She shrugged. "I suppose I do. But they said horrible things about you."

"Well, I'm not that good with people. I misjudge them a lot and have a tendency to say the wrong things. Perhaps I said the wrong thing to the King while I misjudged him?" He sounded tired.

"Yes, but, you see, they said you were a traitor. Plotting against England!"

"I am most certainly not an enemy of the Crown. I want nothing but to see the people of Britain healthy and prosperous. The King wants otherwise, from where I sit."

"I . . . " Polly was bright, even gifted, but at just that moment the intricacies of imperial politics were more than she wanted to understand. "I believe you. I don't fully comprehend, but I believe you."

"Good. Because you will find yourself in difficult times soon, Polly."

"What do you mean?"

"In six years the world will change, to what possible end I cannot predict. There are those trying to guide that change in one direction; I seek another. That is why the King's Guard hunt me—for what I know, and to steal that knowledge, so the change will come only as the King wills. And though it pains me to say so, on this the King is wrong."

Polly pulled her blankets close to her chest. This was something new and difficult to grasp . . . *and frightening*, she thought to herself. "Will you start teaching me again, now that you are back?"

Overton stood up. "But I'm not back. I must take a different path, one that leads away from London. You must study by yourself now. And you *must* study, Polly, for you have gifts, and a role to play in what is to come."

"But how can I? They took all your books, and all your devices, and I've not seen their like anywhere else. Why did you come back, if only to tell me to do the impossible?"

"A girl who can open locks with her mind should be less quick to use that word." This time Overton's smile was unalloyed. "I give you one piece of guidance, knowing you do not actually need it. Find the Society of Numbers and make your place within it."

"But—"

Polly stopped. She was speaking to an empty room. In the blink of an eye, her tutor had vanished. She threw herself back in the bed, flopping her arms wide. "Isn't that just a polt in the muns," she complained to the empty room.

Part 2:
A Book

*About a book, in many parts,
that contains singular secrets*

1757

INSTRUCTIONS TO BENJAMIN FRANKLIN ESQR. One of the Commissioners appointed by the Assembly of the Province of Pennsylvania to obtain Redress of those several Infractions of the Royal Grant and Proprietary Charter, and other Aggrievances, which the People of this Province very justly complain of.

In Assembly March 31st. 1757.

You are to proceed immediately to Great Britain in the first Packet Boat that sails from New York, or by the next convenient Opportunity after your Receipt of these Instructions.

If thou shou'd be taken by the Enemy, you are to advise the House by the first opportunity . . .

Aboard
the Packet Boat
General Wall
Nearing England
July 16th
❖ ❖ ❖

✦ 13 ✦
Out of the Way, Mr. Franklin!

Seagulls circled above, but that was deceptive. Gulls, Ben knew, often flew as far as eighty-five nautical miles from shore—though even that much distance would be good news, he supposed. After six weeks shipboard, including months lost waiting for the Connecticut coast to clear of French privateers, Ben was eager to stand once more on dry land, and breathe air flavored more of smoke than of salt water.

Taking another endless, meandering stroll around the deck—any excuse to escape the confines of his tiny cabin, and the increasing complaints of his son—Franklin paused when he spotted Captain Lutwidge on the poop deck. The Captain held an ornately decorated three-draw mahogany and brass graduating telescope to his eye, with which he scanned the horizon.

Ben called out, approaching, "That is an exquisite piece of craftsmanship! Is it a Pyefinch?"

The Captain replied with a single terse "Aye," seeking to discourage further conversation without being completely disrespectful.

"Pyefinch's glasses are fine, very fine." When the Captain did not immediately respond, Ben squinted and stared up at the clouds. "I wouldn't have thought gulls would be out this late in the afternoon. All things considered, might we be closer to land than our last chart estimates indicated?"

"No, Mr. Franklin," the Captain sighed. "They sleep on the water if it's a calm sea." He lowered the glass and turned to shout at his crew. "Hard to port! Tack hard! What word, barrelman!"

"Horizon is clear, Captain!" the sailor up in the crow's nest called down.

"Fascinating," Ben said, grabbing the railing as the ship shifted underfoot. "I knew that gulls could fly this distance, but I never dreamt that they took up a kind of residence as well, hunting and sleeping so far from land."

Captain Lutwidge managed a half-smile. "I would more say that they come this far out for sport."

"Sport?"

"Give it a moment, you'll see. Tack *harder*! I want us back five miles from the Channel in the next hour!" There was a splat on the deck next to the Captain, which he indicated with a tilting glance at Ben. "See, Mr. Franklin? Sport. I think we're a moving game to them."

"Ah." As he realized the Captain's point, he found himself looking up more warily. "Speaking of motion, sir, why do we withdraw? We were on direct course for our landfall at Falmouth. This change you just ordered will delay that."

"We're too close to land. We need more time."

Ben held the deck railing tightly. "*Too* close? How is that even possible?"

"French ships. This stretch of water is one hundred and seventy miles, port to port. From sunup to sundown, even this ship can sail that distance. But a faster vessel, at twenty knots an hour, can make it here from France in plenty of time to raid our side of the Channel and be back for dinner. We don't have the firepower to outrun such an enemy, so I propose to sneak past them instead—*if* they are there, which for our safety I must presume." As he spoke, Lutwidge never looked away from the horizon. "Now if you don't mind, sir, I would rather focus on the task at hand than spend more time explaining my decisions."

"My apologies, Captain, I was not trying to undermine you. I was more hoping to gain some understanding of the logic of seafaring decisions, since this war has changed the rules of maritime travel. I only asked in the spirit of inquiry."

"I understand, Mr. Franklin. To you this is a long and uneventful voyage, with not nearly enough to occupy your attention. But the worst you have experienced, so far, is the *General Wall* moving slower than you might prefer. That is not the case now: we are at actual hazard. At any moment a black dot could appear on the horizon—something entirely insignificant to you—and I and my crew would immediately be in a life or death effort to escape an enemy with superior firepower. Therefore I find your questions distracting, not deleterious to my standing. Perhaps you might care to wait belowdecks?"

"Ah. Again, my apologies. I'm afraid I need the air. But I promise to watch quietly, and be no hindrance to anyone."

The Captain frowned but said nothing further.

The next few hours were a practice in staying silent, as Ben camped out by the aft railing and just observed. In that time, Captain Lutwidge ran several drills, getting the crew ready for night sailing into a harbor. As the sun dipped lower in the sky, the *General Wall* sailed hard north, then tacked southeast to position itself to hook due east out of the Strait of Saint George. Watching, Ben gathered the Captain's plan was to put Ireland at the *General Wall*'s back, then use the setting sun to cover them—hoping that any French ships waiting in the Channel would find it impossible to see the small postal packet against the sun's great disc.

The western tip of Cornwall came into view, just a shimmer in the shadows, right as the sun's lower rim touched the horizon.

"Ship sighted!" The barrelman yelled down from above.

Lutwidge cursed and slid open his glass, scanning the eastern horizon until he found the vessel in question. "All quiet on the deck! Looks like . . ." the Captain quietly counted to himself, "fourteen guns, I'd wager. Converted schooner—fast-running, based on her trim. No sign they've seen us yet, so we're going to go in riding the mirage line. With any luck, by the time they load their guns we'll be blowing right by them. Have all passengers and belowdecks bodies crowd the stern wall!"

On hearing that, Ben started to speak, but Captain Lutwidge broke in first. "Say nothing and you may remain to watch, Mr.

Franklin. I imagine you'd just try and sneak back up the minute you thought we weren't paying sufficient attention, anyway."

Two sailors ran below to relay orders, and the deck fell silent. Ben had grown used to the rowdy chatter of sailors at their work. By contrast, this sudden quiet was eerie; as they sailed into the Channel, dusk nipping at their heels, all he could hear was the rhythmic slap of waves against the coursing hull, the snap-and-rustle of the packet's sails, and the thin high cries of the gulls overhead. Through it all, Captain Lutwidge held their bearing, signaling his commands through hand gestures and whispers to the bosun that were passed down the line in further whispers as well.

The ship sped on. As it approached land, Ben could clearly see the French merchantman-turned-privateer sailing at an angle away from them—Lutwidge's tactic had worked. The *General Wall* had gone undetected.

As the sun finally vanished below the horizon, and the world tilted from day to night, the packet slid smoothly into shallower waters below a series of camouflaging cliffs.

Ben grinned and shook his head. The world was full of wonder, to his perception. It had been a honor and an education to witness such seamanship. Catching Captain Lutwidge's eye, he bowed with sincere respect, then headed below deck to relax.

The ship's night captain, Captain Kennedy, stopped him as they passed each other in the narrow passage outside his cabin. near. "No lights tonight, Mr. Franklin," he spoke softly. "There is still danger that we might be overrun before morning."

Ben nodded. "As you direct. But I don't understand, please, why are we being so quiet? Surely they are far enough away?"

"One would think so, but it is surprising how far sharp noises can carry across open water. The French might not hear what we say, or where we are, but an unfortunate noise could alert them to the fact that they are not alone. So, we stay quiet. Once we near Falmouth, they will not follow. We have the larger navy; they won't risk trying to catch us in sight of the coastal forts."

Ben nodded. "I understand. Thank you."

He headed into his cabin, one of two besides the Captain's. William was already in his hammock and inclined towards convivial discussion, whether from relief at their safe passage or proximity to their voyage's end, or both, Franklin could not say. He was simply grateful to feel a natural warmth to their connection again for this while, however long it might last.

Hours later he stared out the cabin window, from the rear of the ship, at the dark waters of the Channel. It was a rarity for him to have trouble kipping down when he wished, but despite being tired, sleep was proving elusive. Perhaps it was the hushed voices of the crewmen on watch that kept him up, or William's snoring; whatever the cause, it was quite a long time before he finally felt himself nodding off.

At that moment a light flashed across the water behind the ship and the loud ring of a bell echoed across the water. Then came Captain Kennedy's voice, a series of shouts at the top of the man's lungs, slicing through the constant *slap* of waves hitting the hull. "Hard starboard! Cut the mainsails tight, full jib! Ready about! Now, now, *now*, lighthouse port!"

William remained oblivious, but Ben's eyes snapped fully open, all chance of sleep banished. He threw on a coat and, struggling with creaking knees and a hip that refused to cooperate, limped his way up to the main decks.

The boat, which had been all but asleep a moment before, was fully active now. Captain Kennedy took just enough note of Ben's presence to wave him aside. "Out of the way, Mr. Franklin." Kennedy spoke quietly, but his manner brooked no debate. Ben nodded and scurried to the back railing, grabbing hold. The coastal lighthouse and cliffs loomed above them, far too near for safety.

Kennedy leaned all his weight into spinning the boat's wheel and grunted, yelling "Hard alee!"

Ben was almost thrown over the railing by the force of the tack, barely catching himself in time. Kennedy spun the wheel fast in the opposite direction and the *General Wall* did something Ben wouldn't have thought possible—as it hit a wave coming back off the shoreline, the ship tilted precariously, then seemed to almost jump into the air. The coastal winds caught the sails and the packet slammed forward, speeding away from the rocky doom that had nearly wrecked it.

Just as Ben regained his balance, he heard a boom and a splash. "Is that a *cannon*?" he shouted at the Captain.

Kennedy glanced back in exasperation. "*Please*, Mr. Franklin. Go belowdecks! We will let you know when it is safe to come up."

A second boom and splash sounded, closer this time. Instinct took over in response to imminent danger. As Ben fumbled his way towards the stairs, barely able to stand on the pitching deck, he stretched both arms to the sky, fingers cramping as if the very air was cloth that he could seize and hold and pull. In his mind's eye he saw a vast grayness descending on the sea; and, as he pushed with everything in him, as he had once pushed against lightning in a storm, he commanded the single word, "*Nebula.*" With that, the energy to stay awake flooded out of him, and he dropped to his knees in a dizzy stupor. Hunger surged as if he hadn't eaten in days.

Sailors ran around him, desperately manning rigging and righting the ship as a fog bank overcame them from nowhere. In seconds, the air was so thick it was hard to see more than a few feet in any direction.

"Father?" Franklin felt William's hands on his shoulders. "Do you need help? I awake to a ruckus and find you up here. What is wrong? Are you ill?"

"Food," Ben muttered. "Cabin."

William struggled to get his father standing.

"All quiet!" Ben heard Captain Kennedy command. "The fog plus the darkness will cover us."

The two Franklins stumbled downstairs, William propping up his unsteady father. Once back in their cabin, William settled Ben into his hammock. Weak beer from the pail and some hardtack would have to do. Dipping the bread in the beer, he offered it to Franklin, who consumed it eagerly. He slowed down once the feeling that his stomach was going to cave in on itself subsided. The relief of this sensation, combined with general exhaustion, overcame him, and he fell into fitful sleep.

Some hours later, as an unseen dawn lit the fog with a light gray glow, Ben woke. He saw that William had not returned to his own hammock, but was instead asleep on a stool, leaned back against the wall. How he didn't fall over, Ben wasn't sure. He chuckled quietly at the sentiment. Above him he could hear telltale sounds of sailors moving around on the deck. They were making no attempt to maintain silence, so all danger must be past.

Over the next few hours, the ship came fully alive. Soundings revealed that they were near land, so they proceeded carefully through the fog. Ben felt giddy. Soon he would be standing on the shores of England once again. Even William came up to enjoy the morning air and check on his father. As much as he had protested that this journey was not one he wanted to undertake, in his heart of hearts he was beginning to feel otherwise.

The soundings kept showing that they were closer, and Ben kept glued to the bow, checking his pocket watch and watching the gray fog before them. It was just about to strike nine o'clock in the morning when the fog lifted, rising from the water like the curtain over a stage. As it did, it revealed the town of Falmouth, surrounded by the greenest of fields and resplendent with life and commerce, its welcoming harbor full of ships.

All the activity around him ceased. To the crew, having seen nothing but water for long weeks on end, there was something magical about arriving. Forgotten was the war, the ceaseless rocking of the waves: here, at last, was England.

" ... The bell ringing for church, we went thither immediately, and with hearts full of gratitude, returned sincere thanks to God for the mercies we had received: were I a Roman Catholic, perhaps I should on this occasion vow to build a chapel to some saint; but as I am not, if I were to vow at all, it should be to build a lighthouse."

~ Letter from Benjamin Franklin
to Deborah Read Franklin, July 17th, 1757

Wiltshire County
England
July 23rd
✦ ✦ ✦

❖ 14 ❖
Do You Hear That?

The road from Amesbury to Stonehenge was smooth and regularly maintained by the Duke of Queensbury. William and Ben watched the landscape roll by, each observing from opposite windows. No matter the circumstance, the two never seemed able to share a view. They had changed to a smaller carriage, leaving their slaves and bags behind on the waiting high flyer, in order to enjoy a detour from their trip to London so they could visit the legendary stonework.

Grass so green it seemed ready to jump to blue covered the turf, broken by the occasional farmhouse jutting up from the plain. The warm air smelled of the grass, of distant leaves, and even of the further distant ocean. It smelled clean in a way a city never could.

"This is very exciting; I've always wanted to see the henge. Didn't make the time when I was here last, which was foolishness." Ben never took his eyes from the passing scene, hungry as he was to see everything. "Always make time, William. It may seem that you are too busy to accommodate your small desires, but you should never let them pass by unattended."

"Indeed, Father." There was a hint of something deeper on his son's mind, but Ben was too distracted to notice.

"I cannot wait! It is a marvel, no doubt. A testament to what the kings of old could build." He shifted in his seat, trying to get a better view ahead of the carriage.

"I'm sure it will be most astounding," William agreed without thinking. When his mind was elsewhere, but social obligation bade him speak, his habit—unknowingly learned from his father—was to declaim. He did so now. "I have recently reread the translated *Historia Regum Britanniae* in anticipation of arriving here. Monmouth believed that Merlin constructed the rings with rocks from Africa at the command of Aurelius Ambrosius. He calls them the giant's dance. It is said the stones traveled from Africa to Ireland before they were eventually moved here."

At an earlier time Ben might have complained about the interjection of folklore, but now he paused. Given the events of the last few years, and the odd powers he himself now possessed, though in small measure, who was he to say that a tale of Merlin was mere fancy? "As I recall, wasn't it a tomb for Arthur? Or Uther?"

"It was for Uther, yes. Arthur is lost, but, according to myth, Stonehenge covers the bones of Uther, Aurelius, and Constantine the Third."

"There it is!" shouted Ben. They rode in silence the remaining way, as the carriage passed the embankment ring and then pulled to a stop. Ben's eyebrows knitted in surprise. There was a faint but persistent—and familiar—hum in the air, from the direction of the henge.

"Do you hear that?" he asked his son, already suspecting the answer.

"Hear what?"

"Never mind."

William reached past him and opened the door. The two climbed out of the carriage, and Ben stopped to gaze around in purest awe. The massive stones of the inner horseshoe were wider than a person and over twice as tall.

William stepped around him to address the coachman. "You'll just wait here?"

"Yessirs." The coachman tipped his hat. He had already dismounted and started tending to his charges. "Take yer time, I'll brush down the horses and be ready when you are to go back to Amesbury."

The Franklins hadn't bothered packing a lunch or doing anything special, since the monument was only a twenty-minute ride from the town. They had even left Peter and King alone to have some quiet time at the inn. The morning sun was cresting overhead as they approached the monument from the side of the horseshoe shape in the center. Walking forward slowly, both were speechless at what they saw.

Ben scratched at his ear. The faint humming hadn't gone away, and thoughts of Merlin and ancient magic seemed less preposterous by the second.

The two men split, each intent on his own exploration of the site. Ben walked under the archway of the outer stones, drawn to the larger ones at the center. They pulled him along until he stood before the head. Tentatively he reached out and placed his hand upon it.

The stone felt both cool and warm to him. It vibrated subtly under his touch. His brow furrowed in thought. The sensation was not unfamiliar. In kind it was much like touching the Key, only less present in the moment: fainter, distant, as though there had once been great power in these stones, but now it was only a memory.

Curious, Ben thought. He pulled a kerchief and his slip-joint knife from the pocket of his coat. Chiseling a few shavings from the stone immediately wrecked the blade, but it was a worthy sacrifice in pursuit of knowledge.

"What are you doing, Father?"

Quickly folding up the kerchief, he turned, "Simply testing the hardness and character of the stone. What of you—uncovered the door to Uther's tomb yet?"

William quirked an eyebrow but let the comment go. "Nothing so interesting. It is an extraordinary monument, to be sure, but I will soon have had my fill."

"That quickly? Have you even touched the stones? Felt their history?" Ben offhandedly tapped the headstone with the ruined slip-joint knife. The resulting sound was a humming clang that echoed between the stones, pulsing harmonically with the faint humming tone.

"Well, that I heard." William perked up interestedly and came to examine the struck stone.

"Apparently, I have happened across a trait of the stones." Ben stood back, tapping the megalith in a different spot. It made a hollow-sounding, deeper sound.

William ran a finger along the rough surface, studying it intently. "It reminds me vaguely of your glass harp."

"Indeed. I keep meaning to fiddle with it, too, but I cannot find an arrangement I like." Ben suddenly shook his head and looked around sharply. As plain as the sun in the sky, he knew—*knew*—that someone was watching him; and the fact that there was no one in view for miles save William and the coachman did not dull that absolute certainty one whit.

For his part, William observed his father acting even more strangely than usual, and, after his own experience of the last several years, grew quickly concerned. Though this time there had been nothing to see, he was reminded of the strange events surrounding the close inspection of the bell, and how drained and ill his father had been for weeks afterward. He reached out to take Ben's arm and led him to the carriage. "Come, Father, shall we?"

"Pshaw," Franklin said, waving the hand away. "I'm perfectly capable of moving myself to the post-chaise, William. For once, my knees don't even hurt." But the truth was that every instinct in his body was suddenly screaming at him to run, to hide, to get away from this place as quickly as possible and never return.

No matter where he looked as they walked back to the cart, the sensation persisted, though there was no possible visible reason: just the mute, motionless stones, and the good English countryside stretching away in all directions.

Ben could take it no more. He held up his hand and snapped his fingers, borrowing a motion from the Great Gasparini. "*Slæp.*"

Both William and the driver slumped to the ground. Even the horse's head drooped, he noted proudly.

Ben, with great care, walked back to the stones. Using the sleep spell had tired him, but he was growing stronger in his manipulation of the arcane laws. As he walked into the circle once more, he waved a hand and focused his intent behind saying the word, "*Revelare.*"

The air shimmered and Ben began to hear faint sounds of . . . a battle? It seemed to be coming from a thousand years away. Electrostatic sparks of purple and blue jumped from stone to stone. One caught Ben and knocked him to his knees. He struggled to regain his feet, leaning heavily on his cane, swatting away more of the sparks.

"Hello?" He backed away warily. No one answered. Fire ringed the inner stones, erupting from nowhere and consuming the monoliths.

Either there was someone here messing with him, or there was no one here and he had accidentally triggered some primal force of the henge. Ben turned and ran back to the carriage as much as his bad hip would allow him to. He had to move William and the driver to safety before he faced down this... whatever it was, and figured this out.

He urgently wrestled the limp William into the interior seat, then managed to get the driver up onto the perch. As he turned back, the flames and noise vanished. Stonehenge was once more just a series of megalithic rocks forming an ancient monument.

Ben stood stock still, intently studying the formation. *What just happened?*

Behind him, and a bit above, the driver woke. "How'd I get up here then?"

"You collapsed, and I thought it best to move you up to the cushion than leave you laying on the ground," Ben lied.

"Well, I feel fine now. Drowsy, but fine."

Once back in the carriage, Ben leaned into the cushioned seat and closed his eyes. With a simple "hyup" from the coachman, the horses and carriage jostled into motion. As the stone circle fell further away to the rear, Ben could feel his nerves clear, and he idly wondered if insanity was the price for practicing magic.

As the carriage rattled off, a middle-aged man with angular features and pudgy cheeks, wearing the finery of a noble, stepped out from behind the monument's headstone, gazing after the departing Franklins. "How very weak he is. Surprising." He muttered to himself, then walked away, headed away from Amesbury.

The
Collinson Home
Ridgeway House,
Mill Hill, Middlesex
July 25th
✢ ✢ ✢

❖ 15 ❖
Thy Best Interest
at Heart

William thought they were stopping for the night at the Bear Inn, where in the morning they could catch the Marine coach for their final leg into London, but it turned out his father had other plans. Ben directed Peter and King to shift the party's luggage to a newly hired post-chaise, and informed his son that after their meal they would be continuing on to a secret destination that Ben had determined to visit even before leaving Philadelphia.

In the dining hall of the stable yard, William sought to make plain his dissatisfaction. "I do not understand, Father," he said, sitting down to a tolerable meal of leek potage and brown bread. "Why don't we simply take rooms here for tonight and proceed tomorrow to the lodgings Mr. Charles has secured for us in the city? It is late. I am tired. I would much prefer to rest and prepare myself to enter London in proper form in the morning. Whatever else could you possibly think sensible?"

Peter and King, eating their own meals nearby, remained attentive to their masters' discussion.

Ben smiled and gestured with his spoon. "I suppose I've kept it to myself long enough. London, as you will soon discover for yourself, is an exposure that takes some getting used to. Before we surrender to it, I am determined to go where one of the greatest gardens in England is being nurtured. And, having never met Peter Collinson face to face, I will not be turned from that happening as quickly as possible."

Peter and King glanced at each other. King rolled his eyes, and Peter shrugged in response. They went back to eating.

William glanced uncomfortably at the two slaves, then back at his father, who was now wholly occupied with his food. There really was nothing to say. He dipped his bread and took a small bite, unhappily resigned to having his wishes ignored yet again.

The rest of the meal was eaten in relative silence, filled only by the conversations of the tavern's other patrons.

When all four were done eating, they left on the chaise. It was a speedy carriage, with room for two inside and two on the back, plus the cargo tucked on the lower back. The drive kept them on a steady pace. Inside the carriage, William maintained his silence, and Ben let him, content to look ahead in pleasure as they rode. In what felt like much less time than it actually was, for Ben—and much more than actual for William—they neared their destination. They were beyond the city and its pervasive smells. The fragrant scent of blooming flowers was on the night breeze, and everywhere around them botanical skill was evident in the moonlight. They had left central London and arrived in Mill Hill, one of the better tended suburbs.

The post-chaise brought them to the entrance of Ridgeway House, a modest three-story manse with steepled roofs and expansive gardens in back, where Peter Collinson grew his rare plants. The ground floor was red brick; the top two stories white trimmed. Ben was the first out of the carriage and bolted to the door, despite his various aching joints.

He pulled the bell handle and waited expectantly. The door opened and a man with a severe expression and intense eyes opened the door. On seeing who stood before him, his visage immediately brightened.

"You can only be Ben Franklin."

"Just so. And you, Peter Collinson," Ben ventured happily. "I have been waiting for too many years for the pleasure of shaking your hand!"

"The pleasure is all mine, all mine," returned Collinson, eagerly returning his guest's firmly enthusiastic grip.

"I will not have anything acknowledged but the debt of gratitude I owe for your boundless generosity. I would never have wandered into my electrical experiments if you had not sent me that pamphlet and glass cylinder. And, as I remember it, that book was *not* part of the Library Company's order that season. You added it like you've added so many generous gifts to our humble endeavor over these many years."

Collinson continued to smile as he turned his attention to William, who was now approaching.

Ben held out his arm to his son, proudly offering him for review. "This is my son, William Franklin. William, I am pleased to introduce you to Mr. Peter Collinson, Fellow of the Royal Society of London, brother printer, ahem, and master botanist."

William reached out his hand and shook Collinson's with clear pleasure, "I have heard your gardens are a wonder to behold, and I see that I was not misled."

Collinson received the compliment graciously. "Thank you, though what you see out here is but a minor sampling. Wait till you tour the rear gardens! But that can wait until morning. Ben, dearest friend, I have made arrangements for you and your son, and your servants as well. You will rest well here."

Ben tapped the tip of his cane against the ground. "Please let us not discontinue all conversation. I am eager for your insight on how to facilitate His Majesty's government annulling the powers of the Penns and creating Pennsylvania as a Crown Colony."

"Thank you, sir," William gently chided his father by displaying better manners. "I confess I have great need of the offered arrangements, after so long a day, and lengthier journey."

Ben was of another mind. "Surely not straight to bed for you and me, Peter. We have so much to discuss. So much!"

"It's to be business straight away, instead of books and flowers? If only you'd arrived in daylight I might have kept this sortie at bay." Collinson laughed heartily. "Well then, your servants can attend to unloading the baggage and seeing your son and themselves off to bed. For myself, I keep late hours, and am ready to match you subject for subject as we please."

Once Peter was sure the guests were being assisted with the unloading of the carriage, he motioned for Ben to huddle close, then continued the conversation. "As for your business in England, Ben, the Crown may feel that the colony's name says it all. Most of the powerful socialites come from landed estates, and cannot help but think of Pennsylvania as a landed estate of the Penn family. As they would be loath to have their own ancestral lands disposed of without a clear and cogent cause, they would be, I think, wary to act in such a manner against the Penns. Your cause is not a popular one here. It is not noble, and it is not wanted. It is only on the strength of your own renown that you may carry your cause forward to any degree."

"But the Penns have barely been in Pennsylvania for eighty years," Ben answered with a wicked glint in his eye, though his lips were pursed. "Some few of the Lords in court were alive before there even *was* a Pennsylvania. Most have outhouses older than that! How 'ancestral' can it be, as a land goes?"

Collinson chuckled. "A fair point, and if not for other pressing issues, it may have been fairly considered."

"What other issues do you mean?"

"You know that the Penn family lives a life that is not strictly abstentious. William was a man very different from his sons."

"They plunder Pennsylvania and live in pomp," Ben scoffed. "This is well known, I can assure you. It is one of the many grievances the people of Pennsylvania have sent me to discuss with the government. Our coffers are drained without defense, and the Penns are exempt from taxation and overrule us in our own Assembly. It is disgraceful."

"Have you not considered that the Penn family's use of frill and finery is not so much a decadent outcome as a well-developed tool? Something which supports their real goal? Do not underestimate Thomas Penn."

"I am not sure what you mean," Ben said, both annoyed that he did not understand something he felt he should and keenly interested to learn what it could be.

A woman's voice came calling from further inside the house. "What is all this, then? Our guests are being made to stand in the entryway like strangers? Come, Peter, you know better than that!"

"My dear . . . " Peter began sheepishly, as his wife Mary Collinson walked up to the group. "You are completely correct. May I introduce

Mr. Benjamin Franklin and his fine young son, William Franklin, both late of Philadelphia. Mr. Franklin and William, this is my beautiful wife, Mary Collinson."

Mary took their hands, beaming with pleasure, "So glad we can enjoy your company as you begin your tour of England, Mr. Franklin. And William, I believe this might be your first visit? I hope it will be everything good that you might have considered. I can't imagine how difficult your journey must have been. Think upon how shocked we were when the main body of your luggage arrived in England so many weeks before you did. How they must have shuffled you about—I mean, your possessions set sail without you, for goodness sake!" As she spoke, Mary managed to get William to let her take his arm, so she could lead him into the house.

It was a complex maneuver, and one the young man had not previously experienced, to find himself in the lead while, in all actuality, being led. Mary glanced back at Ben and her husband and winked, then finished whisking the young man away.

Collinson raised an eyebrow to Ben as the two moved inside, with Franklin following the older man to his study. "Please, sit here," said Collinson as his servant, Jemmy, brought in a tray of refreshments. "Lemon water and small biscuits. Both very good. Do not fear, I will return to the object of your inquiry, but for the moment I believe these will help revive you somewhat. I assure you that your son and servants are being similarly encouraged."

Ben happily surrendered to his host's offer. The lemon water was a treat he rarely tried. It was slightly sweet at room temperature, with just a hint of tartness, and surprisingly refreshing. "Tell me," he asked. "Do you have tea water delivered, or are you far enough from the city that you can draw on your wells?"

Peter shook his head. "We still have to have it delivered. So long as you are in London or its environs, my advice to you is simple: if it doesn't come out of a cask, or hasn't been boiled first, don't drink it."

Ben nodded and sipped. "It was the same when I was here before. In the Colonies we only have to worry about that in city-center. Tea-water and swill farms aren't as common."

"Fascinating." Collinson leaned against the edge of his desk. "The structure of the young cities out there is so different. Which means different problems must be accounted for, it would seem."

"That is a marvelous way of stating it—young. And so true, though a bit narrow. I think it is a question of age. The populations are younger, lacking the centuries of sharing space that European cities have." Ben gestured with his cup. "Through time comes density. A city is a generational boat that carries our bloodlines from past to future, becoming ever more compounded, and complex, as the deckhands repair the hull and sails."

"I like that imagery. And obviously learning and ideas grow along with the generations of families, and governance becomes more complicated. Amid the labyrinthine solutions the population implements, so too must that population's rulers create more detailed machinations and methods to stratify themselves and retain the power of rule." While Ben sipped and chewed, Peter deftly returned to the topic they had left before. "For instance, there is the game the Penns play. In London, the most effective way to influence the rich and powerful is to be equally rich and powerful, or at least to appear so. Old money has a natural distrust of young money—and the Penn fortune is only aged to a vintage of three generations, so they overspend to compensate. You can meet in a patrician's fine house, but if he can never meet in yours because it is too simple and utilitarian, then he will never take what you have to say seriously. Oh, he'll *listen*, if you are connected to powerful enough people, or if he thinks inviting you to one of his gatherings will be useful to him in some manner, either political or social. But will he consider? Will he act?"

Collinson smiled wryly at Ben. "These are things you must consider. As Commissioner Franklin, I imagine you will get invited to many a gathering, because of your name, your reputation, and your temporary value as a curiosity. But if you do not act like them and live like them, they will never truly consider you one of them."

Ben sat still for some while, considering this advice in silence. As a Quaker, Collinson was accustomed to such rumination, and comfortably left his friend to his thoughts. While Ben pondered he let his gaze wander, truly taking in the room. It was an exploration he could have continued for days, for Collinson's study was packed with the tools and record of a lifetime in search of discovery. What must have been a thousand books crowded shelves that stretched along two walls from floor to ceiling, and partway along a third. Etchings of flora, cardiovascular systems, maps, and even some occult symbolism filled the little bit of wall space remaining. Framed to the side, in a place of apparent honor, Ben spotted the *Pennsylvania Gazette* article in which he had written up the methodology of the kite and key experiment.

When Ben finally spoke, it was to change the topic. "Let us leave Parliament and the Penns for the moment. I see you have been holding out on us, you fiend." His tone of mock severity was clearly in jest. "Here I thought you were generously searching the dusty attics of England to send us poor unenlightened souls in the New World the best books you could find. But no. What do I see here? A collection that makes any private collection in the Colonies pale by comparison. Even my own!" Ben lowered his face to both hands as if shamed and disgraced.

"Thank you for your horror and detestation, Ben. A finer compliment I could not hope to receive, from such an old friend I have never before met."

"I loathe your collection and yearn for the day I can steal it from you, Peter," Ben continued jovially. "If only I could unlock the wonders in my own library, as I am sure you can here."

Collinson gave Ben a long and thoughtful look, as if he were trying to make up his mind about something. This obvious change in demeanor surprised Franklin.

"May I be more serious for a moment? I have wondered, Ben, if you realize that I sent you the most precious of all my collection in that batch I shipped in the Spring of 1752. Yet in five years I have heard nothing from you about them. This has confused and concerned me, but I dared not refer to them without risking exposure to the wrong parties."

Ben's hand shook with a sudden rush of memory. For just a moment he felt himself back in his workshop, rendered the next thing to unconscious by an idle flick of an intruder's hand. *Gasparini.* He realized that he had not thought of that morning in some time.

"I am sorry to report, Peter, that not that long after you sent them, one was destroyed. A mysterious man broke into my home and incapacitated me. What he did with the book in question, which he was examining when I caught him, I cannot explain, nor would you credit me if I tried. Suffice for now to say that it no longer exists. But the others remain safe. He showed no sign of being aware of them."

Collinson's eyes widened in concern. "I never meant to put you in such danger. I had only your best interest at heart." It was his turn now to compose his thoughts. Ben gave him the time he needed by reading the spines of the books on the nearest shelf to his right.

Eventually Collinson continued, "I had hoped the strange script would intrigue you and impel you to understand its contents."

"The journals were clearly written in one hand, but many languages. I recognized one of them for Latin, but it appeared to be a cipher; those portions of the text were in no Latin I ever studied. I spent a good deal of time with them after the attack, of course, trying to puzzle out the mystery. But like you, I felt constrained to keep their existence to myself. And much as I have enjoyed our correspondence, and believed I could trust you with any knowledge I might have, once written down words are at risk of wandering. After what I experienced . . . well, as I wrote in *Poor Richard's Almanack*, 'Three may keep a secret, if two of them are dead.'"

Peter looked at Ben sadly, slipping into the familiar Friend's language of plain speech for a moment, "I believe thee had no choice."

"Peter, it was the only time in my life that I have ever felt powerless." Ben set his glass of water down and refilled it. His throat was uncharacteristically dry. "I know you meant me no harm. I do feel that you are all that is benevolent and good in this world. So please tell me—why did you send me those volumes? What was your purpose?"

Collinson's gaze intensified. "Do you know the story of how I came to be accepted as a fellow of the Royal Society?"

Ben shook his head.

"In October of 1728, I wrote to Sir Hans Sloane, then President of the Society, about some odd events I witnessed in Kent. Within a month, he had proposed me for fellowship."

Ben placed his empty glass of lemon water on the tray and gave his friend his fullest possible attention.

"It turns out they were receiving many reports of strange goings on, with each reporter looking for answers that the Society could not provide. Something about my report stood out. It convinced them that I would be able to offer an explanation to the Royal Society, even though it be one unpalatable to the world at large." Collinson paused. "I would be less than credible if some of those reports became public."

He shifted in his seat, thinking carefully on his choice of words, "I have done my duty here and found that I have been able to be of some service to the Royal Society and to my country in the endeavor. But reports out of the Americas continue to grow, and we have no means to investigate them, much less mollify the reporters or resolve the described experiences. I thought you might be the right person to take up those duties in the Colonies, Ben. I still do. I cannot think of any other person so well positioned, or so well suited to the task. People genuinely like you. They will talk to you when they might not to others."

Ben looked aghast. "I cannot imagine what you mean. I am a businessman, a philosopher, a thinker, not a—" He stopped, then started again. "Yes, I am embarrassingly inquisitive. Yes, I tend to root into a problem, any problem, until I solve it. I cannot bear to be left in the dark when the light is but a step away."

Peter nodded encouragingly. "Go on."

Ben thought, *Dare I tell him? Will he actually understand? My Debby does, just perhaps. But William now entirely disapproves. I can no longer share any of this with him.* Thinking of Debby and Sally, and the rest of what he left back home, he suddenly understood that William's diversion by Mary was neither incidental nor an accident, but rather a full acknowledgement of Ben's particular predicament with his own son. Somehow, they knew.

For a moment he stared at Peter Collinson in frank astonishment. "*This* is why you proposed me for membership? This is what the Royal Society wished of me when they elected me as a fellow last year? Not for my research into Natural Philosophy and the electrical fire, but to help them study and lay bare the truth of occultism, magic, and the supernatural through a deistic approach of study?"

"You were my recommendation to receive King's George's grant, yes, and he approves of you. The work is more than that, for certain, but as beginning descriptions go, I have heard worse."

"So while I am here attempting to unwind the struggle between the Penns and the Assembly, you will share with me the discoveries into the occult the Society has made?"

Collinson nodded. "Of course. But why do you assume the two are separate?"

London, England
July 30th
✣ ✣ ✣

✧ 16 ✧
No Secrets

Ben chose to travel to Craven Street by dog cart. His house slave Peter sat next to him, staring in wonder at the sights. London was quite literally twenty-five times the size of Philadelphia, and Ben knew his slave had never seen anything like it.

No, Ben thought, *not slave. Here I must abandon that word.*

He was well aware of the fact that more than fifty years earlier, English courts had struck a blow against the slave trade by ruling that any negro coming into England was automatically free: as Chief Justice Holt had put it, "One may be a villein in England, but not a slave." It was something his abolitionist friends spoke upon, missing the greater truth that the merchant courts ignored the ruling.

He noted with mild surprise that this change in Peter's status did not displease him—the relentless speeches against the practice of slavery that Isaac Norris and a few others had made were apparently taking hold. But it raised a thorny issue. If on English soil Peter was free, now, then to take him back to Pennsylvania and slavery would make Franklin himself complicit in that freedom's loss. It would be as if he had personally caged Peter and put him on the block.

Ben ignored the sights and smells of London, musing instead on this conundrum. It had never been a secret that he did not personally favor the practice of slavery, and yet he owned slaves and had allowed his own paper to run advertisements for human sales and trades. Yes, grants of freedom for all his household slaves were included in his Last Will and Testament; but that act had been a sop to conscience. Suddenly the grand moral pride he had felt when making that choice seemed pure hypocrisy; the act itself a small, shameful thing, too late by three-quarters and then some.

If he were to truly begin to investigate and report upon the secrets of the occult world, as Collinson had proposed, must he not also lay bare his own flaws and secrets? After all, only a coward would choose to hide in silence when wrongs cried out to be made right.

The dog cart bounced over the cobblestones as they passed Hanover Square, coming ever closer to the shores of the Thames.

"Peter?"

"Yes, Mr. Franklin?" Peter was comfortable enough with Ben that he didn't look back, instead keeping his gaze locked on the city's passing wonders.

"I plan to send William traveling while we are here, to expand his circles." Ben sighed. "He must learn and grow as his own man, 'stead of riding the tails of my coat. But I am unsure that he is ready for it."

"I don't think he'd see it that way, Mr. Franklin. Young Captain Franklin would say he tends you, so as you don't get lost in your own ideas."

"Indeed. And what do you think of William and his opinions? You have no need to blunt your tongue. Not here, not now. Truth is a far greater currency than sparing my feelings."

Peter glanced back in surprise. "I don't think I understand the question."

Ben shook his head. "You understand perfectly well, you're just attempting to avoid it because you think I will not like your answer. Please, go on."

Peter's jaw clenched. "Captain Franklin is *proper*." Ben started to speak, but Peter put up his hand, begging a moment. "Insists on being called master, as is his right. Dresses in a manner that no one could comment on. He has earned his officer rank at a young age. True to him, he is a perfect example. But I think he looks down on everyone. He may act proper, but I doubt he thinks about other folk proper. He and King, well, I'm surprised you left the two of them alone back at the inn."

"I thought we could square away the new lodgings better by ourselves."

"Probably right," Peter nodded and continued. "But I also understand where you worry. Neither of them likes the other. If Captain Franklin calls King 'boy' or 'negro' and the two of them are alone, I can't tell you what might happen."

"Why would that be a problem?" Ben asked in surprise.

Peter worked his jaw for a second as his own words caught up with his ears. "Aw, Shango forgive me. I overstep. Never mind, Mr. Franklin."

"Peter," Ben paused, gathering the thought, "what do I not understand here?"

Peter shook his head. He hadn't meant to open this sack of rot, but what was done was done. "Please don't take offense at this. A man must love his son, and take pride in him. That's as it should. But Captain Franklin and King, they're just like a striker, one of 'em flint, the other one steel. They spark each other."

"Surely any problems are King's fault."

Peter just stared at Ben, saying nothing.

Well, I asked him for truth, Franklin thought. He blinked. "How did I not know this was how you felt?"

Peter shifted uncomfortably on the dog cart's bouncing seat. "Do you know the opinions of the cats that hunt mice in your scullery?"

Ben shook his head. "It's not that bad, surely."

"Yessir, it is. But as much as the two of them hate each other, and they do, that's not my biggest worry. What scares me most is that neither of them trusts the tricks you can do now."

"Tricks? What are you—I—" Ben found himself suddenly speechless. It was not his natural condition, which made it all the more discomforting.

"You know what. I don't have to say. Guess I was most grateful for the fog—don't mind admitting I was pretty scared, hearing those French cannons and thinking we were about to sink. But you fixed that."

Ben found his voice, but it was less certain than usual. "I thought within the family only Debby and William knew. You know too?"

"Yes, Mr. Ben. We all do. Sally, Jemima, everyone in the house except King knew before we left, and it's plain obvious King knows now. Sally even runs around mimicking you, yes she does. King, though, he's stopped talking 'bout you to me, but I see it in his eyes. And except for him . . . well, we that know, we all work hard to make sure you aren't discovered."

"I . . . " Ben hesitated. "I have no secrets, do I?"

Peter shrugged noncommittally. "You think you do."

"Craven Street!" The driver called back.

Peter leapt down off the dog cart and released the steps. As Ben exited the conveyance, he did something new to him. "Thank you," he said.

The door at number 7 Craven Street opened. A slightly stout, immaculately dressed woman came out onto the steps. "Mr. Franklin, it is indeed a pleasure to meet you. I have been told much of your more creative characteristics and find them delightful."

"You must be the Widow Stevenson," Ben bowed slightly. "It is a pleasure for me as well. Mr. Charles spoke quite highly of you, and I am most excited to see the domicile. 'No more neat and tidy lodgings will you find in the city of London,' he said." Ben smiled warmly. "Allow me to introduce my man Peter to you."

"It's a pleasure to meet you as well, Peter," Mrs. Stevenson replied.

"Thank you, ma'am." Peter ducked his head.

"As to the quality of my lodgings," she went on, "quite right. Me and my ladies keep a right proper arrangement. Respect the house, and the house will provide."

"Respect the house? That I shall." Ben studied the outside of the home and the surrounding street intently. "I see that your curtains are sheer, but I can't see in from here—a nice trick of differing light. I presume you can see out through them from the inside?"

"Indeed, Mr. Franklin, indeed." There was a slight twitch of one of the shades, and Mrs. Stevenson shook her head. "The effect provides great privacy to the occupants. You can't even see my daughter, Polly, who is watching us intently this very moment."

Ben waved to the curtains and they twitched again, exposing the secret watcher.

Mrs. Stevenson laughed. "Oh, you'll do just fine. Just fine indeed. Mr. Charles was right about you."

"I do find the apparition you call your daughter a bit unsettling. Will we ever meet her, or shall I simply assume a ghost will always be watching my morning airings?"

Ben spoke with so serious a tone and expression that it took a moment for Mrs. Stevenson to realize he had been joking. "You hear that, Polly?" She called out while ushering her two guests into the house. "You're an apparition now."

The narrow main hallway had beautifully polished hardwood floors, and midway down its length there was a stairwell and bannister leading up to the next floor. At the top of the stairs, Mrs. Stevenson turned right and pointed out the sitting room, with its window facing the street. The room's most prominent feature was a large fireplace. Placed carefully about it, and positioned to receive equal warmth, were three chairs and a divan. Directly opposite the window was a closed door. Ben wondered briefly where it led, but he assumed he would be told later.

Stepping into the room to take a closer look, he was astonished to discover that he could detect, just at the edge of the audible spectrum, a faint and familiar hum. Without thinking he pressed his right hand to his chest.

This, in my offered lodgings? he thought. *Either the wildest of coincidences, or no coincidence at all—but in either outcome, my first study for the Royal Society would appear to have announced itself.*

"Peter, this is Hannah," said Mrs. Stevenson, pointing to a plain woman in her early twenties. She stood midway up the stairs to the next higher floor, and wore a simple household uniform and cap. "Hannah will you show you the back ways around the house."

"Yes, ma'am," Peter replied, following Hannah up the stairs.

Now Mrs. Stevenson beckoned Ben to follow her in turn. "This way, if you please."

"Right you are," he said, allowing himself just the barest glance back. The persistent hum faded only slightly.

"Back here, through the garden, is the portion of the house I stay in. And should you wish a midnight snack, our kitchen is here. I believe you will find it well-appointed," Mrs. Stevenson said with evident pride.

There was a time that fire and heat had fascinated Franklin as much as electricity. He therefore examined the kitchen with a critical eye. The fireplace, he noted with approval, was complete with swinging iron arms to position cook pots in and out of the flames as needed. The arrangement reminded him of the multi-armed optical lens device he had designed for his experiments back home. He rounded out his review by noting the kitchen's heavy chopping block, the large, well-arranged pantry, and the big sink with hooks suspending four full-sized buckets over it.

"Very modern, Mrs. Stevenson. I approve. Just inspecting it is whetting my appetite." He rubbed his belly, "Not that it needs particular help."

"Thank you. We are going to be one of the first houses in the neighborhood with a water pump right in the kitchen—just as soon as they can connect the pipes to the master well. No more water deliveries for us, then."

"Will the water circulate throughout the house?" asked Franklin, enticed. He tapped the walls, his inventor's mind trying to puzzle out how that might work.

"I'm sure it won't yet," answered a suddenly wary Mrs. Stevenson, watching her strange new lodger get lost in his own head. "It will pump here to the kitchen only. Is something not to your liking?"

Ben became aware of his unintentional insult and immediately set to correct it. "Mrs. Stevenson, I apologize. I find no fault with your extraordinary kitchen. Indeed, it has inspired me—overtaken as I was by the spirit of inquiry, I found myself looking ahead to a future where London homes shall have running water, rather than water from runners."

She smiled graciously at this witticism, which pleased Ben. Apparently all was now forgiven.

"May I look at our rooms? If they are as satisfactory as all that I've seen so far, I'm sure we will have no difficulty coming to equitable financial arrangements."

"The rooms are on the second floor, sir, which is actually third up from the street. There's a box of books waiting for you already."

"I'm sorry—books?"

"Your friend Mr. Collinson sent them. The accompanying note said it was to get your library started. It also said something very strange, after. 'Tell him this will give him a good start, and he'll have to work hard to catch up.' *Beautiful* penmanship. No idea what he meant, of course, but I'm sure you do."

"Nothing too serious," Ben assured her. "From the beginning of our communication, Collinson and I have enjoyed setting each other challenges. I imagine he shall pester me horribly, and I him, now that there isn't an ocean between us to mitigate these impulses."

As they walked back toward the stairs Mrs. Stevenson noticed his slight limp, even though today his cane was more affectation than crutch. Concerned, she made inquiry. "Will the steps be a problem for your legs, Mr. Franklin? I should have asked sooner."

"Not at all, not at all! A healthy diet and plenty of exercise are the true secrets to a long life. As you will be providing delicious, healthy fare, it will fall to me to walk these stairs and the streets each day, providing the physical exertion."

Mrs. Stevenson paused at the banister. She raised her eyebrows at him quizzically, then continued up. It was plain as day that she found him odd, but charming regardless.

He followed, focusing on placing one foot correctly in front of the other on the steps. The exertion was not enough to overcome him, but with his bad knees and hip, plus his weight, it wasn't the easiest climb; and coming from street level to the first floor had already strained him. "You know," he called up to Mrs. Stevenson, "when I was younger, I had every opportunity to be physically active, and was quite the fit man. Maybe it's the air here that is giving me such pause."

"It's just London, Mr. Franklin. You'll get used to it. We all do."

At the top of the stairs Ben was short of breath, though not completely winded. Mrs. Stevenson kindly pretended to not notice. He resisted the temptation to draw strength from the Key, knowing how the counterbalance of hunger and exhaustion would swing against him later; there was nothing for it but to wait until he recovered naturally and accept that all the pleasantries in the world couldn't make him one day younger.

His brow furrowed as he closed his eyes and leaned his head back. The faint humming that was so like the Key—and the Bell too, he remembered—was *stronger* here.

"Thank you for your patience, madam. I believe I am ready."

Still breathing a bit hard, Ben followed Mrs. Stevenson into the simple room that was being offered for use as his library. It was filled wall to wall with empty bookshelves, and a comfortable desk and chair were set to one side of the small fireplace that was connected to the main chimney.

Sitting at the desk was an eighteen-year-old woman in a simple yet elegantly fashionable dress. On hearing them enter she looked up from the open book on the desk, and her eyes locked with Franklin's, clearly taking his measure. Ben, in turn, saw within her gaze both profound intelligence and a considerable gift for mischief. In spirit, she reminded him deeply of his own daughter Sally. So strong was this reaction that it took him a further moment to see the small brooch she wore as a pin. It was a miniature metal scorpion in a jade setting, and there could be no question—it, and it alone, was the source of the humming.

Ben sought to control his features. He hoped the girl had seen nothing in them, but doubted his success.

"Mr. Franklin," said Mrs. Stevenson, "may I introduce your apparition, my daughter, Polly." Polly stood and curtsied prettily.

Ben sketched a bow in keeping with their respective ages. "My pleasure, Miss Polly. I see you are reading the newest work of Mr. David Hume. I have not yet had the opportunity to consider it."

"Mr. Franklin," Polly beamed. "I am honored to meet you. Please say you will choose to lodge here, and that you will fill these shelves with even more books to read. They have been empty for a very long time, and bear occupancy. I've taken the liberty of unpacking the crate of books your Mr. Collinson sent over earlier, so you would be able to examine them without delay, and then I saw that *Four Dissertations* was amongst them. I have been simply desperate to read this book, and could not resist, though I know it was rude of me to do so without asking first. May I ask you now?" She spoke quickly, one hand fidgeting with the edges of the book all the while.

"Polly," Mrs. Stevenson interrupted. "Please allow Mr. Franklin a moment around your words." She glanced at Ben somewhat ruefully. "Forgive my daughter, sir. She can, at times, be overly helpful, especially when there are books concerned."

Ben forced himself not to stare at the brooch, however much it now dominated his thoughts. "No offense taken, Mrs. Stevenson. Your daughter's intelligence, education, and thoughtfulness have certified my decision, and Mr. Charles' recommendation of this house. You both make me feel as though this is my home, and I am coming back to a warm family. Young Polly, you must let me initiate correspondences between you and my own daughter Sally, who also has a great love of books."

"That is most kind of you to say," Mrs. Stevenson said, with a small sigh of relief. "I'm sure Polly would love to correspond with your family in the Colonies. I am not a great letter writer, myself."

"Then it is settled. Peter and I will go fetch the rest of our party and arrange for our belongings to be delivered, so tonight we can eat our first meal together in our new English home. And perhaps *after* dinner"—he favored Polly with the most challenging look he could muster—"there will be time for chess. Tell me, O Ghostly Spirit: do you play?"

The Stevenson Home

Craven Street
London, England
August 10th

✣ ✣ ✣

❖ 17 ❖
Letter to Mother

Benjamin Franklin, Esq., commander, general, and strategist, studied the battlefield in the parlor of his Craven Street lodgings with exquisite care from inside his cocoon of warm blankets. He was certain of victory, for his troops had fought well, but it was not the victory he wanted. The brooch that his opponent wore had proven an impenetrable mystery. It still tugged unceasingly at his attention and sounded in his ears, but over time he had begun to grow used to the feeling. Resigned to it, more accurately. Neither Polly nor her mother admitted knowing anything of the brooch's origin—a trinket purchased at a street fair, the girl had claimed, with a face so guileless that Franklin suspected her all the more.

"You should study the chessboard more than you study me," he said softly, seeking to avoid overtaxing the raw throat and hurting chest that accompanied his current mild malaise. He had forgotten how much he had disliked the summer colds he always suffered in England.

"I completely disagree, Mr. Franklin. The more you carry of knowledge of your opponent, the more you control their moves." Polly looked at the battlefield between them and bit her lip. The board was from a traveler's set, about the length of a hand from side to side, and the tiny pieces were red and white in the current vogue, as opposed to the more traditional black and white. "Or is it too forward for me to control your movements, sirrah?"

155

William choked on his beer and coughed, inadvertently spitting on the pages of the law book he had been studying. His cheeks flushed as both players turned to stare at him. "I wouldn't move the queen if I were you," he said to Polly, seeking to recover his dignity. "He does that a lot, you know—threatens a piece he has no intention of trading for just to gain some positional advantage."

"Give away my secrets, would you?" Ben cried in mock outrage.

"Oh, I don't know that he is giving away anything, Mr. Franklin. At least not anything that hadn't already been clearly exposed to one who is looking." Polly tucked her chin and hid her mouth with one hand, as though embarrassed at court by a suitor. But her eyes twinkled.

"I approach this sport of the mind with a singular focus," Ben complained, this time a shade more seriously. "The *bon-vivanterie* that you both display is very distracting."

"Don't let him fool you," William shot back. "He could have won three moves ago. He's more interested in improving your game than in maintaining his. I cannot tell you the number of times I wanted to throw the board into the fire because I knew he was playing *with* me and not, as a true opponent should, *against* me."

Ben addressed his son. "You learned, did you not?"

"I am not sure. I still lose more games against you than I win."

"Just like everyone else, as it should be," Ben replied off-handedly.

"Such overwhelming confidence," Polly said, sliding one of her rooks forward. "Check."

William and Ben stared at each other for the briefest of moments. The girl was, in ways, schooling them both in the art of conversational warfare over the board.

Polly blew an errant hair from her forehead. "Your move, I believe."

This was a game two could play. Ben put his hand on hers, gently but commandingly. "Are you sure that is the move you should make?" he asked, sliding a bishop three angled squares, but keeping his fingers on the piece.

"Father, really," William said condescendingly. "She has made her move, let her suffer the consequences. Don't seek to intimidate her by showing what you *might* do. I always hated that!"

"Silence, my boy," Ben replied. "Red's Brigadier is still thinking. She has not answered."

William rose from the divan. "Nor have you taken your hand from hers, Father. I guess you like moving her as a player too. You two enjoy yourselves, I think I'll go write a letter home to Mother and Sally, and my dearest Betsy. I promise to include quips about knights moving by night, just for you."

Ben moved his hand back to his blanket covering and frowned. "What a dutiful son you are, my William. Shall I see you tomorrow to accompany me to the Royal College?"

"I will, Father. Enjoy your games." William took his book and mug with him as he left.

Ben frowned, "Sometimes I wonder about that boy."

Polly looked over at the door through which he had departed, then turned back to Ben. "I don't. He would have been tricked by the forced-attack trap I laid. You saw right through it. Unfortunately, he seems a bad chess player who thinks he is good. And no, I do not withdraw my rook, nor do I fear your bishop." She grinned at him ferociously. "Now attend the board, please, and do try to learn, or I shall have to charge you for the lesson."

"Ha. Such overwhelming confidence indeed," Ben said sternly, but his eyes twinkled.

The Home
of Thomas Penn
At Hitcham,
near Maidenhead Bridge, Bucks
August 20th
✣ ✣ ✣

✤ 18 ✤
A Lifetime of Favors

Heads of Complaint; to be known to the Penns

1. That the reasonable and necessary Power given to Deputy Governors of Pennsylvania by the Royal Charter, Section 4th. and 5th. of making Laws with the Advice and Consent of the Assembly, for Raising Money for the Safety of the Country and other Publick Uses, "according to their best Discretion," is taken away by Proprietary Instructions enforced by penal Bonds, and restraining the Deputy from the Use of his best Discretion; tho' being on the Spot, he can better judge of the Emergency State and Necessity of Affairs, than Proprietaries residing at a great Distance; by Means of which Restraints sundry Sums of Money granted by the Assembly for the Defence of the Province, have been rejected by the Deputy, to the great Injury of His Majesty's Service in Time of War, and Danger of the Loss of the Colony.

2. That the indubitable Right of the Assembly, to judge of the Mode, Measure and Time of Granting Supplies, is infringed by Instructions that injoin the Deputy to refuse his Assent to any Bill for Raising Money, unless certain Modes, Measures, and Times in such Instructions directed, make a Part of the Bill;

whereby the Assembly, in Time of War, are reduced to the Necessity of either losing the Country to the Enemy, or giving up the Liberties of the People, and receiving Law from the Proprietary; and if they should do the latter in the present Case, it will not prevent the former; the restricting Instructions being such, as that, if comply'd with, it is impossible to raise a Sum sufficient to defend the Country.

3. That the Proprietaries have injoined their Deputy, by such Instructions, to refuse his Assent to any Law for raising Money by a Tax, tho' ever so necessary for the Defence of the Country, unless the greatest Part of their Estate is exempted from such Tax. This, to the Assembly and People of Pennsylvania, appears both unjust and cruel.

The Proprietaries are now requested seriously to consider these Complaints, and redress the Aggrievances complain'd of, in the most speedy and effectual Manner; that Harmony may be restored between the several Branches of the Legislature, and the Publick Service be hereafter readily and fully provided for.

~B Franklin,
Agent for the Province
of Pensilva.

Ben was grateful to be approaching this home so soon. From the way Peter Collinson had spoken on Franklin's arrival, Ben had thought that a private meeting with Thomas Penn would take him at least a year of effort, bribery, and subtle pressure to achieve. Instead, all it appeared to require was the right word from certain mutual acquaintances. It was a result Collinson had found no less surprising than Ben himself.

An impeccably dressed servant answered the door. Though of simple cut, the doorman's uniform was made from a rich plush velvet of a quality with Ben's own favorite suits. In terms of the social display of prosperity, at least, Ben saw that Collinson had been entirely correct. But he could not help but wonder if this was also a means for Thomas Penn to show the Pennsylvanians—more specifically the Pennsylvanian now standing at his door—where the balance of power actually stood. The thought increased his wariness over the coming conversation.

Franklin was relieved of his hat and cloak, but decided to keep his cane. He was still not well-recovered from his recent affliction, and, ever since his arrival in London, his breath had been shorter than preferable. Far shorter.

Left waiting in the house's main hall, Ben gazed at the paintings hanging on the walls. He recognized the likeness of Thomas Penn himself, and of course that of his famous father, William Penn, founder of the colony of Pennsylvania. There was also a large painting of William with a group of men, among whom Ben thought he recognized George Fox, Thomas Janney, and Robert Barclay. Much to his chagrin, the remainder of the portraits were entirely mysterious to him—he suspected the names of some, but not enough to hazard a guess. Interestingly, no pictures of William Penn's other children were on display. It was as if Thomas Penn's brothers and sisters did not exist.

Ben fought back a fit of coughing as his breath wheezed in. The muscles in his back clenched, his ears rang, and everything hurt as the world, for a moment, spun in place. When the coughing finally subsided, he held his left hand over his chest and muttered "*Medicor.*" A tingling wave flowed from that point through all his limbs, easing the pain and allowing him to take a deep, clear breath.

He shook his head.

The ringing persisted in his ears, but all other symptoms fled. He would pay for this temporary relief later, of course; he had come to understand that magic always extracted its price. But for now he was in need of his wits and the semblance of health.

The most prominent painting in the hall showed a woman, dressed in a fashionable gown of soft gray silk, standing next to a fireplace that held a large silver vase of flowers. The wall behind her was covered in ornate blue wallpaper, and the artist had clearly enjoyed contrasting a studiously sylvan picture above the fireplace with the more realistically painted tree and sky that were visible through a background window. Franklin was quite taken by the picture's technique, and by the knowing, slightly bemused expression on the woman's face.

"I see you have settled your eye on the portrait of my wife," said a voice from close behind him.

Ben resisted the sudden startlement, managing to remain stock still. "So, this is the Lady Julianna Penn," he said without turning, continuing to focus all his apparent attention on the painting before him. "Quite admirable."

"Yes," said Thomas Penn. Out of the corner of his eye, Ben saw the man step to his side and join in contemplation of the work. He wore finery far beyond anything Ben would have deemed practical, dressed head to foot in a silken suit of brown, gold, and silver. What was most striking about him was that even through the pudginess of age Thomas Penn still had strikingly sharp eyes and cheekbones.

Ben tilted his head in acknowledgement. "Mr. Penn."

"Mr. Franklin."

"A most handsome painting."

"It was done by Arthur Devis, to celebrate the occasion of our marriage. Julianna posed for it in her father's house on Albemarle Street, in London. Many an admirer has stood where you now stand and commented on her beauty."

"For obvious reasons; you are a fortunate man. But if I may inquire about a different piece...?" Ben turned to the group painting, "This one, with George Fox and your father."

"Oh, that's a flight of fancy my father commissioned. It never actually happened. These are the men foundational to the creation of Pennsylvania. George Fox was always good for causing a stir, wasn't he? Much as you and your people are now with the Crown." He gave Ben a questioning look, then turned and began to walk away, after first gesturing for Franklin to follow. "Isn't it funny how far we've come since the days I was your patron, sending you parts for the clever engines of experimentation you built? But you did not come all the way from the colony to discuss art and the past, Mr. Franklin. I am in receipt of your draft complaint. Let us retire to the sitting room and discuss matters over a pot of tea, as gentlemen."

Ben took stock as they proceeded in silence. Having heard from mutual acquaintances that Thomas Penn was a cold, distant, even taciturn man, he mistrusted this warmer-than-expected reception.

Servants with an elegant silver and china tea service awaited them in the sitting room. Ben took the setting in with both admiration for the handicraft he saw, and irritation at its excess: there was more wealth on display than he had ever before seen in a room this size. He felt a very long way from his own humble beginnings on Boston's Milk Street.

Penn did not jump directly into important matters; instead, as their tea was laid out in silence by his help, he began by discussing interesting but less vital matters from Pennsylvania and other colonies, and the war effort in Europe. Ben was surprised to discover that Penn was not only well acquainted with the minutiae of political and military events in the colony his father had founded, but that he was informed on more mundane matters as well, especially those that involved Franklin himself. As they sipped hot black tea calmed with generous dollops of milk and sugar, Penn expressed deep appreciation for the work Ben's paper and press had done to increase the prosperity of the colony, quoted obscure yet clever quips from *Poor Richard's Almanack*, and offered praise for Ben's work with the Library Company, the College of Pennsylvania . . . and even his adventures forming and then participating in Philadelphia's volunteer fire company.

By the time the tea was near gone and the dregs cooling in their cups, Ben felt he understood the game that was being played; apparently Penn thought his poor colonial guest could be lulled and deflected through simple flattery. Such underestimation, in Ben's judgment, was both mildly insulting and of enormous potential use. As he listened, he contemplated various ways to take advantage.

"But enough of pleasantries, Mr. Franklin. Do you mind if we move to the more formal portion of this meeting, in order to outline the basic position you represent?"

"Please, Mr. Penn. I would find it most enlightening if you did and would be much obliged," answered Ben.

"Then please join me in my study." Penn rose from his chair with ease; Franklin, with a little struggle. He wished he could take a moment to once more boost his vitality, but that was impossible in Penn's presence. He followed him down the hall to a large room with even richer appointments, including an ornately carved formal table, a Venetian mirror, and elaborate Italian chandeliers with hand-blown glasswork.

Thomas's younger brother, Richard, was waiting for them there, already seated. The informal Heads of Complaint that Ben had drafted was on the table before him, and Ben could see that Richard had been reading it and taking notes.

As they sat down in their own well-upholstered chairs, Thomas cleared his throat and spoke.

"Please allow me to introduce the other quarter vote of the proprietorship, Mr. Richard Penn. I am told the two of you share natal days. Such coincidence!"

"January 17th?" asked Ben.

Richard Penn smiled. "The actual one."

Thomas looked momentarily confused. "Pardon me?"

"Let me clarify, brother. Mr. Franklin and I were both born in the same month, January. But when the calendar was aligned five years ago, he was among those who chose to adjust his date of birth in consequence."

"It was only sensible," Franklin offered. "The calendar was wrong by 11 days."

"This again?" Thomas put his hand over his face, rubbing at his eyes. "It was bad enough, the placards and protests. Can we not move past this, Richard?"

"Parliament agrees with you, sir. For my belief, this misnumbering of days is but the whim of a dead pope, and while I must put up with it in law and commerce, I will not submit to it in my person." He nodded cordially enough to both of the other men, moving on with grace. "But surely we are not here to rehash the lost days...?"

"No, we are not," said Thomas. He turned in his seat to face Ben. "Please correct me if anything I now say is misinformed or inaccurate. It seems to me that you represent a group that is deeply upset at the hereditary rights granted to myself, my family, and the other established and settled estate owners in the colony. Furthermore, you feel that much of this power over the politics of Pennsylvania is unjust—as it is not power exerted in the best interest of the colony or the Crown, but rather merely for personal gain. Put simply, you believe a more equitable means of apportioning power must be developed, so those who are active in the colony's daily affairs would have authority commensurate with their abilities, accomplishments, and proximity. And should this not happen, you believe that the actions of our appointed office will harm the colony and people therein."

"That," agreed Ben, "fairly expresses the basics of the Assembly's point of view. I would further state that the Assembly and colonists would have no problem at all, were it not for the tax exemption of large portions of the incomes of these settled estate owners. Specifically, your ownership and refusal to be financially accountable in a time of war makes it difficult to run our colony. Especially in light of your refusal to acknowledge and represent that two thirds of the Assembly are pacifists and will not muster troops."

"Very well then," said Thomas, firmly. "I agree that things must change."

"Excuse me?" Of all the words Ben might have imagined coming from Penn's mouth in this moment, these were not among them.

"The point you make is a valid one. Most of the proprietors don't even live in the colony. What could we know about how to properly defend it from French or Indian attack, or negotiate a trade deal? Might as well ask your Speaker Norris to do something about John Wilkes bribing his way into office in Aylesbury."

"That is a most enlightened way of viewing the matter."

"Thank you," said Penn, smiling warmly. "Of course, your main problem lies with the Quakers, and the fact that they refuse to even mount a defense. Rather than putting able-bodied young men into service, and arming them, they would have us buy treaties with the aggressors to the west. This is weakness. Their pacifism will get them killed. Why should they have a voice in the Assembly, then, if they are unwilling to pay the cost of all that they now receive? Please, convince me otherwise, but the way I see it, I will still own my land after their rejection of a reasonable course puts them, and many others, in the grave."

Ben's eyes narrowed, and his jaw clenched. "Do not mistake pacifism for weakness, sir. Your own father bent the knee to no church and all the while raised the fist to no man. In this world there must be a place for those who refuse to fight, as much as for those who do, and in my observation it takes *far* greater strength to put down a weapon than to pick one up. Your family founded this colony, and its Assembly, to protect this ideal."

Richard waved Ben's words away, looking bemused. "The Charter expresses no such thing. My father needed more money. He got it."

"Your father's Charter expresses *exactly* that, in its first section."

Ben made no effort to disguise his irritation. "Just as its second section establishes the Assembly, and enumerates its powers. We Pennsylvanians have the same rights as any free-born subject of England."

"Yes, yes, Mr. Franklin," replied Thomas Penn. "My father promised a lot of things. I don't really care about that. The Charter of Privileges is a worthless document, granting rights which my father was not, by the Royal Charter, empowered to grant. Nothing can be claimed by it, and as you have already pointed out, a new arrangement is necessary. That is the essence of the document you have placed before us, is it not? Something *new*?"

All vestige of illness faded from Ben's awareness as he felt heat course through his veins. His face went flat, expressionless. Those that knew him well knew that when he was emotionless, he was at the height of his anger. Thomas Penn did not know him at all. Calmly, quietly, Ben continued. "If your father had no right to grant these privileges, with the Throne's support, and published all over Europe, with the Throne's pound, after his father's rescuing of the King—well then, those who came to settle in the province on the faith of that grant were deceived. Every last settler who came on his word and the *King's* word were cheated and betrayed. Surely this is not the position you are intent on taking. No sane person would accuse the Throne of that."

Thomas Penn's demeanor was as cool and aloof as Franklin's. "You assume culpability where there is none. The settlers should have looked to the laws, and to the Royal Charter. If they *were* deceived then it was their own fault; they should have learned to read and utilized that capability. It is not the Penn family's fault they were fools. And fools who are on the wrong side of the law."

Before Ben could speak, Richard Penn held up his hand and coughed politely. Ben turned to face him, understanding that this was part of their game, having arranged the room so that he could only look into the face of one Penn at a time, whereas both could always watch him. "My brother appears to feel your proposal to be too forward, and lacking in the appreciation our father's memory deserves. I take a more practical view. To me this is not so—shall we say, deep?—an issue. It is just that we, the proprietors, do not want to give up the political power which serves to protect the financial benefits we now receive. That is the real issue. Of *course* you want more power. And there is a way for you to have it, should the Assembly be willing to consider a solution along certain lines."

Ben regarded the younger Penn warily. "And what lines would those be?"

"We might be persuaded to give up all extra-legal rights we now possess as a special class in the colony . . . in return for a binding guarantee that our lands will not be taxed. Ever."

"Unworkable, sir. Your holdings represent too much of the land value in the colony to be allowed so complete an exception. Indeed, if—"

Richard Penn lifted a forestalling hand. "Then let us be less complete. Naturally, as loyal subjects to our monarch, should His Majesty declare a war and the colonial Assembly vote to support it, then we would allow our lands to be taxed. But *only* as much as others in the colony, and *never* more than ten percent, no matter what appalling burden the rest of the colony chooses to impose upon itself."

Ben looked from Richard to Thomas and back, slowly, gauging their expressions as he thought through the implications of the offer. In Richard Penn's eyes he thought he saw something of the common hog-trader, willing to drop price if necessary to complete a deal; in Thomas's he saw only boredom and disdain, with no hint of compromise. And Thomas held the dominant position in the proprietorship.

"Many would object to the Penns not having to pay taxes except in time of declared war."

"No doubt," said Richard Penn. "But Pennsylvania is growing. As it does, the lands available for taxation will increase."

"A clarification, then. Can I presume that your proposal would apply *only* to the lands the proprietors hold now? And that any future holdings you might acquire in the colony will be taxed at normal rates, instead of joining the exemption?"

"It will be difficult to persuade the other proprietors, but I sense that without this concession you could not bring the Assembly to agree. Is that correct?"

"I wouldn't even try," replied Ben.

Thomas Penn spoke next, and once more Ben had to turn in his seat. "It will be difficult, but I think I can make it work so long as any such an agreement is guaranteed in a way that all will find inviolate. An act of Parliament, for example, signed by His Majesty."

"You could get Parliament to act on such a matter? I find that hard to believe."

"It would mean calling in a few favors, but I have a lifetime of collected favors, and not all that much lifetime left in which to spend them." Thomas laughed at his own joke, and Ben found it diplomatic to laugh with him. "It might be best to use some of this personal credit to settle the issues that threaten the peace of our colony. Under the right circumstances, I suspect we could have a draft agreement out of the House of Lords and on its way to the Assembly in less than a month, in order to avoid placing it on the desk of a judge. Always assuming . . . "

An uncomfortable silence followed—one which, clearly, neither Penn intended to fill.

"Yes?" asked Ben, finally yielding.

" . . . assuming your further cooperation, of course," said Thomas Penn.

"I speak for the interests of my colony, gentlemen. I will not yield to proposals which are not to their benefit, and you already ask much."

"Oh, this has nothing to do with the colony. Richard? If you may, please?"

Richard Penn opened one drawer of the desk and removed from it a paper-wrapped packet, tied in string, which he placed on the desk. Pulling the knot loose, he unfolded the paper, unveiling a neat stack of old, leather-bound journals. He lifted one at a time from the stack, distributing them in a pattern across the desktop that reminded Ben of the way self-proclaimed seers spread cards for divination.

Thomas Penn read the shock in Ben's eyes with evident pleasure. "Recognize them, do you?"

Ben spoke slowly, and with care. "They appear to be quite similar to a set of rare volumes I last examined in my home in Philadelphia."

"We may speak freely. They are not similar—they are the same. But of course you already know that. Printer and collector that you are, I'd wager you memorized every nick, scratch, and stain on their bindings while you had them in your possession."

Ben's anger flared and his expression went cold once more. "You are *admitting* theft, then? Nay, proclaiming it?"

"These did not belong to you, sir; there can be no theft in arranging to return them to their proper owner."

"Who is—"

"No one you need be concerned with," said Richard Penn.

"I rather think I should be the judge of that," said Ben, grimly.

"Come," said Thomas. "I understood you to enjoy a good performance; forgive us this small piece of theater. We are prepared to reward you with everything you ever realistically hoped to win for your Assembly, in a manner that cannot be revoked or broken, in return for our own guarantees and the answers to three simple questions, which we will convey to the true owner of these journals. First, from whom did you get them? Second, how much—if any— have you gleaned of their contents? And third...there is one missing. Our agent was quite thorough in his search, while your family enjoyed time with you in New York, prior to your coming here to test your wits against our will. *What happened to it?*"

Ben calculated carefully. There was too much at stake for the colony. His shoulders slumped, and he spoke. Every word he chose was true, while still revealing nothing. "They were procured as part of a lot sale from an estate. They are written in too many languages. I have to date, been unable to translate them. As to the fate of the final journal...it was, sadly, destroyed."

Thomas studied him intently, then smiled. "Noooo...I don't think I shall choose to believe you, Mr. Franklin. We cannot do business with a dishonest colonial. Richard. Destroy the papers. Consider the offer revoked."

Ben stood, his spine a ramrod despite discomfort. "I was reluctant to trust your offer, sir, but hopeful to trust you. Clearly that was an error in judgment. Thank you for the tea and entertainment. I will see myself out." Stone-faced, he bowed just half an inch less than was proper and left without uttering another word.

"Ta, Mr. Franklin. We shall see you around."

Middle Temple Hall & the Home of Thomas Fermor,

First Earl of Pomfret, London
September 15th

✦ ✦ ✦

❖ 19 ❖
Satan's Work

William was deeply absorbed in a book on imperial law, and its application in border disputes with foreign powers, when one of the Silks of the King's Counsel tapped him on the shoulder. The sunlight streaming through the stained-glass windows of the Middle Temple's library was warm on his cheek and neck, and the smell of fresh buns with currants filled the air. In all, he could not imagine a better place to pursue his studies, and any interruption—even so quiet an invasion as this—was hard-borne. On reading the Silk's note, however, he took firm hold of the reins of his emotions. For a student barrister, turning down such a request was *not* an option. He would simply have to leave immediately, and best foot forward while at it. Anything less could be deemed an insult.

"A moment only, please," he said. He closed the book, carefully marking his place, then stretched his idle limbs and nodded. "Shall we?"

The Silk led him deeper into the Middle Temple Hall, through areas still mostly unfamiliar. Multiple wings extended from the central portion of the building, which served as a church every Sunday, and each wing was marked with high ceilings, ornately decorated walls, and rich oak wainscotting. The oak had been polished so many times over the centuries that William could see a dim reflection of himself in some of the panels. Eventually they came to a stair to the basement, which they descended. At the bottom, William found himself standing before a door unlike any he had ever seen.

It was both tall and wide, and very old, with a red stain to the wood that was so dark it might as well be black. The bindings and hinges looked to be made of antique brass, dingy with age, while the handle and lock were of a curiously different metal that appeared to be gray and silver at the same time.

William opened the door and walked through.

The unsigned summons had been a curious thing. He was far more confused, however, to open a basement door and find himself in a brightly lit room, with sunlight shining in from high windows along three walls. Seated at a desk in the center of the room was a man he knew only from printed reproductions.

For the first time in William's acquaintance, the Silk spoke, offering formal introduction.

"Presenting Captain William Franklin. Captain Franklin, may I present the Honorable Thomas Penn, Esquire, doctor, proprietor of the Pennsylvania Colony, son of the Honorable William Penn, Esquire, founder of the Pennsylvania Colony, and grandson of the Admiral Sir William Penn."

Thomas Penn looked up and smiled. "Ah! Captain Franklin. I'm afraid I haven't much time now, but wanted to introduce myself while we were both here." He scooted back from the desk and stood, then stepped around it to approach the younger man. To the Silk he said, "Wait outside, please, until we are finished; and do close the door."

William took in his surroundings. The room was even larger than it had appeared at first. Bookshelves twice the height of a standing man lined the far wall, each shelf packed with leather-bound volumes of various sizes; exquisite tapestries, richly framed paintings, and glass-boxed animal skins hung on the other walls, and artifacts from around the globe were positioned strategically around the room. It was an impressive display.

Penn coughed gently into his balled fist.

William shook off the room's momentarily overwhelming effect and focused on the man before him. "Mister Penn, the one true Proprietor? I am, I must say, surprised to find you here."

"Ah. Please call me Thomas, as I hope you will let me address you as William, unless your father has already turned you against me. No?"

William shook his head.

"Good. Despite the opinion of the senior Franklin now habiting London, I am certain that you know I am more than just this dispute over taxes. I had therefore hoped that a sensibly reputationed gentleman such as yourself would be amenable to a meeting. Hence my invitation."

William raised an eyebrow, uncertain just what to say. "Your invitation? My apologies, Mr. Penn ... Thomas ... I mean no harm, nor to diminish you in any way, but on receiving an unsigned summons from a member of the King's Counsel, I had naturally expected, um, the ... " He trailed off as he realized how foolish it must seem for him to have expected a meeting with the King. "I'm sorry."

Thomas threw back his head and laughed. "You have no need to apologize. This *is* the King's study at the Middle Temple, after all. Only a very few of us who have the King's ear have permission to use this room. Knowing you were at the Middle Temple this morning, I decided to avail myself of it. We have much to discuss, you and I, if you are amenable."

"You do me a great honor, sir."

"Pshaw. Nothing of it."

"No, of a certainty you do," insisted William. "But I hope you will understand that I cannot work against my father's wishes in any way, no matter my own opinion on a given point of politics. I am not an appointed Commissioner for the Colony. I hold no sway over any member of the Assembly, nor any local influence worth giving the name. In short, I do not see what value you may find in taking conversation with me."

"You may rest easy, William," said Penn, his tone warm and inclusive. "All I wish from you is perspective. As I said, I am more than the dispute. It has been years since I was in Pennsylvania, and though I believed otherwise until a short time ago, I fear I am now English, through and through. The proprietorship does not understand the colony's current set of mind. It seems ... *foreign* to us, if I may say so. Even the French are more sensible, to be perfectly candid."

"My fellows can be damned hard to understand sometimes, at that. I often struggle with colonial attitudes, if I'm to be forthright."

"There. You see? You offer precisely what I need." Penn rapped the desktop once for emphasis. "There is a gulf between our worlds. If I am to find my way to a solution, I must somehow bridge it."

"An admirable goal," agreed William. "But I am still not clear on how I might be of assistance."

"Simple enough. I am in London all this week on business. Come dine with me tonight at my father-in-law's residence, and let us talk, simply talk, about the colony. I want to see it through *your* eyes. I want to understand it as *you* do, having been born and raised there. Your perception and insights regarding your home might seem obvious, even trivial, to you; they will be anything but that to me. Indeed, by some measures they may make all the difference between success and failure in this endeavor."

"I . . . I hardly know what to say."

"Say yes, then. I promise you a splendid meal, and even my aging company is tolerable for a single evening."

"You do yourself a disservice, sir. But . . . yes. I will come. And thank you for the invitation."

They spoke for another fifteen minutes before Penn, pleading prior obligation, had to excuse himself. After that, the waiting Silk, as silent as before, led William back to the library, where he picked up the book he had put down, turned to the marked page, and found himself utterly unable to focus on the text at all.

The Home of Thomas Penn

At Hitcham,
near Maidenhead Bridge, Bucks
September 15th

✛ ✛ ✛

✣ 20 ✣
A Famous Father's Son

William had ordered King to commandeer his father's hired coach so that he could arrive in at least a modicum of respectability. On the ride to Albemarle Street he instructed his servant on the fine points of the evening and the standard of behavior he expected King to meet. Just because the boy was technically free on English soil was no reason, in William's consideration, to be lax. He made it abundantly clear that if King was not on his absolutely *best* behavior, it was off to a Carolina plantation for him—English law or no. William disliked having to resort to threats; it really was distasteful. But tonight he had no time for King to be up to any sour looks or tomfoolery.

King rapped the knocker and the door was opened by a household servant dressed more elegantly than William was, which took him instantly aback. *At my finest I'm less than a servant of the proprietor,* William thought. *Why do we engage in conflict with these people? We play at power but don't understand how powerless we are.*

Despite these misgivings, he maintained a pleasant—even commanding—demeanor as the servant relieved him and King of their cloaks and hats, then led them to their respective destinations. King was given a seat in a side hallway and told to wait until the servant could return to take him to the kitchen; after which William was taken into the most private sections of the house, where Thomas Penn awaited him.

William entered the calling room with an air of confidence that he hoped would ingratiate him with his host. For the first time since earning his captaincy, he felt himself his own man, instead of merely being a famous father's son.

"William," said Thomas Penn, buoyantly. "How marvelous to see you twice in one day. I am glad you were able to keep our appointment."

William was delighted to be received in so open and friendly a manner. He carefully modulated the depth of his bow to offer respect to a non-royal, without crossing over the line into obsequiousness. "Chief Proprietor," he said in earnest, "I am, humbly, at your service."

"Oh, please, let's not stand on such formality. This afternoon I was Thomas; pray let me be Thomas again." Penn had not moved as he received his guest, but put out his hand so that William could advance the distance to shake it.

William closed the gap with vigor and took Penn's offered hand. He gave it his best grip, firm and decisive, and was well pleased with the manner of his handshake's return. "You are kind, sir, but your family is well above my station. I do hope to someday be called to the bar here, and must know my place. So I will surrender to your wishes within these walls, or else otherwise in private; but outside them or in company I shall call you Mr. Penn. For my own comfort, and for propriety's sake."

Thomas Penn considered this speech and appeared to judge it worthy. He smiled more warmly than ever, the very model of congeniality. "Agreed, then. As before company I shall never omit your own well-earned title, *Captain* Franklin."

"Thank you." William bowed his head.

"It is only your due, young man. And now that we have obliged the niceties, perhaps you would like to eat?"

The meal, as promised, was splendid—easily the best William had yet had in London—and the smooth perfection of its serving, spectacular. William was glad to think of King watching within the kitchen as the household staff progressed from course to course: perhaps he might learn something useful from the experience.

The conversation had also been something to savor. Penn had not leapt immediately to colonial matters, choosing instead to open London's doors for his visitor. William had made a point of following both business news and the doings of society since his arrival in England, but hearing this information from Thomas Penn's lips was vastly more compelling. William was entranced, and not least because the man knew the stories *behind* the stories—details and secrets that provided extra layers of meaning, spice, humor, or outrage. William found this experience almost as intoxicating as the brandy.

Before dessert was presented, the nexus of discussion finally jumped westward, across the Atlantic, to Philadelphia and the many challenges comprising life in Pennsylvania. Now the balance of give and take shifted, as Penn retreated to the role of questioner, and William happily answered his probing queries at length. He was taken by the diversity of the man's interests, the precision with which he ferreted out details and sorted them for relevance, and, above all, by the *concern* he showed for William's fellow colonials. Before this evening, William would never have questioned his father's views on the Penn family. But he could hardly deny the evidence of his own experience. Sadly, he knew that his father's stubbornness and biases had led him astray, at least on this topic.

Later still, William was quite surprised to see that the elegant clock above the fireplace was nearing eleven o'clock.

"My God," he said. "Look at the time. I have horribly abused your hospitality, Thomas."

"No," said Penn. "You have simply confirmed my good judgment. I am grateful to you, and happy to count one Franklin, at least, among my friends."

William swelled at the praise, an emotion boosted only slightly by the evening's drink.

"I do admit that this entire day has been . . . unexpected. Such a strange introduction, and then your invitation to a private meeting. You know, before coming here I wasn't sure that I should, considering the turbulent nature of your relationship with my father. But I'm glad I trusted my own instincts in the matter."

Thomas Penn nodded. "I would hope for you to trust me."

"I do, sir."

"Then may I trust, in turn, in your circumspection? For there is one element of recent events that we have *not* discussed, at least not yet, because I was not certain you might be ready." Penn's tone was serious in a way it hadn't been earlier in the evening. With that, William understood that he was once again standing before a door, and that the entire day had in some manner been a test of his worthiness to enter.

"You have my attention, Thomas, and my promise. Any secret you choose to share will be safe with me."

"And if that secret is one you *already* share, what then?"

William frowned and his brow crinkled, confused. "Excuse me?"

"I speak of something I know has troubled you. Sadly, I can confirm that you are right to be concerned."

"Please. It is late, and no, I don't know what you are talking about."

Penn studied William for what seemed a very long time. "I fear I have come upon the matter clumsily. Your reticence is understandable—even admirable. Let me earn your further trust, then, by sharing a great secret first. What you are about to learn is known by very few."

The dining table had long since been cleared of everything but their two brandy snifters. Now Penn opened a bureau drawer and withdrew a roll of paper. William noted, with some amazement, that the roll was held closed by a blob of red wax bearing King George's seal. Penn quickly broke the seal and rolled the sheet out on the table, weighing down both of the mildly curling ends with the brandy snifters. Penn motioned William over to examine the paper closely. It was a strange map of sorts, of the English Isles, with blotches of color that in no way aligned with any cities, counties, or shires.

"Tell me what you make of this, William."

He studied the map intently. But much as he longed to pierce Penn's mystery, and prove his usefulness, the meaning of the image eluded him.

"The map is obvious enough, though the markings are not. I can offer this, however. Idle representations do not merit the King's seal. Whatever this map records, it is something the Crown fears." He paused. "Or desires? What might that be?"

Penn looked at him solemnly. "This is a map showing areas where—and I grasp hold of my heart as I say it—good Englishmen and women are taking up magic, to the destruction of us all. Each stain you see is such a concentration."

"Of *magic*." William blinked, trying to hide memories of the late night experiments of his father's from being exposed by his expression.

"Yes."

William pulled back from the table. "There is no such thing."

"That won't do," said Penn sharply. "We both know better."

William was not yet ready to yield. His thoughts spun wildly in his head. *Father . . . if what Thomas says is true . . . if what has happened to you is happening to others, as well . . .*

"All right," he said, turning to face Penn. "You have proposed magic. I grant you the notion, and ask what seems most obvious. How is the Crown dealing with this? Have trials begun?"

"We are not superstitious Puritans, William. We do not summarily execute people for their beliefs. This is a different time— Deists control the Royal Society despite the King's grant, Quakers bend the knee to no church and get their own colonies, and magic is abroad in the land once more, growing stronger. So we watch. We observe. We catalog and record, and on order from the Archbishop of Canterbury, when there is nothing else for it, we simply imprison these poor unfortunates until such time as they repent and declare loyalty to the church."

"I don't understand. The Bible says 'suffer not a witch to live.' Is not our duty to take a stronger stance?"

"That is under some debate," said Thomas, with a brief shake of his head. "It has been two hundred years since a member of our Parliament, Reginald Scott, advanced the theory that 'witch' was a mistranslation from the Hebrew word *mekhashepha*, which he felt more accurately meant 'poisoner.' And it has been over twenty years since our good King repealed the old laws. Here, witchcraft is no crime."

"So the Archbishop does not believe this is Satan's work?"

"The Most Reverend Thomas Secker is wise. All who promise their life to the Lord are welcome in His church, so long as they repent and live a life of virtue. At least, that is what he says from his pulpit."

"Convenient." William frowned.

"This is not Satan's work, but neither is it the Lord's work, William. It takes from the land and the Throne for personal gain. This makes it evil, no mistake, even if it is not directed by the hand

and will of Satan—men can be evil enough on their own, without inspiration from that quarter." Penn stared straight into William's eyes, challenging him. "And I am sorry to have to say it, but your own father, as you well know, is one of those engaging in these selfish practices."

William said nothing, but Penn read acquiescence in the young man's sudden change in bearing.

Penn continued. "The loved ones of those we have uncovered bear a special burden. I'm sure you have been more than a little troubled by his efforts in this realm, both on his behalf, and of course out of concern for the greater good of Englishmen everywhere. But do not fear—" Thomas Penn took William's hands within his own, as if they were praying together. "—Our gracious King has asked me to personally enlist your aid in his quest to defeat this evil and return England to its proper glory."

"I'm sorry . . . you said the *King* . . . "

"He has created a charter in support of Archbishop Secker. We will bring these people back to obedience unto God and destroy any magics they have left behind."

"I knew," William admitted. Speaking the truth to Penn felt liberating. "I knew that what Father was engaging with was not in good order. He was always one to test the boundaries, but these forays into magic were never seemly. He calls them arcane laws, but they are not just another philosophy. They are witchcraft, and they never felt right to me."

Penn finally released William's hands, but it seemed to William that he could still feel the gentle pressure of the man's touch. William, once started, found it difficult to stop. He told Thomas Penn of the night of the kite experiment, the Key and how it was oddly bound to his father, and—at great length— the unease he had felt since then.

Thomas nodded sagely, looking with compassion on the young Franklin. "Your father is a mage, William, and it is up to us to save his immortal soul."

The Stevenson Home
Craven Street
London, England
November 24th
✣ ✣ ✣

❖ 21 ❖
Immediately!

William bent over the desk in his Craven Street room, sealing a letter. His jacket was draped across the back of his chair, but the rest of his clothing was crisp and formal, as usual. With a sigh, he cocked his head to the side, listening.

Nothing could be heard.

"King," he said loudly. "I called you! Attend! *Attend*, blast it!" He finally heard the sound of steps approaching the door and turned to it angrily. "When I—"

But instead of the sullen, resentful face of King that he expected to see, he was confronted instead by the friendly smile of Polly Stevenson.

"I heard you calling. I wondered what might be—"

William interrupted her, "I am not much interested in what you are wondering. Truly. I am just working at my studies and *trying* to make sure . . . " William stopped, his dignity failing him. "I just . . . "

Polly looked at him thoughtfully. "It's King again, isn't it?"

William glowered at her for a moment. Despite his father pushing for him and Polly to come to a closer acquaintanceship, the truth was that he disliked the uppity girl. To his mind she was too full of herself by half, and he was certain that her friendly manner concealed a disaffection every bit as strong as his own.

He stood up, holding the letter behind his back. "You wouldn't, by any chance, know where he might be?"

Polly smiled. "I do."

So irritating. "Then share, pray tell, for I would like to know."

Polly tapped one forefinger to her lips, and let her gaze drift momentarily heavenward. "Well, to be precise, I don't know *exactly* where he is at this moment. More the general direction . . ."

"Please stop shillyshallying and tell me what you know of King's whereabouts."

"Ah, well," Polly demurred, "perhaps I shouldn't. I don't want to get him in trouble."

"He is already in trouble, Miss Stevenson. Constantly, as he is an incompetent buffoon. Just get on with it." William's jaw tightened. He could feel the heat rising in his face, betraying a lack of control which was an embarrassment in its own right.

"As you wish. Your father desires Peter's assistance with his present condition, which has required steaming hot water vapors to assist his breathing all morning. More medicine must be procured, so Mr. Franklin sent King off on that errand."

"How ridiculous," William fumed. "Father knows that King does not have Peter's facility for finding his way around London. He will get lost in no time."

"Possibly. But how is a person supposed to improve if they are never allowed to venture a task? Do you always speak so poorly of those you refuse to empower to grow?"

William glared at Polly. "People do not grow to be more than they were born to be. Our capacities are as set and prescribed as the pieces on a chessboard."

Polly tilted her head to the side, clearly amused. "Just as you say, William. That is why we cannot promote a pawn to be a queen on the board. Oh wait—we can do exactly that!"

"Play whatever word games you wish; you know the truth in what I say." He longed to end this unintended conversation. "When was he sent out, pray tell?"

Polly looked away and slid a finger along the doorframe, as if checking for dust. She continued to ignore how piqued he was as she pretended to inspect her fingertip for grime. "Oh, now that I think on it, I believe he has been gone some considerable amount of time. Certainly much longer than should be expected." She glanced back with a wicked grin. "What is it you have there, behind your back? Is it a love letter?"

Exasperated, William sought to shove past her through the doorway, and in the ensuing tangle Polly managed to snatch the letter from his hand. She was laughing as she did so, but when she saw the name and address on the envelope she stopped in surprise; which gave William the chance to grab it back.

Before he could give vent to his anger, he was interrupted by King's voice, calling up from the stairs.

"Mr. Franklin, sir? I'm back. They tell me you've been calling—"

"Never mind that. Come up here at once." Turning his back on Polly, William met King as he reached the top of the stairs, and handed him the letter. "You will deliver this immediately—and I *mean* immediately—to the address on the envelope. Just leave it with whomever answers the door. Do not detour or dawdle on the way and return here directly afterward."

Polly looked on with big eyes. "Weren't you just talking about how incapable this man is, William? How is he to find his way?"

"He already knows the way, you stupid . . . " William stopped midsentence, taking firm control of himself. He refused to allow the girl the pleasure of baiting him in front of his own slave. "I will *not* have this. King, see to your task at once. Miss Stevenson, please leave me to my studies." With that, William returned to his room and closed the door firmly behind him, resisting a strong compulsion to slam it shut.

As King started back down the stairs, Polly called to him and held out her hand for the letter. "You have already been abroad once today, King, and it is very cold. Why don't you give that to me while you stay in and assist with the cooking? I can have Jemmy deliver it for you."

King looked at her for a moment longer than she was entirely comfortable with, his face wary. In this instant the young slave seemed both older and more certain of himself than Polly had ever observed. "I don't think that's a good idea, mistress," he answered her. And with that, he turned and descended out of sight.

The
Stevenson Home
Craven Street
London, England
November 24th
✤ ✤ ✤

❖ 22 ❖
Not Who You Think

Ben sat upright in bed, re-reading the latest in a series of dissembling letters from Thomas Penn. Like the others of its kind it was a sham, couched in formal but affable language, that pretended to deal with matters of practical substance while never mentioning the real conflict between them. Franklin allowed himself the pleasure of composing a blunt reply in his mind, knowing that it would never be written down or sent, and that his actual answer would be no less false beneath its surface. There might yet come a time to use stark words, plainly stated; before then he had much to uncover and learn. Now if only his bloody body would cooperate! He pulled the warm orange cover-up close round his neck, snuggling into it, as another cough racked his chest.

As it subsided there was a knock on his door, and then Polly came in with his evening meal. She was in a simple house dress, proper but unassuming, and she wore the brooch that always drew his attention. The tray she carried had simple fare on it, steaming porridge and equally hot tea, with root of the licorice to soothe his stomach. He frowned and sighed, putting the letter to the side.

"This is Peter's task, Polly."

"I prevailed upon him to let me look in on you. How are you feeling? I see you are still laying about as though you haven't a care in the world." She took a good look at him, plainly worried despite her lighthearted tone of voice.

He watched as her gaze drifted to his own necklace, then quickly darted away. *Interesting,* he thought, but kept his reply jovial. "Nonsense. Can't a man rest, after jousting all day with Jack Slack?"

"Might as well name your croup after a boxing man," Polly said, placing the tray on the bedside table. "It's laid you out same as he would."

Ben harrumphed, but smiled. "This plague is the devil's own, I grant you. But I will outlast it in the end. Another day or two . . . or three . . . and I shall be fine. Never fear. Now out with it, please. Why are you *really* here? You have the look of someone with words that want saying."

"It's probably nothing," Polly said, pouring the infused tea from pot to mug.

"Nothing enough to interrupt me in my sickbed? Go on, go on," he said, taking the steaming mug from her hands.

"Oh, rot!" Polly squared her shoulders. She moved the room's chair nearer the bed, then sat in it, placing their eyes at near-level. "The letter you were reading when I entered—it is from Thomas Penn, is it not?"

"Yes. But you knew that. You were here when it came in the post." Ben stared at Polly with increasing curiosity. Something was clearly troubling her, and he had no notion what it might be.

"As I've said, it may be nothing. but I feel bound to tell you. Earlier today I saw William send King out to deliver a letter. And while it was a London address—Albemarle Street, as I recall—the name on the envelope was unmistakably Thomas Penn's."

Ben was sitting bolt upright now. "He *what*?" The shocked exclamation was followed quickly by a coughing fit. When Ben finally had his lungs under control again, he wiped his hand against the blankets and started all over. "I'm sorry, I must have misheard. *The damnfool boy did what?*"

Polly sighed deeply. "No, no. Ben. I knew I shouldn't have told you. But I also knew I had to, even though I shouldn't. Oh, this is impossible!"

"You needn't put on the pretend flummoxed act, Polly. I think you fully understand what this means. But why in the world? *What* in the world would William have to communicate to Thomas Penn's household?"

"When a promoted pawn moves back up the board, it is no longer a pawn. But it is still being moved by someone's hand." Polly paused, giving Ben a sad look. "I think, Ben, that William is not who you think he is."

Ben looked at her blankly, then shook his head. "He is my son. I know him far better than you do. I love you as I love my own daughter, Polly, even in this short time we have known each other. But make no mistake—William is a Franklin. He's always been a bit of a popinjay, I'll grant you that, and more rigid in his thoughts than I might prefer. But he and I, we always have the grandest adventures."

"Which only makes this worse." Polly took Ben's hand, seeking to both console and convince. "I'm so sorry, Ben, but you need to know the rest. It was clear this was not the first time King had been to that address."

Ben looked away from the girl, wanting to find thoughts and words to counter her. But as he considered the truth of his own experience, he could not. The rift between father and son that had been born years earlier, in the aftermath of lightning; the change which he had forced himself to ignore had only grown larger during all the time he had avoided seeing it. Over the last few months, in particular, William had seemed more distant, ever since starting his studies at The Honorable Society of the Middle Temple. Ben had been eager to advance his son's opportunities by opening the way for him to be called to the English Bar, and for William to someday be a barrister. When William stopped joining him in visiting salons and coffeehouses around London, he had ascribed it to William's naturally intense desire to be considered entirely upright and respectable in the eyes of his fellow students. But this additional piece of news that Polly had delivered altered Ben's view of everything.

Polly waited patiently as he struggled through the implications. When he finally turned back towards her, she sensed a wound in him she feared might never heal.

"He really is a bad chess player, isn't he? If he had troubled himself to write anywhere but here, we would never have known. It's so frustrating, having no grand society connections like the Penns do."

"You? No connections? Are you daft?" Polly squeezed Ben's hand. "If that's really how you feel, it's time for you to get better. There are some people I want you to meet."

1758

The Turk's Head Coffeehouse
London, England
January 22nd

❖ ❖ ❖

✤ 23 ✤
Get a Number

Ben stood stiffly in the coffeehouse cloakroom as Polly removed and hung his greatcoat, then neatened his coat and cravat. "All is well in the name of decorum," he complained, "but had I really gotten that far out of order?" His breath puffed in the air; it was still chill in the vestibule, though not as cold as the street outside.

"Tsk," Polly fretted, making sure every line in his garments was just so. "You get into all manner of things as you walk, Ben. You make a fine gentleman, but you're so, so . . . *colonial*, sometimes."

His chest puffed out in pride. "I am proud to be an Englishman from the American Colonies."

"You know what I mean." She stepped back and gave him the up-and-down. Tonight needed to be perfect—it was to be her introduction of him into her philosophy club, the Society of Numbers. Further, it was his first real night out after almost three months of being bedridden with a shortness of breath and lassitude that she had feared at times would prove deadly. "All right. You're as ready as I can make you."

Ben lifted a wry eyebrow but did not directly address her comment. Instead he gave voice to a greater concern than the sartorial. "You are certain that these friends of yours can be of assistance?"

"They have given me much. After they have taken your measure, which they will do in their own fashion, we will learn what they may be willing to do for you. There are no guarantees," she admitted. "But I promise an interesting evening."

Taking his arm, she led him through the interior doors and into the coffeehouse proper, which was bustling with activity. Long tables ran from the center of the room up to the windows, separating the counter and coffee-boy near the entrance from the private rooms in back. At the counter they ordered and were served, after which they headed for the private areas in the back. Many of the patrons looked askance at Polly, but she studiously ignored them. "My penny is as good as theirs," she had explained to Ben when he had expressed surprise at the announced location of their meeting.

The back area in the Turk's Head was as large as the public front, though the space was used differently. In addition to private booths it had three private rooms, each with its own closable door, where parties could sit and discuss what they would without having to overcome the boisterous noise of the common area.

Entering the central room, Ben and Polly found seven people waiting: two ladies and five gentlemen. The assembled company showed a wide range of style, indicative of diverse backgrounds. Some wore modern fashion, to at least the standard set by Polly and Ben himself. The most elderly man, who was speaking as they walked in, wore tights and a purple velvet coat with brass buttons. The woman on the far side of the circle—whom Ben was startled to realize he already knew—was dressed in observant Quaker plainclothes, with a white cap and a blue dress. Despite this apparent hodgepodge of social levels and backgrounds, the group shared a common air of education and expectation; and it was clear that their interrupted conversation had been lively.

"Mr. Franklin," Polly said, "may I introduce you to the Society of Numbers. Society of Numbers, Mr. Benjamin Franklin, Esq., late of the colony of Pennsylvania, now lodging here in London."

The elderly man, who was at least two decades older than Ben, leaned forward over crossed legs and gestured to two seats. "Please, please, feel welcome to join us, Mr. Franklin! We are so very happy to receive you! Sit down, sit down, and you too, Lord Twenty-Three."

Something scratched at the back of his mind, like a terrier digging for a bone, but Ben couldn't get at the detail buried in his memory. He let go of the elusive thought for the moment and focused on the group. Bowing his head slightly and embracing the seemingly freeform style of the group, Ben smiled warmly at the Quaker woman across the circle. "Mrs. Payton. It is an unexpected pleasure to see you here!"

"Hello, neighbor Franklin. It is a pleasure to see thee as well. It has been, what, three years since thee and Debby received me and Samuel Fothergill in Philadelphia, has it not? But please, leave names outside. In here I am simply Lord Seven."

"Yes, yes," the older man interrupted. "Please, be seated that we may continue."

"Thank you, Lord Five." Polly made sure that Ben was comfortable before sitting herself. Then she led him through courteous introductions to each attending member of the Society in turn. They were Lords Five, Eight, Nine, Thirteen, and Twenty-Eight for the men, and Lords Seven and Twenty-One for the women. Plus, Polly as Lord Twenty-Three, of course. It made for much to remember, and Ben felt slightly distracted by the task, even as he waded into general conversation with the group.

So many questions . . .

Ben chose to start with the most direct. "Is there a Lord One?" he asked. The whole group quieted, not-so-subtly watching their oldest member to see how he would answer.

"Indeed, there is, Mr. Franklin," said Lord Five. "Or perhaps the correct word is 'was.' We don't know which it is, for we have not seen our founder in many years. Lord Eight is the last member for whom he shared in the voting. But this is minutiae of the oldest provenance, and irrelevant to where we are today. I fear I may bore you by continuing."

"Not in the least," said Ben. "Everything about your group is of interest to me. Consider your naming convention! How came it to be that Polly—" he was briefly hushed by looks of discomfort and disapproval, so apologized earnestly. "Forgive me. I am still unused to the custom. How came it to be that Lord Twenty-Three is not *Lady* Twenty-Three?"

Lord Twenty-One spoke up. "As one of the three women here, I would like to answer that. At our founding it was decided that for the purposes of discussing matters in a complete and open nature, it would not do to have anything but complete equality. Otherwise we would be likely to fall into the customs of our upbringing. My own included."

"And the focus of our purpose was so important," added Lord Five, "that it suggested we should discuss matters in a new way. Thus here, within our Society, there is perfectly equivalent rank and identical title. Our only individual distinction is our numbers."

"And how does one get a number?" asked Ben, genuinely intrigued. "Is it a matter of one's importance in the group?"

"Not at all," said the one called Lord Nine, who looked to Ben like a printer. "It is simply a matter of when you joined. For instance, if you were to honor us with your presence on a regular basis and we approved you to join, you would become Lord Thirty."

"How *does* one join?" Ben asked.

"Simple," Polly answered. Ben smiled, trying to imagine ever calling her Lord Twenty-Three. "Every other member of the Society must approve, upon your recommendation by any one of us."

"A *liberum veto*," Ben said, knowing the practice well, having used it himself for the Junto. "That is an excellent way to keep membership down."

"And trust up," added Lord Five.

As the evening's conversation progressed, sometimes involving the entire group, while at other times splitting apart into eddies of communication among smaller subsets of the attendees, Ben was fascinated by the range of topics covered and the depth of knowledge on display. It was without question the equal or better of the best intellectual discourse he had previously experienced. But it was also frustrating, in its own strange manner, for it felt to him as though he were witnessing an act—as if, indeed, his presence brought with it a singular distortion that was guiding the group away from matters they would otherwise have devoted themselves to. Heeding Polly's earlier caution, he said nothing, though he still wondered.

With the hour growing late, several members settled their accounts, indicating the impending dissolutions of the night's discussions. As he himself did so, Lord Five gained everyone's attention, then turned to Polly. "Before the evening entirely gets away from us," he said, "I understand that you have ventured to bring Mr.

Franklin among us because you felt he had some affinity for our *raison d'être.*"

Lord Sixteen gazed at Ben intently. "Is it time to consider this matter?"

Polly nodded. "I, Lord Twenty-Three, would like to request a clearness committee to consider that which we know to be now together but soon apart, and align our efforts with the forces for good within light of Emræs."

One by one, round the circle, each of the Lords placed their left hand forward, palm up.

Ben blinked a bit at the strange phrasing but made certain that his demeanor remained warm and open. Inside, he felt his stomach drop as he finally remembered the troubling thought. Gasparini, and that cold morning five years ago, came to mind. As memory returned, it was of the magician speaking a phrase. *"One of the lost journals of Myrddin Emræs. One chronicling the founding members and numbers of his society, no less. How odd to find it here."*

His mind raced, and his pulse quickened.

A quick glance at Polly revealed that she was smiling.

Apparently, thought Ben, *I have passed muster.*

He raised his own left hand, but differently, in the manner of a schoolboy seeking to ask a question.

"Yes, Mr. Franklin?" said Lord Five.

"Well, nothing ventured, as the proverb says." Using both hands, he untied his cravat and loosened top buttons of his shirt sufficient to reach in and pull forth his necklace, holding up his own hidden object for all to see. The resulting look in all their faces confirmed everything he had begun to suspect. "Does this mean we can talk about the secret things now?"

The Stevenson Home

Craven Street
London, England
February 28th

✤ ✤ ✤

✤ 24 ✤
I Will Not Be Spoken to in This Way

With William due back any day from his long-planned tour of the countryside, accompanied by King, Ben thought it high time to indulge in some long overdue London shopping. The hunt had been a great success. So much so, in fact, that come late afternoon of his second day of shopping he sent his overstuffed carriage home to Craven Street under Peter's supervision while he stayed at the glassworks shop to oversee the crafting of some special lenses and other experimental equipment. Having completed this, he had overseen the packing of his purchase, then hired a sedan chair to carry him home. He held the wrapped goods carefully on his lap, eager to return to his rooms so he could begin his new experiments.

As Ben climbed out of the sedan chair, however, Peter hurried out the front door to meet him. Ben was surprised to see that his normally imperturbable servant was deeply agitated.

"Is something the matter?" Ben asked.

"Yes, sir. Master William is here, and very upset. He has commanded me to bring you right to him and not say a word."

Ben's mouth opened, then closed, followed by a deep knitting of the brow. Finally, he shrugged and motioned for Peter to lead the way, while carefully holding his lenses under his other arm. He

211

followed Peter into the house, then upstairs and into the main sitting room. There he found his son sitting in his favorite side chair, a plush and comfortable short legged lounger. William's hands were clenched so strongly his knuckles had gone white, and his face was red. "Leave us, Peter," he directed, with evident heat. When the slave was gone he rose from the chair, bypassing common civility in a way Ben had never seen before, and launched straight to his point as he jabbed a finger in the air at Ben. "Father, it is all your fault. I can't believe you let this happen! No, made it happen!"

"I beg your pardon?" Confused, Ben took a moment to think by walking to the window and gently depositing the cloth-wrapped parcel on the end table. "What exactly is my fault, William?"

"It is your lax attitude with the slaves that has caused this to come to pass. You treat them like they are something *more*, and they get ideas. You cannot deny it!" The young man's tone was haughty and supercilious; an aspect of his nature that showed itself rarely, and which always troubled Ben when it did. He found it keenly repugnant.

"Watch your tone, boy." Ben spoke quietly, stoically, as felt his own passion rising to meet his son's. The observation gave him pause. He felt suddenly certain that this was one of William's transparent chess moves—he was *trying* to work Ben up into anger, so he would be unable to respond as rationally as he might later wish.

But why?

"How dare you call me 'boy'! Like I'm just one of *them*," William screamed, gesturing in the direction of Peter's exit. This was part of some game on William's part, he understood, but it was also a direct response to real or imagined provocations. Just as so many of his moves in chess were simply a response to what he saw on the board, with no deeper strategy or thought involved, William was throwing out anger to see what response could be drawn.

Oblivious to the shift in his father's demeanor, William continued shouting. "I will not have our family made the fool by your inability to behave as a proper English gentleman. You are the product of a primitive colonial culture, and as much as your charisma has blinded some to your smallness, I can no longer sit silently at your side, watching real power and the real world be lost to your hidebound philosophy."

Ben watched his son, quietly clenching his jaw. Not a muscle in his body so much as twitched.

"Do you have *nothing* to say?" William's face was growing angrier with each moment Ben failed to respond.

"I am unable to account for what has brought this tirade on. It does not seem to me you wish a response, but rather an audience. So, I shall be an audience."

William once more jabbed an accusing finger at Ben. "Are you truly unaware that King has run away? Are you that simple?"

Ben's blinked in surprise and chose to ignore the insult for the moment. "He is not with you?"

"No, he is not. Three days into my journey I received a missive from the household stating that I was to send him back immediately—that your poor health had returned, and you required his assistance. Had you not done that, he would not have escaped."

Ben stared at this stranger who wore his son's face. The anger created an ugly mask, but Ben suspected that the mask was letting the true William out, rather than concealing the William, Ben wished he was. There was nothing of his beloved child to be seen; not even a shade.

He sighed heavily, but answered, "I ordered no such letter. Nor can I imagine the circumstances under which I would have done any such thing. Think, William. Were I ill, why would I send for help that would be days in coming, when there is aid aplenty for local hire?"

William frowned, wrestling with this unconsidered but inarguable truth. "I don't . . . I . . . I can't understand how *King* could have been able to arrange such a subterfuge."

Ben spoke in his calmest possible voice. "I should think you would be relieved to be done with him. You complained incessantly about his uselessness and constantly whined that he was a source of mischief and dismay around the house. Your hatred and disdain for him were palpable at times."

William's face went red again, "That is exactly the sort of trivializing response I would expect from you at a time like this. One does not *hate* a possession, one simply gets frustrated when it does not function as intended. This is exactly what I mean when I say you are a backward colonial. You have no sense of propriety or station. I have already inquired into the services of an agent who assures me that King can be found and returned to us with a minimum of fuss and only moderate expense. None of higher station ever need know that our property ran."

"Billy—" he began, but was quickly interrupted.

"My name is William. Do not trivialize me as you do this situation, old man."

Ben took a deep breath. "William, then," he said, accepting the correction in his most neutral tones. "I am truly perplexed as to why you would wish to pursue this particular line of action. Although King was meant to be your man, you despised him, finding him troublesome and useless. You said it repeatedly. You were unhappy. He was clearly unhappy. Why must we go to so much trouble and expense over someone you don't really want back into the household?"

William shook his head. "It is unbelievable to me that a man as smart as yourself could be so stupid about these things. He must be recovered, and made an example, or our family will lose the precious good opinion of people of worth. Only punishment will serve. As for expense, I propose we recoup the cost of his recovery by selling him to whichever Carolina plantation will pay the most. Let him regret his actions for the rest of his days."

Ben was quite done with this absurdity. "People of worth don't earn their value by taking advantage of other people, whether they own them or not, you fool. What in the bloody hells do you think we are here fighting for? Pleasantries?" Ben drew himself up and raised an admonishing finger. "I will not be spoken to in this way, *Billy*. He was your slave, and you handled him badly while he was with you."

William opened his mouth to retort but Ben's chilly gaze froze the words in his mouth.

"People of worth don't seek out and hurt other people just to make themselves feel better about being petty. There is no need to disparage me when it was your management that induced him to behave so. This vindictiveness you indulge in does not suit you, and is far more a stain on the good name Franklin than any mercy shown would be—*even if that name is colonial*. I shudder to think who these people are whose good opinion you favor over mine, if such behavior is their standard and requirement. People of worth don't skulk around caring more for other people's damned opinions," William reeled back at his father's words, "than for their own humanity. I see now it was a mistake to have you take up study for the bar at the Middle Temple, for it has taught you to mistake richness for worth, and act like the damned Penns, bloody worthless vultures that they are."

William slammed his hand into the wall, leaving a gaping hole in the lath and plaster, with cracks spiderwebbing outward for several inches. "Do not ascribe my thoughts to the Middle Temple, you addle pate. It is with my own power that I have sought out the truths you would keep hidden. I have developed a good understanding with the Penn family, and I see now how you would burn to the ground all that they have built, rather than allow them the profit they deserve from it. If you intend to set the Colonies aflame, you must do so without me. I will take my leave of this house and of you, *sir*."

When Ben said nothing in reply and simply stood stock still, expressionless—William bowed and departed the room.

There was a queasy feeling in the pit of Ben's stomach. His pulse thundered in his temples. He wanted to run after William, but whether to beg forgiveness or lash out himself in turn, he could not say. Instead he stood absolutely still as the window light slowly faded with the day, sick inside with the certainty that there was no way back from this moment. The words echoed in his mind, *"I have developed a good understanding with the Penn family, and I see now how you would burn to the ground all that they have built."*

Ben calmly walked to the window and twitched aside the curtain, watching the sunset over London, thinking. He finally understood.

You think this is me burning you down, Thomas? You've taken my son for this? You've seen nothing yet of the flames I command. Behind him, in the mantle, the wood caught fire and lit, though no hand touched it. Warmth radiated from the fireplace as Ben studied the imaginary chess board in his mind.

The
Stevenson Home
Craven Street
London, England
March 11th

✢ ✢ ✢

✤ 25 ✤
For the Riders

Ben stared at the blank foolscap in front of him, quill in hand, his thoughts elsewhere. Light from the Betty flickered, but the room was well lit and warm, the fireplace behind him at a full roar.

He had been reflecting on his skirmishes with the Penns. The fight with William had changed everything for him. He realized now that he had been taking a purely reactive position, hoping for compromise. The only thing that ever happened when playing to a stalemate was that neither side won, and that had been a mistake he made with the Penns. Here, in their domain, that style of passive play would never prevail. Thomas Penn knew the English game board and pieces far better than Ben ever could, even with help from Peter Collinson, or from Polly and her fellows in the Society of Numbers.

He needed to give the Penns other troubles to deal with. The most direct way to do that was to expand the field to include Pennsylvania, forcing them to distribute their efforts and their resources. They had taken it a step too far, turning his own son against him. Now he would hit the Penn family where it hurt them most, in their balance sheets, and not just this generation of Penns but future ones too. But he must simultaneously shore up the finances of the colony's government in order to make this an effective strategy.

His thoughts composed, he dipped his quill in the open ink bottle, and began to write.

General Post-Office, March 10, 1758

Whereas the News-papers of the several Colonies on this Continent, heretofore permitted to be sent by Post free of Charge, are of late Years so much increased as to become extremely burthensome to the Riders, who demand additional Salaries or Allowances from the Post-Office on that Account; and it is not reasonable, that the Office, which receives no Benefit from the Carriage of News-papers, should be at any Expence for such Carriage: And Whereas the Printers of News-papers complain, that they frequently receive Orders for News-papers from distant Post-Offices, which they comply with by sending the Papers, tho' they know not the Persons to whom the Papers are to be directed, and have no convenient Means of collecting the Money, so that much of it is lost; and that for Want of due Notice when distant Subscribers die, become Bankrupt, or remove out of the Country, they continue to send Papers some Years directed to such Persons, whereby the Posts are loaded with many Papers to no Purpose, and the Loss so great to the Printers, as that they cannot afford to make any Allowance to the Riders for carrying the Papers: And whereas some of the Riders do, and others may, demand exorbitant Rates of Persons living on the Roads, for carrying and delivering the Papers that do not go into any Office, but are delivered by the Riders themselves.

What that would look like in the long term, Ben did not fully know; but in front of him was the beginning of a policy that could make a difference.

The trick lay in designing a new strategy for deliveries, beginning with newspapers and expanding from there, that would continue to provide the means for the colonists to communicate things widely, yet also simplify the method of delivery while generating systemic profit. By establishing a set price for shipping goods—as the Quakers were apt to do with delivered store-bought items—rather than one negotiated by the delivery riders, then regularity and predictability could be provided, and the change he sought begun. As Deputy Postmaster General for the British Colonies, a position he had been appointed to in 1753, Ben had the power to make this happen.

He continued:

To remedy these Inconveniencies, and yet not to discourage the Spreading of News-papers, which are on many Occasions useful to Government, and advantageous to Commerce, and to the Publick; You are, after the first Day of June next, to deliver no News-papers at your Office (except the single Papers exchang'd between Printer and Printer) but to such Persons only as do agree to pay you, for the Use of the Rider which brings such Papers, a small additional Consideration per Annum, for each Paper, over and above the Price of the Papers; that is to say, For any Distance not exceeding Fifty Miles such Paper is carried, the Sum of Nine pence Sterling per Annum, or an Equivalent in Currency: For any Distance exceeding Fifty Miles, and not exceeding One Hundred Miles, the Sum of One Shilling and Six pence Sterling per Annum; and in the same Proportion for every other Fifty Miles such Paper shall be carried; which Money for the Rider or Riders, together with the Price of the Papers for the Printers, you are to receive and pay respectively, once a Year at least, deducting for your Care and Trouble therein, a Commission of Twenty per Cent. And you are to send no Orders to any Printer for Papers, except the Persons for whom the Papers are to be sent, are in your Opinion responsible, and such as you will be accountable for. And you are to suffer no Riders, employ'd or paid by you, to receive more than the Rates above mentioned, for carrying any Papers by them delivered on their respective Roads; nor to carry and deliver any Papers but such as they will be accountable for to the Printers, in Consideration of an Allowance of the same Commissions as aforesaid for collecting and paying the Money.

And as some of the Papers pass thro' the Hands of several Riders between the Place where they are printed and the Place of

Delivery; you are to pay the Carriage-Money you collect for the Riders, to the several Riders who have carried such Papers, in Proportion, as near as conveniently may be, to the Distances they have been carried by each Rider respectively.

~ Franklin and Hunter.

Perfect. He was sure that people would prefer that arrangement to overpricing which depended on the whim of the delivering rider. And once the policy was expanded beyond newspapers, and the Penns sought to challenge it, he knew he could incite the common people against them. He imagined mobs of Pennsylvanians boycotting goods from the proprietor's estate, or blockading the roads to their properties—all ignited by pointed newspaper articles penned by Silence Dogood or some other identity from his collection of writing monikers.

This was a long war against the Penns he was beginning, but damned if he was going to lose.

He stretched for a moment, working out the kinks in his muscles. There was a positive side, too. This new policy wasn't solely about retribution. It provided an actual, measurable benefit to those living in Britain's colonies in America. Where so many of his efforts in England seemed to be stymied and deflected at every turn, his efforts in the Americas invariably produced fruitful and satisfying results. This would be one more.

He returned to the work of completing his letter, smiling at the seed he knew it would plant.

Simpson's Tavern
Cornhill Street, London
April 21st
✤ ✤ ✤

✤ 26 ✤
There Are Worse Reasons

Polly had enjoyed a dinner out with Ben at a new but popular eatery, barely a year old, where they were now giving their chess skills some exercise. Their emptied plates of Prussian sausages, bacon, and calf's liver had been removed, but the aroma of those and other meals still lingered as they played. Now the diners in Simpson's Tavern, watching, whispered at their tables as the two exchanged moves over the board. Being the focus of this mildly scandalized attention made Polly smile to herself: the wanton abandonment of public propriety that her current favorite person embraced was, to be frank, quite thrilling to her.

He appreciated her using this time to share, quietly, the latest information collected by the Society of Numbers. He had been fascinated, that first evening, to discover Polly's group was working on the same issue for which Peter Collinson and the Royal Society had recruited him—the growing expression of magic throughout the United Kingdom. Though they themselves had little or no skill in the specialty, they did hunt rumors of occultism and magic, and sought to either procure mystical items or debunk them. The primary differences were that their organization was smaller than the Royal Society; they kept their entire existence secret, disdaining public work that might distract their attention—and they operated under no grant from the King—just a founding directive from the mysterious Lord One, whose identity Ben had made no progress on penetrating.

In her own turn Polly enjoyed the stories Ben chose to tell of his inventions, his work in the Colonies, and his mad adventures during his first visit in London, some thirty years before; most definitely including the frugal strategies he had devised to improve his condition.

"There was so much on that trip that is so vivid I think I will remember it for years to come. It changed the course of my life. Conversely, I believe," Ben said with a satisfied sigh, "that on this trip I will go bankrupt, spending my fortune sampling the offerings of every coffeehouse and restaurant in London." He patted his belly. "And as the last pennies of my fortune melt away, I'll be all the happier for it."

"There are worse reasons to enter bankruptcy, I would wager," Polly shot back, and both laughed with the genuine mirth that comes from easy companionship.

Ben looked out the window. The sun had set, and dusk's deep gray blanket, with just hints of gold and crimson lighting the tops of the London skyline, was now a memory. Full night was on them. "I do believe we should head home quickly, Polly. Your mother will not take kindly to my keeping you out later than is her wish. She might put limits on future excursions, and neither of us wants that."

"You are the soul of courtesy, Mr. Franklin. Does this wish to retire early have nothing at all to do with the fact that you are losing?"

"We shall, of course, continue the game from the same position. I was up a knight, yes?" Ben helped her with her cloak.

After retrieving his greatcoat, they headed to the door. "Why yes, you were," Polly pointed out, "if by up a knight you actually meant down a rook."

"Right," he agreed as they passed the restaurant's threshold and closed the door behind them.

Both were immediately struck by a sense of grave disquiet. "Hhmm..." Ben trailed off, forgetting his rejoinder. Ben felt his heart skip a beat. *Something is not right*, he thought, suspiciously scanning the alleys that they passed.

"We should not tarry, I think," Polly said. "It would seem you feel the same disturbance that I do."

"I concur," Ben agreed, leading the way with a pace a younger man would have envied. Despite being encumbered by her shoes' protective pattens, which gave slippery purchase on the damp cobblestones, Polly's youth stood her in good stead, and she kept pace.

They continued for several blocks at this rapid stride, when suddenly Polly grabbed Ben's arm and stopped them both in their tracks. "I have lived in London all my life and never seen the streets this deserted. Even in the midnight hours, there is someone around." She glanced around quickly, eyes narrowed, seeking motion in the darkness, and found nothing.

"Nor any sound at all," Ben said. His voice seemed unnaturally loud to him in the stillness, and he couldn't help but drop to a whisper as he continued. "Perhaps my imagination is getting the better of me, but in the wilds, when a predator has been detected, all the animals will go quiet. I fear we may be someone's prey in this moment."

Polly, too, could feel someone watching. Her shoulders tensed as she considered what to do.

"Excuse me, Ben," she said, making sure her speech was loud enough to carry. "May we take a moment? This brisk walk has loosened the strap on my patten, and I must adjust it." Then quietly, for his ear only, she whispered, "Pray do me the favor of speaking no Latin before I am done."

"Of course." He looked at her curiously, then shrugged, waving his hand as casually as he might if they were standing on the Brighton Walk at busiest mid-day, instead of Cornhill Street on a deserted night. "Take your time, my dear. I'll just watch the creepy empty streets for us."

Polly knelt, pretending to apply herself to her footgear. She knew that to any outside observer she was under Ben's protection, a misunderstanding that she could work to her advantage and the observer's detriment. That Ben shared in this misconception was endearing; she knew that his chivalrous nature would compel him to defend her and based on what he'd told her fellow Lords he had significant capacities in that regard. But tonight, she was determined to be the one who would protect *him*.

She reached out with her mind as her fingers worked the straps of her right shoe patten. There could be no normal reason for what was happening on the street, *ergo* it must have been organized by magical effect. Her thoughts spread away from her in waves, gently touching on the subtle webs that bound the world, noting the spots—*here* and *here* and yes, *over there*—where they had been tampered with. Cautiously, so as not to give herself away, she traced a path back along the rippling alterations, towards their source. Careful not to make direct contact, she flitted all around that the source, gleaning what she could. It was a man, though she could not tell his age or anything else about him, other than a sullen ill intent which flared at his edges like wisps of smoke. And he was not alone. There were others with him, also men, of no magical capacity at all, but full of thuggish vigor.

Their collective intention was clear enough to Polly, if not their motive. It gave her great pleasure to charge the strands she had used to trace their presence with the full force of her anger and her will. How dare they wait in ambush!

One street away, four men of the Bow Street runners waited patiently. They had been guaranteed a conviction if they apprehended these two, and convictions paid.

"Bloody quiet out here." The largest of them spoke, though in hushed tones.

"Shut up, Doxer," said the man peering intently around the corner.

None of them noticed that the shadows were beginning to swirl around their feet.

"Why do I gotta shut up? Why don't you, Georgey?" Doxer sounded sullen.

"I'm the leader, that's why." He held up a hand, warning everyone back. "They's takin' their time to tie that damn shoe. Maybe we oughta just g—" A shadow wrapped around George's throat, cutting him off mid-word. The dark tendril yanked him back, sending the thief-taker plowing into one of his compatriots.

The night came alive; shadows frothing and bubbling, like a rabid octopus morris dancing, with inky tendrils snapping to and fro. The last man standing was Doxer. He threw down his truncheon and held up empty hands. He begged, "Please?" The darkness swarmed over him, stifling his scream.

✛ ✛ ✛

One by one they fell, insensate, vanishing from her mind's sight, while her ears detected a most satisfying collection of pained cries from a block or so ahead.

"There," she said, standing back up. "All done."

Before Ben could say anything to her, a loud thunderclap broke over the city and, with it, rain began to fall. Oddly, now that rain was pattering down, people began to make their way out of buildings and on about their business as if nothing had been detaining them. In minutes the street was populated at normal levels for the hour.

"Ah," said Polly as she pulled her hood over her head. "One of those unexpected London thunderstorms I'm sure I will remember fondly in years to come. How fortunately coincidental, for now you must hail us a carriage instead of making me walk home to Craven Street. *You* should try that in pattens sometime."

Ben looked at her thoughtfully. "Indeed," was all he said, though his eyes were full of questions she knew he would not let her avoid answering.

Once the two had faded into the night, the wall shimmered. If one looked *just so,* a stack of boxes turned into a door, and a rotten piece of fruit the handle. The door swung open and Thomas Penn stepped out, surveying the group of downed thieftakers. "Interesting," he mused. "Franklin appears to be getting stronger."

The Collinson Home

Ridgeway House,
Mill Hill, Middlesex
April 24th
✢ ✢ ✢

❖ 27 ❖
Valid Concerns

Ben's carriage jounced along the road as he approached the home of his closest friend in England. The trip was a welcome distraction. Over the last weeks, despite his hard work and Polly's bright company, his fight with his now-absent son weighed heavily on his spirits. He and William had exchanged letters as William traveled, but there was no longer anything personal in what his son wrote—just curt and simple presentation of details. Ben almost dreaded opening them. When not otherwise occupied by pressing matters, he had begun taking long solitary walks through the London streets, missing Debby and Sally, missing Philadelphia—though he was careful not to let melancholy overpower him. Above all he must be mindful of his campaign against the Penns.

He had taken this day to head out to Mill Hill, then, to break his dour mood and the lure of downcast behavior it encouraged. Arriving, he knocked on the door with his cane. A servant admitted him, after which Mary Collinson promptly took him in tow. "Peter will be delighted you were able to make it, Mr. Franklin. He's waiting for you in his study."

After a short walk, Mary opened the door to the study, revealing a diligent Peter Collinson writing in a journal.

"You've had an interesting time of it, Ben," said Peter, looking up from his notetaking with a warm smile for his friend.

"No question. Much more than I had understood when you first introduced me to some of the complexities of the current situation." His eyes reflexively scanned the room's bookshelves. There were always at least a dozen, sometimes more, titles he had missed on earlier trips.

"But your health, at least, has improved. That pleases me."

"I'll need it, to get through, as I need your continued insight. Which is why I am here. Well, that and you invited me." Ben frowned seriously. "There is new information to make you aware of, the sort I can't even hint at in our correspondence."

Collinson prepared himself for taking notes, switching out which journal he was writing in. "Best start, then."

"Where to begin, where to begin? I feel like a man with a scattering of milled parts, and no guide for their assembly. As you already know, the Penns and I are at war on multiple battlefronts. They have stolen my son from me; I have made changes in the Colonies that will affect their authority and cost them a great deal of money. They have stolen the surviving journals you sent; I have identified some of those they employ in their search for magical tools, tracing the pattern of their operations, and still hope to uncover the robber."

"That will be an achievement," said Collinson.

"I do not hold with thieves, plain and simple."

"Go on."

"You remember Polly, my landlady's daughter?"

"That's the young woman who introduced you to the group that parallels our own secret work. Their motivation seems admirable enough. I should like to meet some of them, when the time is right. Depending on their character it might be logical to work together on occasion; or at least to avoid accidentally working at odds."

"Yes," Ben said. "I was of the impression that none of their number were much able with magic, despite their knowledge of it. But Polly *does* have this power. Her aptitude seems more in line with my own—if not stronger—and she demonstrated it to me two days ago, by dealing handily with a presence that appeared to be threatening us. I have no idea who was responsible for that. The Penns? Some other player in this game, perhaps, who has not yet revealed himself? It troubles me . . . no, it *vexes* me not to know, Peter." He took in a long breath.

"It's true I've never seen you this out of sorts before," Collinson agreed. "Perhaps you should stay with me and Mary for the rest of the week. The air here would do you continued good, there is peace in the gardens, and we could devote ourselves each evening to your issues and your further education in the Royal Society's secret work."

"It sounds a wonder. May I decide later?"

"Of course. Meanwhile, I have some news for you of my own. It may ease your mind in some ways, though I suspect it will give you pause in others."

Ben smiled at his host's slight formality. "Whatever it is, I welcome the diversion—every time I think I have my feet under me, these last months, something new comes along to knock me askew."

"This may do that. Your man King is at the home of a woman in Suffolk—of some independent means—called Widow Eversleigh. She is keen on making him a Christian and improving him by means of education."

Ben was dumbfounded. "Peter, to what purpose would she try and do that? King is by no means able to absorb that sort of complicated information."

"You subscribe to an unenlightened opinion, my friend. As a means of correcting your very base error, consider this—she has not only taught Mr. King to read and write, but also to play violin and French horn. At a beginner level, to be certain, but I am told quite credibly for the time spent." Collinson held up a letter that had been sitting folded on his desk, and offered it to Ben. "She delights in the idea of being able to end his time of servitude to your family and transfer whatever obligation to herself."

"*Mr.* King? King learning to *read*?" Ben dismissed the notion. "I rather doubt it. He was a sullen boy, more prone to the physical than conversational. No, King is not the brightest candle in anyone's chandelier."

"Nor is he the dimmest, Benjamin. From what I have read here, I believe he only showed you what he was willing to, which was little. In a matter of a few months he has begun learning two instruments and mastered letters. And before you protest again, this is far from the first time I have known of Africans more knowledgeable than the average Englishman on the street. Is it your place to limit what a man may become?"

"But that is the heart of the issue, is it not?" asked Ben. "King is my slave that I gave to William, and therefore his property. But, as head of the household, is he not also my responsibility? I must protect everyone's interests in this matter."

"In England he is no one's property. You know that."

"Yes, but—"

"Widow Eversleigh has given some particulars that lead me to believe Mr. King ran away from a forced and abusive relationship, one that he was neither party to, agreeing to, nor able to alter himself by any means except escape." Peter caught Ben's eyes, and held them in his most serious gaze. "Does not that sound the slightest bit familiar to you?"

It took Ben a moment to realize what his friend was referring to. "That is not the same situation at all," he bridled. "I was not a slave! I was indentured to my brother by my concerned father, to prevent me from going to sea."

"No resemblance? You, like Mr. King, had your labor sold. You, like Mr. King, had no say in the making of the contract. You, like Mr. King, were bound to it. But because of the location of your birth and the color of your skin, you had compelling advantages. You had a date after which you would no longer be held to labor. You had the terms of your labor defined, and boundaries set upon what might be asked of you. You had a guarantee that physical harm would not be inflicted upon your body. Yet even with all these advantages—none of which Mr. King had—you still chose to run away."

"That is not a fair comparison, Peter. If you wish to put things on a sort of balance, I am game for that entirely. For the first, I did not run away from my contractual obligations as an indentured servant. My brother, to further his own ends, quietly discharged my apprenticeship. He didn't wish for me to take advantage of that by running away, but what I did was completely legal. For the second, I do not allow the servants in my household to be beaten. That is not a fair thing to put on the balance on your side—it must be removed. For the third, I found a way around the limitations my brother's jealousy placed upon me, and managed to forward my skills and my understanding even *before* I ran away. By contrast, it is commonly known that Africans are constituted in such a way that any serious effort expended on teaching them is wasted. That, in fact, it is a kindness we provide, giving them a chance at a civilized life."

"So you have allowed the legend that you ran away from your indentured servitude to run rampant, uncorrected?" Collinson looked closely at Ben, "Indeed, you may have encouraged the report yourself, if I know you. But back to the matter at hand. We must keep the point of being beaten on the balance. It is a strike against the institution of slavery. *You* may not have beaten him, but can you say he has not been beaten? Or that your son William has not done so, behind your back? Or that if you were to suddenly take ill and pass, Mr. King's next owner may not beat him? We both have dear friends our age who have passed recently, and that number will only increase. Your longevity is not ensured."

Ben opened his mouth to start again, but Peter politely held up one hand. "I'm not done yet, Ben. As for his capacities: unlike you, King has been constrained. You and your family told him what he could do, and when he could do it, limiting his ability to gain new skills in the manner that you did. It is obvious that you have never provided your slaves the means to better themselves. Should you have the right to control any outward improvement your servants might wish to pursue? Can you claim to know what they are capable of merely because you don't believe in expending time or resources in that direction? Is it even honestly about them, or just the fact that improving their lives would provide you no benefit?"

"Dammit, Peter. Am I on trial here?" Ben slapped a hand against his knee in frustration. "Just because we differ in opinion does not give you the right to convict me."

"I assume no right, Benjamin—rather, I must help you shoulder a responsibility. The institution of slavery puts us all on trial. As your friend, I must speak to your condition, and I tell you this—you have a chance to be better than you are. I must encourage you to take that chance, even if it requires making plain the worst in you."

Collinson watched his friend carefully.

Ben's hands were draped over his cane, and he rested his chin on his hands. This was not the easiest thing for him to hear. The only reason he didn't outright reject it and leave was that over the last years he had already begun thinking about these very things, prodded by Speaker Norris and others.

"That Mr. King pursued learning his letters, and other forms of improvement, shows capacity. That he did so without your approval—indeed, against your passive will—shows remarkable character and desire. How can you deny this man his right to further himself now that he has found a home where such efforts are welcome?"

Ben finally looked up. "I admit that you speak compellingly. That King has found a place where he learns is amazing to me." Ben reflected carefully before he spoke his next words. "I confess that I did not believe—no, I was not interested in cultivating these skills in my servants. That was my decision. But how can I abandon him? He is my responsibility."

Peter Collinson smiled, "Mr. King is in a very good home, being looked after by a kind woman who is comforted by his presence. Widow Eversleigh reports that he is strong and clever, and when a man like that gets to keep all that he can earn, he starts earning a far greater amount that any lash could hope to bring out." He held his hand up again, forestalling Ben's automatic protest. "I know you use no lash. I know. Consider it a metaphor. Truly, Ben, you should be grateful for this rarest of opportunities."

"And what opportunity might that be?"

"To experience hard evidence of your own ignorance," Collinson said. "This is exactly the sort of circumstance you are mostly likely to benefit from, if you are to continue to improve your quality and virtue. God shows you a path and gives you an opportunity here."

"Always the Quaker, Peter?"

"Always."

Ben knew when he was bested. Collinson had not only shown him his own ignorance, but a way through it to greater knowledge. It was exactly how Ben himself preferred to angle his machinations and arguments.

"I accept that your side of the balance is weightier than mine, and I will take your counsel to heart. King can stay, with my blessing."

"I will write Widow Eversleigh tomorrow to tell her so."

Ben stood and stretched, full of emotions he could barely understand, let alone name.

"May we talk about simpler things now, Mr. Collinson—like magic, and what the Penns might be up to with those journals, and why in heaven's name you haven't yet offered me any lemon water?"

Montagu House
Bloomsbury
London, England
June 17th
✠ ✠ ✠

✤ 28 ✤
The Rarest Botanicals

During the previous November, when Ben had believed himself well mended from his illness, both Franklins had attended a feast with the Royal Society. The affair had been formal and splendid. Unfortunately, it was closely followed by a relapse that had interrupted Ben's participation in subsequent events. Now, at last, he had a chance to make up for lost time—in response to the letter he and Peter Collinson had penned outlining their latest occult discoveries, he had received an invitation to another gathering, this one less formal, at Montagu House in Bloomsbury. Montagu House would soon harbor the new British Museum collection (a gathering of art and artifacts rather unimaginatively to be named "the British Museum Collection at Montagu House") and was currently undergoing renovations. Ben was particularly excited to attend because he knew that when the Royal Society met in out-of-the-way places like this, it was to discuss their non-public concern: the proliferation of magic and its theorized causes.

The day had already been a busy one.

In the morning Ben had gone to Rawthmell's, one of his favorite coffee houses, to attend a gathering of William Shipley's Society for the Encouragement of Arts, Manufactures and Commerce—a group more commonly called the Premium Society, after the medals and monies it gave out to individuals who successfully met that Society's published challenges. The gathering had included three men in particular with whom Ben made close connection, after finding that two were fellow members of the Royal Society, and that the third, an artist, had also been invited to attend this evening's event.

While beginning to part ways from Rawthmell's, the four had quickly decided to share transport to Montagu House later, in order to continue their conversation. Thus Ben found himself traveling with Henry Baker, author of *Employment for the Microscope*, who had proven highly educated on the subject of lenses; Gustavus Brander, a naturalist and trustee of the British Museum; and William Hogarth, the artist, who was an enigma all around. Not only did he have a special invitation, but he had brought with him the same pug dog he had carried around all morning. Ben rather liked the pug, who was spirited and friendly. The little dog had spent a good portion of the day snuffling hands and collecting not-so-covert pets and table scraps from everyone he charmed.

The main entrance to Montagu House was sealed for the renovation, so the carriage dropped the four men at a roundabout entrance to the garden front. They climbed out, and for a moment took in the sight. The house was a four-story design with two large wings flanking a smaller central manse. A long gravel walkway stretched from the roundabout to the manse, with lavish gardens on either side and a massive circular fountain in the center.

After entering, they made their way up the grand staircase, which featured some of the most ornately beautiful paintings and decorative treatments Ben had ever seen. Not only were the walls adorned with fine scrollwork, but the ceilings themselves were painted with murals of daytime clouds and sky, so that the sun cheerily shone indoors above their heads.

Hogarth, Ben noticed, paid no attention to this lavish display. His eye was completely committed, instead, to examining each attendee. It was if he looked at the people in the room through one of Henry Baker's microscopes.

Ben spotted Peter Collinson in the far corner of the room, chatting with a man who, by his dress, was also a Quaker. Ben took leave of his travel companions, promising to return. He took a glass of wine from a passing tray and was stopped twice—first by John Hadley and then by Thomas Birch, both of whom asked him to come find them later—before he finally made it to his friend's side. On the way he was amused to see the two Quakers politely refuse the passing wine tray. Of all the vices, a nice nip to the King now and then was one he knew he could never abstain from; nor would he want to.

Quakers, of course, did not participate in the loyal toast, having special dispensation from the Crown out of respect for their religious convictions. But having the right was not the same as social acceptability; members of the Society of Friends often avoided events such as this one, where they might be exposed to misunderstanding. Ben knew that Collinson generally disliked public parties for just that reason.

"Thanks for coming tonight," Ben said to him. "I was afraid you wouldn't be able to tear yourself away from your gardens."

"Indeed," Collinson laughed. "There was good reason to stay. I have just received the latest box of seeds from John Bartram. His drawings and descriptions of the plants they would grow into were fascinating. He always finds the most amazing specimens for me to propagate."

The man sitting with Collinson interrupted. "Are these medicinal varieties or merely decorative?"

"From his descriptions, a combination." Collinson turned towards Ben. "But I forget my manners: introductions are due. Mr. Benjamin Franklin, I have the honor of presenting Dr. John Fothergill. He is the man who supplied the treatment recommendations I passed on when you grew ill."

Fothergill looked Ben up and down, swiftly reading the indicators of his condition. "Mr. Franklin, have you continued the cinchona bark treatment I recommended? Your health is not something to let slide."

Ben pulled a face, capped by a sharp eyebrow, "I still follow your regimen, mixed with wine as you suggested. But it is really quite terrible. A glass a day is punishment, though I know not the crime I committed."

"Better than being ill, I am sure," Peter observed, clapping the laughing doctor on his shoulder. "I'll continue to grow the rarest botanicals for you, John, so long as you keep finding clever uses for my plants."

"All for me to be able to drink the most foul concoctions. But I do thank you, doctor. You know," he continued, changing topics, "I met your brother Samuel in Philadelphia several years ago. He was traveling in the company of another Quaker minister, a woman named Catherine Payton." *Or Lord Sixteen*, he thought to himself. Ben might have wondered if Samuel or John Fothergill were part of the Society of Numbers as well, if he had not already been informed that Miss Payton was the only Quaker in their small community.

"I have heard good report of her," Fothergill said, "though our acquaintance is entirely secondhand. As for Sam, he is back in England now, pursuing his good works here once again. I see him often and would be happy to convey your greeting if you wish."

"Please do," said Ben.

They heard the clinking of metal on glass from the front of the room, as George Parker—Second Earl of Macclesfield, and President of the Royal Society—gathered everyone's attention. He smoothed down the velvets of his maroon suit, which stretched over an expansive belly. Once he knew that every eye had turned to him, he lifted his glass and called out the loyal toast, "Gentlemen, the King!"

"The King!" All but the Quakers raised their own glasses, returning the toast in unison, then drank.

"The first matter at hand," Lord Macclesfield began as the group settled, "is the taking of the roll. Call out to our secretary, Mr. Birch," at which he nodded to a gentleman seated at a table, "so that he may enter it into a record of our proceedings."

In the end, fourteen Fellows and three invited guests were accounted for in rapid succession.

"I appreciate all of you answering my special request. We have important matters to consider. But for the moment," he said, dabbing at his brow with a white silk kerchief, "we will continue a period of open conversation as we prepare the *materia* for tonight's demonstration." With that Lord Macclesfield removed himself to attend to details, and the room's attention was no longer required.

"By all the—Benjamin Franklin, I'm delighted to see you here!" called out a voice resonant with a deep Scottish accent.

Ben turned to see one of the three special guests, the Scots astronomer James Ferguson, bounding toward him with such energy that it made Ben feel older with step the man took.

"How goes your progress with the clock, James?"

"Oh, excellently. I believe I have improved your design to the point that it may actually work!" James laughed as he clapped Ben on the back. The astronomer was a full head taller than anyone else around, so Ben was looking up into a huge smile. "And these two fine gentlemen? Ah, Mr. Collinson!"

Ben took care of the introductions. "You and Peter obviously know each other. The gentleman with Peter is Dr. John Fothergill, physician; and this very tall, rather Northumbrian fellow is James Ferguson—astronomer, instrument maker, and author of *Astronomy Explained*. You can set the world's clocks to the tiny levers and gears this man works with."

Fothergill smiled as he shook hands with the eager Scotsman. "I am delighted to meet the author of the work that finally made Sir Newton's works accessible to my understanding. Wonderfully done."

"'Tis my pleasure to meet you, doctor."

Peter reached out his hand as well, saying, "Lovely to see you again, James, as always. Perhaps we can catch up more in a bit? For now I must beg everyone's pardon—things are about to get going, and I have a part to play in the proceedings." Ben blinked. That was news to him—he had thought Peter was only attending in order to accompany him.

As he left, a nearby argument became heated enough to interfere with all other conversation in the vicinity.

"Who are those two?" whispered Ben.

Ferguson answered in a voice slightly less loud than his usual, the closest his nature came to being discreet. "Oh, those two. The most pompous people in attendance, I would say. They get into it at every banquet. That one there," he said, pointing, "that's Mark Akenside. Thinks he's God's gift to poetry, though he butters his bread as a doctor. And the other one's Thomas Anson. Most people'd be happy enough standing for Litchfield in the House of Commons, but no, the man can hardly speak a sentence without reminding you that his brother is *Lord* Anson, or that his second cousin is *Lord* Macclesfield, our esteemed host. God spare me insecure elder siblings—"

At that moment, as if cued, Anson's voice carried through the room.

"My brother George is First Lord of the Admiralty! I will not have you imply that one of my rank could ever be so—"

"I'll say what I bloody well want about your family, you—"

Ben leaned toward his tall Scottish friend. "This is better than the mummers and seasonal players who pass through Philadelphia. Will they try to sell us cure-alls after the fight?"

"Aye, 'twould seem they might," James shook his head sadly. "But it's right dreary on regular rotation."

"You *idiot!*" Anson shouted.

"Come," John Fothergill spoke up. "For those of us new to the display, this is most entertaining."

It was Akenside's turn now. " . . . one who rides on his brother's coattails without embarrassment, and is an amateur at *everything,* and master of *nothing,* should not speak as if he were—"

"Gentlemen!" A very big man, even larger than James Ferguson, came up from behind them and easily separated the two arguing men by placing one hand on each of their shoulders.

"Who would that be?" Ben asked.

"Shukburgh Ashby. He was made Sheriff of Leicestershire in the same decree that named Hutchinson to Massachusetts and Haldane to Jamaica last January. I rather think Akenside's 'bloody' got his attention." James shrugged. "And the curtain comes down . . . "

Ashby's grip had rendered both men sullenly mute, though each still glared at the other. He squeezed hard and was pleased to see them falter. "Gentlemen—more respect, please, for the importance of this assembly; and for our patron, His Majesty, King George the Second." Akenside and Anson eyed one another for a moment, but now seemed disinclined to continue their argument. When Ashby released his grip, they quickly moved off in opposite directions.

Lord Macclesfield called out again from the front of the room. "Thank you, Sheriff Ashby. I appreciate your assistance in maintaining order. Assembled gentlemen, please take a seat in the provided chairs. The proceedings are about to begin."

James commandeered a nearby table and pulled out chairs for himself, Ben, and the two Quakers.

Behind the Earl of Macclesfield stood four easels draped with white cloth. To his left were three chairs occupied by Peter Collinson, William Hogarth—still holding his pug—and a man Ben did not recognize. In front of the Earl was a plain table with four neat glasses of water, and a silver pitcher.

"I will now put forth a framework for our discussion. When I am done, then Mr. Collinson, Mr. Askew, and Mr. Hogarth will present their evidence and information in this matter."

Ben settled in for what appeared likely to be a long and somewhat stodgy introduction. He could not have been more wrong.

"The Royal Society has long been engaged in the study of things, which our fellow Englishmen believe to be fairy tales, or the talk of those addled by madness. We know truths that they do not—and each and every one of us here has taken pride in our secret knowledge, as is only human nature. But there are orders and domains of knowledge. A philosopher of physics and a physician may respect one another's work and enjoy mutual discourse; they have nothing in common beyond two spoken syllables."

He paused to clear his throat. "Well . . . those of us who have guided our Society from its inception—its inner circle, as you will— have had the privilege, and the *responsibility*, of knowing a truth the rest of you did not, because its very importance required that it be kept from you. Tonight that division ends. Tonight we bring the whole into the light."

Ben blinked in astonishment. Around him he heard furtive whispers and hushed exclamations; the sound of questions leaping to the front of more than a dozen brilliant minds.

Lord Macclesfield held up his hands, palms down, then waited for the room to quiet before continuing. "The basis is this—where the arcane is concerned, the philosopher of physics and physician do not occupy separate worlds. There is an *underlying cause* that unifies their particulars. That cause unifies the idea of a *philosophiae naturalis* and a *philosophiae* praeternaturalis into a singular *principium*. That cause is nearly upon us and is of grave concern."

He took a long moment to examine the faces of his audience. They, in turn, saw how absolutely serious he was. The silence was profound.

"I speak of the proximity of Mr. Halley's comet, which the inner circle has proven to be instrumental in causing outbursts of magic and mysterious happenings that do not align with the norms we can expect at most times and most places. Further, we now know of a certainty that the comet's influence has increased with each return. We theorize that as shavings fall from the comet to the Earth, more of the arcane laws are accessible, even between the comet's orbits. This does *not* mean we expect the comet to hearken the 'end of the world,' as superstition and some ha'penny newspapers would have it, nor the second coming of Christ—Sir Newton calculated that event to be several centuries away, using his mathematical method. But we know the magical havoc the inner circle had to overcome in 1682, and we feel certain that this time, it will be worse.

"Halley himself thought the comet would reach us in late 1758 or early 1759. We have a bare few months, then, to galvanize ourselves and find ways to mitigate a potentially catastrophic disaster. Which makes what our three speakers are here to tell us of the utmost importance. I urge you to let them proceed *without* interruption." At this, Ben was sure he saw Lord Macclesfield cast a stern look in his cousin's direction.

"I will not waste any more of your time when these other gentlemen have so much to make clear to you. Mr. Collinson? The floor is yours. Please begin."

He took his own seat as Peter Collinson rose and stepped to the fore.

"Thank you, Lord Macclesfield. Ahem." Collinson coughed into his fist. "My esteemed colleagues of the Royal Society, a little over three years ago the Society funded me to complete a botanical survey of rare plants in and around the areas of Salisbury and Hampshire. Some of you may have read the paper I published—we collected some extraordinary samples of burnt-tip orchid, field fleawort, and bastard toadflax, among many others. What I did not include was that the real purpose of my journey was to investigate long-hinted connections between Halley's Comet and certain specific locations, beginning with Salisbury Cathedral."

"The construction of the cathedral in Salisbury began in 1220, and the historical record indicates that the comet returned a mere two years later, in 1222. This appearance was, of course, taken as a great portent, especially since its passage was accompanied by a larger than usual number of falling stars, and the concurrent discovery of large chunks of anomalous geologic material through the Salisbury region. Our suspicion was that this unidentifiable debris might have been cast-off material from the comet itself. Further, we theorized that an unknown quantity of it might have been taken up by the foundry workers and stone masons of the day and included in the cathedral itself."

He sipped water from one of the glasses on the table, then continued. "This was not a search at random. It was inspired by reports of certain strange phenomena that all had Salisbury Cathedral in common and that mapped neatly against the known periodicity of the comet. Again and again, since the 13th century, as the comet approached our sphere, these anecdotal reports increased in number; and as it departed, they decreased in turn. Within the last decade the pattern appeared to be repeating. In its simplest form, it can be described thusly: an unsuspecting soul grips the knob of a door in London, or Liverpool, or Little Bushey Lane in Hertfordshire—the starting points in these accounts varied wildly—and then, upon opening the door and walking through, finds himself *standing on the other side of the cloister door at Salisbury.*

"Yes, I know how that sounds," he said in response to murmurs from his audience. "It gets stranger. Those who held onto the knob and immediately went back the way they came, closing the door behind them, remained safely where they had started. They were startled, to be sure, and quite a few went straight round to their confessor or their alehouse, but otherwise they were unaffected. By contrast, anyone who let go of the knob was stranded; no amount of opening and closing the cloister door would yield a passage back. This left these people in considerable straits, being so inexplicably far from home and unequipped for travel.

"I inspected each component of the cloister door in detail, making detailed sketches of the knobs on both sides. There was no lingering trace of the occult, nor could I discern anything radically out of the ordinary. The substance of the doorknob did look *slightly* unusual to my eye, but I am no metallurgist; it might have been common as lead for all I knew. So I took samples from the knobs, though many of them appear to have been replaced with a different pattern over the years, and each separate piece of metal on the door, and gouged sample splinters of the wood. These I gave over for analysis to Mr. John Hadley, Professor of Chemistry at Cambridge University, who reports no clear results."

Hadley was in attendance. Collinson nodded to him, and the chemist rose for a moment to be recognized.

"I next went to Stonehenge, to look into testimony of ghosts, strange lights, and noctambulism on the Salisbury plain. I was unable to document any such activities at either first- or second-hand; at present they remain no more than rumor. Once again I took some small samples for Mr. Hadley."

Ben thought of his own samples from Stonehenge, and the strange echoes he had felt when visiting there. Though he understood why Collinson had never mentioned this research to him, he wished it could have been otherwise, and resolved to follow up at earliest opportunity.

"Winchester Castle was my next destination. Specifically the Great Hall, built as an addition during the 1222 passage of the comet. As I am sure some of you already know, an ancient replica of Arthur's famous table hangs on the wall there; and local legend has it that whenever a comet is at its brightest, King Arthur and his knights and the actual Round Table appear in the middle of the hall. The castle itself was built upon Roman ruins that can be dated to a calculated comet pass circa 66 *Anno Domini*. As with Salisbury, we suspect the castle itself was begun in 1067 using *materia* we believe to have been impregnated with debris from the comet's 1066 passing. Once again I found no direct evidence, just talk and local superstition, but some of it was compelling." He paused for another sip of water.

"Regardless, I took samples from the Great Hall and attempted to take samples from what I believed were remnants of the original castle. I did not dare take a sample of the round table, though I wish that would have been possible.

"At each stop, canvassing the local population revealed consistent patterns, such as distress at the imminent arrival of the comet, anecdotal reports of legends coming to life, and an increase in people claiming to have experienced ghostly visitations and other bizarre experiences similar to stories told by their grandparents and great-grandparents, i.e., tales dating back to the last passage of the comet.

"Excuse me..." Collinson unfolded a slip of paper from his vest pocket and, squinting fiercely, scanned the notes he had written on it. "Ah. Sorry, sorry... completely forgot Montisfont Abbey. Much the same, really. Recent reports of ghostly monks in what had been the nave and the cloisters, nothing directly observable while I was there, some samples for Mr. Hadley, the usual local talk. The results of the surveys seem to be consistent." He refolded the scrap and tucked it in a different pocket. "Thank you all for your time, and I invite Mr. Anthony Askew to take the floor."

Looking relieved, Collinson returned to his seat, taking his water glass with him. There was a smattering of polite applause. As Ben glanced around to his fellow audience, he read mainly skepticism and confusion there.

The third man, the one Ben hadn't known, waited until the clapping ended before he finally stood. He was lavishly dressed, as if for a more formal occasion, and, unlike most of the Society's fellows, he wore an elaborately coiffed and powdered wig. He bowed respectfully to the gathering.

"My friends. Though the collective knowledge of our Royal Society is vast, the portions which concern the comet are still mainly theory and conjecture. We do not know why it returns as it does. We do not know why it makes magic blossom in the world, the way that rain makes our gardens bloom. Above all, we do not understand why this fostered, amplified magic takes on so many different forms, and does so many different things, nor why these are all too often terrifying and harmful; perhaps even malignant. I'll not bore you with the details of the research and vetting I have performed. Suffice it to say that I can vouchsafe for the information brought to you by the esteemed Mr. Collinson and our celebrated guest to my right. The observations made are accurate, despite our lack of knowledge as to the how. What is most interesting, though, is that it is possible there is someone who already possesses this knowledge. Someone we must find."

It was almost impossible for those present not to gasp at this. Even Ben found himself taking a deep involuntary breath.

"I now require the assistance of Mr. William Hogarth, the celebrated artist, who is here tonight as a most valued and respected guest. If you please, sir?"

Hogarth put down his pug and left his seat, taking up position next to the first draped easel. The dog followed along happily, sniffing the floor with great interest.

William paused, studying the room with a smoldering intensity that reminded everyone present of his youth, and the subsequent tremendous talent that accompanied it. His right eyebrow twitched up as he simply said, "Exhibit one."

A Silk, the lone representative of the King present, stepped up from the back wall and lifted the drapery off the easel, revealing a framed portrait in an antique style. Ben carefully kept his comportment, though the presence of the Silk, and the task delegated to him, seemed odd. He tried to ignore it for the moment and focused on the painting. The subject of the portrait was an intelligent-looking man in his mid-thirties or so, visible from mid-chest up, wearing fine clothes of perhaps a century before. At the man's neck, just under his long beard, was a jade brooch that carried an indistinct metal *something* at its center—the artist had not bothered to detail that portion of the painting to the same degree given the face and, especially, the eyes.

Ben shifted in his chair and came to full attention. He knew that brooch very well, or one uncannily like it. And the man was oddly familiar, though he couldn't quite place him.

"Presenting a work in oils by John Riley, painted in *Anno Domini* 1682—the last passage of the comet. The name of the sitter is not known. Next, please."

This unveiling revealed an older, larger painting than the first. This was a full figure of a man wearing elaborately brocaded Elizabethan court dress. Allowing for the difference in styles, the man captured here was virtually a twin of the first—and at his neck there was a jade brooch.

"We discovered this one hanging in Windsor Castle and arranged to borrow it. It is dated 1607, yes, another year of the comet, and was painted by Isaac Oliver. Mr. Oliver is primarily remembered as a court miniaturist for Elizabeth, and then James the First, but he also painted larger works. I'm grateful this was one. As I am sure you have already guessed, the name of the subject is recorded nowhere."

Hogarth nodded to the Silk, who removed the third drape.

This piece was very old indeed: a cracked wooden panel perhaps eighteen inches high, showing a highly stylized face, from the neck up, against a nighttime sky. The signature feature of that sky was a bright ball, done in gilt, at the head of three wavy, retreating gilded lines. There was no great talent in the work, and either the varnish or the paints had been poorly made, so there were cracks and ripples everywhere and several large patches of the picture had simply fallen away. These imperfections made it hard to say from the rendered face alone whether this was the same man as in the other two portraits. But the jade brooch at his neck was unmistakable, and the streak in the sky could only be the artist's interpretation of a comet.

"I have no idea who painted this, or when it was done—by materials and style it could be anywhere from 1200 to 1500. But it takes no leap to assume it was painted in a comet year, and the ever-present brooch completes the connection." Hogarth pointed to the detail in the painting.

Anthony Askew leaned forward, knuckles resting on the table, and addressed the room once more. "The only thing that Mr. Robert Hooke and Sir Isaac Newton agreed upon was that the secret to everlasting life, the philosopher's stone, was a mystery none could understand. I'm no longer certain they had the right of it. In these paintings we see evidence of a man who has lived at least 300 years, possibly more than 500, unchanging, a man who seems only to appear when the comet does. This cannot be coincidence. I reject that idea. There *must* be a connection, and I propose to you, my fellow members, that we must locate this man and ask him for ourselves. The last veil, Mr. Hogarth."

During this last exposit, the pug had finally wandered away from its master, eager to seek what fallen crumbs it might find in the vicinity of the refreshments table. Hogarth didn't notice, being keen on coming to the finale of the demonstration.

He grasped the veil covering the fourth easel, but did not immediately lift it. First he addressed the audience once more. "This is my own painting, based on a drawing I did of a person I noticed in a coffee house two months ago. Mr. Askew saw it when visiting my studio and insisted I bring it here tonight."

With that Hogarth removed the veil, and everyone in the room understood why the painter was present.

"He does not have the brooch," said Askew, "and appears to have more the appearance of an eccentric than a fine courtier. But the similarity of these likenesses cannot be denied. "

Ben lifted a hand, feeling only slightly like a child in a schoolroom.

Anthony Askew stepped forward. "Yes, Mr. Franklin? What is your question?"

"I have two, actually," said Ben, raising the volume of his voice enough to reach the whole room.

"Continue."

"Our unnamed Methuselah obviously sat for the first three portraits. Mr. Hogarth caught him a fourth time by unknowing accident. But why would a secret immortal betray himself by leaving such evidence? And Mr. Hogarth, what drew your eye to him in the first place? Wouldn't such a man, to survive, become practiced at *not* being noticed?"

Ben deliberately chose not to mention Polly's brooch, or the persistent sense that the man in the paintings was familiar to him. Those things could wait until he had actual answers to share with his fellow Society members.

Askew nodded at Ben with respect. "Astute questions, and exactly why I requested Mr. Hogarth's help. His eye for realism in portraiture is matched by none. It is to him I look for authentication."

Hogarth shook his head emphatically. "You have it, Anthony. The man I saw in the coffee house is certainly the man in these other paintings. I would stake my life on that. As for your question, Ben—" Hogarth shifted his attention to Franklin—"What caught my attention was the odd way that everyone moved around him without even looking. You know what a crowded coffeehouse is like. Might as well visit Bedlam, most times. But he stood in complete silence, examining the menu, and everyone parted round him the way water flows past a rock in a stream. I called my sketch *A Study in Stillness*."

"We have set a watch on that coffeehouse," said Askew, "since learning Mr. Hogarth's story. Our mystery man has not yet returned."

"Assuming he even will," said Hogarth. "A man of that nature, with such depth of experience, I am sure he would have seen me sketching him. That alone might have driven him away."

"Which brings me to my final point," announced Askew. "I would like everyone in this room to join me in devising ways to find our quarry. But at no point should any of us engage with him directly, either physically or in conversation. With His Majesty's gracious permission, arrangements have been made for the King's Guard to handle the task of isolating this man so he can be questioned. We shall play the role of the King's hounds, as it were, baying after the fox—but once he has been treed or run to ground, we must let the King's *hunters*, his Guard, take lead."

"Thank you, gentlemen!" called out Lord Macclesfield from his seat. "That is the presentation for the evening. Pray discuss it amongst yourselves at will and come to me or Mr. Askew if you have any questions."

As it happened, Ben left in different company than he arrived. Tired and deeply thoughtful, he decided to return to Craven Street before Baker, Brander, and Hogarth were ready to leave. Hogarth's pug seemed eager to depart, but its owner overruled the excited small dog.

John Hadley was also determined to go back to his work, so they took a hackney coach together.

"You are unnaturally quiet, Ben," he observed after a while.

"The world is upside down, John. I have always taken pride in the flexibility of my intellect, but it is sore challenged in this moment."

"Easier for me, I suppose," agreed the chemist. "I didn't know about Collinson's portion until he brought me the samples for testing, but I've been after our stranger longer than Askew has. Not that he agrees, because he didn't think of it first. But I know I'm right. It's the only explanation that makes sense."

Ben stared. "I fear you have lost me."

Hadley leaned back, beaming. "Do you know what the Royal Society was called before the Royal Charter was signed?"

"Wasn't it just known as the Philosophical Society of Oxford?"

"Only for a few years. For nearly a century beforehand its members called it the 'Invisible College'—a group of curious men who exchanged letters, held secret meetings, and all sought exactly the same end."

"Which was?"

"Uncovering the secrets of Merlinus Ambrosius, of course—he who conquered the philosopher's stone, learned the secret of immortality, and spent the last several thousand years amassing magic. Whom else could our eternal be?"

Bedford Court
Craven Street
London, England
July 1st
✤ ✤ ✤

❖ 29 ❖
The Entire Time

Ben convinced Polly to go for a walk without much difficulty; it took further persuasion to convince her to wear the brooch. At first she resisted, uncertain at his sudden insistence, but it soon became clear that refusal would simply confirm she had something to hide. She yielded, assuming that the issue, whatever it was, would soon become clear.

Ben told her, as an excuse, "I can say only that I have learned something interesting about that trinket of yours—something you might wish to know as well. And it's such a splendid sunny day, it seems a shame to discuss the matter inside when we could be appreciating its subject in the fullest natural light."

A brisk breeze off the coast had cleared the London air of some of the lower-hanging stench and smoke. The city, when the air was cold and all the coal furnaces were belching, was not a place for leisure walks. But after a strong breeze to clear the air, as it were, it was marvelous. They had been meandering here and there, Ben letting Polly take the lead, since he still didn't know his way around much past Durham Yard to the Thames, each just a few moments from Craven Street. He was determined over this walk to bring up magic and the things he had discovered at the meeting of the Royal Society.

"Polly, may I see your brooch please?" He turned to her, leaning against the railing on the edge of the walkway beside the river.

She touched a hand to her chest, covering the green and black bauble with the tips of her fingers. "It's quite a pain to remove. Can you just ask me what you wish to know?"

"I'm afraid I must inspect it. Please Polly, this is important."

Her hand hovered there near the brooch, and she looked unsure.

"It will simply take me a moment to confirm what I am thinking."

With a minimum of fuss actually removing the charm, Polly relented and handed it to Ben.

He inspected the brooch closely, exhilarated to finally be allowed a proper examination. The second it touched his skin, he felt a jolt. It was definitely an object of power, though what it did he had no idea. Jade circled the brooch, creating a small disc, on which the black scorpion was mounted. Whatever artificer had built this trinket had been a grandmaster. The fusion of the inky black metal and jade was seamless and the two materials seemed to just melt into each other.

His suspicions about Polly seemed accurate. Like him, she was a mage. Once the path was clear of other pedestrians, he hefted the brooch, palming it in his other hand, and cocked his arm back to throw.

Polly reacted instinctively, throwing out a hand, fingers splayed, "*No!*" while her other hand furiously made an intricate set of signs and motions. Invisible tendrils of force wrapped around Ben's arm and locked him in place, mid-throw.

"I knew it!" Ben stared at Polly. He extended his other hand, turning his palm up and exposing the brooch hidden there.

Glaring, Polly snatched away the trinket. "That was not something a nice person would do, Ben."

"I merely feigned the throw, harmless enough. You have lied to me, though. You can perform acts of the arcane nature and have kept it hidden from me."

"Hardly." Polly glanced up from repinning her brooch long enough to flash him a dour look. "I dispatched ruffians in front of you, while pretending to tie my shoe. That was an invitation to talk with me openly, Benjamin, not to accuse me."

Ben sat silent for a moment, thinking through what young Polly had said. Finally, he looked up and met her eye. "I was wrong. I am sorry. You were inviting me, and I was too caught up in the, I don't know, *espionage* of it all to realize that."

She turned her back to him, walking by him to lean against the railing.

"I was telling the truth about the brooch, Polly. I've seen it in three paintings, over the course of hundreds of years, and all of them were of the same man."

"Can you show me this man?"

"I cannot," he shook his head. "I do not have access to the paintings."

"Do you know how to cast a *glamour*, Ben?"

"Truthfully, I have no idea. I can do fog and lightning pretty well. There are a few tricks to stave off hunger and illness I have as well."

"Dangerous spells, those. Hm." Polly stared out over the Thames. Finally, she turned back and faced him. "Might as well show you the rest, then. Apology accepted."

Ben's lip twitched with a half-smile at his young friend, "I promise not to try anything like that again. I just needed the truth. What might we as well show me?"

"Two things, in fact. Tonight, I will teach you to cast a glamour, as well as give you more of the fundamentals. Being self-taught is very dangerous. The second is that we are very near a place I haven't been to in a while. It is the rooms we have taken for the Society of Numbers so we could store our collected books. We used to meet here, but it has proven inconvenient. One of our core missions is to seek out ancient journals to discover what secrets they may hold. We found a fair few, over the years." Polly spun about and put her hands on her hips. She raised an eyebrow, "But there are more than just those found at estate sales and back alley bookstores. In particular, my old tutor had many journals that I hid there. Would you like to take a look? Of course, you would. When did Mr. Benjamin Franklin ever turn down a chance to satiate curiosity?" If she was being overly lighthearted and playful, it was simply in an attempt to balm the sting of wounded pride over the tongue-lashing she had just received.

"You know how much the written word in all its forms fascinates me. Ancient texts sound particularly intriguing. I've had a few myself, over the years," Ben nodded and smiled deprecatingly, playing into it. "Especially if they relate to that brooch and hint to the secrets of magic. And it is true enough that I always feed that particular hunger. Yes, let us go."

They reached the building, an unassuming closed shopfront on a side street, and climbed the stairs to the residences above. Once inside, they went up to the next floor and Polly began poking around in a plant next to the door. "Oh no, it looks like someone has taken off with the key. Someone always forgets to put it back. Luckily, there's a trick to popping it."

"Pick the lock?" Ben looked at Polly and slowly moved his hand toward the doorknob, "Might as well give it a try? Nothing ventured, nothing gained." He waggled his eyebrows and twisted the knob, muttering in Latin under his breath as he did. Ben kept a deadpan expression as the door opened easily, swinging silently inward. Even more surprising, they saw a man surrounded by books and materials he had pulled from shelves and trunks around him, oblivious to the state the room was in, and unaware of their entrance. He knelt, digging through one of the trunks.

Polly pushed past Ben and stood behind the stranger indignantly, "How dare you? These are not your rooms. I shall have you arrested for trespass and thievery!"

"Oh, hello Polly." The man glanced back, only half interested. He went back to rooting through the scattered papers in the trunk. "I have every right to be here. Even more than you. Or, should I call you Lord Twenty-Three instead of Polly?"

"Who? What? I know you—" Polly tilted her head to the side, a quizzical look on her face, "Mr. Overton?" Her fury was temporarily forgotten in the shock of being confronted by her old tutor's face.

Ben stared also, tilting his head this way and that, squinting his eyes, with the nagging thought, *I know him from somewhere.*

From amidst the things gathered around him, Mr. Overton motioned dismissively, "Forgive me if I do not get up to receive you. I'm looking for something, and I'm not quite sure where it is."

"What are you doing here?" Polly's brows furrowed. She was deeply perplexed. "And how did you know I was Lord Twenty-Three?"

"You are cleverer than that, Polly." Mr. Overton sighed, then stood up and made his way out of the chaos he had created. "Because I am Lord One. Of course. It is clear your education has lapsed considerably for you to have been unable to arrive at that conclusion yourself. Even with the glamour I've cast." He waved a hand casually. "*Animan.*"

It was like a fog began to lift and the ball dropped for Ben, though his thoughts were still fuzzy. *Its him! The man from the portrait!* He gaped.

Polly reddened, and, where she had seemed at first delighted to see Mr. Overton, now she pulled herself back. Something felt familiar to her about him, and yet also off. "Why did you abandon me?"

"You're . . . You . . ." Ben pointed.

Overton regarded them both for a moment, then glanced toward the fireplace, though it held no fire.

"It's more than half useless talking to you two until the spell finishes wearing off anyway. What would you have of me?"

Polly ventured, "You were Lord One the entire time. And you knew I joined the Society. Why the subterfuge? Was it necessary to hide from me?"

"Necessary?" He seemed angry. "Then you are even more naïve than you were as a child. I hoped to see you grow into your power, into who you could have been. Instead, I watched you prattle about with my hounds. They are my dogs, only meant to find things for me. And," he continued, standing, "this is all very much necessary."

Polly reddened at the insult.

Ben finally found enough faculty to speak. Every moment, more of whatever Overton had done cleared away. "I know who you are now. I've seen the paintings of you. Desist with your badgering, Merlin. You'd think that after millennia alive you'd have learned some manners."

"Is that what those fools of the King's think? You couldn't be more wrong, there was no Merlin. Just a confused soldier drinking with Geoffrey and starting a legend. And, frankly, you are not the one to command me," Overton answered back.

Ben and Polly both tried to talk over each other, and Overton sliced his right hand through the air in an angry motion. "Silence. All of this is irrelevant," and in a sudden inversion of his motion, Overton waved his left hand and a blast blew Ben against the back wall. Shelving and books collapsed atop him. He struggled to rise, his head swimming.

Polly looked at her former teacher through narrowed eyes, mumbling, hands behind her back.

"None of that." Overton walked over to her. "*Slæp.*"

Polly froze, unable to even move her eyes.

Bloody hells. Gasparini?? Ben stared, wide eyes, as his muscles stopped responding and he slumped down.

"I had hoped that you would grow to be so much. Just as I hoped he," the magician gestured to the moaning form of Ben, "would stay on the other side of the ocean. But you both disappointed me." Overton unclasped the brooch from her bodice. "The Royal Society and the Society of Numbers were the best you two could do? You don't deserve this, I'm sad to say. I had hoped you would become an ally."

He turned, walking toward the fireplace.

The second his back turned, Polly began moving her fingers again. Her jaw clenched and sweat dripped from her brow.

"After today you won't see—" Overton began, then stumbled as Polly's mental pressure overcame him.

Ben watched in awe as Overton struggled to stay upright. Ben fought his way vertical, regretting the stiffness and heft of old age every second of the way up. There was a force, like waves, coming off the angry Polly. Even behind her, Ben fought to not be pinned to the wall. Her hands were working what looked like a simple mathematical count as Overton became red and began to steam. He dropped to his knees.

A primal scream began to build as a gut-wrenching sound ripped its way out of Polly's chest. It tore through the cacophony of silence ringing in all their ears. Ben finally realized what he was witnessing—a battle of raw will between two equally gifted mages.

Ben forced his arm up and held a hand out to Polly, doing the only thing he could think. "*Præsidio,*" he muttered. The sleep spell shifted, hitting him full force, and he slid down the wall, exhausted.

It was enough. Polly stepped forward, marshalling all her strength in the second Ben had bought her.

Overton grabbed his head. His face became redder and redder, his breathing coming in great gasps. He toppled, unmoving, and all the pressure in the room dissipated.

Neither Ben nor Polly moved. Polly wasn't even sure she was breathing. At any moment, she was sure Overton would leap back up and blast them both.

After a few moments of continuing quiescence, Polly walked over to Ben. She laid a hand on his forehead and muttered to herself. The exhaustion lifted, and Ben's eyes went from barely open to wide.

"I don't understand something. How were you using magic without speech?" He could see that she was hurting, struggling with the conflict and betrayal, and was attempting to distract her.

She leaned against the wall, steadfastly ignoring Overton. "Oh," she said as she looked absently at her fingers, "it's like reading using a finger to track the words. You don't need it, it just helps."

"I see. Some of my assumptions were incorrect then. When I first began to learn the art, my Debby suggested Latin and it worked. I had assumed it was part of the composition of a spell." Ben stood, shakily, and cautiously stepped over the detritus to get to Overton, glancing at Polly as he went.

She looked exhausted and haggard but nodded at him to continue. Getting no reaction from Overton as he nudged him with his finely shod foot, Ben knelt next to him. "I think," Ben began, "I think he is dead."

Polly blinked. She shook her head. "But, I—" Her jaw clenched. "Lobcocks."

Ben jerked back in surprise at the foul language. The stress and emotional tool of the situation was just a little too much, and he began laughing. "Lobcocks? Really?" He wheezed through the laughs.

Once the dam was broken, it was infectious, and Polly began laughing too. Hers wasn't a laugh of joviality, but rather had a knife's edge of hysteria under it. Ben recognized the tone from his own suffering at loss and knew what was coming next. He regained his feet as his laughter died down and stepped to Polly, folding her into a hug. Her laughs became tears. "It's okay to cry, Polly. I understand that's a lot you've had to deal with." He patted her back.

She shoved him away. "I'm not crying because I'm sad. I'm crying because I'm angry. Just give me a moment. Tenderness is a poor cure for fury. Retrieve my brooch, please."

As Ben stepped back over to the dead mage, a change came over Overton's body. In that moment he became completely desiccated, and his body collapsed into a pile of dust. Ben stood, agape, wondering at this rapid transformation. He had no conception that Polly's magic was nearly this powerful. To think: he had assumed his magic was the most advanced.

"What have I done?" Polly gazed in horror at the pile of ash that was once her teacher, her hands shaking.

"I think you saved our lives," Ben said. "Thank you." He used some of the strewn papers to sift through the ashes.

"For years," she spoke softly, "I longed for nothing more than to see Mr. Overton again, to show him how I had progressed, so he could applaud my efforts and perhaps teach me more. He told me that I would have to be ready. That there was a struggle coming. I had dreams of being a hero, a mage, like in the tales of Arthur. And now I've killed him and, with him, killed my own dream. All I've left us is questions."

Ben turned from the pile of dust. "A dream can turn into a nightmare, Polly." He glanced back at the ashes then shrugged. "Unless I am mistaken, Overton was not interested in you or your growth. Apparently, he was interested in your brooch. I don't think it is here," he said. He couldn't feel the artifact. "Now that I consider it, the hum from it vanished sometime in the middle of the fight."

"That was the only gift he ever gave me—at least that I was allowed to keep." Then she paused and looked at Ben, "What hum?"

Ben looked a little sheepish but was glad that her natural curiosity had momentarily diverted her from her distress. "Certain objects give off a hum that, apparently, only I can hear. Your brooch was one of those objects. From my first day in your house I knew there was something special there and have been curious. The brooch does not appear to be here now though. It must have been destroyed in whatever just happened to his body."

Polly began to move toward him, but Ben held up a hand, "I assure you, it's not here, and it doesn't seem worth it for you to engage in such a disturbing examination. I can tell you with certainty that it is not in this room."

"Are you saying that you could, essentially, sense where I was at all times?" asked Polly.

Ben hung his head, looking sheepish, "Not really. I can kind of hear it, but it has to be close."

Polly shook her head, "I don't know what to think of that, so I am going to ignore it for the moment. This makes no sense. I am not a powerful mage. I am not nearly as powerful as he was. How could I have done that to him? How could I have incinerated my brooch at the same time?"

"I was thinking the same thing," Ben's eye narrowed. "You weren't using heat magic, were you? The body maintained its integrity for a moment before it turned to ash."

Polly shook her head, "No, I was trying to make him dizzy, maybe have vertigo or a headache. My goal was to render his casting useless by interfering with his mind. He taught me at a young age to apply a magic to the smallest spot to achieve the greatest effect."

"Interesting. Much like the principle of a level." Ben walked around the body, still studying the ashes. His eyes darted back and forth between the pile of ashes and the walls as he silently measured the room's dimensions.

"Accurate." Polly nodded, staying back and watching. "Just as natural philosophy dictates the rules by which our world operates, there is an underlying group of taxonomies and sciences inherent in supernatural philosophy, as well, that dictate the operation of magic."

"I had noticed that my systems of experimentation have produced similar effects when using them in the casting of magic. Look here, he was kicking over the piles of papers he had been stacking before. As I recall, he seemed to have a fit of apoplexy," Ben said thoughtfully as he traversed his memory to recall Overton's appearance and actions at the end. "Perhaps whatever you did overtaxed his brain?"

Polly frowned, "That doesn't explain the way his body turned to dust like that. It was long after he died, and I had stopped casting. I think he would have kept his grip on me and not put down his guard. Or he would have turned to ash immediately. It makes no sense."

"You are right. It makes no sense. But I have a thought," Ben said as he walked over to the fireplace. "I was in a house in Surrey once that had been a Catholic residence, and the devout Anglican owners delighted in showing the concealed space the previous owners had installed to protect priests. That priest hole had been concealed at the side of the chimney of the fireplace." Ben began searching the sides of the fireplace. "If you look carefully, the dimensions of the room don't add up. There seems to be more space for the mantle than the fireplace is actually using. Aha!" He felt a slight give. A narrow door, just under the height of a man, opened. Inside, Ben found what he least expected: a stack of books that looked exactly like the journals Gasparini had stolen from him.

"What is in there?" Curiosity overcame Polly's contemplation of

Overton's motivations and her culpability for his death, and she joined Ben at the fireplace.

He stared in silence.

"What are those?" Polly asked.

Ben exhaled heavily and looked at Polly. "I know now where else I knew him from. I thought it was him, but these confirm it."

Polly looked at him quizzically.

"He broke into my home in Philadelphia and destroyed a journal identical to these right in front of me. He called himself Gasparini, performed real magic as a side show, and spoke English with an incredible Italian accent. He was able to immobilize me with one word. The same word he used on you."

He pulled the journals out and handed one to Polly. A quick perusal showed that though the language changed from book to book, the handwriting remained the same.

"You have a lot of questions to answer." Polly stared at Ben intently. "But for now, perhaps we should take these to the house and then we can discuss the rest."

"Indeed," Ben replied dryly. He had some questions of his own he was hoping to get answers to before too much longer.

As the two left, the wall shimmered and a form detached from the shadows. *Perhaps those two will be useful after all,* Overton thought as he rolled the brooch through his fingers.

Ben prepared for himself and Polly small glasses of sweetened rum. She had said she was fine as they walked back after their encounter with Lord One/Overton/not-Merlin, whatever his real name was, but Ben had doubted it. They were both still shaken. Or at least, he was. If she wasn't, then she had nerves of oak.

Since they had returned to Craven Street, Polly had sat at the small table in his library and study quietly. She stared at the stack of journals.

Ben smiled at her as he slid the glass in front of her, knowing this investigation would distract them both from the disturbing events. He patted the seven journals on the table. Ben held up his glass, "To discovery."

Polly raised her glass, "To discovery." They both took a drink. Then Polly raised her glass, "To friendship."

Ben grinned, raising his glass, "To friendship." They both finished their drink with a smile.

Polly looked at the stack of seven journals, "One thing I will say, these look exactly like the journals I once found on Overton's desk. I was a young girl, and curious. The King's men seized them. Took away all his property."

Ben nodded. "Yet we found them in the Society of Number's secret stash. He mentioned they were his hounds; it does seem logical to think these are what he had them seeking. And I watched him destroy one of them in my own house. Three separate occasions of these books."

"I can make no sense of it. Why destroy them? Why be so cruel about it? No thread that I can spot ties them together." Polly ran a finger along the cover of the top journal as she spoke.

"We'll start, then, by making general observations about these journals before we try to find the ties to others. I will make notes as we go, to record our thoughts. A moment while I prepare my quill and ink." After he had his paper and pen ready to go, he said, "What is the first thing you see?"

"They all look of a sort. Similarly sized, similarly constructed."

"Yes," Ben said, as he scratched some notes. "They remind me of my quire books. I would say they are four folded sheets of parchment with eight leaves providing sixteen sides. Then those are sewn together to make a journal of, what, one hundred pages or so. I wonder what method was used to manufacture this paper? It seems fairly uniform. More uniform than should be possible for its age."

After he noticed Polly's look, Ben laughed, "Neither here nor there. I am still a printer at heart."

"Other than this stylized Yggdrasil emblem in the lower corners, I see no particular markings on the covers, front or back," Polly said, looking around the outsides of them. "Again, though not identical, the person who had these made was striving for a certain sameness. Maybe to make them easier to store?"

Ben nodded, "That makes sense. These are identical to the journal Gasparini destroyed in front of me in Philadelphia. The emblem is in the same spot, even. I managed to keep two held back, though Thomas Penn stole them."

"Did you learn from those journals before the theft?" Polly asked.

"Sadly, no. Not even what language they were written in, but I have since seen similar writing in Anthony Askew's collection and know that it was runic Anglo-Saxon. So, very old indeed. Maybe from around the time the Normans invaded."

Polly smiled eagerly, finally fully distracted from the earlier trauma. "Shall we see if these are also Anglo-Saxon riddles?"

Ben nodded, and each of them picked up one of the journals to peruse. After a few moments he said, "Interesting. Some runic Anglo-Saxon, but also Latin alphabet Old English interspersed with, well, a lot of things." He showed his journal to Polly. "Do you think these journals are written by the same hand?"

Polly nodded, "I do."

"Let's look at the others," Ben suggested.

"There seems to be a variety of language," added Polly as she scanned the next one. "I noticed bits in Greek, Latin, Hebrew, and what I think is Arabic as well as one other language I am uncertain of."

"I think those were Chinese characters," Ben added. "I also saw mathematical equations of some sort."

All the journals were written in the same hand, though in a strange variety of languages mashed together, and in every way seemed to be part of the same set.

Ben took the last journal from her and placed them all in a stack, "I am sure there is someone in the Society who can read them completely."

"You can't read it?" Polly asked.

"No, but I know people who can. We have to get this to Peter and the Royal Society."

Polly looked confused, "The Royal Society? What do they have to do with all of this? As a matter of fact, you mentioned them before, as did Overton."

Ben looked at her seriously. "There are more players in this game than the Society of Numbers. The Royal Society has also been investigating these magical phenomena and seeking answers. They will have the right resources to make sense of these journals and perhaps discover something we can use to determine a course of action. We are living under this sense of imminent doom, but have no clear idea why we all feel that way."

Polly nodded, though clearly disappointed. "We didn't get to discover anything."

Ben laughed, "Not true. We discovered that we need some help!"

"All right. Shall we go?"

"Please." Ben held up his hand. "I'm getting older. I would like a little bit to rest and recover before we take a carriage to Peter's."

Polly laughed, "Shall I set up the chess board then, old man?"

"Please," Ben said, "do."

The two idly played chess and talked of the events of the day while also occasionally glancing through the journals. "I was thinking tomorrow, but I do fear we must make every effort to have these journals deciphered. It is a matter of some concern to me."

Polly studied the board intently. "I agree. And I'm curious. Shall we wrap up and go visit your friend?"

Ben picked up the last journal and turned the pages. Finally, with a tired sigh, he replied, "I need to find a way to regain some of the energy of youth. Yes, let's go ahead and get moving."

The
Collinson Home
Ridgeway House,
Mill Hill, Middlesex
July 22nd
✣ ✣ ✣

✤ 30 ✤
I Did No Such Thing

Ben waited in Peter Collinson's sitting room. He paced nervously. Peter simply sat quietly, attending to nothing in particular. Vibrant hues of the sunset, seen through his frosted glass windows, warmed the room and Ben's mood. His familiarity with his friend, grown carefully over years of correspondence, had bloomed into real knowledge and affection in their time together in England.

"It's not easy for you, is it?" Peter asked gently.

Ben paused, suddenly startled. Then he gave a wry smile. "I've always despised waiting. I know I've spent a lifetime counseling patience, counsel I sincerely believe in, because I know how much it would help me if I could only heed it. Some days I feel my life is filled with giving advice I can't hope to follow myself." He looked at Peter sheepishly. "I do admire how calmly you can sit there as we wait for the others to do their assessment."

"Benjamin, we would not have to wait outside if you had been able to keep your curiosity in check. You couldn't let the poor man concentrate on his effort. It isn't his job to teach you Old English."

"But I should be in there," he fretted.

"You were. But you were not helping the matter with asking him what he had learned every minute or so."

"I did no such thing," Ben protested.

"My dear friend," Peter smiled. "I counted the swings of the pendulum myself. We could have set the clock by your pacing and questions."

Ben opened his mouth to object, then thought better of it and pursed his lips in a thoughtful frown. "I suppose there may be some truth to that. Do you think he's done yet?"

Peter laughed. He shrugged, then returned to quiet contemplation.

What seemed like an eternity later the door opened and an excited Anthony Askew walked out, holding an open lexicon of language, marking his spot with a finger. "I will need more time to decipher this properly, Mr. Franklin. I must say I would never have thought to find such documents in my life. It is so much livelier than the Bibles and formal poetry I have been familiar with from my collection. Most documents created in Old English were not diaries or journals as we in this modern era have adopted. They were more instructional or biographical. These are something far different."

"Have you yet discovered anything of use to our cause, Anthony?" Peter asked.

"Honestly, there's just so much. These do seem to be the journals of the man in the portraits, from what I've been able to translate so far. Where did you get these, Mr. Franklin?"

Ben glanced at Peter. "He sent them to me, years ago."

"To my recollection, they were part of the library of the chemist, Reginald Eversleigh. I bought his library, and his soil physic formulas, from his widow."

"Could we interview her? Perhaps see what other sundries this chemist has left behind?" Anthony leaned back against the doorframe while he talked, mindful of propriety, but still making himself comfortable.

Ben glanced to Peter once again, who replied, "Sadly, I do not think we would be well-received should we try. Ben has had recent dealings with her, and upon recognizing her name I had already attempted to inquire as to making social calls. She rebuffed those attempts, quite politely, but quite firmly."

"Pity, that." Anthony clicked his tongue and frowned. "Ah, well. At least we have these journals now. I can confirm that there is description of the comet, the regularity of its appearances, and the consequences of these appearances being magical in nature. I'm seeing references to the city of Winchester and its cathedral and castle. In another passage, Salisbury city and that cathedral. It appears to speak directly to the reports you recorded, as well as how it all ties to the comet, though that is only the beginning. In truth, there is far more in here than that, and it is just easiest to look for familiar things for me."

"I'm most pleased to hear that. If it truly is him, are there clues to the nature of casting? Which of the interpretations is correct?"

"I honestly haven't gotten that far. It seems to talk about power in the body, which may point to the Hooke interpretation being more accurate than Halley or Newton, but I'm not sure. Oh! It also has some mathematical formulations that I don't understand, and some of its sentence structure seems to be idiosyncratic to the writer. Top all of that off with the flowing nature of the text's transitions between tongues and it makes it near impossible to translate without large amounts of guesswork. Please understand that I don't speak all the languages. I'm able to understand about three parts in five. This is going to take some time to thoroughly decipher. I would say years, but I know we have little time. Perhaps if I rush with just a few months I can have enough translated."

"But you *can* translate them. That is good news, Anthony. We appreciate your efforts."

"Is there nothing else you have gleaned?" Ben asked, looking between the two men.

Anthony pursed his lips. "Well. Maybe. I believe that one of the books has a large section musing on the population density, at least I think that's what it is. One of the mathematical tables seems to indicate that perhaps one in every several million people can use magic, but when the comet is in the sky it is more like one in two?" He looked up, a sparkle in his eyes. "It talks about holding star metal in your hand to gain its strength. '*Who holds the star metal holds the power and gains the power,*' is the rough translation. I'm not sure the writer knows either, and that's even if I'm translating this properly. These books truly are a treasure."

Peter put a hand on Ben's arm and addressed Anthony. "We will give you the time you need to speak more authoritatively. Do you require any assistance or further resources to continue your work?"

"I am actually concerned that the content of these journals not break out of the circle of people prepared to understand. Some of what I am reading frightens me. I think I will have to work alone, perhaps setting down a few phrases for others to help with, but I don't want to raise too much curiosity."

"Indeed, we have already seen where that can lead. We will give you all the time you need," said Peter ruefully, "so long as it is in the next few months, before the arrival of the comet."

Lodging House
Tunbridge Wells, England
September 3rd
✣ ✣ ✣

✦ 31 ✦
Plans Change

Honoured Father

I miss'd writing on Friday and Yesterday no Post went from hence, otherwise I should before have acknowledged the Receipt of your Favor of the 30th. Mr. Jackson is prevented from setting off from here so soon as he intended by reason of the matrimonial Affair he mentioned to us not being quite settled. He says he has Letters from the Parties almost every Day, and was he to leave this Place, they would not know where to direct to him; however he expects by Wednesday next to have Matters quite adjusted. Mr. Bridges goes with us as far as Mr. Rose Fuller's, where it is intended to stay a Day or two. In a Fortnight from hence Mr. Jackson thinks it will be proper we should set off on our Norfolk Tour, and therefore proposes being in London some Days before. I am extremely oblig'd to you for your Care in supplying me with Money, and shall ever have a grateful Sense of that with the other numberless Indulgencies I have receiv'd from your paternal Affection. I shall be ready to return to America, or to go any other Part of the World, whenever you think it necessary. We have chang'd our Lodgings to the House next adjoining, but much for the worse, tho' somewhat cheaper. Mr. Hunter is now acquainted with a pretty many Persons, and is as fond of this Place as he was before averse to it.

Your Letter of Yesterday, with the agreeable News of the King of Prussias having defeated the Russians was very acceptable. It contain'd some Particulars which no one else had, and I had an Opportunity of obliging several by communicating them. Rather than a proper journey beyond Scotland this winter, to the aforementioned other Part of the World, I wish to return to London to spend the turning of the year with you. My companions have graciously allowed me grant to come back to Craven Street and reacquaint myself of them early next spring. The rest of the Family desire to be kindly remember'd to you, as does Mr. Hunter.

I am, Honoured Sir Your ever dutiful Son,

~Wm. Franklin

The
Stevenson Home
Craven Street
London, England
December 2nd
✦ ✦ ✦

✤ 32 ✤
Back in Town

Ben led the way as he and his son climbed the stairs to their Craven Street rooms. Ben was much slower, with the cold winter air wreaking havoc on his stiff joints. William patiently accompanied him as the elder Franklin grunted his way up.

"Back in town for less than an hour, and you can't simply unpack this mysterious treasure and bring it down to show me, Billy?" Ben paused to address his son. It was too much of a struggle to talk around his climb.

"It's worth the trek up the stairs, Father. I swear, how do you do this nightly?"

"I don't suffer this nightly. It's this damn fog that's rolling in. Whenever there is a barometric pressure change, I stay downstairs. But fretting is for the feeble. Up we go, yes?" He grunted and kept moving.

Ben was taking his time. He hadn't seen his boy in months, and then he shows up and vanishes to his room for an hour. All Fall, Ben had been working on how to talk to him, but he was sinking into the mire that most parents face when attempting to communicate with a child: all he had was hope. He hoped to finally get an admission from William as to his having formed an alliance with the Penns. He hoped his son was prepared to renounce it. Never having the heart to bring it up, Ben hoped William's conscience was inducing him to return to his filial duty.

They finally finished climbing the stairs, and he thought it was odd the door to their sitting room was already open, but stepped through anyway. As they crossed the threshold of their darkened rooms, William gave Ben a little shove and closed the door behind him.

"What the?" Ben exclaimed, as he quickly turned to open the door again, but opening it did not deliver the expected results. He found himself staring not at William but at a big black void. As his eyes adjusted to the light, he realized he wasn't in their rooms at all. He stared down a long dark hallway. Suddenly, a candle was lit, then another until he could see, sitting at a desk a good forty feet in front of him, Thomas Penn.

Thomas stood and opened his arms wide as he got up from the desk and walked over to the astonished Ben. "So, the master of the quip has nothing to say? Perhaps a little rejoinder aimed to barb my sensibilities over the tax situation? Mmm?"

Ben drew himself up, straightening his back and posture despite the pain in his hip and, with all the dignity he could muster, spoke simply and coldly, "Where am I?"

Thomas considered Ben for a moment and gave a modest shrug. He looked more disappointed than anything else as he said, "You are in His Majesty's Royal Palace and Fortress of the Tower of London. You should prepare yourself, because I am taking you to see your monarch."

"So be it. Let us go meet the King."

Thomas's eyebrows raised. "I'm impressed. No 'that's not possible' nor other exhalations of disbelief from the exalted Mr. Franklin. Just the simple sentiment to get on with it. Very well then."

Ben stared at Thomas, wary, senses heightened. Everything inside him screamed at him to run. He did not. Instead, he calmly followed behind Thomas as they went down a corridor.

As they made their way down the passageway in silence, candles located at intervals on alternate sides of their path burst into flame. They did not provide abundant illumination, but it was adequate. This was no home, or temple, they were in. The walls were stone, and they were *old. Parlor tricks meant to make me uneasy,* he thought, but then noticed beads of sweat dripping from Thomas's temple despite the chill.

He is casting a spell, Ben realized with a start. "Is this dramatic approach really necessary?"

Thomas didn't even turn to acknowledge him, "It is, according to His Majesty. And that is all you should concern yourself with at the moment."

Thomas Penn stopped before the only door at the end of the passageway. Two guards stood, one to either side, and both nodded to Thomas as he and Ben halted. "For all your purported cunning, you have always seemed to lack the right sort of understanding of your place in the events that surround you. Your fame is transitory. Your wealth is transitory. *You* are transitory, Mr. Franklin. Remember that, as you stand before the Crown, and understand the truth." Thomas opened the door and held it for Ben to enter. "Or don't. At least I'll get a laugh out of it that way."

Ben straightened his jacket, glancing coolly at Thomas. He felt... *power* on the other side of that door. Raw, immense power. Steeling himself, Ben walked in cautiously. The source of the sensation he had felt became immediately obvious. The number of magically imbued objects in this room was in the dozens. It was, in truth, overwhelming.

He collected himself quickly, glancing around the room. It was stone walled, just as the passage, though this room was well lit. And standing in front of him . . .

"May I present his Majesty George the Second, by the Grace of God, King of Great Britain, France, and Ireland, Defender of the Faith, Duke of Brunswick-Lüneburg, Arch-Treasurer and Prince-Elector of the Holy Roman Empire." Thomas walked past Ben into the room.

Ben stopped in his tracks, fighting his hip and knee to bow. It was just a moment too long for Thomas to endure.

"I know you are a simple colonial, but I didn't actually expect you to take the first option." Penn's disdainful tone was voiced from a distance that came from the gap in social experience between them more than the physical space. "Surely they must have taught you how to show basic respect to your King, even across the Atlantic?"

Numbly Ben went down on one knee in front of his monarch, George the Second, by the Grace of God, King of Great Britain, France, and Ireland and various territories around the globe including, but not limited to, the thirteen American colonies. Ben couldn't even settle on which immensely long title to assign to him.

George the Second was old, in his late seventies, but fit. He had less of a stomach than Ben and strong shoulders under the finery of his office. Perhaps years of avoiding books in favor of stag hunts had served his physique well in his older age. What Ben noticed first, however, was that though the King always wore a slight smile, he had intensely sad eyes.

Off to the side to the right, not far from where he stood, there was an odd construction. It looked like some sort of temporary altar set up on the floor. Candles were arrayed among objects in front of a deep etching in the wall. The carving appeared to be an astrological chart or alchemical table, albeit not one the likes of which Franklin had ever seen before. The objects of power surrounding the etching were of varying sizes, but included an almost comical spread of oddities. There were door handles, coins, shoe buckles, and even a Jew's harp. A suit of armor and an ornate standing mirror were the largest items in the collection. A familiar hum, so familiar that Ben usually just tuned it out nowadays, strongly emanated from that tableau.

They set this up for me. They want me to see this and be over-whelmed. The tactic was working, but just the knowledge of the effort being put into him strengthened Ben's nerves.

King George either didn't notice, or chose not to notice, Franklin's overly long but somehow still inadequate bow—and immediately seconded Thomas's derision. "Well, I suppose that is the most we can expect of such. Colonials." Even after decades of living in England with only brief sojourns to his homeland, George still carried a strong German accent.

Thomas gave a deeper bow that was both more respectful to the King and insulting to Ben all at once. He glanced back briefly and winked.

"Forgive him, my Lord. He is merely the son of a chandler. You may need to set aside the privileges of your rank for this conversation to progress. At your discretion, of course."

The monarch studied his subject, and in a flash Ben realized the King didn't see him as a person, but rather as just another prize amongst his many toys.

"I hope he can learn." Though George's words were soft, his body never relaxed. "He seems rather a simpleton. Is everyone in the Colonies like this?"

Despite the man in front of him being his King, Ben felt his hackles rise. They were playing a game, baiting him. Franklin's anger had always burned cold, making him calmest when he was at his angriest. He stayed quiet, letting the two get whatever this was over and done.

Thomas shook his head. "Sadly no. Mr. Franklin is considered among the best and brightest of the colonials, Your Majesty. He is even a member of the Royal Society."

The two both turned to see how he would react, silently appraising him. Once the silence got uncomfortable, Ben drew a measured breath and spoke. "I may be a poor, ignorant colonial, but at least I am true in my loyalty to the Throne and my love of being an Englishman. This one," indicating Thomas, "only cares for himself. So, call me simple, but I do have my pride. Your Majesty."

"You have no idea how true those words are, but you will," George the Second said carefully, dangerously. "Let's keep this simple. You are to recover the journals from Lord One and his society, along with whatever magical artifacts you and your associates have managed to acquire. Like all those Fellows that run about in the Royal Society. Books, books, books, all the time. They took our grant but kept to themselves. Couldn't even find a damned journal. You're not to do that, hear? Anything you find you will place into the care of our loyal servant, Thomas Penn."

"Your Majesty, I don't have any magical artifacts or journals that I am aware of possessing." Ben paused. "I did *have* journals, kept in my office in Philadelphia, but somehow Mr. Penn ended up with them. Somehow."

Ben was taken aback as both George the Second and Thomas Penn broke out in genuine laughter. It took a moment for them to recover, but finally Penn said, "Did I not tell you it was thus, Your Majesty? The great luminary, Benjamin Franklin, whose legend is known far and wide, even across Atlantic, is quite underpowered in the current climate and completely ignorant of the situation at hand. Do you understand, Mr. Franklin, what it was you possessed and what you could help us gain? The journals contain the knowledge of Merlin, and show us the proper path to power."

Ben remained stoically calm, but under the surface thought, *Someone isn't as smart as he thinks.* He noticed something he had failed to see previously, when being ambushed at the Penn estate. Thomas's eyebrows furrowed a bit when he lied. So, the question of the hour for Ben was, what was Thomas lying about? If Thomas was lying, what did that say about the King? "Beyond the journals . . . I know nothing of what artifacts you seek."

Thomas waited for a nod from his monarch before replying.

"These artifacts are created by people who have found themselves temporarily enabled by the arrival of the comet to imbue objects with magic that are created from star metal. They imbue it with their intention, an intention that can be detected and used by sorcerers. By mages. Since these objects were created by those who could have no knowledge of the result, they are unstable and can cause harm. Any artifacts that we have not managed to gather before the arrival of the comet will become even more powerful at that time, and these objects will become even more dangerous and unpredictable. These objects, accidentally wrought, can be used by people with true power and control. They are a hazard to the citizens of this land, and they need to be collected and kept in a safe place until the comet has passed."

"Are you saying this is my chance to aid my country? I don't understand what you expect me to do." Ben watched them both carefully.

"To be clear, His Majesty George the Second, by the Grace of God, King of Great Britain, France, and Ireland, Defender of the Faith, Duke of Brunswick-Lüneburg, Arch Treasurer and Prince-Elector of the Holy Roman Empire, is also the current head of the Round Table, Apprentice-Select to Merlin, and Hand of the Martyr on Earth— though we don't use those last titles in public." Thomas smiled tightly. "We are aware, Mr. Franklin, that you have the ability to sense star metal when you are near it. We need you to use that skill for the good of England."

"What about beyond England? What about in America?" Ben asked.

"By concentrating the star metal that has been worked here, we will be empowering our Sovereign and King to protect us all. Until the Key turned up, we were unaware any imbued star metal was in the Americas. I don't think there is much that could be there."

Ben nodded, "I see. I'm still not sure what it is you would have me do." He knew damn well what they wanted, but there was no way he was going to reveal the truth about the Assembly Bell to Thomas Penn. King or no King; he had his limits.

King George's humor fell away as quickly as it came. He turned back to Ben. "We are perfectly aware of what you once had in your possession, and your profound inability to retain what you had gained through no effort of your own. What we want to know, and what we need to understand, is where you got the Key. We have a careful catalog of all known objects infused by *materia* from the comet. Recently, these objects have been disappearing at an alarming rate, but never among the objects known to be created with star metal is a key at all, much less a key like the one you possess."

Ben blinked, uncomfortably aware of the weight of the Key around his neck. George knew . . .

"We need to know where the Key came from, how you came into possession of it, and if you are aware of any similar artifacts in the Colonies. It is your duty as our subject to deliver to us any information that is required for the preservation of the Crown and the defense of this Kingdom. The great and almighty God has manifested his power, stretched out His hand to shower upon us all the blessings of peace. We will take up that power and the responsibility of bearing it, for there is no one else so suited to the concern."

King George took a step forward and Ben took a step back. For being seventy-six, the King emanated power and control.

"Bring us whatever star metal you can hunt down. Deliver it to Thomas Penn. If you have not brought us any more star metal in two months' time, by the first day the comet appears, we will assume you have committed the treasonous act of refusing to obey a direct order from your King. If you attempt to leave London in that time, again, we will assume you have committed a treasonous act. In either case, we will then provide a warrant for torture and see if *peine forte et dure* will loosen your tongue."

Ben contemplated His Majesty for, again, a moment too long, and Thomas Penn stepped forward just as King George's ire began to make itself further known. "If I may, Your Majesty." King George waved his arm toward Ben.

"His Majesty is prepared to ensure your success and the success of your family and friends. Assist and aid your sovereign and King in his just cause, and he has commanded that I relinquish the arguments I make for the proprietors' absolute power over Pennsylvania and provide the Assembly the freedoms they seek. Additionally, he will assist you and your son in rising to the highest levels of society. He is prepared to grant you land for your own colony beyond the Appalachians, larger than any currently in place. All this, though he could command it as your King and offer nothing in return. He could even offer you a quick death for disloyalty should you refuse him. This is something you would do well to remember."

Ben appeared stunned. "I hardly know what to think about His Majesty's offer. I don't know how much help I can really be, but I will make the effort to locate the star metal. I appreciate His Majesty's kind and gracious nature and value the effort he is willing to take on my and my son's behalf, things I could never even dream of accomplishing. I have seen some of the effects of this star metal, and I agree that it is extremely dangerous."

"Excellent," Thomas said carefully, "I appreciate you understanding the seriousness of the situation, and what is the correct thing to do for King and Country. You have but one question left to answer: where did you get the Key?"

Ben had not done well against Penn before, but he gambled by once more relying on absolute simple truths to tell many lies. "It was given to me. I received a crate from London with journals as well, delivered from the Royal Society. The Key was imbued with Divine Spark when I performed my electrical methodology to pull fire from the heavens. A man broke into my house and destroyed the journal." He glanced acerbically over to Thomas.

"I see." Thomas turned to King George, "Your Majesty," he said as he bowed, "do I have your leave to return Mr. Franklin to his home?"

The King waved absently, nodding.

Ben also bowed to the King, then Thomas walked Ben to the closed door and, after a moment, pulled it open for him. Ben saw the hallway of his own lodgings and gratefully stepped through the doorway as quickly as he could.

After Ben had departed, Thomas returned to the chamber and

bowed to his King as he asked, "Are you certain it was wise to offer to reward him with rich lands, Your Majesty? His loyalty has not been won. He could bring you a stirrup while hiding a carriage. Much as he did while not telling us where he got the Key—or even that he still carries it."

"I noticed that he relied on the truth to hide what we sought, yes. He is not an unclever man. Yet," King George turned to Thomas, "remember, what I give the father will in time pass to the son, should either of them survive what is coming. The son is far more suitable to our purposes. Sons often are."

Thomas Penn thought about his own father and smiled. "Your Majesty is wise in all things. Why not allow me to simply pry that information from him and take the Key?"

"Everything in its own time, Thomas." George the Second walked slowly to the carving and knelt before it, tracing a finger along its ridges. "Have you heard of the man who carved this star chart?"

Thomas walked up beside him. "Only in passing. I can't recall his name."

George the Second nodded. "His name was Hew Draper. He was born on the 26th of August 1531. The night of his birth, the comet was overhead, and he was born to the power. Everything I've read of him in the journals and communications of the early Invisible College say the man was a true sorcerer. He confessed to knowledge of magic but denied practicing sorcery. After his power was stripped mostly away, he was imprisoned here in 1561."

Thomas leaned down and studied the carving in the wall. "What is the purpose of it?"

"No one knows. I believe he was attempting to predict the next passing of the comet. It is based on this that we begin the first part of the ritual at Christmas. It is rumored that he died in 1606, sitting below this carving, less than a year before he would have seen the return of his full power." King George dug the tip of his cane into the stone floor and shook his head. "Do you understand?"

Thomas shook his head. "I do not, Your Majesty."

The King peered at his protégé, then sighed. "Only a damn fool trusts in books and spells. Use people against themselves. Use your own muscles. We have three months to complete the ritual and bring the comet close enough. Until we possess it all, relying on magic for anything other than that goal only gets us where Hew Draper ended. And that's why we will seize it all. You outthink them, then you outfight them, then when the magic is all they have left, you take that away too."

"I understand. We will let Mr. Franklin do our work for us, and even the act of his hiding things will reveal to us that there is something to be hidden. And with that, we can learn the truth."

King George the Second nodded. "Exactly."

1759

The
Collinson Home
Ridgeway House,
Mill Hill, Middlesex
January 13th
✢ ✢ ✢

✣ 33 ✣
The Last Passing of the Comet

Him bið swā þām trēowe þe bið āplantod nēah wætera rynum, þæt selð his wæstmas tō rihtre tīde, and his lēaf and his bladu ne fealwiað ne ne sēariað; eall him cymð tō gōde þæt þæt hē dēð. Ac þā unrihtwīsan ne bēoð nā swelċe, ne him ēac swā ne limpð; ac hīe bēoð dūste ġelīcran, þonne hit wind tōblǣwð. ᚠᛁᚷ · ᚻᛖᚱᚢᚳᛞ ᚹᛁᛚ Þȳ ne ārīsað þā unrihtwīsan on dōmes dæġ, ne þā synfullan ne bēoð on ġeþeahte þǣra rihtwīsena; for þām God wāt hwelċne weġ þā rihtwīsan ġeearnedon, ac þā unrihtwīsan cumað tō wītum. *Sealm* ᚹ

ᛗᛜᚱᛞᛞᛁᚾ

Ben sat in Peter Collinson's study with those, and only those, he trusted to be included in what would now become at least a conspiracy, perhaps even a rebellion. Peter stood to the side of the of his desk, listening intently.

Ben wished that he could have invited other members of the Royal Society, like Ferguson and Sir Pringle, but was hesitant to involve either of his two friends who lacked the knowledge his arcane experimentation. In the end, neither of them was a close enough compatriot to cross this bridge.

And then there was Polly.

Polly sat in a comfortable blue-upholstered oak visitor's chair to the side of the door. She had hesitated only briefly when Ben said her mother could not be included in their discussions, but she had decided to move forward even if that meant excluding Mama. Polly, ever the pragmatist, had to admit it was unclear where her mother's loyalties would lay.

Her struggle with her loyalty to her mother made Ben painfully aware of the one person he most wished could be with him. He swiftly banished the sentiment. His son could not be trusted in this matter. Maybe someday he could be, but that day was not now. That left three people, including himself, to deal with what Ben had learned from Thomas Penn and the King in the Tower of London. After concluding his tale, Ben was greeted with bare incredulity from Peter and a curious and engaged demeanor from Polly. "As I said, he mistook his previous victory over me for me being an inferior intellect to his."

"This is terrible news," Peter said at last. "I don't see how this can be."

"Are you sure it was actually the King?" Polly asked. "Could it not have been a *simulacra* spell of some sort? Perhaps a glamour?"

Ben smiled at the incisive question and the lack of fear the workings of her mind revealed. "I wondered much the same thing. Though I cannot say for a certainty, if it is not truly the King, perhaps Thomas Penn controls the only public-facing form of King George. If that is true, then as we unravel this conspiracy, we will find ourselves saving the King as well as the kingdom. But I do not believe this to be the case. Conspiracies rarely hold up to the light and are often dispelled by the simplest applications of research and logic. Unfortunately, there is more."

Peter's already troubled expression became even more sober. "More?"

"I have a summary of the translated journals from Anthony Askew. I have let Polly read it already, and I think you need to see it as well," Ben said, handing a letter to Peter. "Considering the contents, Anthony has had them removed to a secure location in hopes they can be protected. It has become apparent why they are so sought after."

Peter put down the pages and nodded grimly. Polly was not surprised when Ben spoke first. "As you can see, it is pretty clear why the King and his faction are so desperate to get their hands on these journals. And why they lied to me."

"I can hardly believe what they relate," said Peter, obviously shaken.

"I can," replied Polly. She sounded sad. "It makes so many other things that have happened so clear."

"What do we actually know?" demanded Peter. "I mean, so much of this letter and your report of the King's bargain must be taken on faith."

"Peter, I'm afraid we know a lot more than it may feel we do. Let me tie together what is in those papers so that you may read them later at your leisure." Ben answered gently as he held up a hand and started ticking off points, "From Anthony: this book appears to be written by a man who has been alive since the time of the last Anglo-Saxon king of England. From the Royal Society, this man, then known as Myrddin Emræs, later became known as Merlinus Ambrosius. We thought he was millennia old but may have gotten his age wrong."

Ben glanced at the other two, then continued, "Per Myrddin himself, he was drunk with Geoffrey of Monmouth when they concocted the Merlin myth. Per the Society of Numbers and others: in our own time, he has adopted the monikers 'Lord One,' 'Gasparini,' and 'Mr. Robert Overton.' Once again, from Anthony, as well as our own observations: the handwriting is remarkably similar throughout all the journals, written by a polyglot who employed an idiosyncratic mix of Anglo-Saxon, Latin, Old French, runic Norse, Old English, Elizabethan English, and more modern usages—thus debunking the different writers idea."

Peter breathed deeply to calm a shaking hand and took a sip of lemon water.

"Judging solely by appearance, the journals run the gamut from truly ancient to merely old. They can be easily dated as they incorporate known events in history, minor and major, as well as unknown events of seeming import. Our newly gained insights also explain Myrddin's efforts to find and destroy the journals. The destructive force the comet can unleash is terrifying, and the King wants that power. Desperately. The King who, I will mention, was born just after the last passing of the comet."

"I know all of this." Peter shook his head. "I am sorry for my attitude. I just don't want to believe it."

"I feel so very sorry for Myrddin," Polly interrupted. "He discovered magic before anyone in the known world. He discovered the power of the star metal that falls with every passing of the comet. He made the connection to how much danger the world would be in if that knowledge and power ever got into the wrong hands. He's almost prophetic in how he describes what will happen and the consequences for later times. And then he apprenticed the man who would try to steal that power from the heavens."

"I am afraid that might have been a self-fulfilling prophecy: by describing the dangerous power of the star metal, he essentially created a manual on how to use it for evil; he taught the power-hungry how to use it to gain power," Ben sighed. "I once commented, to much public delight, that with these pretty systems we build, it is only a matter of time before we must be called up to destroy them."

"We often create what we most fear," agreed Peter. "It is poetic, even if I disapprove of the practice of quoting oneself."

"It's such bad poetry, though." Polly was indignant, as only the young can be, at the machinations of life that seem so obvious and trite to the old. "He gathered a group of people attuned to magic to help him protect the world from its abuse, and those same people and their descendants plotted to become the abusers. Myrddin created the situation where the King's faction could hope to take advantage of the star metal's power, unconcerned that it would destroy the countless lives. It's rank. It's rotten. It's just so *unfair*."

"All very true, Polly. But now we must clean up his mess or, if these journals are to be believed, perish." Ben continued, "Myrddin has expressed a great deal of bitterness in his more recent journals, but I don't see how he can blame anyone but himself. He trusted the wrong people. He made bad choices. Now we have to figure out how to undo the damage and prevent catastrophe."

Polly shifted uncomfortably. "So, if the King's faction is merely trying to gain more power, isn't that what nations and empires always do? They have more powerful tools, I will grant you. Any advantage they can get would always be irresistible to them."

"Indeed," agreed Franklin. "What I can't understand is why they would choose the path they have. When they use the comet to cast their dark spell, it will destroy the world as we know it. The world will know only fear and suffering. Supposedly, it will call forth monsters and creatures from other realms and worlds beyond our understanding. A return to the times of giants and fairies, dragons and mages is what he says. It will be Hell on Earth. And this will be done so the elect will be able to create what they believe will be an immortal empire, where the most evil and selfish desires of favored members of the King's faction live forever. They believe they will be able to do as they wish, to whomever they wish, for well-nigh unto eternity."

"They will divorce this world from God's creation," shuddered Peter. "They will deny themselves, and all who dwell upon the Earth, any hope of salvation. They will create Hell so they may rule it."

"It is clear from those journals that Myrddin believes that without that metal, the King's faction won't be able to cast its spell," Polly said. "I say we steal their hoard of star metal artifacts and make sure they can never even try to do this again."

"But, Polly," said Peter, "that means we will have to move directly against the King. And steal from the King's holdings. That's treason. That way is madness incarnate."

"Begging your pardon, sir," Polly said respectfully. "The way I see it, if I have to choose between a King who doesn't care about me and is satisfied to let most of the world die for his personal gain, it's not a hard choice."

Ben nodded in agreement. "The King's faction's heartfelt belief is that they are the only people who are worthy to live. I shudder to think what they will do with that much magic. Are we to simply sit back and let the world be destroyed because an evil man was crowned king?"

"Bloody hells, this argument is pointless." Polly slapped the desk to get their attention. Peter winced at the use of profanity, but he didn't interrupt. She grabbed the papers and quickly scanned through them. "See what Anthony says here: one percent of one percent of one percent are born with magic in their veins. That means there are what, four hundred people, maybe, who can use magic in the world? Look, here. At least a dozen mages are here in London. It's disproportionate, but either or both of us is on that list. What's worse is that of those that can't, one in two will pay the price with their lives if the King casts the spell Myrddin is talking about in the journals. That is hundreds of millions of deaths across the globe. That's half a million deaths just in this city. He isn't a man, he's a *bloody* monster."

"Ben, Polly, this is treason. I cannot simply agree to treason. Can you not see that? At least not without more proof. We are taking Myrddin's story as true; we are holding that your conclusions of your experience are all there is to know about things, to understand the truth. The Truth is not usually so easily named."

"We must oppose evil, Mr. Collinson," Polly said. She truly didn't understand why he was being so cautious, so obtuse. "Surely that is what God demands of us. We see the evil. Now we must stop it. Or try our best to. Anything less is to be a part of the evil, should we refuse to stand against it."

"Thee has so much vigor, so much passion, Polly. But I cannot be swayed by thee. It is thy very passion that will divide thee from the Lord's path and blind thee to the Lord's will. I cannot so quickly discern what the Lord's will is in this matter." Peter Collinson rose from the table. "I am used to sitting with my fellow Quakers and having their aid in understanding the Lord's way forward, but I cannot expose any of them to the consequences of this undertaking. I must sit in silence and wait for the Spirit to light the way to life and darken the path that leads to death. I cannot turn my back on the Truth, no matter where it leads, but first I must feel that I know the way forward in Truth. Please forgive me. I will send Mary to attend to your needs. Understand, I want to oppose this, to know more before we act in such a treasonous way, but I cannot listen only to my own wishes in this matter." He clasped Ben's shoulder and smiled sadly to Polly, then left quietly.

"Sit in silence?" asked Polly.

"He will seek an inward retirement so that he may open himself to the voice of God," Ben replied. "Quakers believe that if they are sufficiently still, the Holy Spirit will guide them in all matters. He must follow the path he feels God is guiding him to take. He must not act in his own will, but instead he must be obedient to the guidance he is given. We must respect his faith."

"Fine, but I don't need to sit in silence." Polly jabbed a finger into the papers. "We must stop them, King and all."

The
Collinson Home
Ridgeway House,
Mill Hill, Middlesex
January 13th
✤ ✤ ✤

✢ 34 ✢
Let's Save the World

It was several hours before Peter returned. Mary kept Polly and Ben well-fed and well-watered with fresh breads and cheeses complemented by the Collinson house favorite, lemon water. With the late hour, tea had also been offered. Everything in the home was warm and inviting, from the smells of the baking breads to the cozy drafts of the fire and the fragrances of the indoor flora. Mary had further engaged them both by bringing a chess set into her husband's study and sitting with them for a couple games. Late that night, when Peter opened the door, both Polly and Ben looked up from their game with a start, and then turned to him expectantly.

"I have listened to the Holy Spirit, and I have spoken at some length with my wife. I feel quite clear. The way forward is assisting in preventing the planned calamity, but I am afraid that I cannot take part in an action that will lead to violence. I cannot support it," Peter said.

"You're saying we should give in to their evil plans?" Polly demanded.

"I am afraid you do not yet quite understand the Quaker mindset, Polly," Ben interjected. "If I may illuminate," he asked looking at Peter, who nodded his consent as he took a seat next to them. "He cannot join with the King's faction because he would be supporting actions that would very likely lead to the harm and death of many people. It would be the same whether he voted for a military appropriation or stabbed a man to death personally. Quakers don't hold much with doing things by halves, and even peripherally engaging in violent action would violate his deeply held convictions. That does not mean there aren't other things he could do, by way of opposition, as long as it didn't devolve to violence."

Peter nodded, "I do find myself at a crossroads, but my time of private retirement has eased my sense of burden somewhat. I am prepared to see what aid I can offer to this effort to prevent the downfall of everything familiar."

Ben turned to Peter. "You could just withdraw from this affair. I think the King's faction would not be concerned if you simply stepped aside. He held the Royal Society in less than high esteem."

Peter held up his hand. "I know that I must oppose this group. They would use this force of magic to warp and weave the will of men. They are turning away from the Light, turning against the will of God. Whether a man is deprived of free will via a court, shackle, lash, or magic, such are of this world and not of God. They must be opposed, for I must oppose both the physical enslavement of the children of God and their magical enslavement as well." He paused and looked troubled. "Oppose without resorting to violence against another, of course."

"How are we to even consider doing this without violence?" Polly asked.

"By being strong. By choosing the path that God guides us to take."

Polly stared absently, chewing her lip, deep in thought.

"Of course, Peter," Ben said, speaking to his long-time friend. "I suspected as much from you. You would not shy away from a task no matter how great the danger or how terrible the power that opposed you. No one will ask you to violate your convictions. It is that very strength that is one of the qualities I admire the most about you. You will stand fast before any power that seeks to harm."

"Power is not all that troubles me, Ben. Nor is it all that should trouble you. Understand what we would embark upon. Shall we stand against the Throne? This is the Throne we have been loyal to our entire lives, unquestioningly up to this point."

Ben regarded both Peter and Polly, then said, "I'm loyal to the

Throne. Always. I'm only loyal to the King when he deserves my loyalty. He is the one that betrayed the Throne and the land, not us."

"I concur." Peter nodded. "Just as a church is not God, the King is not the Throne."

Ben looked and saw they were all in agreement. "Well good, then. All we have to do now is invent a way to oppose a secret and powerful organization armed with both vast political power and legal authority, as well as potent magics we know little of. We will need to do this not understanding the scope of their power, the precise outline of their plans, or the resources they will be able to bring to bear."

Polly cleared her throat. "Is it that hard? They need the star metal to perform the ritual, according to the journals. If we want to avoid violence and confrontation—"

"I have no problem with confrontation. Only with violence," Peter interrupted.

"Yes, well," Polly continued, "be as that may, if there is confrontation, it could lead to violence, so better to avoid it. So, as I was saying, why don't we figure out where all the artifacts are and just steal them?"

"As easy as that?" Peter mused.

"As easy as that, Mr. Collinson. Right, Ben?"

"I believe we have the beginnings of a plan. And about two months to execute it." Ben raised his lemon water high, "To magic and treason."

"To God, the Truth and the Light," Peter responded, lifting his glass as well.

"Let's save the world," said Polly.

Part 3: A Bell

About a Bell, which must be rung,
that a new world may be born.

1759

The
Night of the Comet
March 13th
✢ ✢ ✢

Kensington Palace
London, England
✤ ✤ ✤

❖ 35 ❖
Funny You Should Say That

"I'm not sure, Mr. Collinson." Polly Stevenson and Peter Collinson walked toward Kensington Palace with the moon high overhead. They had left Craven Street a little less than an hour before. Most of their journey had been in silence, but as they were drawing close to their destination, Polly finally initiated conversation. "It seems foolhardy to split up. I know we've been searching London for weeks with no results but... Just like a game of chess, we need to attack the center of the board."

"Three thoughts come to mind: the first being that the King is the center, and it would be foolhardy to attack the King." Peter turned to Polly. "The second being that we have two people capable of performing magic, three final locations, and one night. Those are not good odds. The third, and final, being that if we were all in one place and something went wrong, then there would be no one to continue the efforts. I'm not the chess player that you are, but the weakness in playing against a superior opponent and simply attacking the center is that it is what one always does. Doing what one always does is too predictable, and I can only think that the reason that they are so confident is because they are waiting for the attack to the center. When you are cleverer at people than deep strategy, you learn that you can interchange them."

Polly glanced sidelong at Peter. "Funny you should say that. That is how I insulted William the first week the Franklins lodged with us."

"It's not meant as an insult. And from that, I take it you play the player as much as the board?"

She nodded.

"Then let's look at it this way—King George and his cadre, especially Thomas Penn, understand exactly how Ben thinks. As clever as he is, as sociable, and as well as he normally navigates politics, Penn has been far ahead of him every step of the way. So, by avoiding the way that Ben thinks, we are shifting tactics. Our strategy cannot change, but our tactics can. We will go to the left, as they expect Ben to go to the right." Peter pointed up. "We're out of time. The comet is overhead."

"Yes, and, is that the palace?" Polly pointed ahead as a great lawn opened before them, with gardens to either side and wrapping around the palace to the rear. The palace itself was a three-story monstrosity that had numerous wings and over one hundred rooms. She gulped. "This place is larger than all of Craven Street combined. I believe that is the servants' building over there."

"Indeed it is." Peter peered at a small sketched map, then folded it up and placed back in his jacket pocket. "Shall we?"

As Peter and Polly made their way to an entrance on the far side of the second set of apartments, between the main building and the far lodge, Polly began making her calculations, obscuring them from the vision of anyone who may be watching. It wasn't enough that they were being silent. They couldn't risk discovery at all, so once they were close, she used a glamour to hide them completely from the servants and guards, though they could see each other. They listened to the general chatter.

One of the older maids chatted amiably with a bored looking footman, "I know the King has let the place go a bit, but it has only been since his good wife Queen Caroline departed this Earth that he has been this way. I think they should let a man have his grief and not harp on him for this and that."

They snuck past the two, only to turn a corner to another conversation.

"Mistress, I know. It's the wildling. He frightens me. Why allow the man-beast to roam here? The thing is touched by the fairies. I thought it was supposed to be at the farms. It gives me the creeps."

"Pah. Superstition. The thing was cursed, but the devil's been cast out of it. They gave it a good Christian name. Peter, they calls it now. Avoid it, and it'll avoid you, I'm sure the King'll move it back as soon as he's noticed it's wandered back to the palace."

They moved on. There were a few near-misses when people nearly ran into them, or when Peter Collinson accidentally knocked something, that made things a little nerve-wracking, but soon Polly saw what they were looking for: a well-dressed lady's maid purposefully striding by with a freshly laundered gown carefully draped across her arms.

Polly gestured to Peter silently, and they began following her. When a housemaid came too close, the young woman sternly commanded, "*Aus meinem Weg, Bauer.*"

As they passed, the housemaid pulled a face behind the back of the lady's maid and muttered, "Damm'd Germans."

Peter nodded emphatically to Polly, and they continued on their way. They exited the servants' lodge and walked across the gardens to the main house. Finally, the lady's maid led them to an apartment in the private residences at the palace. They followed her into a dressing room, where she set out the dress carefully and was turning to go when they all heard a commanding voice. "*Friedegunde, was hast du getan? Verlassen! Aus!*"

Friedegunde gave a little squeak, and with a rapid curtsy, said "*Entschuldigung, Gräfin Amalie Sophie, Entschuldigung, Bitte,*" and scampered as quickly as she could from the room.

"*Ich weiß, dass du hier bist, kleine Maus. Wo sind sie? Oder bist du eine englische Maus?* I will not have my private rooms invaded so rudely. Who are you? *Jetzt!*" A woman walked into the room wearing a long yellow gown and carrying a small black terrier. She had piercing black eyes and long brown hair that framed soft features.

Polly put her finger to her lips and indicated to Peter to go look for the artifacts. She then uncloaked herself, curtsying deeply, "My lady Countess, my name is Mary. I am seeking a great sorceress. I felt there was one here, and my seeking led me to you. I was hoping you would take time. Talk to me. I mean, take time to talk to me!"

Amalie Sophie Marianne von Wallmoden, Countess of Yarmouth

stood regally, slowly petting her terrier and regarding Polly, "Really? Why would I do any such thing?"

Polly came out of her curtsy. "There are so few of us. I had hoped you would be able to teach me. I would apprentice myself to you and provide whatever assistance you require."

Amalie Sophie's eyes narrowed dangerously. "*Gib mir deine stärke, Teiwaz.*" She snuggled her dog into the crook of her right arm and pointed at Polly with her left. "I am not much interested in teaching vagabonds to rise above their station. Nor am I interested in talking with little liars who are trying to deceive me." She snapped her fingers.

Polly rocked back as the invisible slap reddened her cheek.

"Now truthfully, girl, why are you here?"

Polly froze, then carefully let tears spring from her eyes. "Forgive me, Countess. I just thought, maybe, I just thought—"

"You thought what? That I couldn't tell the difference between a girl with homespun talent from someone who rises with the comet? That I wouldn't be offended by lies?" She snapped her fingers again, and the terrier began to growl.

Polly braced herself just in time, but the second slap still stung.

"Please stop, Countess." Polly rubbed at her cheek.

"One does not stand before the storm and beg it to stop, *Wicht.*" She started throwing her hand forward snapping her fingers in rapid succession. With each snap, another blow landed on Polly. "When the storm rises, you *run.*"

Polly crossed her arms in front of her face, taking the pounding for the moment. She saw in her peripheral vision when Peter returned, shaking his head.

"And don't think," Amalie Sophie said, "I am so ignorant as to think you are here alone!" She raised her hand and snapped as Polly began a series of rapid calculations and the air between the two women shimmered. Peter watched on helplessly, as even he could feel the change in the atmosphere of the room. The Countess looked directly at him. "*Die Hölle??* Who are you?"

The door crashed open and a man unlike anything Peter or Polly had ever seen crashed into the room. He had curly black hair and wide features, looking like he belonged in the wild, not in a castle. He wore a green jacket and no shirt, but a wide, dirty leather collar bound his neck. "George! George! George!" he screeched.

The Countess held up a hand, fingers splayed. Heat shimmered and sparks danced along the barrier between the two mages. "Hush, Peter, my little Wild Boy. It is aright. You are safe."

Collinson watched, stunned, and Polly kept trying to break the barrier as the wildling jumped in place, shouting George's name.

An irritated Countess looked at Polly, "I don't have time for this, and now you have robbed me of my chance to be properly dressed for this evening, *du Nagetier!*" Then Amalie Sophie Marianne von Wallmoden, Countess of Yarmouth, mistress to the King of England, sent a blast at Peter the Wild Boy, sending him flying into the two intruders. She sped to the closet door and went through it with her little terrier in tow.

Polly raced to the door as the scared wildling rolled himself away and huddled, but when she opened it, she saw only a closet for gowns and no exit. "Lobc—" Polly turned to Peter the Wild Boy and froze, addressing Peter the Quaker. "Um. I can't believe it. She has a Manydoor. Overton taught me about these things. I might be able to figure out how to work it, but what do we do with him?"

Collinson walked up to the wilding, unafraid. He stroked the man's hair, calming him. "It's okay. I know who you are. I know Dr. Arbuthnot. He helped the men from the Royal Society. Do you remember? You got to eat cake."

Peter the Wild Boy nodded.

Collinson smiled warmly. "Good. Can you go to the kitchens and get food? Are you hungry?"

The wildling nodded uncertainly but seemed calmed as he left.

Peter turned to the amazed Polly. "I believe you were going to figure out how that woman vanished?"

She nodded mutely and turned to the closet door, studying the portal.

The White Tower, Tower of London

London, England

✛ ✛ ✛

✢ 36 ✢
Tonight Was the Night

The night was eerily silent, brightened by the moon and the comet overhead. It rained gently, despite the lack of clouds in the sky. Myrddin was afraid. It was an odd sensation. It wasn't that he didn't have every right to be afraid, or any reason. Over the years he had witnessed and endured events that had, until today, largely disconnected him from that emotion. He had never thought the world a friendly place. People were bastards. They used each other, they hurt each other. He would have called it all long ago, and just been done with the human race, except that amid the deepest perfidies, he found people overcoming them with compassion and self-sacrifice.

Life was—complex.

And now he found himself afraid not for himself but for the world. It was a *tord* place to be, but no one else was going to stand up and try to save everyone. There was also a deeper truth that, in the tiniest of ways, all this might have been his unwitting fault. He didn't know if he was going to succeed, after all these centuries of planning and effort, but it was time to step out of the shadows regardless. He was out of time and so, perhaps, was the world.

Funny how the mind works, he thought, *living in the past when it's afraid it's going to be snuffed out in the present.*

He had fought on ancient battlefields with swords swinging and

327

arrows flying. Starting with Harold Godwinson, he had watched kings, queens, cities, and nations rise and fall. He had seen many more thousands perish in the natural course of events, felled by disease, accident, old age. All in the normal order of things, a normal order of chaos and greed and selfishness. And because of this cursed star metal, he had lived through it all, a poor soldier who watched his own king slaughtered. He shivered, pulling his cloak tighter.

So why was he afraid now? He was approaching the Tower of London, anticipating a battle with those he had once believed to be fighting on his side, on the side of order and normalcy. Of his two apprentices from the last coming of the comet, one had rejected magic and retired to the country as a simple chemist, choosing to run. The other was a King, and oh, what he could have done . . .

He had been betrayed before; perhaps that should not have bothered him. He had met many of these same people in this same place, the White Tower in the Tower of London, where he had shown them Hew Draper's carving, explained most of its import to them, and shown them how to use the Manydoor. He had given them every weapon they now had trained on him. And still he feared, because still he had hope.

This time, entering the Tower would be a very different experience. He would walk right in. He could not use the Manydoor, *Monegumdór*, not until he found a replacement handle, or the one stolen while he was in the Colonies. Instead, he must remove obstacles.

He walked up to the main gates of the White Tower: The Tower of London. The name was misleading. The Tower of London was not just a singular tower jutting up into the night. It was a vast walled compound with more than a dozen towers in the two concentric walls surrounding the main "tower." The White Tower had been built as the fortified new home of William the Conqueror. He hated it; it reminded him of the oppression of the conquering Normans. Walking to the front gates, he dropped his cloak to the ground, revealing resplendent robes of blue and red, clasped across the chest by a jade and black brooch: the same one he had taken back from Polly when she had thought she killed him.

He touched the brooch lightly, muttering, "*Eorlgewæde.*" Wind swirled, nipping at his heels, then gusting up along his robes. Each tiny fiber of cloth welcomed in the wind, grabbing tiny gusts with errant strands, until finally the gusting settled to stillness. The breeze hadn't departed, but rather had settled on him, an invisible secondary cloak.

"Halt! Who goes there?" A voice carried from the entry to the tower. A single guard rushed out, but at the cry of *Halt!*, several more followed. Myrddin was immediately surrounded by guards wearing the red robes of the King's personal force.

"I am Merlin Ambrosius, known to some as Myrddin Wyllt, of Caledonensis, of Aurelianus, protector of England and Wizard of the court for his Majesty Arthur Pendragon." One lesson he had learned over the years—a little theater never hurt and, with the comet directly overhead, he was at the height of his powers. He could put on a show. And a night like tonight, this was why he had gotten Geoffrey drunk and spun this story. He spread his arms wide. "Stand aside, or I *will* move you."

The guard laughed. "Right then. Nice to meet ya, Merlin. Off ya go, ya drunken sot, before we throw you in a cell!"

"When the day comes that you talk of this night, tall tales told to your grandchildren, tell them that tonight was the night Merlin spared your life." He tilted his palms upward as the guard laughed and in his deepest voice, declaimed, "*Þunorrádstefn!*"

The wind swirled in his palms, invisibly, building more and more pressure as it spun so fast it left a vortex in the center of each of the tiny cyclones. As the guards watched in confusion, Merlin breathed deeply, dropping his palms, then exhaled as he slowly pushed his palms forward from his chest. The two invisible cyclones collapsed and a massive boom sounded. The shockwave caught the laughing guard full in the chest and knocked him backward off his feet. He slid along the ground, unconscious, coming to a gentle rest against the Tower's wall.

All three guards carrying crossbows leveled the weapons and loosed bolts at the mage. The bonded wind released from the threads of his robes, snapping the bolts as they struck him and grinding them to splinters just inches from his flesh.

Enough guards had gathered, and close enough, that he was pretty sure he could hit them all with one spell. "*Slæp.*" A series of thumps sounded as the guards all hit the ground, fast asleep.

He walked through the bailey, leaving the guards in the entry field, but stopped before he was even halfway to the White Tower. He shook his head, then tilted it to the side, listening. What he wanted was to the right. In the Salt Tower.

Of course that's where he put it. Of course. He shook his head and strode to a section of the castle he knew all too well.

The Salt Tower entrance was protected by a locked gate and two guards—nothing more. The guards gladly opened the gate for the King, or so they believed, and then swiftly fell asleep. It was only when he entered the tower complex itself that he saw another living soul: a man tending to the lamps in the tower who paid him no heed.

Myrddin had no problem finding his way through the Tower. He had been there when it was built, and he had been a regular visitor over the years, in one capacity or another. Myrddin moved down the darkened hallways, illuminating his own way just enough to avoid any hazards. As he came closer to the King's inner sanctum, candles had already been lit, and their flickering light greeted him, showing him the way he already knew. Myrddin stopped in front of the doorway, took a deep, sad breath, and squared his shoulders. It was time to put an end to this.

St. James's Palace
London, England
✤ ✤ ✤

❖ 37 ❖
No One Could Do More

Ben, having successfully enlisted the aid of his man Peter, made his way towards St. James's Palace with his servant by his side. The regular clicks of Ben's cane sounded steadily on the cobblestones.

Tap, Tap, Tap.

The early evening air was crisp and chilly. From Craven Street, it was only a fifteen- or twenty-minute walk, for which Ben was extremely grateful. He had been trying to reserve his use of magic for any offensive or defensive maneuver he might have to engage in, rather than easing the discomfort of his leg and hip. He wasn't sure the pain itself wasn't costing him more than he could afford to lose, but no matter.

"Mr. Franklin?" Peter asked.

"Yes, Peter?"

"Is this the only way to protect things? Are you sure we can't tell someone else what is going on? Have them call everyone to account?"

"Sadly, there is no one who could do more than we, which means we would be sad excuses for men if we opted to do less."

"There's no one? Can't we just tell everyone then?"

"That," said Ben, glancing up at the comet overhead, "would be lovely. But in England, there are no authorities to turn to that would actively work against the King."

333

"The people are not an authority?" Peter asked, surprise obvious in his tone.

Ben paused and sighed. "I sometimes forget how insightful you can be. No, sadly. Not in the way we would need them to be. Politicking and back room bargaining? Englishmen can do that all day long. Acting to remove a king who is a menace to life and liberty? That is not a path they wish to follow again. Unfortunately for us, we seem to be the ones called to this action."

"I see that. I really do. I just guess I wish it wasn't so." Peter stood a little straighter. "But that is neither here nor there, is it? If no one else can stand against the King, then we stand for them, yeah?"

"That is so," agreed Ben. "And we stand as tall as we can. Or limp, in my case."

"So where is it that we are going?"

"We, my friend, are going to St. James's Palace. It is where the King holds court and is also where he and his mistress have each their own apartments. We hope that we will find what we are looking for there, and this business can be concluded."

"We're looking for things that make power, like that key you had?"

"Just so, just so." Ben nodded.

As they approached the palace, they were startled to hear a voice calling Ben's name. "Benjamin Franklin! What in the world are you doing here?" Ben turned to see Sir John Pringle descending upon them.

"Sir John, what a surprise!" Ben offered a little weakly. He subtly motioned for Peter to stand slightly back.

"Are you headed to St. James's? If you are, I am happy for the company, for I head there myself!" Sir John was full of energy. "I imagine you are on your way to see William. He has been there nearly every time I have needed to visit. It is amazing how the King has taken to him—you must be so proud."

Ben blinked for a moment, then said, "Indeed, I had hoped I might be able to see him. Unfortunately, I do not have an official invitation. I was merely taking my chances. Should I not be so lucky, it is just a nice nightly walk for me and my man here."

"Then the good Lord is looking out for you, and your chance is right in front of you!" Sir John was overwhelming in his excitement and effervescence. He walked them directly into the palace, the guards not taking any notice of them. "I believe he has been frequenting the King's Presence Chamber. Let's see if we can locate him."

Sir John led them through the many halls and chambers of St. James's with the certainty that only considerable familiarity would bring. Ben began to feel more than a little disquiet. "Sir John. You have much more familiarity than I would have expected. Is there something I don't know?"

"Why would there be anything you wouldn't know, Ben?"

"I am just surprised at the alacrity with which you are walking us through the palace. I thought we were friends, but this doesn't feel very friendly."

"We are the best of friends!" Sir John laughed as he led them forward through gilded halls, past suits of armor and portraits of the long-dead. "The Royal Society operates under the King's grant. Why would you think we didn't communicate our findings to the King? Accept his benevolence, my friend, and the King will reward you."

Ben shot a warning glance to Peter, who nodded quietly in return.

Sir John led them into an audience chamber. The room was two stories tall, with a six-foot-tall fireplace on the long wall interrupting the tan wallpaper and gold trim. Unlike the other rooms, there was less decoration in this room. Ben understood why it was called the Presence Chamber now. A dozen people milled about, talking, but there was no throne in the room.

Peter tugged on Ben's sleeve and whispered, "There's Mr. William, just over there."

William was indeed there—dressed in his best finery, which still looked drab next to the white- and gold-fur trimmed velvet suit the King wore—in a private circle, talking to George the Second. Ben saw William gesture toward them, and the King turned to look at them. George lazily waved a white gloved hand and the man to his left politely, but rapidly, emptied the room of everyone but William, Sir John, Ben, and Peter.

The King walked to the fireplace, resting a hand on the mantle. "I do not see, Benjamin Franklin, that you have brought any of the things I asked for to me. Your payment is due, and yet you do not remit. What can you mean? I did tell you what the penalty would be."

Ben bowed, then said, "I was unable to find these things. I told you I had them once, but they are no longer in my possession."

The King slapped his hand down on the marble mantle. "It is not what you currently possess. It is your knowledge. What do you know of the star metal that Merlin ferreted away? The Key was a piece of it, but there is considerably more. You must have some knowledge. I will have that knowledge. *Now*."

Ben raised his hands and took a step back.

William bowed, and stayed bowed, while he interrupted his father's protestations. "Your Majesty, forgive the interruption, what are you asking about? You and Mr. Penn only told me you sought my father."

King George turned to him, "You told us your father had possession of a key made of the star metal. I am aware that it was cast from artifacts that had been melted down. The Key does not account for all that was lost. In fact, it is only a tiny fraction of it. Though we cannot seize that lost metal, I am positive your father knows where the rest has gone."

"Oh," said William, interrupting a second attempt at protestation from his father. "That. I know where that is. Why didn't you ask *me*? The Assembly's new bell and father's Key were cast at the same foundry here in England. Mr. Loxley told us all about it when he gave father the Key."

The King's eyes grew wide. "Where is this bell?"

William looked from the King to the Ben, who shook his head, and then back to the King, "It is in Philadelphia. At the Assembly Hall."

"*Gib mir deine stärke, Tyr,*" King George muttered, then smiled at William. "Thank you, William. I knew you would be useful." He waved his right hand toward him, sending a bolt of lightning smashing into William's chest. William went flying sideways, crunching into the wall, then fell to the floor where he lay unmoving.

"William!"

Peter ran to the younger Franklin and knelt.

"*LUX!*" Ben shouted as he ran forward. Lightning arced from both of his hands in great fiery bolts, sputtering with deadly intent and ripping apart the air between Ben and George.

George the Second waved his left hand, and the white lightning jumped into his palm. It wrapped around his arms, lovingly pulsing around his body like a serpent, beginning to crackle. He threw back his head and laughed. "Fire from the heavens? You know nothing of the old gods. Before there was Christianity, there were the gods of the Hanovers." He thrust his right hand forward. Ben flew up nearly to the ceiling as the lightning smashed into him. He hung there for a moment, then George swiftly lowered his hand, and Ben crashed to the floor, hard. He felt the floor hit the side of his head, then everything went black for just a second. Everything hurt and the world spun about as he lay there stunned.

The King turned to Sir John, "I believe we are needed at the Tower. Who is that?" He paused and pointed to Peter, who carefully tended William and tried not to attract notice.

"It's just the Franklin slave, Majesty." Sir John bowed, then went to the door of the chamber. He put his hand to the door, then said, "The tower is ready."

King George strode to the door as Sir John opened it. On the other side, Ben could just see the room in the Tower of London where he had seen the artifacts. Eight weeks of searching, assuming they would have moved them to keep the location hidden, and all along they were in the *tower??* Ben groaned. Every muscle in his body hurt, and if that wasn't enough, he had just sustained a major blow to his pride. Through the door there were flashes of light and a loud boom. George the Second and Sir John looked at each other, then Sir John ran through the entry. The King followed immediately behind him.

The door shut, and the two men were gone.

Peter ran to Ben, quickly assessing his injuries. Blood gushed from Ben's nose and he seemed to have numerous broken ribs. His right arm and his right leg were both broken badly, and, when Peter tested it, Ben had no feeling in the fingers of his right hand. Peter sat down carefully and put a hand on his shoulder. He had seen far lesser injuries prove fatal many times.

"Peter," Ben said weakly, "help me up. We must hurry to the Tower." There was a slight whistling gargle coming from his chest every time he breathed in.

"Mr. Franklin, you are not going anywhere," Peter said sorrowfully.

Ben turned his head to the side. "I see. William?"

"He's fine. He'll wake in no time," Peter lied.

The door George had departed through opened again. Peter's shoulders slumped. He was prepared for it to be the King again, come back to finish the business, or perhaps the King's Guard. Instead, it was an old woman in an unusually plain dress reminiscent of a mountain skirt and huge boots, like a soldier wore. She was clad the clothes of the working class yet carried the demeanor of gentility. White hair was tucked up under a cap, and she sported a kerchief and apron. She stomped into the room, squinting and looking down her nose at the scene. "Well. Isn't this untidy."

Someone was holding the door open for her, he realized. It was . . . *King?*

Peter gaped, "King, you young fool, where have you been? What have you done? Am I ever so glad to see you, but how—"

King held a large black leather book in his hands. "I have work to do." He glanced once more at Peter and Ben, a little balefully, as he flipped open the book. Ben's breathing was ever more shallow, and his eyes drifted closed. "I must hurry."

The former Franklin slave knelt next to Ben, looking down to the Bible he held, and began to read the first Psalm: "Blessed is the man that walketh not in the counsel of the ungodly, nor standeth in the way of sinners, nor sitteth in the seat of the scornful. But his delight is in the law of the Lord; and in his law doth he meditate day and night." A golden glow began to surround King as he read, "And he shall be like a tree planted by the rivers of the water, that bringeth forth his fruit in his season; his leaf also shall not wither; and whatsoever he doeth shall prosper—"

Peter backed away in awe, still on hands and knees. King continued and the glow spread, its soft light moving gently out to encompass Ben as well. The old woman turned to Peter, holding out her hand. "Come away now, young man. I am the Widow Eversleigh, and you are going to help an old woman stand steady."

Peter nodded and shuffled to his feet. He stood next to the widow, and she looped a hand through the crook of his arm. "Much better, thank you!"

"How? How did this come to be?" Peter asked in hushed tones. "He can read now?"

"Eh?" The widow glanced askew at Peter. "You believe that malarkey too? Pah. He's a bright young boy. Just like my nephew

Stephen, he only needed to be taught his letters and given a good Christian upbringing. And to read my Reggie's secret notes, of course."

"In just a year, he's come this far? I'm sorry, I have so many questions. He can use magic? Are you a witch?"

"Ha! I'm sure there's plenty as would like to call me a witch, but no. My family tends to the cloth, with the exception of my granny. Did I mention my darling nephew? He's a vicar. What a good boy. Learned to tend his letters from me and his religion at Salisbury Cathedral. You know, even with the comet overhead, I don't have the skill King has, nor the talent. My husband, God rest his soul, did though. Trained under Merlin himself. I listened carefully to my granny and learned hard everything she taught. It was simple enough to teach it to King, between what Reggie left me and my own family secret. Yes indeed."

Peter shook his head. "That makes no sense. How did you come to be here?"

"You think I let those journals slip out of my hands? No. When my dear husband, who loved studying those, died—I sent them far and wide, all thirty of 'em, to make sure we'd have help stopping those as would hurt people. It ain't how we came to be here, it's how you came to me."

King kept reading, but at this point the glow completely covered both of them.

The Widow Eversleigh kept on talking. "We paid attention to the portents, and whatnots, of course. Can't be too careful with portents. Never know when they're gonna lead you astray. When the time was right, we activated the Manydoor. My nephew, did I mention him? He brought me a Manydoor from the cathedral. He's a good boy now, though—stopped all the thieving and studied to become a Vicar. This," she waved her hand, "is what I was meant to enable, by the Lord's grace."

Peter was stunned by the cessation of verbal onslaught, but at the same moment King concluded his recitation. The glow receded, and Ben sat up, looking at King in wonder.

"Thank you." Ben patted himself down, in shock that all the bits seemed to be in place. "What of William?"

"You're welcome," King said dryly and closed his Bible. He looked over at William, still unmoving. Slowly he stood and walked over to the younger Franklin. "A good Christian holds forgiveness in his heart. I will try to forgive him. But he is gone. There may be a way, but not yet." He nudged the prone William with a toe. "I'm sorry. He was a crap master and a crap person, but still, I'm sorry for you."

Ben stood stock still, ignoring the tears streaming down his face. His jaw clenched. His back straightened. At his sides, his fists clenched until his knuckles popped. "I am going to kill the King." He said it simply, a statement of intention, and to no one in particular. Ben wiped at his eyes with the back of his sleeve, then looked at the Widow Eversleigh, "Can this Manydoor get us to the Tower of London?"

The Salt Tower, Tower of London

Tower of London

London, England

❖ ❖ ❖

✤ 38 ✤
Meiko!

"So, it's finally time, is it?" the pompously dressed man said.

Myrddin just looked at the stranger, unimpressed. "I assume you are one of George's ridiculous lackeys. He was always good at surrounding himself with the worst."

"Lackey?" The man's lips went thin and his eyebrow twitched. "I am Thomas Penn, the True and Absolute Proprietor of the Province of Pennsylvania. You will yield, Merlin Emræs."

"My name, minion, is Myrddin. Merlin is a myth I created for the masses, which you purport to not be."

"So, all that outside?" Thomas inquired.

"Just a show to grow the legend. But enough talk, where—"

With a swift motion, Thomas flung his arms wide and white fire erupted from his hands. It landed where Myrddin had been, scorching the walls and floor, but he had vanished.

"*Æris.*" Thomas turned just in time for an airborne lamp to hit him on the side of the head. He was knocked off his feet, and hot wax burned his cheek below the slice on his temple. From his prone position—without pause—he took out a small silver horn from under his shirt and blew into it. No sound was heard, but Myrddin knew the artifact. The horn was an artifact of war, used to summon others to one's aid.

He smiled grimly and slapped his hands together in a booming clap. "*ABRECAN!*"

The horn crumbled to ash, a big enough surprise that Thomas froze. They had thought the metal indestructible. Myrddin made no such mistake. "*Æris.*" He started wildly flinging his hands, using the fairly-easy-to-maintain spell to hurl everything he could see that wasn't bolted down at Thomas Penn. A stanchion, dragging rope, clipped the back of Thomas's skull as he tried to regain his feet.

The proprietor curled into a ball, stunned, trying to protect his head.

The door opened, revealing a Manydoor, and a regal-looking woman stepped through with a terrier in her arms.

Thomas grunted, struggling to throw off the daze and rejoin the fight as he was pelted.

The Countess didn't wait. Flinging her hand forward she snapped, focusing her gaze on her target.

His air armor protected him from physical attack, but not magical. Myrddin threw his left hand up to cast a defensive spell but was too late. The force blow the Countess had thrown landed between his legs, and he doubled over in pain. "*Boardrand!*" He grunted and slapped his thigh.

He straightened up, his shield spell protecting him as the woman rained invisible blows down with each snap. "*Æris babilónum,*" he gasped through his tears. In the normal course of events, Myrddin didn't need his hands to cast; but controlling so many threads simultaneously was too taxing. He needed the extra focus.

Myrddin waved his right hand at Thomas, sending him flying across the room just as he was about to regain his feet. Simultaneously, he waved his left hand at Amalie Sophie. She was lifted bodily till she was pinned in the air. He left her suspended there, his left hand held up while he wove his right hand in a pattern around his left. "*Handfaestnung!*"

The terrier fell from her arms as the spell took hold and immobilized her hands. It ran at Myrddin, growling and trying to bite his heels, where it drew blood from his ankle. With a grunt he kicked it. The terrier yelped once before it was silenced by impacting the ceiling.

"Meiko!" the Countess screamed. The terrier whimpered at the sound of its name. When Thomas tried to stand, yet again, Myrddin closed his right hand with a muttered, "*Basengen,*" and a flash of light erupted around Thomas. He screamed in pain. From the hallway, six men in courtly attire—Fellows of the Royal Society loyal to the King—ran into the room just in time to see the flash. They all shied away, agog at the scene of destruction in the room. It was one thing to see small parlor tricks and know magic was real. It was a completely different thing to see wizards battling and wish magic wasn't real.

Myrddin grunted, scanning them for any visible artifacts. If he could destroy enough of them, the King's spell would misfire. Even though they were all a hundred times stronger with the comet overhead, it wouldn't be enough. Proximity counted, and there was only so much casting a single person could do before they started consuming their own body to power the spells. None of the cowering men had anything visible.

Before Myrddin could act further, the Manydoor opened again, and this time a burly man burst in, quickly followed by King George, resplendent in his white furs. As King George quickly took in the scene, he hurled a lightning bolt at Myrddin. "Don't just stand there, you fools," he barked at the Fellows from the Royal Society. "Rush him!"

Countess Amalie began screaming, writhing against her invisible bonds.

The electrical fire shattered against his shield, but Myrddin was beginning to sweat with the exertion. He released the fire around Thomas and turned his attention to the King.

Sir John moved toward the King. "My Lord, the Royal Society does not seem so use—"

"Useless." King George gathered more lightning from the air and hurled it against the invisible shield protecting Myrddin. "Don't talk. Fight."

Myrddin had let his left hand drop down, sending Amalie Sophie, who had begun shrieking as soon as King George told them all to rush Myrddin, dropping to the floor. She landed with a sickening thump. She moaned weakly and didn't get back up. Meiko the terrier limped to her side and began nuzzling her face. Myrddin then brought both hands forward in a grasping motion. Speaking the words, "*Æris babilónum!*" he lifted the charging Sir John Pringle into the air. As John struggled, his feet dangled, face turning red.

Myrddin turned his attention to King George. "*Wæhþoll!*" He stomped a foot down just as the other man threw a third bolt of lightning. An invisible fist slammed into the seventy-six-year-old king's gut, and he went down.

Myrddin dropped his prisoners and rolled to the side, the bolt missing him by only a couple of feet.

George rolled over, gasping. "*Gib mir deine stärke, Wurdiz.*" He was an old man, but the toll of the battle was heavy, and his now-sunken cheeks and gray skin made him look easily like he was over a hundred. In the time it took Myrddin to recover his feet, the King held out his right hand toward the still-gaping Royal Society members. John collapsed, then his body rapidly desiccated, turning nearly instantly to dust. In quick succession each of the other members of the Royal Society were quickly consumed by the King's spell. George stood back up. "I've learned a new trick, teacher." Gone were the sunken eyes, the pallor, the near-death exhaustion. The King looked like a man of forty again.

George held up a hand, and Myrddin felt his shield crumble under the other mage's will. He fell to his knees, using all his strength to keep the crushing will from consuming him. He had nothing left to cast with. "A tiny version of the comet spell?"

"Don't." The King walked up to Myrddin and slammed a right hook across his jaw. Myrddin spit blood, gasping and fighting to not fall over. "Talk." George whaled on his former mentor, taking out decades of frustration and anger. "Fight."

Thomas Penn had recovered enough to stand, though his visage was burned and horribly scarred. He held his hand to the Countess and helped her recover her feet as well. Without a word, Thomas advanced toward Myrddin and stood beside his monarch.

The King snorted in obvious contempt. "Look upon him, Thomas," he spoke. "The great Merlin Ambrosius, discoverer of all the mysteries of the comet, first among sorcerers, too cowardly to use its power, but foolish enough to think he can stop his betters from doing so. Everything about him is a lie. Your time has long since come to an end."

"My name," said the ancient sorcerer, "is Myrddin Emræs. I am a soldier." He rolled over onto his back, coughing weakly. He spat the pooling blood from his mouth.

"Yield now or face His Majesty's wrath," Thomas ordered.

"I've seen the comet ten times, each holding a stretch of years longer than you have been alive between them." He rolled onto his side and spat out more blood.

"No. There are no terms of surrender," the King ordered, sounding very much like the soldier he had been before becoming king. "The Crown will have the pleasure of delivering its wrath personally. Hold him down, Thomas. Feel free to get your fists dirty."

As Thomas knelt over the prostrate wizard, leaning with all his weight on a knee pressed against Myrddin's neck, King George walked to the Countess Amalie. Licking his thumb, he rubbed a spot of blood off her cheek.

"I'm fine, my love," she said, sitting with her back to the wall. "I just need a moment to recover. Go tend the moment at hand."

He nodded, softly stroking her hair, then strode across the room and opened the far door. Hew Draper's cell lay on the other side. George opened his arms, and at the clenching of his fists, the gathered artifacts flew toward him. The star metal artifacts swirled through the air around him, then several of them settled onto his person: the suit of armor, rings, and the sword from the East. Even a halberd floated at his side as if prepared to be his second.

Once he had adorned himself with the wearable and usable objects, he moved his hands toward center and brought them together as if crushing something between them. The rest of the objects came together, then melded into a solid mass, extraneous material burning off or dropping to the ground. With a few twists of his hands, they formed into a semblance of a sash, which wrapped itself over his shoulder and around his waist.

"Move away, Thomas."

The King's vassal struggled to the side as he stood. He was cold and calculating, watching the gasping Myrddin like he was an insect. A blast of pitch-black smoke poured from his raised hand, boiling through the air toward the slowly rising wizard.

Myrddin raised his hands. "*Heaðusigel gebærdstán.*" The two words created an orb of brilliant light in front of him that dissolved the smoke before it approached. He was panting, struggling.

From where she sat, the Countess snapped her fingers again, and the blow caught Myrddin on the bottom of the chin.

Thomas stepped forward, held his wrists together in front of him with his palms held wide, and shouted, "*βελοσφενδόνη!*" which was quickly followed by a flaming dart erupting from the empty space between them and speeding toward Myrddin.

Myrddin struggled up to one knee. "*Heofonfýr!*" A tiny bolt of lightning hit the dart, which exploded in a shower of bright sparks.

Myrddin was dripping in sweat and breathing hard, while it seemed that his opponents were barely exerting themselves at all. He had been spiritually, magically, and physically beaten down. All too quickly Myrddin found himself being surrounded and squeezed by the smoke tendrils of the King, who also took the opportunity to send the halberd into the fray, taking swings at Myrddin as he tried to cast spells to dodge.

Myrddin could smell his flesh beginning to burn. *This is it,* he thought. *I can't defeat them; others will have to.*

The King and Thomas, smelling blood, closed in. The King held up his hand to Thomas, pausing him mid-stride. Like a conductor with his baton, George's hand came down, and he sent smoke and flame at Myrddin. The intense heat made them both cover their eyes and protect their faces. When the incendiary blast receded, they saw the kneeling form of Myrddin seemingly cast in gray stone. As they approached, Myrddin collapsed into a pile of dust.

George didn't even pause. "Let's go. The rest of the star metal is in Philadelphia. We need to collect the Assembly Bell and complete the ritual."

Thomas put his hand upon the door and chanted, "*Φιλαδέλφεια.*" He then opened the door and bowed. The King and Countess passed through, Penn following behind. The door closed, leaving an empty and battle-scarred chamber behind.

As soon as they departed, the wall shimmered. The wallpaper seemed to ripple, then reality just bent to the side by about three degrees. A human form slumped forward out of the distortion, collapsing to its hands and knees. Myrddin looked up, panting. He could feel his life force ebbing. With a groan, he stumbled to the second chamber.

He had made a difficult decision in admitting to himself that the best hope to defeat George and stop him from bringing the comet crashing down was Polly's group of friends. She had trained under him, as had George and all his vassals, but the others—they were different. Magic was a vastly different and personal experience for each wizard, as he well knew. That they would be able to do things that George couldn't even conceive of was their biggest strength. It could be the way they would succeed where he had failed. Could be.

Reaching out his hand toward Hew Draper's alchemical carving, oblivious to the blood running from his nose and ears, Myrddin closed his eyes and concentrated. The carving appeared to be pulled from the wall, a three-dimensional set of glowing lines of purple and black, almost folding in on each other, hovering just above the floor. The sorcerer and the object began to glow as it floated closer and closer to the door the King had exited through.

King George had been his second-best student, but he didn't know all the secrets. The Manydoor could connect to any door that had a matching clasp, so long as the wielder had a handle from the Salisbury Cathedral, where the artifact had originated. There was a second way to use it too, when the comet was overhead. Hew, Myrddin's best student, had known that. You could use the extra magic the comet produced, almost like it was *æther* that infused the very air and connect all the clasps. But the price was high. The highest. He would only have one more chance, if this worked, to stop George and the ritual.

Myrddin Emræs, originally a vassal of Gruffydd ab Rhydderch of Deheubarth, who sought his fortune in the east of England as a blade for hire after his ruler's death, had ended up fighting at King Harold's side out of loyalty and admiration. For all of that, it had only been to watch yet another ruler fall, and the conquest and destruction of all he had known to unfold before him. He was ready to return to the Earth from whence he came. And it was a small price to pay in order to spare others even a small bit of what he had experienced.

It stops now, he thought.

He concentrated all the power he had ever felt or known, all the love he had ever felt or known, all the joy he had ever felt or known and whispered his final word, "*Álisendas.*"

The Manydoor burst open, the alchemical stone carving hurtled through the opening, and as the Manydoor slammed shut, Myrddin's body consumed itself. His cheeks shrunk in on themselves and his skin went gray. In the space of just a few seconds, he starved to death and collapsed as his soul left this world.

Kensington Palace
London, England

&

The Franklin Workshop
Philadelphia,
Pennsylvania Colony

✢ ✢ ✢

✤ 39 ✤
Either Way, Something's Happening

Peter Collinson kept watch, carefully peering out into the hallway through the slightly ajar opening to the dressing chamber, as Polly made her best efforts to activate the Manydoor. He breathed in deeply. Magic, treason, adventure—none of this was what he had expected when the Royal Society made him a fellow. But God's will was God's will, and he would follow the path laid out before him.

"I don't know, Peter," Polly said. "I've heard of these things, but I haven't actually seen one before. I can't really imagine how they work—" Just then, the door started glowing faintly. Polly stepped back. "Um, I think I did it? Did I do it? Either way, something's happening." The portal flew open.

Peter left his post and rushed to Polly. They both peered suspiciously through the door. They couldn't make out anything beyond a latticework of glowing blue lines in the inky-black portal.

Peter stared through the entry with more than a fair amount of awe. "Will it take us after the Countess?"

"Not sure," she said, "but I think we have to go through it."

Peter nodded. He held out his arm, and she placed her hand upon it. They crossed the threshold of the Manydoor. He wasn't sure what he had expected, but the sensation that he felt when crossing through was no different than any other door.

It was an oddity to feel—nothing.

The world that greeted them on the other side of the door was a stark contrast to the refined lady's dressing chamber they had left. They were in a home that, while genteel, was decidedly not royal. It was a simple hallway.

"This," said Polly, "is not what I expected. Not at all."

"No," said Peter grimly. "But I suspect this is where the Lord needs us to be."

A glow coming from under the door caught her attention, and Polly pointed at it, then reached her hand out slowly toward the handle. There was a shriek on the other side.

Polly closed her eyes and took a deep breath, then rushed in, Peter on her heels. The room on the other side of the door had been a study, or perhaps laboratory. Now it was a scorched wreck. Small fires still flickered in one corner on an empty plate, and a charred workbench next to a desk was now good for nothing more than kindling. The only undamaged thing on that side of the room was an oddly articulated brass arm with a myriad of lenses attached, clamped to the edge of the workbench.

"Are you okay?" Peter had spotted, in the corner, two older women clutching each other. It appeared to be the home's mistress and her house-slave. In front of them, a young girl had taken a defensive position with a fire iron. All three were focused at something across the room, where the wall had been destroyed. It appeared to have been blasted out into the street beyond.

It was then that Peter realized he had run headlong into a bad situation. What the women were looking at with so much intensity was a scarred and burned man, who held flames in his palms without any apparent harm. Out in the street beyond him was a middle-aged man dressed as finely as any king—staring up at the sky—and the Countess of Yarmouth.

Polly assessed the situation. It didn't appear that the man with the flame hands had noticed her yet, but his gaze had instantly been drawn to Peter when he bolted across the room. She began working a calculation, sweat beading on her brow.

He laughed, flicking fire at Peter with a gleefully shouted, "διαπυρόω!" Flame splashed against an invisible shield as Polly reacted. Behind him, on the street, the finely dressed man began making a massive swirling motion over his head, rotating his hands and arms in the biggest circle he could.

"Every reaction . . . " Polly made a series of gestures and the flames rebounded, leaping back towards the man. Thomas spun to the side to avoid it. Fog drifted down from the sky.

"What's taking so long, Thomas?" asked the man in the street as he walked back toward the workshop, leaving the Countess further down the street.

"I'm just playing, Your Majesty."

Polly continued muttering to herself, putting up shields around the women. The "Your Majesty" was a surprise. She had thought that the King was much older, but she couldn't really spare it much thought at the moment.

King George walked around the edge of the destroyed wall from the street. "Thomas, leave them. We don't have time for this—the ritual has begun. It will dispose of them. Get us to the Assembly Bell *now*."

The King turned his back to Thomas, clearly expecting his vassal to lead the way. Thomas stood, looking at the tableau of people before him. He had an odd expression on his face, a mix of hatred, anger, confusion, and vexation. He then turned to lead the King to his goal.

Polly, thinking quickly, still hiding in the doorway, focused on his shoes and made a series of subtle gestures. They were just little beacon spells, but they were a tether, a connection. She kept at it, throwing tiny spells at all three of them as they strode away. None of them noticed the cantrips that she laid on their clothing.

Once they were gone, Peter made his way over to the women.

The girl holding the fireplace poker was younger, maybe fifteen or sixteen. She swung it before her wildly. "I don't know who you are, but, be warned, I will clobber you if you come any closer."

Peter held up his hands, passing before the young woman. "My name is Peter. This is my friend Polly. We are here to help."

Polly turned around and, with a couple quick gestures, extinguished the flames.

The girl lowered the poker, just a little, but kept it angled down in front of her. It was obvious she was wary still. "I'm Sally. This is my mother Deborah and our woman Jemima. Thank you for fending those people off."

Polly ignored them all, focusing on the fog that drifted in. She muttered to herself. It was oddly suspicious that the King's trio would leave them alone instead of just killing them and moving on. Never let an enemy into the back ranks if you don't have to. It had to be something to do with this fog.

Peter paused. He looked around, taking note of the surroundings more carefully. His eye lingered on the framed editions of *Poor Richard's Almanack* on the wall. "I'm sorry. Sally and Deborah Franklin?"

Polly really wanted to be a part of the conversation, but the feeling of dread only grew. She began recasting the shields, strengthening them. It was amazing how much magic she could use with the comet overhead. She had never been able to do this before. Nodding to herself, satisfied she had laid every defense musterable for both body and mind to protect each of them, she dusted off her hands.

Debby Franklin recovered herself and, with Jemima's help, stood to greet her guests, all the while favoring her left side—something was painful enough that she grunted as she stood. "My name is Mrs. Deborah Franklin. How may I address you, sir?"

Peter stepped forward, hand extended, "Mrs. Franklin," he began, but Debby took a step back with as much dignity as she could muster.

"Your full name, sirrah," Debby insisted.

"I am Peter Collinson, long-time correspondent with your husband, Benjamin. I know we haven't met, but he has written of you and spoken of you both enough," he added, indicating Sally, "that I feel I know you. This is Miss Polly Stevenson, daughter of your husband's landlady."

Sally dropped the fire iron and sprang forward, fiercely embracing Polly. "My adopted sister from London! Thank you so much for all the books you've sent. Was that you that protected us from the fire that man sent towards us? Are you both able to do magic like Father? Where did you come from? How did you know we needed help?"

Peter's jaw dropped, remembering several times he had been the focus of Polly's rapid questions; and here Sally was doing the same thing. When Ben had mentioned that Polly reminded him of young Sally, it had been no joke. It would be easy to believe the two were related.

While Peter felt nothing but warmth and surprised joy, Jemima watched quietly. Nothing tonight smelled right, and she'd spent a lifetime learning to step the other way whenever trouble came a-knocking.

Debby set her hands on her daughter's shoulders. "Enough, Sally. Let them answer the first question before asking another twenty."

Polly looked at them both. "I am able to cast magic, but Mr. Collinson is not. We can't tarry here. We need to go to wherever the King and the Countess were going. We must stop them. This fog he has called down is only growing worse, and the beacons I laid on them are fading fast. I fear I won't be able to track them."

Peter held up a finger. "They talked about an 'Assembly Bell.' Where would that be?"

Debby looked at the two strangers who had just walked out of thin air and saved them. "I am pleased to meet you both. Ben has mentioned you in his letters, and I am sorry to meet you under such circumstances, but this is all a little much. The Assembly Bell is in the yard next to the Assembly Hall, waiting to be hung into place in the bell tower."

Peter nodded, "Indeed, I am sorry as well. We are in rather a hurry, though. How do we get to this Assembly Hall?"

Debby shook her head. "I really don't know how to explain it, since you aren't familiar with the area. The streets are a little confusing to navigate, even though it is only a few moments' walk. I would take you myself, or send Jemima, but we are somewhat injured. It will be slow."

"I'll take them," Sally piped up immediately.

"Oh, my dearest, that wouldn't be safe." Concern was plainly written on Debby's face.

"But I can do this, just like Father!" Sally held up her hands and showed electricity passing between her fingers. "I've been practicing in secret, every night since Father departed, on the Assembly lawn. I can use the Bell just like he did. Oh, oh! I can do other things, just like in the adventures I read! Mouser, kitty, kitty, kitty. Watch this!" Sally's lips slid into a wicked grin.

The gray and black cat darted out of the darkness around them and ran straight to Sally. As she gave him pets, electricity crackling from her fingers, he rubbed up against her ankles. "I thought of this when I was rereading *Gulliver's Travels.* At least I think this will work." Sally whispered a string of words and focused as the cat headbutted her calf, purring nonstop. He began to grow.

Fur stretched across bubbling skin as the cat simply . . . *changed.* His claws stretched out, hooking into the floor, digging into the wood and tearing up splinters. His tail flicked, slowly lengthening. Purring grew louder and louder till it could be heard as a soft rumbling across the room. By the time he yawned, laying back to start grooming his hind leg, he was the size of a large hound.

The assembled adults stared in shock, though Polly watched Sally rather than Mouser. The surge of power had been *strong . . .*

Sally said proudly to her mother, "Mouser can protect me. I know it! Let me show them the way."

Debby blinked mutely. "Sally . . . "

Polly grinned. "Your father said I reminded him of you. Now I see it." She calmly started laying protection spells on the cat too.

Peter looked to Debby. "I fear we must go. I would say I would look out for your daughter, but I have a feeling it may be the other way around. Have we your permission?"

Debby nodded and pointed out into the night. "Go. Stop them."

St. James's Palace
London, England

&

The Dressing Room
Philadelphia
✛ ✛ ✛

✤ 40 ✤
I'm Sure I Don't Know
What You Mean

"Look, King," Peter implored the former Franklin slave. "I know you weren't much happy with the Franklins, but we have a need to get after King George, and we know there is a door such as this there."

King shook his head. "I do not disbelieve the difficulties to come. I have a certainty about them of my own. I just know it is not for me to aid you at this time. The Widow Eversleigh and I will be taking William through the door back to her home. In the coming conflict there may be a way to save him, and that is my duty—that is *our* duty. Our call. You must follow yours. I don't know whether you open the door to heaven or hell, but it's your door, not mine."

Peter stepped up to King and put a hand on his shoulder. "Please. Don't turn your back on Mr. Ben."

King's nostrils flared and his eyes narrowed. "You think this is me turning my back? Taking that one, after the way he treated me, and trying to save him. This is me *not* turning my back."

"Be that as it may, we're out of time. It's you or none after King George, dearies." Mrs. Eversleigh sadly shook her head. King hefted the still form of William onto his shoulders, activated the Manydoor, and they left Ben and Peter alone in the King's Presence Chamber in St. James's Palace.

King looked back as the portal was about to shut. "Trust in God. And remember, he helps those that help themselves." He pulled the portal closed.

"Do we walk, then, Mr. Franklin?" Peter asked.

Ben sat down on the marble floor and leaned back against the gilded wall. "Please, call me Ben." He draped his arms over his knees and leaned his head back against the wall. "I'm sorry. I'm sorry to have been such an ass."

Peter sat next to him. "I'm sure I don't know what you mean."

"I've dragged everyone into this insanity. The King, *the King— our monarch,* just attacked us with magic. I've gotten William killed, but for the grace of God and the work of King will say if he is to survive. But for you and King, I would be dead too. I don't even know what has become of our compatriots."

"I think you are being too hard on yourself. We are all just trying to stop a lot of people from getting hurt."

"No. It's more than that. We are all at risk. Live together, die together, right? One thing weighs heavily, though, on my mind. It is past time I recognized your contributions to the family. Sometimes it is easier to go with the way of the crowd than to consider the details of that behavior. You deserve your freedom as soon as I can legally provide it."

Peter's eyes welled up, but he kept his distance. "And the missus?"

Ben nodded, "Of course, her too. I should have died back there, and your freedom is bequeathed. Only seems fair."

Peter looked at Ben in perfect stillness for a moment, then cautiously offered, "If that be the case, I would like to be freed of the name I was given as a slave and use the name my grandmother, my *iya agba,* called me—Mobo."

"I will do my best. Come now, Mobo. Help an old man up?"

Mobo laughed as he stood, reaching down. "I'm as old as you are, Mist—Ben."

"Yes, well, I'm fat." Ben arched an eyebrow.

"Come, let us inspect this door the King went through."

Examining the door turned out to be fruitless, but before they could revise their plans, the door burst into light, glowing white, and flew open. Ben tapped his cane twice against the ground. "Well then. It seems we have an invitation. Shall we march off to our deaths like young soldiers answering the call to war?"

Mobo nodded. "Let's go, then."

They crossed the threshold of inky black, stepping through the tight beams of blue light, and found themselves in a closet. It was the changing room of a woman of some modest means—the apparel was by no means wealthy or opulent. Ben looked around, startled. "This is not the Tower of London. Did we land in the closet of the Widow Eversleigh?"

Mobo held a finger to his lips, silencing Ben. "We must be quiet."

"Agreed," Ben whispered as silently he could. "Do you hear someone coming?"

Mobo looked around, nodding slowly. The door opened behind them.

The two men turned, ready for anything.

A woman walked through. "By all that's holy, Benjamin Franklin! And Peter!"

"Jane?" Ben stared in shock.

Mobo ducked a quick respectful bow of the head. "A pleasure, Mrs. Loxley."

Jane looked them both up and down. "I heard the door open. Of all the people it could have been . . . I didn't expect it to be either of the two of you. And from the looks on your faces, I presume this was not where you expected to be. Where is the Lord Magician?"

Ben narrowed his eyes. "You seem less than surprised that we are here. Or rather, that someone is here. Just what part has your hand guided in this, Mrs. Loxley?"

She tilted her head to the side and bit her lip, thinking. "Let it be enough to say that you are not who I expected, but that I do know who the enemy is."

Mobo's gaze darted between the two.

"Who is the enemy, pray? And who do you side with? There are either things you have been hiding from me, and lying to me about, for years—or things have vastly changed here in Philadelphia, and no one has informed me."

"Benjamin Franklin. Why can it not be both?" Her lip twitched. "I work for Lord One and know that King George plans to kill half of everyone to try to become an immortal wizard. Is that plain enough?"

Ben thumped his cane once into the floor, hard. "Do you know how many headaches you could have spared me if you had just told me that seven years ago?"

"You assume too much." She gave no ground. "You had to learn it yourself to get here, I suspect. Besides, I've only put together the pieces myself as this whole thing has unfolded. The whole world does not actually revolve around you, Mr. Franklin, much as it may seem to some days."

"I suppose you are correct . . ."

Mobo coughed into a closed fist, "Mrs. Loxley, Mr. Ben, as good as it is to see you again, and for us to all see each other and catch up on everything—we have no time to tarry. The King and Thomas Penn will be seeking the Assembly Bell. We have to get there quickly. We have to stop them."

Jane seemed a little startled to be addressed so by a slave, but she smiled gently. "You are right, Peter. It is good to know you are both on the side of the angels in this. Let's see what we can do about getting us all to the Assembly Hall."

Ben started, "Oh, and Jane, I should say, I have freed the slave you knew as Peter. He is choosing to use a different name: Mobo."

Jane nodded. "Mobo, I am so glad for you."

Benjamin Loxley walked in behind his wife. "I heard that last bit there. Congratulations on your freedom, Mobo. Was that you that thumped the ceiling, Ben? It sounded like a stick or a cane."

"Benjamin! It was indeed."

"Let me be the first to welcome you back to Philadelphia, Ben. May I also be the first to welcome you to step out of my wife's dressing room and into a more proper environment?"

Ben flushed in embarrassment. "How did you come to be a part of this?"

"When you left for England, Jane started sharing with me. It was quite a shock at first, but I am ready to be a companion in arms." Benjamin Loxley kept on talking as they moved downstairs, not missing a beat. "The Loxley pen is at your service, sir."

Ben walked to the window, staring through the fog at the brief flashes of light above. A storm brewed . . . *and what is a Franklin without a lightning rod?*

"I say, I feel like I'm thinking clearly for the first time in far too long."

Jane *harrumph*ed. "That look always gets my husband in trouble. What are you plotting, Benjamin Franklin?"

Ben tapped his cane twice against the floor. "It is said, those who would seek peace should prepare for war. Well, those who would seek magic should prepare for science! Benjamin Loxley, you so-clever artificer, do you still have my storm kits in your shed?"

"Of course. If Peter—I'm sorry, I mean Mobo—can give me a hand, I will hitch up the horses and have your battery of Leyden jars and the electrostatic machine ready in the back of the wagon, as always, in just a moment or two. We can quickly load up the work cart too, and harness both the horses, so they are ready to be hitched."

Benjamin and Jane led the way down the stairs, where they put on their cloaks. Ben and Mobo had never taken theirs off, so they were prepared for the chilly Philadelphia spring evening that greeted them. Ben glanced wistfully at their cozy home. It looked as if Benjamin might finally have it almost completed.

Hitching the horses was fast work, and in no time they were underway. Mobo drove the wagon with Jane at his side, Benjamin and Ben rode separately in a cart. Even though they kept a fairly slow pace to keep from damaging the electrical equipment, Ben watched the evening sky. The comet was even brighter here than it had been in London, but fog wended through the streets, hiding the cobbles. It was as though some greater power forced a miasma over the eve to force nightfall. Ben felt his eyes start to drift closed and his mind wandered. His father, Josiah, appeared in his mind's eye, looking stern. *"Wake up, boy! Clear the fog!"* The cart hit a bump, and Ben woke. He realized with a start that the carts were slowing and everyone else had drifted off also. Even the horses had slowed to a stop.

He shook his head. *"Purgare corde meo."* He touched his own forehead. Immediately the haze of sleep lifted. He repeated the process for each of his compatriots and the two horses.

Everyone shared uncomfortable looks. Whatever was bespelling the world, it was a potent silence, and it was a true silence, one so deep that even animal sounds didn't pierce it. On the rare occasion they passed someone, the people just stood there, staring at nothing.

"Benjamin," Jane cried in horror, pointing to a group of three desiccated corpses just where Market Street met Third Street.

Ben and Benjamin went up and examined the trio. One was an adult: a woman, by her garb. The other two were children. "It would appear the proprietor has returned with his master and is intent on foreclosing on all his holdings. Somehow these people were different than the others we saw who are just in a trance."

Is this the effect of the great spell? he wondered.

"Why are they here, doing this now?" asked Benjamin as they got back in the cart and followed the carriage.

"The bell Norris has been so concerned about having in place is here and contains the last of the metal they need to cast their spell. They plan to bring the comet down from the sky and gain immortality."

"They believe it will grant them immortality? The greedy fools." Benjamin Loxley shook his head.

"Indeed," Ben said. "And I fear it will cost the lives of half the world to grant it to them."

Benjamin blinked. "You couldn't have led with that? Dear God. We must stop them, no matter the cost!"

"Exactly," replied Ben.

The grim group continued their way toward the Assembly Hall.

The Assembly Hall
Philadelphia,
Pennsylvania Colony
✣ ✣ ✣

✤ 41 ✤
Bell, Book, and Candle

Sally, Mouser, Polly, and Peter quickly made their way toward the Assembly Hall. With Sally's knowledge of the area, they made it in fifteen minutes.

"Here's where the Bell hangs, and no sign of anyone," Sally said.

"I'll be right back." Peter walked up the causeway, peering through the darkened windows.

"Is it?" Polly looked up to the steeple.

"Yes," Sally pointed up, "up there at the top."

Despite the gusting winds, the fog had settled, restricting visibility to the hall lawn. On the way, they had passed several people, all of whom were in trances. The Assembly Hall and the nearby fields were unoccupied. Polly stared up the tower. "So, we break in?"

Peter walked back over. "I don't think we need to break in. I think all we have to do is to stop them from getting to the Bell. We think the journals specified that the caster must be in contact with the metal to use it. So long as we keep the King out of there," Peter pointed at the Assembly Hall, "we will be able to stop him."

"A moment, please." Polly held up a finger. "Did you say *we think? We don't know?*"

Mouser purred and nudged Sally for pets, knocking her slightly off balance as she listened thoughtfully.

She scratched under his chin and the hound-sized cat purred.

369

Peter and Polly both stopped, glancing at the cat. It began to sink in just how large this animal enamored of the young woman was as the rumble of the purr echoed softly on the lawn.

Mouser's ears twitched as he went silent, and he snuggled down to pounce, pointed away from the three. His haunch lifted and his tail twitched. They heard the sound of a wagon on the roadway, with horse hooves clopping along loudly through the silenced night as the fog parted.

"Do we hide? Do we fight?" Sally asked quietly.

"No need. The King did not have a wagon." Peter pointed.

He recognized Ben's man driving the wagon, with a woman sitting next to him. Ben followed in a smaller cart, with a man sitting next to him, engrossed in conversation.

Peter Collinson broke into a grin. "I see we aren't the only ones who made it across the ocean tonight. This is a most excellent turn of events indeed!"

The two girls ran toward Ben, but Sally was far faster, Mouser at her side. "Sally!" Ben looked a little startled at a house cat that came up to his waist, but his clear delight at seeing his daughter again, and her delight in seeing him, made everyone smile.

As Mobo led the horses with the wagon a little out of sight, then unhitched them and removed their harnesses, Ben explained that he had freed Mobo and Jemima, and in turn was delighted to learn that Mouser's transformation was Sally's doing.

"Ben," Polly asked, "do you have a plan?"

Ben shook his head. "No. Yes. Mostly? Benjamin, this is Peter Collinson. Peter, meet Benjamin Loxley. Can you two get the Bell down here with Polly's help? You must hurry."

Peter furrowed his brows. "I thought we had to stop the King from touching it. Doesn't it make more sense to leave it up there?"

"It does and it doesn't. I want it down here, where *we* can touch it."

Benjamin grabbed his key ring and ran to the Assembly Hall door, followed by Peter and Polly.

"Shango, give me your strength that I may make it rain and thunder on my enemies. I will look for Anansi, finding all the places you cannot see." Mobo knelt by the wagon. He stood and turned around, hefting an axe. Ben stared in shock. A silent change had come over the man. It was almost as though a thousand people had been folded into the space occupied by one by some clever artificer, and so long as you didn't stare too hard, your eyes wouldn't start watering.

Mobo's irises were pure white, as though they had been burned away. "I'm ready." He swung the axe in an arc, the head crackling with electricity. His voice sounded completely different. "His *iya agba* told him about old Shango, the god of fire and lightning, the bringer of storm and cloud. You've been a master, binding his spirit, teaching him about being a Christian, Mr. Franklin, but these are the stories that are in his blood. This one is mine, not yours. I have hidden in the secret places in his mind for a lifetime, waiting, and I promised him we would be able to make a difference and bring good into the world. Do you understand me, *ọmọ eniyan*?"

Ben nodded. "I do. He is his own master now. Earlier tonight I found the courage to face him."

Jane walked quietly between them, avoiding both their gazes, grabbing more of Ben's array, and carrying it back to the area they would make their stand.

Shango nodded to Ben, ignoring Jane. "That you did that, and the coming threat, is why you are alive now."

Placing the lightning rods was a precise task with a lot of guesswork, and Ben paused to straighten up and look Shango in the eye. Staring the god directly in Mobo's blinded eyes was disconcerting. He nodded and went back to work.

Mouser purred with a deep rumble and head-butted Shango for pets. The outsized cat was rewarded with scritches between his shoulder blades, then, when Shango went back to unloading the wagon, Mouser darted over to where the people were working and sharpened his claws on the side of the wagon.

Sally giggled and snapped her fingers, "Mouser, no." The cat rolled back and stuck a leg up in the air, unconcernedly bathing, without a care in the world.

Polly, Peter, and Benjamin came back onto the lawn with the 2,000-pound Bell floating between them, held aloft by Polly's magic, with the two men clearing the way for her.

Ben stopped, staring. Of everything that had happened over the last seven years since his accidental discovery of magic, this was the one that just broke his brain—just for a moment—and drove home the reality of what was happening.

Magic was real. A megalomaniacal madman was trying to bring a comet crashing down and kill half the world's population so that he could gain immortality. A vast array of magic and intelligence, strategy and tactics, and even brute strength had banded together to stop the greatest atrocity committed in history before it started. An African deity walked in their ranks. Several of them had been magically whisked halfway across the globe in an instant—and yet it was the damned floating Bell that made it all real.

Ben turned to Peter, a little concerned, "What will you do? I'm afraid there will be violence tonight."

Peter smiled. "I will stand before the Bell in silence and listen until the Lord tells me what to do. It is my way."

Polly led the way to a position that placed Ben, Mobo/Shango, Peter and his quiet, and herself between the Bell and the streets. Fog surrounded them and lightning crackled through the sky overhead, brightening the clouds, though no rain fell. The skies had been overcast and troubled but were rapidly becoming roiling. There was a distinct actinic feeling to the air. Though they could no longer see it through the clouds, they all knew the comet was overhead.

They heard the King's voice before they saw anything. "They die so that their King may live. I didn't understand the reference before, that the veil would be made whole on the Earth, but I think it's this. Everyone is trapped, one foot in the world beyond death, one foot in this." George the Second appeared to be having a casual conversation. He rounded the corner, still a dim shape in the fog, though his armor glowed brightly.

Ben held up a hand and everyone froze. "Get ready!" he mouthed the words. They silently rushed about, and Mouser yawned, curious what the humans were doing.

Thomas Penn's voice came from immediately behind King George, "so when the comet comes down, those with potential for magic all get pulled to one side and those without to the other?"

The defenders at the Bell had seconds left before they would be visible and rushed to finish preparations.

"You idiot," Countess Amalie Sophie said. "Why does it matter? It is holding the spell in place that matters now."

"Unlike you," Thomas rejoined, "I like to understand the things I do to ensure mistakes are not made."

"Stop it, you two." The King's voice sliced through the night, "For years I've listened to your bickering. Attend your King. Igno—Hello. What have we here?"

All three came into view, stopping to stare at the group arrayed against them. The years had melted off them. All three appeared to be in their late twenties or early thirties.

"Well, Your Majesty, we are here." Thomas gestured toward the Assembly Hall.

"Idiot," the Countess shook her head. "Like we cannot see the giant bell?"

Thomas looked over at the crowd, pride stung. "Benjamin Franklin!" Thomas Penn smiled widely. "I don't know how you are avoiding the effects of the veil, but last chance! Step aside now. I've outmaneuvered you at every turn. Leave the board."

"Yes, yes. Whatever you say." Ben watched the King, waving his hand dismissively at the proprietor.

The Countess noticed Polly among their opponents. "*Schatz, darf ich das dumme Mädchen haben*? She trespassed on my rooms at Kensington, and Meiko doesn't like her, do you?" Amalie Sophie gave her terrier kisses on the top of his head.

The little dog stared at the giant cat and growled. The terrier had no scale in its brain for size, it simply saw a cat, and thought . . . *that is a cat, I am a dog. Chase!* So Meiko growled while trying to wriggle out of Amalie's grasp.

The King smiled indulgently, "Whatever you wish, *mein Kuschelhase*. Now, Thomas," said the King switching to a bored tone, "see to the rest. We have a world to recreate in our image, and this will take some focus on our part."

"As you command, Your Majesty."

Halfway through the word "Majesty," Jane held up a candle she had pulled from her cloak, lit it using her magic, and sent a beam of condensed light slicing through the night toward the trio. Thomas held up his hands and as the light struck, his fists erupted into flame. "Thank you," he nodded. He and the Countess began their walk toward the group protecting the Bell.

Amalie Sophie set Meiko down, while Thomas threw bolts of fire.

The dog ran around her legs barking happily, then hunched low, growling at the distant Mouser—who continued bathing, ignoring the battle.

Ben raised his hand to the sky calling down lightning just as Thomas raised his right hand. Fire and electricity met each other, but it was not like anything previously experienced by any party present on the lawn. The electricity, guided by will, probed at the fire, electrostatic tendrils exploring every gap in the flame, while the fire simply tried to consume the bolts like they were so much kindling. Midway between the two, a concussive explosion erupted.

Mouser darted under the cart. He hunched down under the cover, feline eyes darting side to side as he watched the combatants.

The Countess began snapping her fingers, but Jane revealed a secret of her own. With the comet overhead and this close—being yanked toward the Earth by the spell—her minor glamours carried real power. She countered with a wall of light that absorbed the attempt as Polly, positioned behind Ben and to the side of the Countess's view, threw up defensive barriers.

The difference between chess and, oh, say, a battlefield, is that on a chessboard everything is controlled, taken in turn, and carefully planned. On a battlefield, everything happens at once. Further, the difference between a battlefield and a barroom brawl is that at one point, the soldiers on a field were organized and fought in tandem.

This field, like a barroom brawl, quickly devolved into chaos.

Ben stepped forward, squaring off with Thomas. Jane tracked the Countess. Peter and Polly stayed close to the Bell while Mobo/Shango walked to each of the rods in the array and sparked lightning by running the edge of his axe against them. Peter was keeping his hand on the Bell, but Meiko had left the Countess behind to charge at him. The little dog had decided that there was no game with the giant cat. As he nipped at Peter's ankles, Peter reached down and managed to pat the terrier on the head. Meiko calmed immediately, turned, and showed his belly. Peter chuckled and happily gave Meiko a good belly rub.

Ben engaged Thomas with a lightning strike that Thomas was able to dodge as he waved his left hand and said, "βελοσφενδόνη," sending a flaming dart at Ben.

Ben countered with "*Combustio!*" He was already breaking into a sweat.

Thomas did not seem to be feeling the effects of his casting yet.

And no one kept the King in check.

Thomas stood up straight and mockingly bowed toward Ben. "I owe you a sincere apology, Franklin. I kept you out of the King's inner circle out of sheer hatred. The thought of spending eternity with such a pompous, low-born blowhard who dared think himself an equal with his betters was intolerable. I will apologize by killing you as quickly as possible." With that, he brought both wrists together in front of him and shot a bolt of fire from them that Ben dodged, so it hit a brick wall on the opposite side of the commons. The wall crumbled and, at first as if in slow motion and then so quickly the eye could not follow, the small side-building collapsed into the street. If anyone had survived, Ben could not hear their cries. The whole world was silenced by this fog.

Despite the silence ringing them, despite the taunts and barbs, the fight was messy, and spared no one, except, curiously, Peter, who was making friends with the terrier.

Jane threw continuous balls of light at the Countess. One finally hit her square in the chest, throwing her into the building fifty feet behind her. The brick building withstood most of the impact, but one side of the façades and an awning collapsed on top of her. The side wall was completely destroyed, and where the Countess had been was a pile of detritus. Jane also fell to her knees, gasping.

"Are you aright?" Benjamin Loxley asked her as he helped her regain her feet. He was of no use magically, but he could help steady people, and tend to the damage to the rods.

"I am," she replied. "The spell costs me almost nothing unless it connects. I am neither as strong, nor as practiced, as the rest here. And I can ill afford that cost."

Jane kept her eyes on her opponent and Loxley steadied her as she rethought her tactics. She was not surprised to see the rubble of the building tremored slightly.

The detritus began to shake and then it exploded outwards in all directions, breaking walls and windows without care. In the middle of the cleared ruin stood the Countess of Yarmouth. Her yellow dress was dingy and tattered. Her face and arms were bleeding from tiny cuts. But her eyes blazed with fury that suffused her body with the red light of flames that Jane found difficult to look at directly.

Thunder boomed in the sky and bricks flew at Jane.

Loxley spun himself around, his back to the Countess, and held his wife. The spears of detritus from the collapsed building smashed into him, and he stumbled to the side, falling to his hands and knees.

Jane took a trick from the Countess and began quickly flicking her fingers over the flame of the candle. Tiny lights flew off the candle, dancing delicately through the air until they floated about the countess. Like a swarm of fireflies, the lights flickered merrily about her as she attempted to swat them out of the air.

Across the lawn, on the other side of the fights, lightning met fire. Franklin glowered at Thomas. "Months ago you promised me a quick death, Thomas Penn," he said in a voice that radiated power and fury. "But on the lives of all those you have murdered, I promise you," his face took on a savage gleam. It was all an act. His eyes tracked the shadows behind Thomas as he taunted, "Yours will be slow!"

Thomas laughed, the fire around his body swirling. "You're hardly strong enough to imp—" He was silenced by Mouser pouncing on him, bowling him to the ground, and sinking his teeth into the proprietor's shoulder.

King George watched the two sides probing, testing each other. He could feel the Bell's power resonating with his star metal and the comet overhead. Soon there would be enough power to allow him to finish casting the spell that would bring the comet to Earth, ensuring his reign would be an eternal one, and that all those left on the Earth would bow to him and his penultimate magic.

For three months he had devoted hours every day to casting this ritual, nudging the comet closer and closer as it rounded the sun and sped back toward the Earth. Finally, he was inches from his goal. The battlefield well engaged, he focused on concentrating his own power in preparation. One by one he called each of the Hanover gods to him, wrapping them about his own essence. Most those Myrddin taught used the word and gesture to focus their power, but the King held a secondary, stronger, tradition which he and the Countess, his mistress from home in Hanover, had learned from the lore of the land.

There was an African walking calmly through the battle, slicing his own magic into the resonating power around the Bell. The gods recognized one of their own. He was different, though. It wasn't a cloak of power, like George's, but rather an aspect of the man, like the glint of an uncut diamond with pure potential hidden under the surface.

George jerked in shock as a giant cat came out of nowhere and pounced on Thomas, then swatted him like he was a rodent. It batted at him a couple of times, until Thomas hurled both palms' worth of fire into the cat. It darted to the side, yowling in pain. Thomas rose shakily to his knees, gently touching the four slices across his cheek and dabbing at the blood running freely from them. His left shoulder was mauled.

As George finished gathering a cloak of the gods about himself, he reached to the sky and pulled. Burning through the sky, the comet shifted further, answering his call. While doing this, he was bound, unable to participate in the battle. He had to trust, which came hard to him, in others' capabilities.

The colonial, Franklin, had realized that Thomas had only a few moves that he usually repeated in a predictable series. He held his hands in front of him as if holding a ball, shouting phrases in Latin as he filled the space around Penn with lightning. It was like there was a giant chandelier glass ball around the man, filled with churning and frothing electric fire.

Thomas was incredibly strong, but rigid and unable to adapt. Very much the opposite of his courtly persona. George smiled and thought, *This is going to be good; he will be weakened.*

Thomas floated toward the King, screaming and writhing at the center of the ball of lightning. Franklin grunted and fell to a knee, struggling to hold the spell. The little English wench put her hands on his shoulders and George could feel the power surging from her into Ben. How she was able to amplify Ben while also protecting the rest of her flock of combatants with defensive magic was astounding. George, Thomas, and the Countess were Merlin's chosen. These *peasants* should not be able to stand against them.

Across the lawn, behind George the Second, the swarm of fireflies around the Countess Yarmouth attacked. One by one, with no warning, they bit into her flesh with tiny puffs of light, then vanished.

She stumbled back as each one hit her, a thousand points of pain. She stumbled backward into an alley, tripping backwards as the lights attacked.

Trapped and clearly exhausting his reserve, Thomas's hands were at his throat trying to coax whatever bit of air he could into his lungs and failing badly. He looked beseechingly at King George. The King shook his head. It was stupid to do this, but . . . he paused, holding the spell in place with his will, and with just a sliver of his attention he gestured quickly and snapped his fingers. In a bright flash, the ball lightning lost its cohesive force, and Thomas Penn dropped at the feet of his monarch and master.

Whatever was happening with Amalie Sophie appeared to be over. The colonist woman collapsed beside her injured husband, gaunt and exhausted.

The master spell wobbled, and in his mind he could hear a crack, a tiny fissure, form in the body of the comet. Gritting his teeth, he focused, catching the rhythm of the spell again. He needed to get to the Bell: the metal he wore just wasn't enough.

"Thank you, Your Majesty," Penn managed to croak.

"Why are we becoming disappointed in you, Thomas?" the King asked in a dangerously languid tone of voice.

"He is far more powerful than he should be, Your Majesty," cried Thomas.

"Or you are far weaker," the King said with contempt. He stared at the claw marks and realized one had punctured the side of Thomas's throat. He was a dead man and simply didn't realize it yet. "There is no room for weakness in my court." His decision was made for him, then. George released his hold on the spell, only focusing enough to keep the tether there. He had maybe a minute, two at the most, to reestablish his will over it before the comet would break apart under the strain of falling from the heavens.

"Help me, please, Your Majesty. Together we can dispatch him easily, and then I can help you cast the final spell. *Tyr, gehen sie.*" The King swept his hand like a conductor guiding a symphony and a concussive wave caught Ben and Polly—stunning the two as they were bowled backwards.

"We no longer need your help, Thomas. The power that is building within that Bell is more than enough to bring the comet to the earth." King George took two quick steps forward and reached out to the kneeling Thomas, placing a hand on his vassal's shoulder. A serene expression crossed Penn's features . . . until George dug a finger into the puncture in Thomas's neck.

Penn screamed, and in the moment that all his inner walls were down, burnt to dust by white hot, searing pain, George clamped a hand around Thomas's chin and absorbed Thomas Penn's life force. He indifferently watched the proprietor of Pennsylvania crumble to dust. His experience thus far with life force had been one of trickles, a tiny stream slowly strengthening him. This, the essence of another mage, was like a dam burst, and what came crashing through turned out to be pure brandy of the highest alcohol content.

George threw back his head and *roared* in challenge against the comet above.

The Countess staggered around the corner of the alley. Drenched in sweat, she was breathing like a bellows. Blood flowed freely from deeper wounds than before. She visibly held the side of the building to keep her feet. Strength seemed to flow into her as her eyes burned with renewed fury, but her body did not answer in kind. George made a tiny flicking motion, diverting the smallest portion of essence flowing through him into renewing her power.

The glow that had been absent slowly returned and increased as she stood away from the wall on newly steady feet. "*Schatz*," she said in an oddly delicate voice. "I would ask for a star metal artifact. I am facing stronger opposition than I anticipated."

George the Second looked at his lover sadly. "We decline your request. I have fortified you, and this is enough. If you are unable to defeat this commoner, then so be it. If you survive, you will have proved yourself worthy of eternity."

"My King," cried the Countess gasping, her breathing labored, blood beginning to run from her nose. "She's a vile *Englischer Bauer*."

"Prove to me that I chose wisely in you, that you deserve to stand by my side." His gaze was cold, indifferent. "We are monarchs. Act like it."

"As you command, my Liege." Tears of anger ran down her face, but she stood regally in her shredded dress, ignoring the myriad bruises and bleeding cuts covering her body.

The King turned and headed toward the Bell in front of the Pennsylvania Assembly Hall.

The heavens roared and thundered as King George the Second approached the Bell on the lawn. Behind him Shango darted, and as the African god struck the final lightning rod—completing his circuit of them—he turned and strode toward George. A poorly dressed young woman, obviously from the Colonies, ran between the crackling lightning rods, doing something inconsequential. George didn't care; his focus was on the Bell.

Sophie Amalie began snapping with both hands, throwing invisible force at the African. His axe was a blur in the air, catching the blows and deflecting them in showers of sparks. But it was enough to slow him.

The overpowering smell of ozone filled the air, and George smiled. It was an appropriate setting for a transformation from a man to a god. As he approached, the wind roared, and the cover was ripped off the Bell and flung far out of sight. The Bell was glowing with all the power of the comet: all the power George had been directing into it as he drew the comet closer.

The King took out the scroll his family had spent generations and countless lives creating. It left his hand and began unrolling itself before his eyes. The artifacts he had acquired floated off his body and began to orbit about him as his spell grew in power. He looked up to the heavens and raised his hand and a burst of dark energy shot from his body skyward, following the thread of power he had left in place. He felt it envelop Halley's comet, and then draw it down. No longer was he trying to spin it, like a trick shot in billiards, to come close; instead he yanked, forcing it to come to him. The comet's impact would be the greatest single act of magical destruction the world had ever witnessed. Countless millions would die and even more would suffer as the magic crashed in a wave of transformation from pole to pole. This hemisphere would receive most of the physical damage from the impact of the comet. All life but his would be extinguished here, flowing into him as raw power... and across the globe, half of everyone would survive. The subjects of his new immortal empire.

He felt the distraction before it happened. The girl to the side quietly, stealthily, attempted to throw lightning at him. He casually waved a hand, sending a wave of force and fire at her strong enough to crush a wagon. The cat roared a challenge and sprang, knocking the girl aside and catching the attack as a glancing blow itself. It tumbled away, fur on fire, instantly quieted.

"NO!" the girl screamed and ran to her animal.

All that stood between him and immortality was a quiet English gentleman, crouching silently, smiling as he patted Mieko's belly.

He felt the energy he had stolen begin to falter. He tilted his head to the side. The artifacts he had, though potent, would not be enough. No matter. He raised his right arm and grasped toward the Bell, to bring the might and magic of the Bell into his service. He was shocked to discover that it would not come to him. His eyes snapped open.

The man put his hands in his pockets, leaning against the Bell. "Your Majesty." He ducked his head.

"What have you done?" George demanded. No mortal should be able to stand before him right now.

"I've done nothing but ask God to help me show you peace. To help me show you silence."

He threw a bolt of power at the man and it dissipated in the air like butter melting in hot water.

He strode forward and backhanded the man, wiping the smile from his face. The power of the Bell surged into him briefly. As the man stumbled to the side, he managed to catch his balance and once more regain the calmness. George felt the Bell cut off again. He turned and grabbed the man by his shirt, smashing an armor-clad fist into the man's face repeatedly until his form was limp in his hand. He dropped the man and once more reached for the power.

The Bell sat on its stand before the King as all nature screamed in protest at what he was attempting. Slowly it rose, and its glow increased. The King dared not approach, dared not do anything but maintain his spell lest it bring disaster to him. If he didn't complete it, he would not have the strength to begin again and, in fact, the exertion, if the spell were not successful, would probably kill him.

As the Bell rose to over the height of a man, the King saw a man had been under the Bell. It was Benjamin Franklin. The electrical energy suffused him with the brilliance of a thousand suns. The waves of electricity flowed from the man to the bell to the lightning rods and back again.

"We have already cast our spell, Benjamin Franklin. You cannot stop us!"

Ben stood quietly at the center of the maelstrom, ignoring the King's rant, controlling the currents raging around him. It was Sally Franklin that tipped the scales. "You shouldn't have hurt my cat." She said it quietly, then followed it with a phrase in Latin spoken through clenched teeth "*Creui.*" The teenager screamed in guttural fury, wordless now, as she punched upward then brought her fist smashing into the ground. The world responded to her anger as bolt after bolt of lightning rained down from the heavens.

Ben raised his hand to call all the might and fury of nature his daughter called down, amplified by the electricity they had built up with his electrostatic machine. The wrath of nature and the heavens was unleashed, and struck the King full force. Electricity and fire washed across the George, lighting up his armor like a thousand chandeliers. Everyone had to throw arms across their eyes or risk blindness.

"*Exonero,*" Ben commanded, and the electricity from the Bell flowed into the electro-mage. From Ben a burst of pure white energy the exact proportion of the man flashed to and hit the King again and again. The flow lasted for seconds that folded on themselves into minutes and hours. Cutting out as quickly as it had started, a sudden silence filled the air. Everyone conscious was blinded by the light and deafened by a persistent ringing in their ears.

Ben, too weak to move, fell to his knees, spent, and the Bell hovered behind him for a moment, then fell with a massive clang.

As vision and hearing returned, they were greeted by the same sight: the King stood there, panting, hands on his knees. His armor glowed. "Sorry," he looked up, "not good enough."

George reached forward and grabbed the exhausted Ben. Franklin felt the world slip away as George consumed his essence.

The Sundering

✥ ✥ ✥

❖ 42 ❖
Why Not You

"Hello, Mr. Franklin." The dead man he had known as Gasparini, and Overton, and Myrddin Emræs stood before Ben, the swirling fog wrapped around him like old Greek clothing. To Ben's eyes, the edges of Myrddin's form wavered and seemed something less than substantial.

"You!" Ben looked away, trying to see something past the miasma that stretched in all directions. "Where are we? Why aren't you helping?"

"We are . . . *between*, Mr. Franklin. This nothingness is the veil that separates the worlds of the living and the dead. Should George the Second of Hanover succeed, half those now alive will become the sacrifice he needs. They will step through this place into death, and he will live forever. You must stop him."

"Why me? Why not you?"

Myrddin shrugged. "He already killed me."

"Then how can *I* beat him? If I'm between, as you say, then I must already be dying myself." Ben was frustrated with all of this.

"You are here because he has called the veil to the Earth, making it accessible to those who have sufficient power . . . or *had*, in my case. Though yes, you are dying. Whether that continues to be the case is up to you."

Ben's eyes widened with understanding. "I can cross in both directions because of what he is doing with the comet."

"Just so."

"But that doesn't change the fact that he's already beaten me." Ben's shoulders slumped. "The man is too experienced. Too strong. I cannot prevail. I thought I could, but I was wrong."

"When I first sought to incapacitate you, even with all your strength you fell like wheat before a scythe. The second time I tried, you may remember, went rather differently. Because you learned. You grew. Learn more from me. Think back upon the things you have seen others do. *Make their power your own.* And above all, do not attack the King head on, Mr. Franklin." Myrddin reached out and pressed the tip of an ethereal forefinger to Ben's chest. He could see this contact, but felt nothing. "Attack the magic at its source. Borrow the strength your friends are willing to lend and use the knowledge I have given. Attack the *magic*, not the man."

Ben nodded mutely, and suddenly found himself alone.

All right, then. He closed his eyes to shut out the fog and fought his way back through the veil to his living body.

Ben lay on his back where he had fallen. Far above he saw a brilliant flash of light, and a few seconds later he felt a shockwave pass over him. He could feel . . . everything. The magic, the pulse of the battle, all the land around him, and even the comet that crowded the stars out of the sky had grown so large. Splaying his fingers wide, he let all the energy pour into him. "*Et ego recipiam vos,*" he whispered.

Years of being too old, too overweight, too . . . everything, just melted away. He was hurt, but healing. "Shango," he called. "I need you!"

It was a very familiar feeling, then. Magic had been unleashed in response to his call, but now he could sense it, as though feeling his own pulse.

He heard the Countess of Yarmouth scream in pain, then Shango's voice echoing through the night. "Come, my storm, wash this land clean!"

Ben struggled to move. Behind him, the King was locked in position, both palms flat against the Bell, working to complete the deadly ritual.

Shango's axe, afire with electricity, came flying through the air and spun to a halt in the rubble, within Ben's reach. He seized its handle and drew enough strength from the lightning to stand. Trying not to think too hard about it, Ben spun the axe in circles over his head. Electric tendrils arced out from one side of it to each of his companions, connecting them to him in a great skein of force. From the other side of the axe head a flare of lightning jumped to dance among the rods in the array.

George watched in horror, unable to interrupt the ritual and defend himself. It was a race. He turned back to face the Bell, refocusing his concentration, chanting even faster.

The clouds boiled, burning away as the comet ripped through them, consuming half the horizon. Then the electrical maelstrom that blazed around Ben shot lightning upward into the sky, completing a circuit with the storm.

Ben spun the axe a final time. Then, with all of the strength of his body and his fiercely stubborn mind, amplified by the belief and powers of his friends, and backed by a god-created storm, he slammed the axeblade down into the Bell as he shouted, "*ABRECAN!*"

The world shattered.

The spell consumed the Bell, which crumbled to dust in seconds; then it spread like a cankerous disease, rotting away the King's armor; and at last, in the tempest above them, the comet broke into a billion cindery shards that were seized by the winds and scattered across a continent as they burned down to motes that mixed with the air and land.

Ben dropped the axe, then took a single deep breath and fell to his knees. The lightning was gone. The storm was gone. Rain began to fall, pelting everything in sight.

He looked toward the King and saw only a burnt skeletal figure, frozen in the moment of its stolen triumph. As he watched, the rain picked away at it, cutting through the char, dissolving the ugly thing by inches. In moments, what remained of his former monarch was little more than an indistinguishable mound of muddy ash, now slowly washing away.

Of the great Bell itself, there was nothing left to see.

Sally rushed to Ben's side, and her injured Mouser gently licked Ben's hair.

"Did we win, Papa?" Sally asked.

"I'm not certain anyone won, my child. But we survived, and at least one evil is no more, so that's something. Just now, however, I need to rest my eyes for a moment." He patted the back of Sally's hand, then, exhausted, he passed out.

1760

01 A.S.
(Anno Seorsum; or After Sundering)

The
Franklin Home
Philadelphia,
The Sundered World
March 16th
❖ ❖ ❖

✤ 43 ✤
The First Year of Magic

"Pass and Stowe have finished casting a new bell," said Isaac Norris. "I'm on my way there now to inspect it, but I thought it best to drop these off with you first."

Ben looked up from the experimental device he was repairing and saw that Norris was holding a thick sheaf of papers. "Bit on the busy side here for the next hour or two, Isaac. Is it something requiring immediate attention?"

"First land area estimates for the new territories. Be ready to discuss them when the Assembly convenes on Friday, please. I can promise you Joseph Fox will be firing a whole salvo of opinions. You'll want to prepare, and not simply rely on the marvelous Mr. Collinson to whisper observations in your ear as you normally do."

"I'll make sure to study them tonight. Meanwhile, just drop them anywhere on my desk." Ben gestured vaguely to the mahogany monstrosity snugged up against the wall behind him. Not a single surface of the desk showed wood, being rather over-stacked with too many papers and books.

"Easier said than done," Norris laughed. "And here I thought this place was untidy in the before days . . . "

Norris was right, Ben knew. Because of his critical role in current exploration, the workshop had rapidly become a central collection point for every scrap of information gathered about the world they now called home—so like the old in some ways, yet radically, absolutely different in every way that counted.

To manage, Ben had ordered his workshop expanded in size and split into two sections. The left half was dominated by boxes and papers and sample cases and a giant map of the known lands of the Sundered Americas. Tacked to the map were symbol-covered summaries detailing the different types of magic that had been observed so far and the methodologies of their usage. There was shamanism and tribal storytelling to be found here, side by side with Christian and deistic prayer; and shapeshifters, ghosts, and creatures of legend roamed freely. *This surely isn't William Penn's colony any more*, thought Ben. *It is ours alone, and I wonder what we shall make of it . . .*

The workshop's right hall still looked like the domain of an ordered mind, though much of the research now conducted there dealt with subjects once dismissed out of hand as superstition. Right now its most prominent feature was a rig Ben had designed to measure limited levels of magical force, and a series of systematic charts and tables through which he was calculating the physical cost to the practitioner. So far, it seemed that no matter the type of magic, once used, the mage who cast it must refuel by eating. A lot.

Ben turned to his old friend. "Here." He smiled. "I'll put those away myself. Wouldn't want you to vanish into this forest and never be seen again. Give my best to Pass and Stowe. I hope the new bell will sound right."

"Yes," Isaac replied dryly. "Do try to avoid breaking this one."

Ben shook his head. "No guarantees—didn't mean to break the other one. Who knows what creatures could come now?"

Isaac paused at the door. "Well, that is why we have our own wizard to protect the city, isn't it?"

"Indeed, it is. My best to your dear wife!"

"Thank you," Isaac said as he left.

When he was satisfied with the repair he had effected, Ben turned to pick up the papers. Before he could determine the right place to store them, the workshop's outer door once again opened and more people came in, bounding this time. It was Polly and Sally, followed by her large and loving Mouser. The cat was battle-scarred, with only a stub of a left ear and all the fur from that ear to the nape of his neck singed off—but he was whole and refused to be parted from Sally.

"Father! Father! You'll never guess!"

Polly laughed. "Give him space, Sally. But really, Ben, you *won't* guess. It's brilliant."

Hearing their voices from within the house, Deborah Franklin came to the open inner door and called out, "Mind your pattens, girls. I'll not have you two track dirt all over."

"Yes, Mother," they both chimed. With no way back to the old world, at least for now, the Franklin household had welcomed Polly just as Ben had been welcomed into the Stevenson household in London.

Polly handed Ben a package as Sally gushed. "Everyone is talking about it! There is a settlement of people from Norway, only a day's ride away, that has trolls!" She jumped up and down in excitement. "*Trolls*, Papa! Pleeeaaase can we go investigate?"

Debby frowned at her family. "Ben, you are *not* going to let them do any such thing on their own. You must go with them. Trolls, is it now? What next!"

"Of course I'll go. I have a package I'd like to drop off for Mobo and Jemima anyway—we can do that on our way out of town. The trip will also give us a chance to stop by the Countess's cabin and see how she fares in her penance."

"Thank you, Mama," said Sally. She patted Mouser, whose rumbling purr quickly filled the room. "Polly and I promise we'll keep Father safe."

Debby's frown now focused on him alone, Ben noticed; a change of subject was clearly called for. Fortunately, he had one in hand. Unwrapping the package, he announced, "Look here! My new sign has arrived, and, as always, Mr. Loxley has hit it upon the nose."

He held it up for his wife's approval.

"Oh, go on," she said, "Hang the sign."

"Come, Debby—come put it up on the hooks with me. And you two," he said, wagging a finger at Polly and Sally, "are needed for cheers and applause. This is a serious matter; I insist it be witnessed, and all laughter is expressly forbidden."

But of course all four of them laughed, Ben hardest of all, even as

he marveled at the altered nature of his life and the wonders waiting
on the horizon.

The sign read, simply:

Benjamin Franklin
Wizard for Hire